D0670509

Books by Vincent Patrick

THE POPE OF GREENWICH VILLAGE
FAMILY BUSINESS

FAMILY

POSEIDON PRESS
New York

This novel is a work of fiction. Names, characters, places and incidents are either the product of the author's imagination or are used fictitiously. Any resemblance to actual events or locales or persons, living or dead, is entirely coincidental.

A Poseidon Press Book
Published by Pocket Books
A Division of Simon & Schuster, Inc.
Simon & Schuster Building
Rockefeller Center
1230 Avenue of the Americas
New York, New York 10020
POSEIDON PRESS is a registered trademark of Simon & Schuster, Inc.
Designed by Irving Perkins Associates
Manufactured in the United States of America
10 9 8 7 6 5 4 3 2 1
Library of Congress Cataloging in Publication Data
Patrick, Vincent.
Family business.

I. Title.
PS3566.A7869F36 1985 813'.54 85-19151
ISBN: 0-671-46513-9

For Carole

"The tyrant and the mob, the grandfather and the grandchild, are natural allies."

—SCHOPENHAUER

CHAPTER I

THE NORTHBOUND TRAFFIC ON THE DEEGAN SLOWED TO A CRAWL AS VITO APPROACHED THE LANE FEEDING IN from the bridge. He worked the pedals of the borrowed Toyota with both feet, stop and go, his shoes rubbing against one another, and silently cursed the Japs for building dwarf automobiles. On his right, cars poured in from Jersey, filled with suburban, middle-class Jews, he thought, heading for Seders at parents' homes in Riverdale or lower Westchester. He swung quickly into the right lane by intimidating a late model Caddy with a Potamkin sticker on it then pulled off at the One Hundred Seventy-ninth Street exit and circled up behind the old NYU campus. People filled the sidewalks along Burnside Avenue, even in front of the burned-out buildings, but there were few cars on the street. Unless the Puerto Ricans and blacks had taken to celebrating Passover, he thought, there was little chance of running into a traffic jam in this part of the Bronx.

At Davidson Avenue he circled the block twice, then decided that one of the several spaces on Burnside would be safest for the car and for him and Elaine when they walked to it later. He pulled the beat-up Toyota into a spot near a Korean vegetable stand that put him directly under a streetlight and cut the wheels into the curb to account for the hill, wondering, as he felt the tire grab, whether people still cut the wheels into the curb on hills or was it one more sign of advancing age. A dozen teenage blacks lounged on the sidewalk, the boys wearing sneakers, the few girls with dread-lock braids. Vito took Julio's pocket comb off the dashboard and put it into the glove compartment; he remembered at age twelve smashing a car window with a garbage can for half a pack of Chesterfields on the driver's seat, more to impress his friends than for the cigarettes.

You used to be a tough guy, Vito, he thought, and kept his eye on the black kids as he locked the doors.

As he walked through the darkness of Davidson Avenue, as alert as an infantry point man, it occurred to him how crazy things had become. His own comfortable new Cadillac Seville, loaded with every option available, had been swapped for the night for the rusting Toyota that belonged to his employee, Julio; there was no practical way for Vito to bring the Caddy to this part of the Bronx. Something was seriously wrong in the world, he thought, and something was as seriously wrong with his aging in-laws for continuing to live in the neighborhood. He would say it to Nat and Rose at some point during the evening, as he did every year. They would ignore it, and he would talk about it with Elaine on the way home, as he did every year, and she would agree, then point out that they were her parents, not her children, and there was a limit to what she could do with them, being a daughter rather than a son.

He turned into the dark, litter-strewn courtyard and passed between the two chipped-down blobs of concrete that flanked the entrance, for fifteen years now unrecognizable as the two seated lions they had once been.

Mugging victims, Vito thought. A couple of lions don't stand a chance on Davidson Avenue. As he climbed the four flights of dirty stairs he was even more alert than he had been on the street.

He was late. Elaine kissed his cheek and said that she and Adam had been there half an hour. Adam hugged him briefly and patted his back in the masculine way that he did since returning from his travels—five years ago he had considered any sign of affection to or from his father as childish.

Vito apologized for being late. "Don't worry about it, Pop," Adam said. "Grandma put out a couple of gallons of *knaidlach* soup to hold us."

"Traffic," Vito said, then walked into the bedroom and tossed his coat onto Nat and Rose's bed. He returned to the living room and said, "It looks like a scene from *Exodus* out there.

There hasn't been a northbound movement of Jews like this in the Bronx since Co-op City opened."

"His coat's hardly off and he's already starting in on the Jews," Nat said, and handed Vito a folded, white yarmulkah.

Vito read the label in it: THE BAR MITZVAH OF WAYNE GLASGOW. 1976.

"Who's Wayne Glasgow?" he asked.

Nat shrugged. "Who knows."

"He brings the *koppels* home from shul," Rose said.

Vito sat beside Elaine and set the skullcap on his head carefully, thinking that Nat and Rose must open this table into the living room only once a year now, for Passover dinner, the other three hundred and sixty-four days spent as infirm white prisoners in a black neighborhood. There seemed to be endless mahogany leaves that fit into it, leaves stored under their bed between Seders, that expanded it into a ten-person banquet table from a tiny side piece that all year long held framed photographs of himself as a fifties newlywed, pompadour in place, Elaine in an ornately framed eight by ten taken for her sweet sixteen party, highly colored and retouched by a long-defunct photographer on Fordham Road, and Adam in his Bar Mitzvah outfit complete with knitted yarmulkah. Adam's speech, given just when Saigon was falling, had been about the evils of Vietnam, Vito remembered—even then the kid knew what would sell in a synagogue of liberal New York Jews.

Vito looked across the table at Elaine and compared her to the smiling sweet sixteen in the photo, which, for the duration of the Seder, had been moved to the top of the television. In spite of the formal, three-quarter pose in which the photographer had her staring off at some distant horizon, Elaine's teenage exuberance came through in the eyes, the smile, the slight upward tilt of her head. She still had it, Vito thought, as a forty-four-year-old sitting beside her twenty-three-year-old son. She had grown into the earthy, attractive woman promised in the picture. Her hair was still as light an auburn as it was in the photo, maintained through weekly visits to what she continued to call, "the beauty parlor," rather than the hairdresser. The tiny wrinkles around her eyes looked good to Vito.

Sexy as the sixteen-year-old in the picture was, his forty-four-year-old, in-the-flesh wife seated across the table appealed to him even more at this point in his life. She was sure of herself—mostly, Vito thought, because she was pleased with the person she had matured into—so that even with the endless care that went into her appearance, she always looked comfortable and relaxed. Elaine was not trying to fool anyone, least of all herself. Her clothes and makeup made her attractive enough to draw whistles from a crew of young construction workers, yet the makeup never deteriorated into a "disguise." She knew when a piece of clothing or a look simply was inappropriate for a woman of her age. It occurred to Vito that he was lucky, after twenty-four years of marriage, to find at the end of most days that his wife was the most appealing woman he had seen since leaving the house in the morning.

Beside her, Adam's head was bent toward the soup that remained in his bowl. He had his mother's high forehead and blue eyes but his hair color was Vito's, jet black. When he smiled—not often enough for a twenty-three-year-old, Vito thought—Elaine's exuberance animated his face. Perhaps he smiled more when he was not with his parents. This was only the third time that Vito had seen Adam during the six weeks he had been back in New York, and so he shouldn't jump to conclusions about his moods. Whatever conclusions Vito came to about Adam were based on very little current information; during the years of Adam's absence Vito and Elaine had seen him only once, at age eighteen when, having dropped out after a year and a half in college, he passed through New York from Cambridge en route to Berkeley for what he called, "A little time to find myself." The little time had become five years of not only Berkeley but parts of Europe and Asia that had caused Vito to toss and turn often before falling asleep at night.

He broke into his own thoughts and looked at Nat.

"What are we doing here still?" Vito asked. "Next year in Jerusalem. We all said it last year, Nat. We all say it every year, but every year we wind up on Davidson Avenue in the Bronx. Not even Flushing, where you wouldn't need grates on your windows, no less Jerusalem."

Nat ignored him and passed out the slim prayer books, most of them compliments of Mogen David wine. Vito's was a deluxe edition from Maxwell House coffee. Rose cleared a space in front of Nat and set out the compartmented dish of bitter herbs, hard-boiled egg, potato, *karpas,* and the lamb shank bone that always reminded Vito of an archaeological find, then placed two tiny bowls of salt water at each end of the table. The Seder was under way.

The old man had nearly finished saying Kiddush and Rose began to fill each tiny cordial glass with wine when Vito remembered the paper cup. Rose's hand trembled, as always. When she reached across to Vito she spilled perhaps a teaspoonful onto the once-a-year tablecloth and immediately uttered an expression appropriate to the accident.

"Hab a zessin yur," she said, and filled Adam's glass. "Yiddish, Adam. *A zessin yur.* Means we should have a sweet year. Because we spilled sweet wine."

Adam smiled at his grandmother but said nothing. She expected no response from him.

"There's more on the tablecloth than in my glass," Vito said.

Nat raised his head from the prayer book and peered from behind the thick cataract lenses, surveying the stain while he continued to intone the Hebrew prayer from memory. Without missing a beat he interjected, in the monotone he had used with his wife for sixty years, "Rose, you spilled on the tablecloth."

Everyone ignored him.

Vito had never paid attention to the tablecloth before. Now he fingered it. It had to be one of the few family heirlooms, with some touching Isaac Singer story attached to it. Hand embroidered in the heart of the shtetl by the daughter of a famous Reb, then schlepped out by Rose's mother, the ever-present mounted Cossacks no more than twenty feet behind. Snow. There must have been lots of snow. The tablecloth could have inadvertently tripped a Cossack's horse, or hidden the famous Reb's firstborn male grandchild. Maybe even responsible for averting an entire minor pogrom. Whatever—this tablecloth would have done wonders for the Jews. He would ask

Elaine about it when they got home—for sure it was one of the stories she had heard throughout childhood.

Vito studied the half mouthful of wine in his little cordial glass then reached into the side pocket of his jacket and withdrew the paper cup. He squeezed it into shape and rolled it gently between his palms while Rose, Elaine, and Adam watched. Nat, too, looked up and stared, his eyes enormous behind the lenses. He broke into the prayer for a quick aside to Rose in Yiddish. Vito guessed that it would translate close to, "*Nu*, what is the maniac son-in-law up to this year?" Vito dumped his cordial glass of wine into the paper cup, then held the cup up toward Rose.

"Now would you please fill it, Rosie? Every year I ask for a real glass." He tapped the empty cordial glass. "These . . . thimbles you use are not meant for wine."

He turned toward Nat, who had now assimilated it all and was about to speak. "Paper, Nat. It's kosher. You've got no gripe here."

Rose spoke to Elaine, as though Vito was not there.

"Only your husband can't sip wine like other people? He needs such a big glass?"

Vito motioned for her to fill his cup.

"Rose, three hours from now you'll do your little number and tell the table, 'Look, that's his fourteenth glass of wine.'"

"Last year was seventeen."

"Seventeen tablespoons. Now I have my own, seven-ounce, kosher glass. Fill her up please, Rosie."

She reached across and tried to pinch his cheek.

"And after twenty-four years it's still, Rosie? You wouldn't have a stroke if you said 'Ma.' Believe me."

She filled his cup and set the bottle out of reach. Vito took a long draft of wine and smacked his lips loudly.

"I never really had one, Rosie. The last time I called anyone 'Ma' I was seven years old. It's a little late to start now."

She turned to Adam. "Ice in the winter, your father gives."

"And it's not twenty-four years," Vito said. "We're *married* twenty-four years. I've been coming here twenty-three." He turned to Adam.

"For a year they didn't talk to your poor dad."

"Don't live in the past," Rose said.

"Was that a good year or a bad year, Pop?"

Elaine glared at Adam. He sipped his wine.

"Your son doesn't need a monster glass, Vito," Rose said. "Look how nice he drinks his wine."

Elaine looked up from her soup. "Look how *nice* he drinks? He's twenty-three, Ma. He's not eight." She shook her head slowly. "Jesus."

"A little respect please, while I'm *davening*," Nat said in the midst of the Hebrew. "Decorum. Let's keep a little decorum on *Pesach*."

"I don't need a monster glass because I'm half Jewish, Grandma. It kills your taste for alcohol." Adam took the tiniest possible sip from his cordial glass. "I do a lot of cocaine instead."

"Please!" Rose said. "Not even a joke like that."

"Some joke," Elaine mumbled, just as the telephone ring cut off Nat's last few lines of Kiddush.

They sat silently and listened to three rings. Nat brought his watch up close to his eyes.

"Who could be calling?"

Adam rose and went to the bedroom. He returned a minute later, the Seder at a standstill while everyone looked to him for an explanation. Adam stood quietly and let some tension develop, indulging his first whimsical mood of the evening, then turned to Vito.

"Your father, Pop. He wanted to wish us all a good Passover."

Everyone looked puzzled.

"That's Jessie for you. No?" Adam said to Vito.

Vito nodded, still puzzled. "That's Jessie."

Adam read the questions, nicely, Vito thought. Nat interrupted once to correct his pronunciation but Rose stopped him. "Leave him alone, his Hebrew's better than yours." When he finished she asked, "How do you remember so well?" then turned to Elaine and shook her head slowly. "It's *something* the way that boy asks the questions."

"You should have heard me read a few years ago in Berkeley. Knocked out the whole table."

"You went to a *Seder*? In California?" Rose shook her head in mild disbelief. "I thought you were being a beach bum out there."

"Not a beach bum," Vito said. "There's no beach in Berkeley."

"I was crashing for a few weeks at a sort of commune right off Telegraph Avenue. Maybe fifteen kids sharing this huge old house. Anyway, six or seven of them were Jews. But California Jews, not for real."

Nat stopped praying.

"Not real Jews? What kind of Jews, then?"

"Grandpa, there're no *real* Jews raised in California. Real Jews are in New York. Out there the sun turns them into *goyish* Jews. Blond hair, surfboards . . ."

"He knows a little Yiddish, too," Rose said.

"Well, the Jewish kids decided to hold a kind of half a hippy Seder. All the Christians, too. But done right—the bitter herbs, hide the matzoh—the whole ceremony. Everyone read from the books, but in English. Nobody knew two words of Hebrew. It came my turn to read and I rattled it off in perfect Hebrew. Knocked them out. No one knew I was half Jewish. Adam McMullen, that's all they knew. They kept pressing me for how the hell I knew Hebrew. I finally told them, 'You've heard how Jewish New York City is? Well it's *so* Jewish that everybody has to learn Hebrew in public school. Even the Christians. You're not allowed to graduate otherwise.'"

"You don't tell people you're half Jewish?" Nat asked.

"Yeah. I hand out cards when I travel. My mother's Jewish and my father's Italian, Irish, and Cherokee."

Vito sipped his wine. "You're listening to my father too much. His half Cherokee nonsense. Big-time warrior. I'm pretty sure Jessie's mother was a Digger. From California. They're closer to aborigines than American Indians. Whatever, it was some low-life tribe scrambling around in the dirt."

"Cherokee sounds better," Adam said.

As Rose began to clear the empty soup bowls, Vito made

eye contact with Adam and shrugged a silent question. Adam understood perfectly. He rolled his eyes upward, and Vito knew that Jessie's call meant trouble. He barely heard Rose talking to him.

"Well, your son read it beautifully," she said, as she set out plates and filled them with pieces of roasted chicken and slices of pot roast. She paused after loading up Adam's plate.

"A college *graduate* couldn't say it any better, Adam." She found room on his plate for another slice of meat and a mound of carrots. "And talking about college graduates..."

"We weren't talking about them, Ma. You were," Elaine said.

"Somebody's got to. That a boy this smart never finished college is a *shonda*." She watched over him as he started to eat.

"Please, Ma," Elaine said, "don't tell us how beautifully he eats. We can see it for ourselves. Only twenty-three and he gets every bit of food into his mouth. All alone."

Adam looked up at his grandmother and mumbled through a mouthful of food, "Delicious."

Rose continued to fill plates, happy.

After they had finished eating, as Vito started on his fourth paper cupful, Nat completed mumbling a section of prayer and said to Rose, "It's time to let the angel in." She adjusted the extra cordial glass of wine that had sat in the center of the table throughout the meal, then walked to the door.

"Keep the chain on, Grandma. You forget you're living in the Bronx."

"Adam's right," Vito said. "Instead of Elijah, some great big *shvartzer* wearing sneakers is going to come in and mug us."

Elaine pressed the point.

"When are you two going to move *out* of here? There are three white families left in the building. There were empty beer cans all over the stairs coming up."

"They're right," Adam said. "Get the hell out of this place. You're too old to survive here."

He addressed Nat. "Grandpa, how old are the two of you now? The truth."

"Who kept records in our day?" Rose said. "There were no hospitals. No one knows."

"About how old?" Adam asked.

"About means nothing," she said. "You're as old as you feel."

"They'll never tell," Elaine said. "Some crazy superstition about telling their age. They won't even tell you their anniversary. But they're into their eighties. They must be."

Rose stood at the still unopened door and said, "Not such a crazy superstition. All these people... the *kinder*, the grand *kinder*, give them big golden anniversary parties at Areles. Marvelous. But whoever the party's for is dead a month later. They come from dancing the anniversary waltz at Areles, they drop like flies. You don't tempt God by bragging about your age."

Elaine turned to her father.

"You're only a few years younger than your brother David. And he *admits* to eighty-three. He's eighty-three, Daddy, isn't he?"

"I wasn't at his *bris*," Nat said, and returned to his prayer book. He began to *daven* again while Rose unhooked the chain, held the door open for a bit to let the angel in, then closed it and reset the chain. She turned toward Adam.

"This *place* you would like us to get out of, we've been here forty-two years. Your mother was raised in this apartment."

"Anyway, it's not all *shvartzers*," Nat said. "There are plenty of Indians moving in."

"Cherokees?" Adam asked.

"India Indians," Nat said. "Hindis."

"Nat, you sound like it's the Rockefellers and the Whitneys moving into the neighborhood," Vito said. "You think the real estate's going to soar up in the next few years because *Indians* are moving in?"

"They're easier to live with than the blacks. These are not violent people."

"Very nice people," Rose said. "But they don't kill cockroaches." She seemed puzzled. "How could people not kill cockroaches? We're overrun here."

"Bad for their karma, Grandma. It messes up their roach karma."

"Even the *shvartzers* kill roaches," she said.

"They kill old Jews, too," Vito said. "When there's only a few left on the block."

Elaine stood and began clearing dirty dishes. "They want to be the last," she said, and turned to her mother. "You want me to promise we'll chisel it on your stone after the mugging? Rose and Nat Ruden, the last Jews on Davidson Avenue. I'll remember to have the rabbi say it at the unveiling."

Rose motioned with her head toward Nat. "Tell him. He doesn't want to move."

Nat continued reading from the prayer book.

"I can help you with the money," Vito said. "All kidding aside, Nat. You're living in a slum and you don't know it."

"If we move, we move with our own money," Rose said. "We don't take from our children."

"It's no big deal. Business has been decent." Vito winked at her. "Believe me, you wouldn't have a stroke if you take a little help."

"We're not people who take. We give."

Elaine shook her head at Vito. "Drop it," she said. "You can't deal with people who can't take."

There was a long silence, with only the sounds of Rose and Elaine scraping and stacking plates. Rose ran her finger across the wine stain and spoke to Vito.

"Did I ever tell you about *this* tablecloth?"

"Don't tell me, Rosie. Just one question. Did your mother personally shlep it out of the ghetto?"

"No, when we left Russia we had our luggage sent. Everybody in the *shtetl* had their luggage sent. What kind of a question..."

They were quiet for a while, then Adam broke the silence, in his first serious mood of the evening.

"Well I don't care where the money to move comes from, I'm not coming to another Seder in this apartment."

Everyone looked at him.

"I mean it, Grandma. I won't climb over another empty beer can on the steps. I'm not going to walk through two dark blocks to the car with my mother and father, close to the curb so my dad and I have a shot at it if we've got to bust some junkies' heads, and I'm not going to go home and worry about you two getting mugged. You're like a couple of *turkeys* walking these streets. You ought to print up signs and hang them around your necks—mug me, I am a turkey. Well, the five years I've been gone the neighborhood's become a jungle. And I'm not coming to the next Seder unless you're living somewhere else."

Vito raised his eyebrows in surprised appreciation.

Nat insisted upon Adam searching for the matzoh and after a few minutes of refusing, Adam went at it with gusto. Everyone called out, "Getting hotter," or, "Cold," until he homed in on the sofa cushion where he had found the wrapped-up matzoh on every Seder night of his childhood. Nat tried to press a twenty-dollar bill on him, until Adam insisted that, "If I'm willing to act like a little kid and hunt for the matzoh, then you've got to give me a kid's reward." They settled on a five.

Rose opened a box of Barton's kosher-for-Passover candy while Adam played Nat one game of dominoes on the oval coffee table. Vito occupied himself with straightening the half-dozen framed Chagall reproductions that hung in the living room. No one mentioned the move again but Rose seemed in a mild state of shock. She fished out only two newspaper clippings. Vito got a vitamin column. It claimed that excessive consumption of alcohol washed away the Bs and C, and that heavy drinkers should replenish them daily. Brandishing the second one, she interrupted the domino game to show Adam the most recent statistics on the relative lifetime earnings of college graduates and nongraduates. Five minutes later, Vito, Elaine, and Adam left Rose and Nat chained in their apartment.

They walked toward Burnside Avenue, pleased that there was enough of a chill in the air to keep the streets half empty. Another few months, Vito thought, and every stoop and parked car would be filled with beer drinkers blasting suitcase-size portable radios and tossing empty beer cans into the gutter in high sweeping arcs. Now there were just a few small groups of teenagers who looked them over briefly as they passed. They detoured around a small hill of black plastic garbage bags piled against an apartment house. From the outermost bag, the leg of a large dog, a shepard or Doberman, protruded, the fur still shiny. Only the leg had broken through, stiff enough to pierce the plastic. It pointed horizontally, crooked a bit at the knee like a tiny tollgate across the sidewalk.

"The neighborhood's coming up," Adam said. "Five years ago I remember a dead dog on the curb. Now they're wrapping them up at least. Maybe it's the Indian influence."

There was little conversation during the early part of their ride back to Manhattan, Adam seated crosswise in the cramped backseat of the Toyota. Vito drove with the windows cracked open to diffuse the nauseating odor of Julio's several air fresheners: impregnated cardboard cutouts of bare-breasted blondes dangling from the rearview mirror beside a pair of sponge rubber dice. He drove fast, anxious to get Adam alone for an explanation of what the hell was up with Jessie's phone call. Vito realized that Adam must be anxious, too; he sat quietly and never even encouraged Vito to turn on the radio.

"What's the story behind your mother's tablecloth?" Vito asked Elaine.

"What do you mean, story?"

"When she spilled the wine on it I noticed how pretty it is. It had to be handed down through the family and I figured there's a touching shtetl story to it."

"My father found it on the subway. The Jerome Avenue line."

"What?" Vito said.

"She started to tell you but you shut her up," Elaine said. "Forty years ago. My father was coming back from the Lower East Side on one of his errands of mercy. A *mitzvah,* he was doing—bringing some homemade food to an old friend on Rivington Street. Murray somebody, who had just broken both ankles jumping out of a fire in a loft where he pressed ladies' blouses. There must have been three feet of snow on the streets and my mother didn't want him going downtown."

"At least I was right about the snow," Vito said.

Elaine ignored it.

"Anyway, on the way home he found a package on the subway that turned out to be this beautiful tablecloth. My father always used it as proof that God rewards good deeds."

"I'm surprised he kept it," Adam said.

"It sat in the Transit lost and found for ninety days waiting to be claimed," Elaine said. "After three months it became his. The clerks he turned it in to were in a state of shock."

They were quiet again for a while, until Elaine broke the silence, first as they passed Yankee Stadium to comment that it was great that the three of them were together again after five years and that her life had taken on a whole new dimension since Adam had returned to New York. Adam reached forward and squeezed her neck affectionately in the way that he was now able to do, but he and Vito were both uncomfortable with the directness of her affection—it was her style, picked up from Nat and Rose, but not theirs.

Vito mulled it over as he moved fast in the left lane. He envied Elaine her directness at the same time that it annoyed him. Irish and American Indian blood don't make for demonstrative people, he thought. It was too bad his mother had died so early; a little Italian leavening in his upbringing wouldn't have hurt. If he had to do it over again he would make an effort to be more direct in his affection for Adam, yet it seemed to be too late. Their relationship now was between two adults; Vito's opportunities as a father to influence things forcefully had been ripe when Adam was a child. Whatever should have been done differently should have been done before Adam had gone off for five years and, by living independently, established himself as an adult who now dealt with his father as an equal.

He looked in the rearview mirror and saw Adam staring out at the South Bronx tenements. How the hell had Adam supported himself for five years? The question had occurred to Vito often and had been intensified whenever an occasional postcard arrived from Kashmir or Istanbul. He and Elaine would read the card, express concern to one another for Adam's well-being, and carefully avoid saying what was on each of their minds: that their son was running some terrible risks in remote corners of the earth while the two of them behaved like ostriches and shared an unspoken hope that things would work out all right—that mistakes made in Adam's childhood could no longer be rectified. That belief, that it was too late to rectify things, had justified their doing nothing.

Elaine broke the silence a second time as they crossed the Triboro Bridge.

"Wasn't Jessie's call a little odd?" she asked.

From her tone Vito knew she wasn't buying any stories of Happy Passover calls. He shrugged, and asked over his shoulder, "What did you think, Adam? You talked to him."

"Probably just a little drunk and felt like talking to family."

"Jessie?" Elaine said.

They remained quiet.

She spoke to Vito. "I'm amazed that your father would even remember my parents' last name to look up in the phone book."

"Don't sell him short, Elaine," Vito said. "Under that Irish Cherokee exterior there's more warmth than meets the eye." He concentrated on his driving as he said it and resisted the impulse to check out Adam's reaction in the rearview mirror—it would likely be an amused little smile. Elaine let it drop.

Vito eased the Toyota down the narrow ramp into the garage under his apartment house. The young Puerto Rican in the cubbyhole office put down his can of beer and left the tiny television screen after watching the end of a scene that Vito thought may not even have interested him—letting the gentry wait was one of the few areas of self-assertion the kid had available to him. He pretended not to recognize Vito.

"No transients," he said.

"I'm not a transient. I keep the black Seville here. Number eighty-three."

The kid pointed to the large sign of rates and regulations and shook his head sadly. "No substitutions," he said.

Vito nodded. "Is that the little sign right under where it says I pay two hundred and twenty a month to park here?"

The kid shrugged.

Vito dug a five out of his pocket and held it out.

"It's just a painted sign," he said. "I don't see it chiseled in concrete."

The kid took the bill out of his hand gently.

"You're right. We got to make exceptions in this world."

"A philosopher," Elaine said, as the three of them walked up the oil-spotted ramp.

Vito asked her to go ahead of them into the building; he would wait with Adam for a cab. She kissed Adam good night, knowing they wanted to discuss Jessie's call or why wouldn't they have dropped Adam at his apartment first?

Vito and Adam stood under the awning and watched her walk into the lobby.

"What the hell was that call all about?" Vito asked. "A Happy *Pass*over?"

"You'll have to take a little time off work tomorrow. Your old man needs bail money."

"Oh, Christ!"

"Old Grandpa hangs right in there, doesn't he."

"Is it serious?"

Adam shrugged. "A bar fight. But it's an off-duty detective he whacked."

"He hurt the guy?"

"I think so. What the hell, they lock you up for a bar fight, it means somebody got hurt. Grandpa said he kicked the bull's ass the length of the bar and halfway down Tenth Avenue. Those were his exact words. He laughed while he told me."

"Christ almighty, but he just won't let up."

"Doesn't bother me," Adam said. "It's nice to know I've got strong genes. I hope I'm getting pinched for bar fights when I'm sixty-eight."

He waited a moment, then added, "The cop's in St. Clare's Emergency. Not exactly *critical* but his face is all wired up and it needs a lot of sewing. They're also worried about a concussion." He shook his head appreciatively. "Jessie must have gone to work on him something awful."

"Where do they have him?"

"The Tenth Precinct. Twentieth Street. He's in a holding cell. He said they'll bring him downtown to be arraigned tomorrow afternoon."

"Well there's nothing to do for him till then. He'll spend the night in the can."

"He said don't worry about it, the perverts don't want his wrinkled old ass."

"Did he sound drunk?"

"Sounded recently sober. Like the last hour or so. He must have had his own paper cup tonight."

It was the wrong moment to be critical, even in a light, teasing way. Adam was immediately sorry he had said it, then the touch of remorse was neutralized by his father's quick response.

"Well maybe with your strong genes come some other genes, too. You think you're improving the family line by switching from alcohol to those fucking *powders* you use?"

Adam withdrew into an overly posed, superior attitude.

"Freud used coke. And so did Arthur Conan Doyle. Medically..." He let it trail off.

The doorman pulled open the door for a woman walking a black standard poodle on a leash. She stepped out onto the sidewalk and exchanged hellos with Vito. When she was out of earshot, Adam broke the silence.

"Between the two of them the poodle looks like he's got the higher IQ."

"He does," Vito said. "He takes her out for a walk every night."

"Look, Pop, let's not get into this shit now. Jessie's locked up. We ought to get him the hell out."

Vito nodded after a few moments, then threw his arm over Adam's shoulders.

"It was a nice thing you did up at your grandparents, Adam. They might end up out of that cesspool because of you."

Adam shrugged, to let Vito know he was aware of the physical contact.

"I had them over a barrel, Pop. When you know somebody loves you, you've got a hell of a weapon in the relationship."

Vito looked into his face, uncertain at first that he was interpreting Adam's meaning correctly, then said, "Works both ways though, kiddo. If *you* love a person as much, then the weapons are equal, no?"

Adam considered it for a few moments, then reached forward and hugged his father, Italian style. Vito returned it. Adam was slightly surprised, as he always was since returning to New York, that he was a few inches taller than his father and built bigger. More like Jessie, he thought. When they broke the embrace, Adam nodded.

"You're right about the two-way love evening up the weapons. I guess we got a standoff, Pop."

CHAPTER II

THEY HAD AGREED TO MEET AT THE SHOP THE FOLLOWING AFTERNOON. ADAM HAD THE CAB DROP HIM AT THE corner of Fourteenth and Tenth Avenue. He pushed through the heavy doors of the Vitel Meat Packing Co. just before three o'clock, a few minutes early, then walked carefully between two long lines of muscular calf carcasses hanging upside down from conveyor hooks. The cold worked through his unlined leather jacket before he was halfway across the huge room. It was quiet now, the day's work finished. A bundled, white-coated foreman, filling in order forms at a stand-up desk, watched him for a moment then asked if he wasn't Vitro's kid. It pleased Adam that there was enough of a resemblance to be noticeable.

"Yeah. Is he around?"

As the foreman pointed up toward the office Vito walked out onto the stairs, one arm into his topcoat. He descended in a bouncy, one-two cadence, his left hand skimming along the iron pipe railing. His carriage fired in Adam a glow that briefly dispelled the coldness of the still room, a quiet pride in his father's innate physical fitness. Those were some of Jessie's genes carrying Vito down the concrete stairs so lightly on the balls of his feet. Jessie still bragged that he was naturally so light on his feet that his shoes never needed resoling.

Vito, black hair parted carefully and smoothed back over his ears with a touch of fifties style about it, had a nice, direct handsomeness for a man in his mid-forties. Just shy of six feet, trim, his bearing and the lines of his face called out, "knock-around guy." It pleased Adam. It occured to him that it would be hard to look at a father who was short, overweight, and tweedy enough to seem incapable of existing in the New York City meat market.

"You're a lot better about time than you used to be," Vito said.

Adam ignored it. They walked single file between sides of dead, skinned animals, Vito leading. He motioned with his arm and said over his shoulder, "You play your cards right and all this could be yours, someday."

Adam rapped his knuckles against a steer's leg.

"I could inherit a nice, lucrative undertaking parlor too, if I'm really lucky."

"You ever been through the shop that specializes in steer heads? There's a business for you. Thousands of furry heads around, nothing else. His two kids came into the business, too. Happily."

"Some people have all the luck," Adam said. "What the hell do they use heads for?"

"Sausages and frankfurters, mostly. Cheek meat . . . forehead meat. Some of it goes into salami. It's all trimmings."

They exited onto a loading dock and jumped the few feet to the sidewalk, into the warmer air. Vito's Caddy was at the hydrant only a few feet away. He removed a ticket from under the driver's windshield wiper and tossed it on top of several others on the dashboard.

"Another twenty-five dollars," he mumbled to Adam. "Goddamn meter maids. When the cops were still ticketing you schmeared them fifty a week and had your own private space."

He drove through the deserted block and turned right onto Hudson Street. Adam tapped the dashboard.

"Why do you still drive these things? It's a piece of shit for what you pay."

"It's what I'm supposed to drive. You own a place in the meat market, you're supposed to drive a Caddy."

Adam shook his head and tuned in an FM station that was tolerable, but wouldn't drive his father crazy. They moved downtown slowly through traffic.

• • •

Vito led the way into the Criminal Court building through the Baxter Street entrance. The near end of the lobby was crowded with people milling around or leaning against columns, littering the floor steadily with cigarette butts. While his father waited at the arraignment information window Adam moved to an empty stretch of wall and studied the small crowd. They were mostly black or Puerto Rican, there to make a court appearance or to bail someone out, a half dozen of the women with small children or babies in tow. A sprinkling of poorly dressed, undercover street cops waited to give arrest testimony. They blended in perfectly except for the badges pinned to beat-up fatigue jackets or lightweight mackinaws. A bearded cop, just a few years older than Adam, turned to him and asked, "Didn't you work for a while in the one-three?"

Adam thought for a moment, then said, "The thirteenth *precinct?*"

"Yeah."

Adam shook his head, no.

"You're not on the job?" the cop asked.

Adam shook his head, no, again. The cop lost interest and turned away. Adam tapped his arm lightly.

"Maybe you can help me. I'm here to bail someone out. You have any idea how long it'll take?"

"They assign him a docket number yet?"

Adam motioned toward the information window. "My friend's finding that out now."

The cop looked around. "It's not that jammed up. Once he gets a docket number, shouldn't be more than a couple of hours, tops."

"Where would they be holding him now? The Tombs?"

The cop shook his head, no.

"He's back in the holding pens now, if they already transported him from the precinct."

He was silent for a few moments, then asked, "This kid a good friend of yours?"

"Yeah."

"Then bail him out, if you got to hold up a gas station to do it. They remand him and he goes over to Riker's." He shook his head. "They got species of animals over there are fucking extinct on the rest of the planet."

"The stories about Riker's are true?" Adam asked.

As the cop nodded, Vito interrupted them.

"They haven't even finished the paperwork. She said at least two hours until it's called. Why don't we go get a drink and something to eat."

Adam thanked the bearded cop, then he and Vito walked slowly up Baxter Street toward Forlini's. Adam wanted to try a dim sum place he knew of on Pell Street but Vito shook his head.

"Adam, right underneath us is one monster kitchen, maybe eight blocks square. Thousands of Chinks cooking. Every restaurant in Chinatown has a stairway that goes down to it. Doesn't matter which one you pick, all the food comes up from the same kitchen." He steered Adam by the elbow, diagonally across the street. "Forlini's has nice pasta dishes and good veal. And they serve liquor."

They found two empty stools toward the far end of the bar, next to several lawyers whose conversation alternated from Yankee and Met spring training scores to horror stories of judges who sentence capriciously.

"That son of a bitch in Brooklyn last week flipped a goddamn *coin*. In front of a whole courtroom. A *coin*! Then hit the defendant with five to ten."

Vito ordered Scotch on the rocks. The bartender looked to Adam.

"The same."

Vito raised his eyebrows.

"I thought it was rum and Coke."

"I picked up a little class in California."

As they raised their glasses, Vito reached over and clinked his against Adam's.

"It's good to have you around again. You left too young and you stayed away too long, Adam."

Adam hesitated, then touched his glass against Vito's.

"It's good to be back, Pop."

• • •

After Vito's third drink they moved into the dining room, deserted now but for a pair of grossly overweight, neighborhood Italians dressed in work clothes but wearing pinkie rings, seated at a corner booth. Vito and Adam took a table on the far side of the room. Vito sat back and sighed.

"Relax, Pop, it's not armed robbery they got him for. He's not going to do any serious time for a bar fight."

Vito studied him for a few moments.

"Why'd you mention armed robbery? Where'd that come from?"

"I don't know. It popped into my head."

"Did Jessie ever mention an armed robbery to you?"

Adam stirred his ice cubes.

"It's an expression. Like saying, he didn't kill somebody."

"That's not an answer, Adam. Yes, or no, is an answer."

Adam finally nodded. "Yeah. He once said something about a bank stickup."

"Jesus Christ!"

There was a long silence.

"The high point of Jessie's career," Vito said. "His famous Danbury bank robbery. He can't understand why he's not in the thieves' hall of fame for it."

Vito motioned to the waiter for another round.

"When did he tell you about it? At your Bar Mitzvah?"

"He never told me when I was a kid. The first I ever heard about it was a couple of weeks ago."

"You've seen Jessie since you're back?"

"A couple of times."

"What the hell for?"

"Cause he's my grandfather!"

Vito drummed his fingers on the table for a bit.

"I like him, Pop," Adam said. "I always have. Whatever your beef is with Jessie, it's not my beef."

"He'll do nothing but hurt you in the long run."

"Jessie's not looking to hurt me."

"No, he's not. But it'll end up happening anyway."

The waiter set down their drinks.

"Where did you see him?" Vito asked.

"We had drinks together over in Chelsea a couple of times. We sort of double-dated one night."

"Double-*dated?*"

Adam smiled. "He's got a thirty-four-year-old chick he's running around with. A little bit whacko, but she sure as hell looks good. She brought along a friend one night. The four of us bounced around on the West Side, all Jessie's regular spots." He smiled again. "A few of them, you're better off wearing a helmet, but the rest were okay."

"Look, Adam, I love Jessie. I'm glad you love him, too. But the man is crazy as a loon. It took me many years to figure that out. Meanwhile, I got hurt."

"You look okay to me."

"Yeah? And what about twenty-seven months that I sat in a cage upstate? Because of the screwball values that loony tune raised me with. My twenty-second and my twenty-third birthdays I sat out in Auburn. Your grandfather thinks like a Gypsy, Adam. That's the closest I could ever come to his value system. He thinks like a fucking Gypsy."

"There're a lot worse value systems to be raised with. I've met a couple of thousand middle-class kids—moral as could be—and their sense of family and loyalty absolutely sucks."

They sat quietly for a while, then ordered two veal Milanese. As the waiter left the table, Vito spoke, very calmly.

"Adam, I was seven years old. The last year my mother was alive. We lived on Thirty-ninth Street, right off Ninth Avenue. Jessie waited till Christmas Eve to buy a tree. As usual. The prices were going to come tumbling down, they'd be giving them away. My mother kept telling him, buy one now, they'll all be gone. He took me with him Christmas Eve and she turned out to be right. We drove all the way up to Fort Tryon Park. Nothing. Little scrawny trees were all they had left, and Jessie's getting himself all worked up because he doesn't want to face her with some little piece of shit in his hand.

"Near midnight, we're passing an Esso station and Jessie hits the brakes as though a ball had just bounced out in front of the car. The station is all dark and closed up. Right on top of their little brick garage is an absolutely perfect, all lit-up Christmas tree. 'Whoa,' is what he said while he stopped the car. 'What a fucking score *this* is.' He pinched my cheek. 'We even got the lights right on it.' I sat in the car while he climbed up a drainpipe and nailed it, lights and all."

Adam tried not to look pleased.

"What did your mother say?"

"She smelled a rat, but she kept quiet." He shook his head, mildly exasperated. "My mother came from a family probably held up the station two weeks later."

Vito finished his Scotch and switched to a bottle of Heineken. He drank most of the beer before he continued.

"I've got two or three dozen stories a lot like that, Adam. I'll give you just one more. I was twelve. Living alone with Jessie up in the West Fifties. It was a tough, mostly Irish neighborhood. The name Vito didn't do me a lot of good. Jessie was scrambling—driving a hack a couple of nights a week, shaping up on the docks when someone could slip him in—meanwhile running around glomming anything on the island of Manhattan wasn't nailed down. The man will steal a hot stove.

"Again Christmas is coming. He winds up with a temp job at Macy's, demonstrating electric trains for Lionel. The first week he's there, there's some kind of bookkeeping mix-up and he gets a check from Lionel, who hired him, and another check from Macy's. He's like a pig in shit. Told me Santa Claus was finally going to treat us right for a change and took me out to dinner. A big deal in those days, eating out. I closed the joint with him, curled up at four in the morning in an empty booth and sick as a dog on maraschino cherries and a quarter bottle of creme de menthe.

"About ten days before Christmas he tells me to stay home from school tomorrow, he'll give me a note for the nun. Jessie only believed in Catholic schools. He gave me careful instructions—drummed them into me—that had to be followed to a tee. And I damn well followed them. At twelve-thirty on the button, dressed in my Catholic school blue knickers with a red tie, I walked into the Broadway entrance of Macy's and rode the escalators up to the sixth floor. There was Jessie, operating a monster display of trains, maybe six sets running at once, with all the little drawbridges and tunnels, tiny little towns, snow, little traffic lights and signalmen—the whole works. He loved every minute of it. Just like he said, there was a crowd around the setup. He spotted me and he gets everything moving like hell, tooting the whistles on all of them from his little control panel. Sure enough, that drew a lot more people over; they were finally three or four deep. Meanwhile, I had worked my way into the extreme left-hand corner. Next to me, just like he said, there was 'a little carton all wrapped up and tied, with a throwaway handle on it so it's nice and easy to carry.' Trouble was, what Jessie had called a nice little carton was little for one of his dock worker friends. This goddamn thing came up to my waist. It looked like I could have lived in that carton if I had to.

"He does just what he's supposed to—he crashes three sets of trains into each other at a crossing. The place goes wild, people laughing and stretching to see. I pick up the carton to go out nice and slow. I was supposed to count to myself—one thousand, two thousand—so I wouldn't panic and run. Well, the fucking carton wouldn't budge. It had to weigh seventy pounds and I'm twelve years old. I *dragged* the son of a bitching thing across floors and down five escalators, then across the main floor where I got jammed up in the revolving door. All the time I'm counting, up to maybe five hundred thousand. An old Irish security guard helped me get out the door, then called a cab for me. I'm about an inch away from shitting my pants. I got it into a locker at Penn Station. Six hours later, when I bitched to Jessie and wanted to know why the hell it was so heavy, he shook his head at me like I was retarded.

"'The money's in the fucking *engines*, dummy.' That's what he told me. He threw me a big ten bucks for my end."

Adam thought about it for a bit.

"He had a lot of confidence in you, Pop. That counts for something when you're twelve years old."

"You believe that?"

Adam chewed a piece of bread longer than he had to.

"I don't think I'd hold it against you if you had ever shown me that kind of confidence."

Vito felt his anger rise but held it back.

"Well, I can't tell you what to do, Adam, but take a little fatherly advice. Just for once. Steer clear of Jessie. He's not the bargain he appears to be."

Ray Garvey met them in the Criminal Court lobby at five-thirty, carrying an overnight bag and a bulging briefcase. His vest was unbuttoned and his tie loose and off-center. He shook their hands quickly.

"You look terrific," he said to Adam. "You realize how long it's been?"

"At least five years."

"So what the hell were you up to for five years?"

"I was finding myself."

"I hope you got laid a lot while you were looking. Tell me, where did you turn out to be?"

Adam smiled. Ray turned to Vito.

"What's with your crazy old man? He's the only guy I know collects Social Security checks and still walks around kicking ass."

"He wishes he could get Social Security checks. I'm amazed he's not printing his own. It's not like him."

"I'll go back and talk to him. I was in Philly for two days on a fraud trial. I just got in touch with my office from the airport."

He tightened his tie and buttoned his vest before walking into the courtroom. Adam and Vito sat on a bench in the rear and watched Ray disappear into the holding pens. They listened for a while to a cop's arrest testimony against a bewildered, long-haired drug user. He had been collared in Union Square Park on four minor charges. The judge finally agreed to release him on a one-hundred-dollar cash bond. There was no way he could raise it.

As the attendants led him off, Vito said to Adam, "I don't want to press you to the wall on this, but I'm going to be up front. Your mother and I are thrilled to have you back in town,

Adam. We both want to get some kind of relationship going that we never had. The truth is, though, there's no way I'm going to be able to do it if you're hooked up with your lunatic grandfather. Sooner or later Jessie's going to cook up something with you and you're going to wind up in a jackpot."

Adam concentrated on the judge's bench for a few minutes, then turned to Vito.

"I'll be up front with you too, Pop. Number one, I'm not winding up in any jackpots. Number two, I'm not going to lie. Jessie and I already have something cooking. And it's absolutely perfect."

CHAPTER III

JESSIE WAS BROUGHT OUT OF THE HOLDING PEN A FEW MINUTES BEFORE HIS CASE WAS CALLED. HE BLINKED several times, managing to seem bewildered while he searched out the youngest defendants on the side bench, a pair of twenty-year-old blacks. Normally surefooted and erect, with the hint of adolescent buoyancy in his stride that both Vito and Adam had inherited, he now appeared to shuffle through the judge's field of vision. He settled in between the two young blacks, folded his hands in his lap, hunched his shoulders forward, then sat still and looked toward the ceiling occasionally, apparently distracted by the newness of it all. From forty feet back Adam studied him in profile, which always intensified for him the clash between Jessie's Indian bone structure and his Irish eyes and complexion.

Vito sat silently and divided his time between watching Jessie and watching Adam watch Jessie. Some of the admiration Adam felt showed on his face. It came as no surprise to Vito that his father and his son were planning something together, he had seen it in the cards since Adam was thirteen or so, old enough to know that Jessie's value system was different from any other he knew and old enough to sense that he, Adam, took after his grandfather even more than he did his father. Vito's anger rose when he concentrated on Jessie going through his act, knowing that the same acting talents being used for the judge were also put into playing the tune that would lead Adam along behind Jessie Mac, the Pied Piper. The constraint of being in a courtroom, where he could not confront Adam as openly and directly as he might want to, calmed him somewhat. For sure Adam had taken that into account before breaking the news to him. His anger diffused itself even further because Jessie was, after all, in trouble. He was in the clutches of the legal system and Vito, almost from birth, had been taught that fighting off the law at the cave entrance was the first order of family business. All squabbles were to be put aside for the duration. The final damper on his anger was his own ambivalence about Jessie's way of life. While Vito wasn't anxious to see his son go off to do a crime, he still believed in his heart that flat-out honesty was a system for victims.

When the clerk read out the docket number, Ray Garvey had to walk to the side bench and tap Jessie to gain the old man's attention, then guide him to the proper place before the bench.

"Is the judge going to swallow this frail-old-man shit?" Adam whispered.

Vito shook his head, no. "Not if they've run a good B.C.I. check on him. Jessie's like a successful politician; his record speaks for itself."

A crisp, young assistant DA described the charges and the circumstances in detail. It fascinated the judge, who was at least twenty years Jessie's junior. He asked for an explanation of the fight in Jessie's own words, less, it seemed to Adam, for any use it might be in setting bail than to satisfy his own curiosity.

"This little song and dance ought to be good," Vito whispered.

"We argued, Your Honor, and to be fair about it I was as much at fault as he was. One thing led to another and he cursed my mother. When I told him that my mother was a Native-American—an American Indian, Your Honor, a full-blooded Cherokee—he said it was too bad Custer had made such a half-assed job of it."

Jessie shook his head regretfully.

"Well, that did it. I lost all control. I cursed him, Your Honor. I admit I was out of order, but I just lost control. I cursed him."

The judge raised his eyebrows.

"You didn't hit him?"

"No, sir. But I did curse him. I was a thousand percent wrong. And then he went berserk. He tried his best to kill me."

"What did you call him, Mr. McMullen?"

Jessie looked toward the female stenographer.

"Feel free, Mr. McMullen," the judge said. "We hear all sorts of things in this courtroom."

"I called him a son of a bitch, Your Honor."

The young DA interrupted.

"And this twelve-year veteran of the New York City Police Department took such umbrage at that phrase that he went berserk?"

"Yes, sir. It shocked me, too." Jessie turned again toward the judge. "Something obviously snapped, Your Honor. I think he was so furious at my Native American background, he was looking for an excuse to attack me. The man came at me like a trained killer." He paused. "While he was carrying on earlier, sir, he said he had been in Vietnam. God knows what the poor man..." He shook his head from side to side.

"And what did you do?"

"Tried to protect myself, as best I could."

Jessie stepped back from the table to dramatize what had happened.

"As he attacked, Your Honor, I did what I could to keep him away."

He straightened his arms and flailed his fists in front of him, striking an imaginary foe only with his second set of knuckles—little-girl style—shoulders and body rigid, pivoting only his elbows and wrists while he turned his head sideways and squinted, fearful of being hurt. When he spoke he seemed short of breath.

"The scuffle lasted for a few minutes. I did what little I could, for a man of my age."

The DA waved his report toward the judge.

"The little Mr. McMullen was able to do for a man of his age seems to have been pretty effective, Your Honor. The officer has taken eighteen stitches in his face, his nose is broken in two places, and most of his front teeth are gone or soon will be. His head is now wired up because of a dislocated jaw. That's aside from a possible concussion." He turned toward Jessie. "That's what you describe as a *scuffle*, Mr. McMullen?"

Jessie shook his head in wonder.

"I must have been so terrified, Your Honor, that I hit him harder than I knew."

"Mr. McMullen doesn't seem terribly marked up," the DA said softly.

"It was mostly body blows he hit me with, Judge. I can barely pull myself from place to place today."

Adam leaned closer to Vito.

"What the hell do you think Jessie whacked him with, a chair?"

"Probably just his hands. He hits like a mule."

The judge seemed ready to release Jessie on his own recognizance, until the DA read the B.C.I. report aloud. It stretched back fifty-five years, to a three-year reformatory sentence in Oklahoma. The DA pointed out that Jessie's first serious charge had been at age nineteen, in a mining camp in Montana. He had been convicted on an assault charge.

"Your Honor," Ray Garvey said, "I would like to point out that the defendant's son is present in the court. *And* his grandson. His roots in the community..."

The judge interrupted with a hearty laugh.

"Counselor, all day long I hear, 'The defendant's parents are in the court, Your Honor.' I've occasionally been told that the defendant's *grand*parents are also in court. This one—a son and a grandson—is a first."

He leaned forward.

"Bail is set at ten thousand dollars. A thousand-dollar cash bond is acceptable. And I might add, Mr. McMullen, that if I lived anywhere near your neighborhood I would sincerely hope that you couldn't raise bail."

Ray Garvey suggested the bar on top of the Trade Center but neither Adam nor Jessie had a proper jacket. Vito mentioned Spillane's, a bar up on the West Side that Jessie had frequented for thirty years. Jessie dismissed it with a look of disgust.

"I don't go near Spillane's anymore. The guy's running a

fucking geriatric ward up there. There's more pacemakers at the bar than there are broads."

They settled on a small place off Mulberry Street that Vito supplied with meat. Jessie ordered a shot of V.O. with a tall V.O.-and-water chaser, plus two antipastos to pick at while they drank.

"You're lucky Vito had the thousand in cash handy," Garvey said to Jessie.

"I'm lucky he knew enough to bring it along," Jessie said. "He's always got a couple of grand swag money sitting in his safe." He turned to Adam. "He robs the tax collector, your father."

"It was legitimate money. Three thousand petty cash," Vito said. "All of it legitimate."

"What denominations?" Jessie asked. "What size bills did you pay with?"

"Hundreds. It was all in hundreds."

Jessie nodded at Adam.

"Did I tell you? Swag. Nobody keeps hundreds to use for petty cash. That money was being robbed from Uncle Sam." He turned to Garvey. "That raises your tax rate, Ray. And mine. People like you and me foot the bill because of people like him."

He drank down his shot in one slow, smooth motion, then sipped his highball chaser, smacked his lips, and sighed.

"It's never been easy for me, having a thief in the family," he said, and pinched Vito's cheek. "But thank God you had the cash ready for a worthy cause."

"You did a nice job in court, Jessie," Garvey said. "Shuffling around like a case of incipient senility. Those two kids you squeezed in between were perfect."

"I figured they'd set me off nicely." Jessie said. "I looked for the youngest ones there and when they turned out to be pitch black, too, it was like a bonus. Let the judge see this poor, rickety old glass of milk jammed in between the shines."

They ordered another round. It would be Garvey's last, he said, he had no intention of competing with this crew. Adam sipped his drink while Jessie and Vito finished theirs, then asked his father, "How come you drink so good? Jessie's half Indian and you're a quarter. I thought Indians couldn't handle alcohol."

Jessie shook his head gravely.

"Sioux. Sioux and Apaches could never hold their liquor. Cherokees were always good drinkers."

"Could be," Vito said. "Could also be a case of the absolute triumph of strong Irish genes over savages."

"Native Americans," Jessie said.

"When the hell did you get onto this Native American crap?"

"I been hearing it on TV for a while now. I like it. If I'm supposed to walk around calling every spic on the West Side a Hispanic, then I want to be called a Native American. It's got a nice ring to it."

"Did that cop land the first punch?" Adam asked.

Jessie winced. "Adam, I've never been in a bar fight in my *life* where anybody but me landed the first punch. It's a sure recipe for losing."

"Listen to your grandfather, Adam," Vito said. "He's passing on invaluable wisdom."

"You should have paid more attention to it," Jessie said. He turned to Adam. "Your old man got his ass kicked on a regular basis when he was a teenager." He shook his head. "You never had a fast pair of hands, Vito."

"Only with bail money, Pop."

Jessie ignored it. Garvey laughed easily, leaned forward to comment, then changed his mind. He said to Adam, "It's only with this family that I figure I'm better off keeping my mouth shut. And I've known these two for maybe thirty-five years. I still feel like an outsider."

"That's because you are," Jessie said. "Don't ever forget that, Adam. No matter what goes on between ourselves, when an outsider shows up—even a guy as sweet as Ray here—if he goes against any of us, he's the common enemy. I say that with all respect to you, Ray."

Garvey raised his glass.

"To whom should the common enemy submit his bill when this is over?"

"Give it to Vito," Jessie said. "He's the only one in the family's got a buck these days."

Jessie became impatient shortly after Ray Garvey left. He poked at the last slices of cappicola on the antipasto plate.

"Let's get the hell out of here," he said finally. "Another twenty minutes, I'll be pissing olive oil all day tomorrow."

Vito paid the check, handed the waiter a folded twenty, and pushed a ten across the bar on their way out. He left regards for the owner. On the street he answered Adam's silent question with a look of resignation.

"They expect it," he said. "I take four thousand a month out of the place."

"He'll make it up," Jessie said to Adam. "Short them a few pounds of scallopini here, a few pounds of beef there—your old man still knows how to rob when he has to."

Vito didn't comment.

They drove to Doheny's, the bar on Tenth Avenue where Jessie had just beaten up the off-duty cop. Adam had apparently visited it on one of his bouncing rounds with Jessie. Vito had never been in the place but it looked familiar immediately. A large flag of Ireland was draped on the rear wall beside an American flag that contained only forty-eight stars. Both flags needed a cleaning, as did the bar, and, for sure, the kitchen. Under the flags were matching photographs of Jack and Robert Kennedy captioned, PROFILES IN COURAGE, adjacent to an outdated IRA fund-raising poster supporting Bobby Sands, who had died on his hunger strike a few years earlier. Above the register was a print of the marine flag raising on Iwo Jima. Vito guessed that Kevin Doheny, tending bar, had personally hung it just before the end of World War II.

"This is my son, Vito," Jessie said. "Adam you've met."

Kevin Doheny shook hands with both of them, then shook Jessie's hand.

"That was a nice piece of work last night, Jessie. You haven't slowed up a bit."

"Another asshole let the gray hair fool him," Jessie said. "Cocksucker deserved it."

"He did," Doheny said, and turned to Adam. "Thirty years

of coming in here and your grandfather never whipped an ass that didn't need a whipping."

"You get a lot of fights?" Adam asked.

Doheny shook his head, no. "Once a week, tops. Years ago it was a bucket of blood, now it's a nice respectable bar."

He bought the first round of drinks and a cigar for Jessie, then left them alone to talk.

"Nice guy," Adam said.

Jessie lit his cigar, puffed hard, then studied the tip to be certain it was burning properly.

"He's almost a total hard-on," he said. "You got to learn to judge people better, Adam. Anybody runs a serious Irish gin mill and never touched the stuff himself, he's usually a hard-on. That's Kevin Doheny. He'll take customers he's grown up with—heavy hitters who can't control themselves—and spoon-feed booze onto their rotten livers. Makes the register ring." He puffed his cigar again. "I'd rather rob banks."

Several customers waved hello to Jessie but gave the three of them a fairly wide berth. After ten minutes of Jessie's tales about crazies in the lockup, Adam went to the men's room. Vito was alone with Jessie for the first time all day.

"Are you cooking up something with Adam?" he asked.

Jessie sipped his highball.

"Do I look like I'm cooking anything? I'm a man trying his best to enjoy his golden years."

"Bullshit, Jessie. It's eating you up that you'll turn seventy in a year and a half, and let no one say that old Jessie Mac went out lying down. Well, go make your last big score, fine with me. But please keep Adam the hell out of your criminal schemes."

"Criminal schemes? That's a little bit rich coming from an ex-jailbird like yourself."

"Just keep Adam out. I'm not going to watch you fuck up his life, too."

"Too?!" Jessie set down his glass and tapped his finger against Vito's chest.

"First, somebody's got to teach that kid something 'cause you certainly aren't. If you're not careful with a kid he'll end up going through life with his eyes wide and his shoulders all hunched up. Second, anything you ever did with me, you never saw an ounce of trouble out of. When you went off like an asshole on your own and hooked up with that retarded grease-ball couldn't find his way home every day without directions, that's when you wound up in a jackpot. It wasn't *me* got you the twenty-seven months. What you got from *me* was whatever street smarts you're walking around with. You wouldn't know enough to rob the government and fill your safe with cash if it wasn't for me. You should get down on your knees every night next to your bed and thank God that your father was born before you."

They remained quiet while Doheny refilled their glasses. As he left to ring it up, Adam returned. Vito took him by the arm and pulled him closer to the two of them.

"I want you to hear this, Adam. Your grandfather just got through..."

"He's twenty-three, for Christ's sake," Jessie interrupted. "Throw away the baby bottles and..."

"He *is* twenty-three. And I can't stand over him and run his life. But I can give him some advice." He squeezed Adam's arm harder. "It comes from hard-earned wisdom, too. Your grandfather just told me that I never saw an ounce of trouble out of his schemes. That doesn't mean you won't. And even if you don't see trouble, you're not likely to see much money either. Most of it has a habit of winding up in his pockets."

Jessie slapped the bar hard.

"When did I ever cheat you out of a nickel? When?"

"On every goddamn deal we ever did. Starting with when I was twelve. I saw a big ten bucks out of those Macy trains. Ten big dollars. And that..."

"Are you still whining about those fucking trains? I'll buy you a set for Christmas."

He turned to Adam.

"Your old man holds grudges for thirty-five years. That's the Italian genes in him. That don't come from my side of the family."

"Well, it might sound like piddling shit now, but you know

what that means to a kid of twelve? I deserved another twenty-five bucks out of that. You know what twenty-five bucks means when you're twelve?"

Jessie pulled a small roll of bills from his pocket, peeled off a twenty and a ten, and dropped them next to Vito's money on the bar.

"Keep the change. We're even."

"You're just a little late, Pop," Vito said, and pushed the money beside Jessie's glass.

"No wonder your kid ran off when he was eighteen." Jessie looked to Adam for support. "Your father was impossible when he was a kid and he's never changed. I'm telling you, it's the Italian. Don't let it happen to you. Try to encourage the Irish and the Indian genes."

"Native American," Adam said.

"That's right."

"I'm half Jewish," Adam said. "What about my Jewish genes?"

Jessie dismissed them with a wave of his hand.

"What the hell are you going to do with them?" he asked. "Unless you want to be a doctor."

"That might be the first sensible thing you've ever told him," Vito said. "Three semesters of MIT with almost solid A's. In molecular biology—not something people breeze through. Both SATs in the seven nineties. The kid scores as a goddamned borderline genius. I'll tell you, a doctor makes a lot of sense. A hell of a lot more sense than trying to be a criminal by doing a deal with your loving grandpa, Adam."

"The deal is solid as Gibraltar," Jessie said. "And if you had an ounce of good sense you'd jump right in with us. There's enough in it for you to get out of that lousy business you're in. You *hate* it, for Christ's sake. Running a mortuary for helpless animals."

"Another bank robbery, Pop?" Vito asked. "That was your grandpa's moment in the sun," he said to Adam.

"Would you please drop that grandpa shit," Jessie said. "Adam calls me Jessie. We're both more comfortable that way."

He drank down his whiskey and chased it with several long gulps of his highball. The alcohol expanded his mood.

"It sure as hell *was* my moment in the sun," he said to Adam. "Let me tell you—this bank robbery was fucking *elegant*. None of that pushing notes at a teller then runnning down the street in a pair of sneakers like some sixteen-year-old nigger. This was done right."

He warmed up.

"We marched in there like we owned the joint. Halloween masks, surgical gloves, the works. Each of us toting a clean M-one had been robbed from some army depot. You point one of those bastards at a guard and tell him to move, he moves. We didn't rush through it either. Stood right there till it was all in our bags. We didn't leave the feds a *trace*. Not a soul got hurt and we whacked up just shy of a million. Two hundred and thirty big ones, my end was."

He pushed his empty glass forward.

"Where's the money now?" Vito asked softly.

"Where it goddamn well ought to be. It didn't have handles on it."

He spoke to Adam.

"Remember something, Adam, it'll do wonders to improve the quality of your life right into old age. Most people, including your father here, treat money all wrong. They attach meanings to it that really don't exist. Well, when I got rich up in Danbury I did what you're supposed to do with money. I spent it."

"Don't get the idea your grandpa spent it foolishy, either, Adam," Vito interrupted. "Among other investments, he bought what's probably the biggest round of drinks in history."

"Spending money foolishly is the only way you ever enjoy it," Jessie said to Adam. "I went on a four-month tour, the only time in my life. Nine countries in Europe and nobody can ever take it away from me. They can repossess your car, foreclose on your house, but the world can never take back your days of real pleasure."

He smiled at the memory.

"The *QE Two* had just gone into service and I booked a first-class passage. Never forget, Adam—it only costs a hundred percent more to go first class. The first time I ordered a drink at the bar I dropped a fifty. The bartender puts back forty-nine dollars and sixty-five cents. I asked him what the hell that was all about and he explains that on the high seas good booze goes for thirty-five *cents* a pop. Jesus, what a chance to be a sport. I told him to buy the ship a drink. Runty little Englishman gave me the fisheye for a while until I told him loud—buy the fucking ship a drink. The chief steward weaseled around, but I was a first-class passenger. He finally sent stewards through the whole ship—tourist, too—asking people to have a drink with Jessie McMullen. Twelve hundred and fifty-eight of them took me up on it, if those fucking limeys gave me a fair count."

Jessie ordered three hamburgers and had Kevin Doheny move their drinks and money to the deserted front end of the bar where they would have more privacy. Vito took a single bite, then set the hamburger down and warned Adam, "These things violate the Geneva Convention on germ warfare. They not only look like little black golf balls, they taste like them. Try to never eat in Irish bars, Adam. The Irish think that food's something you toss out to accompany booze. They'll kill you if you're not careful."

Jessie smacked his lips and pumped more ketchup onto his half-eaten hamburger. "Eat," he told Adam. "You start babying your stomach at your age and you'll wind up half a fag at forty."

Adam finished his hamburger, then ate Vito's. When he was finished he pulled over a bowl of pretzels.

Vito shook his head.

"There's more roach shit on them than salt," he said.

Adam considered it for a few moments then slid the bowl out of reach while Jessie ordered another drink, bottled beer instead of whiskey.

"You ought to cut back, too," he told Vito. "Stop cocktailing, we've got some serious talking to do here."

"Talk," Vito said. "I'll take littler sips." He stirred the ice cubes with his finger. "We planning your defense strategy on this assault charge? You shouldn't have let Ray Garvey leave."

Jessie sneered. "Forget this assault charge. There's people raping and pillaging out there in broad daylight, for Christ's sake. A nice, old-fashioned assault is a joke in this day and age."

He explained the intricacies to Adam. "They're charging me with Assault Two. It's a class D felony. Without blinking, the DA's going to break it down to a class A misdemeanor and if Ray Garvey presses those pricks like he's supposed to I'll wind up with a dis-con conviction."

"I wouldn't bet on it, Jess," Adam said. "I watched that judge today. What if a jury of your peers decides you're a goddamn menace to society?"

"Where the hell are they going to dig up twelve of my *peers*? I'm half Cherokee. We Indians have special problems you Caucasians can't grasp. Besides, we're not living in Russia; American justice is tempered with mercy. It's traditional. No one's sending a man of my years off to a penal institution just for kicking some off-duty cop's ass."

He examined his cigar, and spoke to Vito. "Let's get down to brass tacks here. We've got a sweetheart of a deal to do. Takes three people to do it. You're a complete dummy if you don't jump in."

Vito looked from Jessie to Adam. They had obviously discussed bringing him into it.

"I spent my childhood doing deals with my father," he said. "Now I'm going to spend my adulthood doing deals with my son? Somebody in this family ought to break the pattern. Kill off the McMullen criminal gene."

Jessie slapped the bar.

"There you go with that criminal gene crap," he said. "You want to see some *big* criminal genes? Go do a scan on the Rockefellers or the Morgans. Those families got criminal genes the size of fucking grapefruits. They did fine with them."

"What the hell are you after *me* for?" Vito asked. "Or Adam? There's twenty thousand thieves live in this town. Highly qualified. And you know them all, Jessie."

Jessie turned to Adam and shook his head slowly, the model of never-ending patience.

"Your old man hasn't smartened up two cents' worth in the

last thirty years, you know that? He still sounds like a fucking hoople head half the time." He moved his face close to Vito's. "You can know somebody for fifty years, Vito. You can save the guy's life twice and he can save yours. He can sacrifice his left hand for you." He waved a finger in front of Vito's eyes. "But you still can't trust him a hundred percent unless you got the same blood. *Blood*, Vito. Get it into your head once and for all. If a deal goes bad—and the best deal on earth can go bad if God's got it in for you—the only people in the *world* who you know won't rat you out are your own blood. Anybody else is up for grabs."

He set his cigar down on the edge of the bar.

"I'm part Indian, so I know about blood. That's what made tribes stick together. It's nice. Nobody can ask any questions, nothing can change, blood is it. People got to go by it. Jesus Christ, Vito, you need *something* in life to bank on."

He took a long draft of beer.

"Blood loyalty makes life simple, Vito. Right, wrong, if, maybe, yes, no—none of it matters. You got something you can *depend* on."

"Didn't I tell you your grandfather thinks like a Gypsy?" Vito said to Adam.

"That's a compliment," Jessie said. "They're marvelous people, Gypsies. Stand-up thieves. Not a hypocritical bone in their bodies."

"And your grandson's being given this golden opportunity because he's blood, too?" Vito asked.

"My grandson brought the deal to me."

Vito turned to Adam, who nodded, yes.

"I don't know what you thought I was up to for the five years I've been away, but I haven't been living like an altar boy, Pop," Adam said. "This deal is perfect. Jessie and I are going on it whether it's with you or somebody else. With you we don't have to take in an outsider. And we want someone who can think on his feet."

"If you were any kind of father," Jessie said, "you'd go along just to keep an eye out for Adam."

"Pop, you'll grab enough on your end to get the hell out of

the meat business. *Out*. The business sucks, you say so yourself. You're on a downhill run. Your business is *shrinking* for Christ's sake. If it wasn't for the cash you're skimming on restaurant sales you couldn't survive. Plus, you hate it—you always have. Well, here's a shot to get the hell out of it. Get into something with a little class, where you can use your brains instead of dealing all day with the lowlifes in the butcher industry. Something, when you meet people socially, you're not embarrassed to tell them what you do."

Vito smiled. "It's not as embarrassing as telling people you just finished a short stretch upstate, Adam. Believe me, I've had that experience."

"Horseshit," Jessie said. "Anybody embarrassed about doing time is behaving like a fucking snob. What the hell is there to be embarrassed about? As long as you done your time nice, you didn't rat anybody out, and you never took it in the ass. You know, Vito, somewhere your values got screwy. When the hell did you get it in your head that it's such a terrible thing to be a thief?"

"What I got in my head, Jessie, maybe twenty years ago, was that it's not *safe* to be a thief. They lock you up for it."

"Safe?! You want to get safe, turn off the compressor on one of your walk-in boxes and go sit in it for the rest of your life. That's safe. You'll never do time, you'll never get hit by a car, you won't even catch skin cancer from too much sun. Who the hell ever put it in your head that being safe is what life is all about?"

He drank down his beer.

"Plus, this is even safer than the green you're robbing the government on, it's that sweet. And it's not peanuts."

Vito sipped his drink and stared through the small window at the trucks moving up Tenth Avenue. After a minute he turned back to Jessie.

"What do you call not peanuts?"

"Forget the money," Jessie said. "I'll get to the money in a minute. Vito, you're not a down-the-line square John. You know it and I know it. Even Adam knows it—and thank God for it—at least you didn't raise him to be a fucking victim. All that

McMullen criminal-gene shit you run on about—well if that's what you want to call it, thank God my grandson picked it up. Nice and heavy, too. You've been honest for the last twenty years or so because you been running scared, not because you bought some line of goods about stealing. People preaching honesty are rich enough to afford it and they'd like to keep the rest of us in line. And how they got rich was by robbing, one way or another. Or their fathers robbed. You know that as well as I do. I *taught* it to you for Christ's sake. You been running scared, plain and simple, and not even liking yourself for it. Well, there's nothing to be scared about here. We're not committing murder, we're not kidnapping anyone. It's safer than riding the Seventh Avenue subway. And to answer your question—what do I call not peanuts—I call it an exact, even, one million dollars, split three ways."

Vito looked at Adam, and raised his eyebrows. Adam confirmed it with a deliberate nod, then waited a few moments before speaking.

"You said yourself I'm not a dummy. If it doesn't sound perfect I'm willing to hear why, but dumb it's not, Pop. You realize that if you don't *use* the money, just invest your end at twelve percent, you'll wind up..."

"I'm not slow with numbers, Adam," Vito said. "Forty grand a year, without waking up in the morning."

Vito finished his drink, slid an empty barstool between Adam and Jessie, and made himself comfortable on it. He called to the bartender to bring him a draft beer.

"Which one of you wants to run down the deal for me?" he asked.

"You tell him, Adam, us Cherokees aren't as articulate," Jessie said.

"If the deal is attractive enough, will you come in?" Adam asked.

Vito thought for a moment.

"I'm not sure," he said.

"Then I don't want to run it down for you. Whatever problems we've had we've always been honest with each other. If you want to learn the details to beat me on the head with them, that's not fair. If you hear the deal and you really think it's bad, fine. Back out. But if you're going to listen then you've got to be ready to jump in if the deal sounds good."

After a minute, Vito nodded. "You've got a point."

"Then why don't you sleep on it for a day or two, Pop. Let us know if you want to hear it out. Meanwhile, let me buy a round of beers and let's just talk baseball or something for a while."

"Starting with Frankie Frisch," Jessie said. "The Fordham Flash. Covered more ground at second base than Kate Smith's shadow."

"Who's Frankie Frisch?" Adam asked. "And who's Kate Smith?"

Jessie looked at Vito and shook his head in disgust.

"I told you, you didn't teach this kid nothing," he said.

CHAPTER IV

THE DOORMAN HESITATED BEFORE SWINGING OPEN THE HEAVY GLASS DOOR, JUST ENOUGH SO THAT Adam was forced to break his stride as he entered the lobby of Christine's building. Adam nodded a thank you anyway; a man of sixty who had to ride the subway in from Brooklyn every day to open and close a door for eight hours was entitled to be pissed off at some kid sharing a twelve-hundred-a-month apartment with an older woman. And Adam's clothes didn't help. He had worked an hour's overtime, wanting to complete the high-speed finishing cuts on a large casting, and then had not bothered to stop at his locker and change into street clothes. Now the doorman, without looking openly at Adam, managed to register his disapproval of the gray work shirt stained with vertical lines of cutting oil that had splattered off the lathe.

Adam emptied the mailbox and waited until the elevator was moving before flipping through the envelopes. Nearly all were for Christine; bills and junk mail. The single piece addressed to him was a postcard from Ambrosia in Berkeley, "Just saying hi—hope things are really together for you," and sending her love, in green ink with an inconsistent slant. He had read once that an inconsistent slant was a sign of madness. She had decorated the edges of the card with a border of minute doodles that might well have been drawn under a magnifying glass; flowers, hearts, and zodiac signs, interspersed with lines of elephants linked trunks to tails. It looked like the work of someone tripping on acid or smoking a particularly powerful species of grass. Or both, he thought. He placed the pile of envelopes on the opened rolltop desk as he entered the apartment, first putting the postcard into his hip pocket, then changing his mind and slipping it into the middle of the stack; it wouldn't hurt for Christine to know that nineteen-year-old California girls were still interested enough to keep in touch.

He did thirty push-ups on the Chinese rug in the bedroom, then showered and shaved. When he came out of the bathroom Christine was in the large easy chair, stretched out in a nearly horizontal position, her feet on the hassock. Her sensible, low-heeled shoes had been kicked off halfway across the dining alcove and a dark brown businesswoman's jacket thrown onto the couch. Adam shifted the jacket away from where he wanted to sit, recognizing her "I've had a bitch of a day" message. She was nearly through the mail, reading glasses low on her nose, the postcard already separated from the pile beside her.

"Did you see the card for you?" she asked.

Adam shook his head, no, walked across, and read it while standing over her. She finished her mail and placed the entire pile on the floor.

"Ambrosia?" she said. "Who in the world names a girl Ambrosia?"

"There are dozens of them in Berkeley. The flower kids in the Haight grew up and had kids of their own. Ambrosias, Starrs, Mountain Girls."

"God. Is she past fifteen, Adam?"

"Almost nineteen. Her parents had her young—they're only a couple of years older than you."

She ignored him.

"Think about it, Christine, you could have a nineteen-year-old Ambrosia if you had started at sixteen."

She left the room to wash and make up. Adam turned on the television, dipped into Christine's open half pound of Afghani sinsemilla, rolled a tight joint on the glass-topped coffee table, and stretched out on the couch to watch a rerun of "Star Trek."

Christine did not want to eat in any of the dozen restaurants they had begun to patronize regularly. She came out of the shower wrapped in a towel and sat beside Adam while she smoked the half a joint he had left, then went into the bedroom to meditate in the darkness for five minutes. When she joined him in the living room she was completely relaxed.

"Let's eat somewhere different," she said. "We're celebrating."

"What are we celebrating?"

"Mr. Myron Shorr—he used to be a client and just returned—he bought a quarter of a million dollars of an over the counter today. That's a twelve hundred dollar commission for me. Plus, he's back in the fold."

"What's the stock?"

"G.Y.A. A little company that went public two years ago. They specialize in old-age homes."

"Is it worth buying?" Adam asked.

"I recommended it highly. After Mr. Shorr raised it as a possibility."

"Should we pick some up?"

She shook her head slowly and said, "No."

Adam turned off the television.

"I'm always happy to celebrate," he said. "But we're not going to retire on twelve hundred bucks."

"There's a second reason. Something coming up that we might retire on. It's going to make us rich, Adam."

"I'm willing to get rich," he said, and waited.

"I'll tell you over dinner. You pick a place. Something nice."

He decided on Sal Anthony's. Christine had never been there and she rarely agreed to Italian food because of the calories. Aside from the food being perfect there were also enough non-Americanized dishes on the menu for Adam to show a little flash in his ordering. While she dressed he lay quietly on the couch, suddenly depressed. He guessed it was the grass. When he closed his eyes his throat constricted a bit and he felt a familiar pressure build up in his chest that meant he was about to be overcome with loneliness. The apartment did not help either, he thought. The walls were too white and too barren and the few graphics on them were too severe and too much of the furniture was made of chrome and glass; it wasn't a place that looked as though someone had settled in for the long haul.

He had been raised in an apartment that always felt like a warm, crowded nest. Christine had her place decorated like a very expensive HoJo motel room. And she was twenty-two flights up. Just knowing that, even without looking out the window and seeing how little the people were and how one-dimensional the skyline seemed, made him lonelier. He realized that he never again wanted to live out of range of traffic noise. The heaviness in his chest would push him close to crying in a few minutes, unless he occupied himself. He wondered for a moment what his mother was doing now—cooking for his father? Likely sitting in the corner of her couch reading the *Post*, a cup of lukewarm coffee beside her on the end table. She still tucked her bare feet under her when she sat with the paper, and it seemed to Adam to be incongruous with the beginning of a double chin and the reading glasses she had acquired while he had been away.

Christine would come out soon, dressed to kill but still looking like a mildly unattractive thirty-six-year-old female stockbroker.

She had looked no better the first time he saw her, even in the dim, party lighting of Robbie Stolber's sprawling Tribeca loft. Adam had been back in the city for only two days, with no money, ready to set up his deal with Jessie and in desperate need of a place to stay. He had crashed with Robbie, the only high-school classmate he would even think of contacting, but had to get out within days. Robbie's girlfriend, an up-and-coming art dealer, didn't want to hear about their days of selling loose joints together at Bethesda Fountain. Christine, leaning against a varnished brick wall beside a large canvas by a Bronx graffiti artist whose work had just been acquired by a major museum, stared over at Adam while she sipped from a glass of white wine. Robbie had pointed out that she had a weakness for younger guys, lived alone in an East Side apartment that could accommodate two comfortably, and seemed to have a fair amount of money. Adam had hurried across the loft, talked to her for an hour, and moved his single, large suitcase into her apartment the following morning.

During their six-week romance he had discovered that she

wanted a younger guy because she wanted to run the show. She would, during dinner tonight, try to lead and advise him. He would resist harder than he should but hover just shy of the point at which she would stay angry overnight. It was a nearly sure bet that something he would say or do would aggravate her. After beating him up a bit emotionally she would make restitution by picking up the eighty- or ninety-dollar check. They would return to the chrome and glass and white walls to get laid, Christine doing a line of coke then acting out whatever madness it might take to wash away her bitch of a day, calling the shots if she chose because she was picking up the tabs.

And because she knew he wasn't ready to walk.

"Why not?" he asked himself, tempted to speak the words aloud; it might force him to answer himself. "It's not just the money anymore."

He could move in with Jessie tomorrow with no trouble. He could, for that matter, move in for a while with his parents. After a few moments of considering going back to the smaller of the two bedrooms in his parents' apartment he grew angry, as he always did when he thought much about them. Why the hell was he so angry with them? He didn't know. Why the hell had he, during the last five years, come into New York four different times on drug deals and never called them? He wasn't sure, he only knew that at the time, sitting in some midtown hotel room waiting for a connection who he hoped wasn't an undercover agent or a wired informer, it would have complicated his life, that somehow he really hadn't *thought* about their feelings—that his parents seemed to him then to be invincible and eternal; there was no pressure on him because he would have forever to works things out with them.

The thought that Christine wanted a younger guy so that she could run the show crossed his mind again, and made him wonder; was he staying with her because he needed an older woman to run the show for him?

As he wondered, Christine came out of the bedroom, dressed to kill, and shook his shoulder.

"Let's go, kiddo," she said.

Adam was thankful for the interruption.

• • •

Anthony's was crowded but Vincent, the maître d', gave them a table against the wall, out of traffic, and lingered for a few moments to ask after Vito. Adam had stopped here for dinner on every one of his secretive New York trips with an admonition to Vincent to say nothing to Vito, who supplied them with meat and was a regular customer. It occurred to him now that on each of those visits he may have been hoping to run into his father.

Adam waved away the menus, then convinced Christine to share an order of fusilli topped with baccalà and to try the chicken oil-and-garlic as an entrée. She took over the wine selection and chose an expensive Barolo that Adam didn't much care for. With Italian food he still preferred red wine from the refrigerator, as his father did. While they drank he had the waiter bring slices of fresh mozzarella with roasted peppers and sun-dried tomatoes, then motioned away the tiny carafe of oil and asked, "Could you bring out some of the virgin green olive oil? The kitchen usually keeps it."

It all worked well enough for Christine to ask, "Where did you learn all this if you're only a quarter Italian?"

"My father," he said. "His mother died when he was a kid but he spent a lot of time with his grandmother. A real old-timer who could really cook. I just picked up the tastes from him."

"Did you know her? Your great-grandmother?"

"Enough so I remember liking her. She was an old lady way into her seventies then. I was maybe eight. They lived in an old tenement on a hundred and eighteenth and Pleasant Avenue. She was married for sixty years to a tyrant. Carmine, my great-grandfather. He was a tile setter, born in Naples, a little bull of a guy who never bothered to learn a hundred words of English. He worked his ass off every day then gambled a couple of nights a week or whored around when he could afford it. If he couldn't, then he hung around the local club drinking vino with friends. Bocci every Sunday. But whenever he got home—any hour of the day or night, no schedule—his pasta had to be on the table within fifteen minutes. God help my great-grandmother if it wasn't ready. The only way she could do it was to keep the pasta pot boiling all day long. Seven days a week, constant. Add water as needed but keep it at a rolling boil. They had a little kitchen that was always like a steam bath, summer or winter. The paint never stopped peeling. I still remember flakes the size of a veal cutlet hanging off the ceiling. My great-grandmother once saw a movie that took place in the Mato Grosso rain forest and she whispered to my grandmother in Italian that it looked a lot like her kitchen. She had terrible arthritis—she always claimed that she got it from the eternally bubbling pasta pot. When she tried to raise her arm or she'd sit rubbing her fingers she'd mumble in Italian, 'Carmine, you son of a bitch, you rotted my bones with your pasta pot.' He was dead by then or she would have kept her mouth shut."

Christine smiled across at Adam.

"Even with that, I'm sure they were very much in love," she said.

"They hated each other for sixty years," Adam said. "They had to drag her to his funeral." He filled his mouth with mozzarella and pepper. "That whole family couldn't stand each other. It's why their daughter ran off with someone as screwy as Jessie McMullen. Marrying into the Irish was close enough to the end of the world, but half an American Indian? They figured she was going off to live in a teepee."

He dug into his bowl of fusilli, concentrating on not staining the Armani shirt Christine had given him a month ago. After a few minutes he took the napkin from his lap and tucked it into his shirt collar. The fusilli began to taste even better. Christine picked at her pasta delicately. She wouldn't like the napkin in his collar, but she wouldn't complain either; the shirt had set her back a hundred and a quarter.

"You didn't get your nails really clean, Adam," she said.

He waited until he had swallowed his food before answering.

"Almost impossible," he said. "The cutting oil soaks right into them. I was machining steel. When you're working with brass or aluminum..."

She closed her eyes and waved her hand at him, pulling her head back as though he were pressing smelling salts on her.

"Please, Adam. I'm not spending at these prices to discuss steel versus aluminum. Your working as a machinist is bizarre anyway. It's perverse, that's what it is."

"I enjoy working with my hands right now. Serious, no bullshit work. It's nice just to build things."

"Perhaps we should invest in an erector set. F. A. O. Schwarz must carry absolute masterpieces. Then, during the day, you could work at something that challenges your abilities and talents."

He put his fork down and leaned forward.

"What talents?"

"You're very bright. Too bright to..."

"I've been hearing that since I'm eight. They used to parade me up in front of my third- and fourth-grade classes to impress every visiting educator, Christine. I was a little intellectual counterpart of Mickey Rooney. 'Watch our Adam McMullen, he solves geometry problems in the fifth grade.' That's not a talent, Christine. Being smart isn't a *talent*. What the hell can I *do*?"

"You could sell stocks for one thing. I could teach you brokering in a matter of months."

"A great job. I could grab twelve hundred here and twelve hundred there just by recommending a stock I wouldn't buy for myself."

Her lips tightened.

"And would it mean supplementing my income by peddling a little grass and coke to my co-workers?" he asked.

"*You* have a problem with *my* morals?" she asked. "You've been arrested for selling drugs. I haven't."

"Give yourself some time," he said. "You'll catch up."

They sat quietly while the waiter set out their entrée. Christine raised her eyebrows when Adam picked up the first piece of chicken with his fingers.

"Do yourself a favor, Christine. Eat this with your hands. You'll ruin the meal for yourself if you use a knife and fork. Chicken oil-and-garlic is meant to be eaten with your fingers." He sucked his fingertips. "My nails will come out clean, anyway."

He selected a few of the tenderest chicken pieces plus a spoonful of perfectly done mushrooms and placed them on her plate; he wanted her to like the food. She used her knife and fork but did stop glaring at him. After a minute she asked, "What about this opportunity I mentioned? Are you interested in listening?"

"Drugs," he said.

"Not drugs—hash."

He shrugged. "Nice distinction." He filled his mouth with chicken and chewed slowly.

A childhood friend of hers, Brian Mueller, had spent his college years at American University in Beirut, fifteen years ago. He had used his weekends and vacations to wander through the northern Lebanese countryside, taking photographs and making notes on what he could sense of the culture. It started as research for an anthropology paper, then blossomed into a consuming interest. On a trip during which his VW Beetle had broken down, he had been befriended by a tribe of hashish growers—the Jaffars—an extended family that numbered in the hundreds who occupied a small village near Baalbek, not far from the Syrian border. For as many generations back as they knew of, their ancestors had grown and sold hashish. Brian had gone there to look over the Temple of Jupiter, which was one of the best preserved Roman ruins on earth. He had gotten to know the Jaffars and had taken to visiting them regularly over a period of two years, actually moving into their huts for weeks at a time and attending their weddings and funerals. When he finished school and returned to the States he drifted into importing furniture and rugs from the Middle East. On six different occasions the furniture had been constructed around a hundred kilos of hashish. Brian now owned a successful Upper East Side restaurant and two boutiques. He was about to open branches of each in East Hampton and was willing to give his Lebanese contact to Christine for twenty-five thousand, payable out of her first profits.

"I can't go over there, Adam," she said. "A woman can't deal with Muslims."

"So I should go into Lebanon, live in a hut with some growers while the deal goes down, and..."

"Six weeks at the most."

"Six weeks in Lebanon. Second prize is ten weeks in Lebanon."

"Are you frightened, Adam? Is that it?"

"Yep."

"It means bringing in two hundred kilos. You know what that's worth," she said.

"Yeah. For me, it's worth eight or ten years of jail time if I have a really first-rate lawyer defending me. It means I do three or four years, minimum."

"I'm running the same risk. And considering the quarter million or so I'd make it seems like a sensible, well-thought-out, calculated risk."

"You're not running the same risk, Christine. For two reasons. One, you have no previous drug bust. I do. Two..."

"Your arrest was expunged."

"It was. It cost me an extra fifteen hundred in lawyers' fees to do it. They threw the case out of court on constitutional grounds twenty-four hours after my arrest. The federal judge said it was as awful an example of police work by the Drug Enforcement people in California that he had ever seen. They violated my rights in *three* separate ways—any one of which was enough by itself to throw it out. So it was dismissed, then expunged. Do you know what expunged means in our legal system?"

She stared blankly until she realized that he meant for her to answer.

"Expunged," she said. "Wiped out."

He shook his head, no.

"It means more like—faded. If I apply for a job anywhere I'm entitled to say that I've never been arrested. I could apply for a job with the FBI and the same thing holds. Theoretically. But it doesn't hold if I'm arrested. Even though it was expunged, the prosecution is allowed to bring it up and the judge takes it into account for sentencing."

"Are you sure? It doesn't seem fair."

"Welcome to the real world. So for sentencing purposes, or even for plea bargaining, if your little Leb deal goes sour, Christine, I'm treated like a second offender. It means I'm looking at eight or ten years for two hundred keys of hash. You're a solid, stockbrokering citizen who gave in to temptation once. Talked into it by me, no doubt. Three years' probation with a good lawyer."

She patted her lips with her napkin and helped herself to more chicken. Adam was pleased that she liked it.

"What was item two?" she asked. "You said there were two reasons we weren't running the same risk."

"Second reason is that you're a woman. It means that if we get busted the nice, bright-eyed prosecutors are going to describe prison to you, tell you about the two-hundred-pound diesel with a smelly snatch who's going to share your cell and how you'll have to go down on half the guards twice a week. And all that need not be, if you'll only rat out the real criminal—vicious Adam McMullen."

She half smiled. "No one could call you vicious."

He realized that she had drunk half a bottle of the Barolo.

"Prosecutors don't know any other way to describe a defendant, Christine."

"And you think I would testify against you to save myself?"

"It's nothing personal, Christine. But my grandfather Jessie pointed something out to me years ago. Do you know how many women's prisons there are in this country compared to men's? Very few. You think it's because females are more honest?" He shook his head, no. "Women don't do time—they rat everyone else out. It's a known fact."

They finished the food in silence, Christine reaching forward to spear the few mushroom slices remaining on the platter. He ordered two espressos and a slice of zuppa inglese, a shot of Sambucca for her and anisette for himself, then on impulse had a fat, three-dollar cigar brought to the table. He ignored the glances and the studied coughing from a nearby table.

"Fuck them," he said to Christine. "I bought the cigar here, let them complain to the management." He puffed on it expansively. Christine watched him for a bit, then said, very low-keyed, "You're my only chance on this hash deal, Adam."

He knew she was right, and made an effort not to take advantage of his position. He lowered the cigar and moved his chair closer to the table.

"I need a man to help me on this, Adam. The Arabs really won't deal with a woman. And I have no one else to turn to."

"I don't want to be unkind," he said. "I really don't. But like the Dylan song says—it ain't me you're looking for, babe."

"It's my big chance, Adam. And yours. I've been selling small quantities downtown for a couple of years now, and I've made good money. Just to be on the safe side, a year ago I visited one of the best drug lawyers in the city, Michael Cunningham. You know him?"

"He's quoted in every other issue of *High Times*," Adam said.

"Well I left Cunningham a thousand-dollar retainer, in the event that I ever need his services. And I asked him a little bit about his clientele. Who are they, really? He enjoyed telling me. 'I don't get hired for heroin cases,' he told me. 'Hash, marijuana, and cocaine—large quantities. It's almost all federal, mostly importation. My clientele is ninety percent flakes, running drugs with only a half-baked idea of what's involved. Middle-class drug-culture kids who when they're busted are amazed that the government treats drug smuggling seriously. They assume that because smoking grass is practically legal that bringing in a ton or so of anything but heroin is pretty much okay. The flakes figure that they're not criminals so they're shocked when they're treated like criminals. Well, another eight or nine percent are desperadoes—career criminals who are tempted to take a shot at one big drug run a little late in life because the stakes are so high. Then there's the one or two percent of solid, calculating, noncriminals who know precisely what they're doing.' Cunningham called them the Joseph Kennedys of this generation—instead of booze it's hashish or marijuana or cocaine. 'They're the guys whose kids might very well run for president of the United States in forty years,' he told me."

"We're part of that one percent, Adam," she said.

"I'm not part of any percent, and I think you're in that first ninety percent flake group Cunningham described so well."

She half slammed her fork down, hard enough for their nearby waiter to busy himself at another table.

"You ungrateful son of a bitch," she whispered loudly, and waited for a response.

"What is it I'm supposed to be so grateful for?"

She picked up her fork and used it to emphasize each point.

"You're living rent free in a very classy apartment. You're eating free in some very classy restaurants. You've got a closetful of very classy clothes for which you paid nothing, including the five or six hundred dollars' worth of stuff that you're wearing right now. That's what you've got to be grateful for."

"You ought to take up accounting, Christine. And if you think that for a bunch of *gifts*, I'm supposed to stick my neck out for a five-year bit on a deal I think sucks to begin with, then you don't have a lot of sense."

They sat quietly. Adam added more anisette to his espresso. He waited for her to calm down—the stockbroker in her would take over, he knew. And this deal hadn't been presented to her in the last few days; it was the reason he had been treated so well. After a few minutes she spoke softly.

"Adam, we net a quarter of a million each. I could leverage that money so that in five years we could live very, very well on the interest. I work like a dog downtown every day—it really *is* hard work. Before this I was selling tax shelters, not an easy job either, Adam. And before that franchises and before that computer time. I'm tired. This is a golden opportunity and I need your help."

"You don't need my help, Chris. You need my advice. You've spent your life walking tightropes on deals that were borderline frauds. All white-collar stuff with no really big risks. You've got a nice criminal streak in you for someone raised in Grosse Point. I admire it—it's one of the real attractions I found in you. But you're over your head in this. It's over *my* head and I'm more a criminal than you are—my inclination is even stronger and I've been exposed to criminal mentalities all through my childhood."

He puffed on his cigar.

"Your parents are criminals?" she asked.

"My mother's a hundred percent honest—as much as anyone is. My father is a thief at heart, but with doubts. He wanted me to be honest and legitimate but deep down he believes that only fools are honest and legitimate so I always picked up a kind of double message. Of the two messages I find it hard to swallow the legitimate one. And my grandfather, who I seem to take after in a lot of ways, is a bona fide, lifelong, fully committed thief. A proud-to-be-a-thief thief."

"So then why not join me on this?"

"Because it's stupid, not because it's dishonest."

"So you're going to continue working as a machinist forever?"

"No. I've got something of my own going. And it's not drugs, Christine. With people who won't rat me out if the cops light matchsticks under their toenails."

She sipped her Sambucca and looked hurt. Adam guessed he would be looking for new living arrangements, as soon as she found a flake willing to sit in some northern Lebanese village for six weeks.

CHAPTER V

VITO LOOKED UP AT THE RED LIGHT THROUGH THE SLOWLY MOVING WINDSHIELD WIPERS AND INCHED the car forward for the third time, impatient to be moving yet not anxious to arrive at the plant. The front half of his car now protruded into Eighth Avenue. Seeing no cars within a few blocks, he ran the light and drove quickly along Fourteenth Street toward the usual five A.M. traffic jam at the beginning of the block-long meat market. The five-corner intersection where Ninth Avenue and Hudson Street crossed Fourteenth was densely packed with tractor trailers and smaller, graffitied, local trucks wanting access to the loading docks of the market beyond. Dozens of trucks at every conceivable angle were locked into a standstill, windshield wipers sweeping, the flat chrome hats of their vertical exhaust pipes fluttering above the cabs while the drivers hunched forward patiently on their steering wheels. They waited for the single trailer that was moving to clear itself, after which everyone would move another thirty or forty feet into a new gridlock. Vito stopped and waited, no longer impatient. The truck inching forward was a huge chromed and polished rig, with Provo, Utah, painted in rich brown script on the orange doors of the cab. The driver crept through a wide arc into the center of the intersection, his bumper clearing other trucks by inches. A New York City bus, empty at the end of its run, backed up a few feet to let the Utah rig clear him, and nearly crushed a white-coated meat handler negotiating a dolly of boxed meat through the narrow corridor formed by the rear of the bus and the front of a truck. Several drivers tugged on their air horns, that sounded, in the predawn air, like tugboat signals. The bus driver slammed on his brakes. The meat handler, high already on a joint, Vito guessed, ignored his near death and zigzagged along to some Latin tempo that he alone heard, his hair glistening in the heavy drizzle. After a few minutes Vito parked on the sidewalk on the east side of Ninth Avenue and made his way through the maze of trucks. The concrete, slippery with rain and a fine film of animal blood, called for work boots, he thought, rather than the leather-soled shoes he wore.

He worked his way carefully through the endless sides of beef and animal limbs hooked onto overhead monorail conveyors. The steel canopies that covered the sidewalk carried bare light bulbs too weak and too high up to do much good. He passed Solomon's lamb house where two handlers nodded good morning. The fronts of their coats, white only a few hours ago, were now dyed to a near ruby red with lambs' blood. Hundreds of lambs, hung by their rear feet from conveyor hooks, were being moved off a tractor trailer and across the sidewalk; whole carcasses not yet skinned, intact but for their entrails, their eyes staring down at the sidewalk. The pork house next to Solomon's was receiving its shipment of hogs, also fully intact, little hundred-and-fifty-pounders dangling upside down beside the army of lambs. Vito was grateful that he dealt in beef and veal; the animals were received headless and already split into two sides or four quarters. It was easier to forget they had been mooing and rubbing against one another only a day earlier.

He entered his shop and paused on his way to the office to observe the benchmen at work, down to a crew of seven, all of them now Puerto Rican or black. He remembered when he ran a crew of twenty on the belt—six Jews and fourteen Italians. The young ethnics would no longer take a job that meant giving up any social life to punch in at three-thirty each morning, then stand for seven and a half hours in a cold refrigerator wielding a knife that didn't forgive a moment's carelessness. Even for eleven dollars an hour plus benefits, which, along with the most expensive electric power in the country to run his refrigerator and freezer space, was slowly breaking him. The final nail being driven into his coffin was the competition of the Iowa

Beef Packing Company's meat, precut by low-cost labor in Texas or Utah or Nebraska and shipped to New York frozen for nothing more than handling before being sent to supermarkets. The market was slowly dying.

The benchmen stood on both sides of a stainless-steel conveyor belt, exhaling little clouds of vapor into the air and boning at the brisk pace set by Al Cutolo, his squat, cranky foreman who hoisted quarters of beef onto the belt. Al pushed two extra hindquarters onto the conveyor and walked over to Vito.

"Everything's running smooth," he said. "Pappas called in an order, said he was probably coming back with us. They must have got one bad eye too many from Fletchheimer."

"What are they taking?"

Al took a folded piece of paper from his pocket.

"Three eyes, a shoulder of veal, a hundred pounds of short ribs, eighty pounds of chopped. He wants the chopped at thirty-two percent, he's got a fat analyzer now."

"COD," Vito said.

"He knows."

"You quote him any prices?"

"He wants to pay a third of the invoice in green. I told him we'd give him a nickel a pound under the market. That it wasn't in yet, you'd call him after you got it."

Vito stood for a bit. He wished he could tell Pappas to find another house to aggravate, but he couldn't pass up the business. This would be the fourth time in six years that Vito had the account.

"By the third order he'll say the veal is tough, this asshole."

Al nodded his agreement.

"What's the story with Torres?" Vito asked.

"He's robbing. I nailed him for sure half an hour ago."

"Son of a bitch," Vito said. He was disappointed. Benny Torres was just a few years older than Adam, a bright, hard worker who had started with Vito three years ago. They had gotten him a union book and he was now a packer at eight-fifty an hour. Vito had taken a liking to him.

"I kept my eye on him from the minute he started," Al said. "At four-thirty I sent him for coffee. I'm sure he smelled a rat;

at his rate I could have it delivered from Sardi's and come out ahead. When he was gone I cut open two cartons he had packed for Jimmy's Tavern. One of them was fine. The other one was marked for twenty pounds of short ribs and thirty pounds of chopped. There were three full eyes in it."

"Son of a bitch."

"About an eighty-dollar difference," Al said.

Vito felt the anger rising in him.

"And Jimmy," he said. "That bastard. We've been doing business for five years. He's probably throwing Torres a big twenty bucks."

"What do we do?" Al asked.

"You say anything?"

Al shook his head, no. "Taped it right back up. It's sitting there now."

"What time does Jimmy's pick up?"

"Nine, ten o'clock."

"Don't say anything to Torres. Send him out again later. I want you to find three rotten eyes in the market—something the inspectors won't let through. Rotted, Al, and overwrap them tight so the stink won't come through. Swap them for the eyes in that box and don't say a word. Let Jimmy and Torres straighten it out between them."

"What about Torres?"

"Fire him tomorrow morning. Not before I'm here. Let him come up and see about it; I'm not giving that bastard his last day and a half's pay. Just make sure you buzz me if he sticks a boning knife in his belt. Ungrateful little pimp."

Al looked unhappy.

"Charlie Backer won't like it, Vito. The kid's got a book."

"Not to steal, he don't. The book's to work at eight-fifty an hour, not to rob my meat. Backer won't give me any noise on this. This kid Torres is lucky he don't get his legs busted."

Vito walked toward the flight of steps leading to his office. Halfway across the room he turned to Al, who was already back in place at the head of the conveyor belt.

"Who the hell is cutting on the rail, Al? I haven't heard a saw running since I came in."

"Julio. He's in the can, Vito."

"Well get him the hell out," Vito shouted, loud enough for the entire crew to hear. "If he's crapping on my time, then he's crapping on me. We're not running a fucking welfare office for the whole South Bronx here."

He climbed the stairs slowly, tired before his day had really begun.

Marie was transferring yesterday's time card hours into the payroll book. Vito said, "Good morning," and sat in the oak swivel chair that had come with the business.

"The market's in," she answered. "Everything the same as yesterday but lamb. It's up three cents."

He tilted himself back on the springs and watched her for a bit as she pored over the cards and the ledger, unaware that he was watching. The bifocals that she had worn for a year now made her look almost matronly. Six months ago she had tied a black cord around them so they could dangle safely from her neck. Now she had them perched halfway down her nose. Even with the matronly look, Vito still found her attractive.

He wondered how he could have carried on an affair with her for two years, saying hello to her husband when she was picked up for a lift home—a nice guy who was some sort of accountant in the Trade Center for a state agency. And Marie knew Elaine a bit; they had sometimes sat in the office over coffee and compared notes on the kids.

"You don't shit where you eat," Vito had heard a thousand times in his life. And believed. And had then gone right on to do it, as had most of the thousand people who had said it to him, he guessed. There had been a brief period during which he had fantasized about leaving Elaine and setting up in some cozy Village apartment with Marie. At age forty. Although he had known deep down that he was not about to leave Elaine he had enjoyed flirting with the idea—discussing it with Marie, agonizing over the grief it would cause Elaine, wanting to believe there were still possibilities in his life and tormenting himself with it enough to justify staying out late and getting slowly drunk, the agonized husband torn between true love and a sense of duty, brooding over a rock glass full of Scotch in bars where he convinced himself he only wanted to drink but in lucid moments knew he was there to nail a stray, two-in-the-morning hungry female as an extra in his life. He had nailed large numbers of them.

Like every other owner in the meat market having an affair, his was conducted at the most unromantic hours. He and Marie checked into motels on the West Side in Manhattan at ten or eleven in the morning and moaned, groaned, shouted, and screwed until noon or one, then walked out into the brightness of midday and crowds of people heading for lunch. Occasionally they would use the shop after everyone had left. He had fucked her a dozen times while he sat in the oak swivel chair that he was now in, on his desk, on her desk, belly up, belly down, with her seated on the two-drawer filing cabinet, on a pallet of corrugated sheets in the shipping room with a fresh lamb skin under her ass, fur side up. Wherever they could dream up a possibility, including one twenty-minute try on an improvised sling hung from a conveyor hook among the sides of beef where they slowly traversed the length of the shop, him walking and screwing slowly, her swaying and screwing, until the forty-degree temperature got to his bare legs and ass, only a few minutes before it would have gotten to hers. They had more than once used the rear seat of his Caddy, parked at a deserted pier a few blocks south, two middle-age people with belly fat, each with a family off about their business, pumping away like a pair of trim teenagers. Two years of sex madness during which he had his affair with Marie and must have gone through fifty one-night stands, all the while maintaining an active sex life with Elaine, who smelled a rat, asked a few questions, but decided to put on a pair of blinkers and wait it out.

He was Marie's first and only extramarital affair, she had told him, and he felt guilty about it—had laid naked beside her and assuaged her guilt before exiting into the midday sun—until several months before they had called it quits, when, over a seven A.M. coffee break with Tony Sausages, who hadn't dipped below three hundred pounds since he was a teenager,

Marie had walked past their booth in the corner coffee shop. Vito had kept their affair a secret, he thought, until Tony closed one of his narrow eyes in a wink at Vito and said, "Lasting a long time with you and her. I don't blame you—she's the best blow job in the whole meat market."

Vito had checked it out with Abie Solomon from the lamb house, for whom she had worked previously. Abie had said she was, "A wonderful girl. A wonderful *person*. Prime. You unzip your fly and she drops on you like a trapeze artist heading for the net. And in three years never a mistake in her bookkeeping. With her the bottom lines balance. I was sorry to lose her, Vito."

It had been over for six years and they behaved with one another as though it had never happened. He had simply lost interest in running around and hadn't slept with anyone but Elaine since, not through any conscious decision but just because women who would have once looked good to him were now never quite appealing enough for him to make a move. His standard for a piece of ass had gotten higher, he had thought, then came to realize that his standards had become so impossibly high that he had, in fact, eliminated the possibility of making it with anyone. He didn't have the heart to lie anymore to Elaine and had decided that he was in the marriage for the long haul. Signed up for the duration. None of them had measured up to Elaine sexually anyway. Vito had recently sat in a steam bath across from a once-a-week acquaintance, tiny towels draped across their laps, and after exhausting their usual subjects—the kids, the cars, how lousy business was, how this overweight garment manufacturer prayed nightly that his son would not have to learn Spanish in order to go through medical school—Vito had expanded the limits of their relationship by telling of his situation; that he simply seemed to have lost interest in other women and that he guessed it meant he had finally settled permanently into his marriage. The guy had shrugged, as he might have at a two-cents-a-yard price increase, and said, "Relax, Vito, it's nothing to worry about. Just means you're turning queer."

• • •

He called Pappas and quoted the day's market prices to him. Less a nickel a pound if a third of the invoice was paid in cash.

"It's good to be doing business with you again," the Greek said. "I can't deal with Fletchheimer. Not reliable. Late on deliveries. My prep men have to break their ass and he's always a drop short on my scale. A digital. Good meat, mind you. And prices even a little better then yours, Vito, but not reliable."

Vito said that he was sure things would work out and ended the conversation. Fletchheimer's meat was nowhere near Vito's quality—the man would blend kangaroo meat into his chopped beef if he could get away with it—he had been one of the group indicted for doing it twenty years ago when the Bronx market was still operating. More than likely the Greek had screwed Fletchheimer on payments. Who knew what really happened? It was in the nature of the business for people to lie. Or to mix kangaroo meat into hamburger if the opportunity presented itself. Vito fantasized for a moment; twenty-five tons of roo meat would help bail him out right now. Even if it were practical, he thought, it wasn't his style. He would sooner take a shot with Jessie and Adam. Pull out the stops and put some hope for the future into what had become a day-to-day grind. Throw the dice for stakes that got some adrenaline flowing, with the promise of a future riding on the pass line. Jessie was not far wrong when he said that Vito had stayed honest for the past twenty years only because he was running scared. It might be time to live a little bit the way his father lived every day of his life.

Which brought him to the cause of his anger with Julio for taking a crap on company time and why he was suddenly jumping lights at five in the morning while he was in no hurry, and noticing the whole lamb and hog carcasses hanging over the sidewalks for the first time in years. He had to deal with his decision about whether or not to go off and rob with his father and son as crime partners.

It was terribly tempting. A third of a million dollars, tax free. If he were to walk away from his business tomorrow, selling it for the last dollar he could and settling his debts, his thirty thousand IRS liability, and his personal charge and credit card bills, he might have twenty-five thousand in his kick. He could scale his life way down. Buy his way out of the remaining two years on the Cadillac lease with Potamkin and trade down for a five-year-old piece of junk that would mean keeping a carton of Sears motor oil in his trunk, funnel and can opener with it, and checking his own transmission fluid. Back to age twenty, with a full set of Craftsman sockets in the trunk for the road trouble that would occur three times a year. Give up the two-twenty-a-month garage and let Elaine devote eight hours a week of her life to shifting the car from one side of the street to the other to comply with alternate-side-of-the-street parking rules. He could continue to rent his East Side two-bedroom for nine hundred a month, a steal in today's market. But not be able to buy his apartment—the building was in the process of going co-op, and it would happen within the next six months. A nonevict plan, thank God, which meant that Vito could continue to rent, but he really wanted to buy at the insider prices being offered. He could begin by giving up Hickey-Freeman suits and shopping instead at BFO. One-fifty a suit instead of five hundred. Beat a retreat with Elaine to second- and third-rate restaurants and eat out only one night a week instead of four, then have to calculate the tip carefully instead of thinking in increments of five. Think about timing any long-distance calls to catch off-hour rates, then watching the clock to see how long he was talking. Forget four-day stints for the two of them in Florida on a whim twice a year. Let Elaine color her own hair and close out the few Fifth Avenue store accounts she had. Cut back from Johnnie Black to a private-label Scotch and hunt through the bins for good buys in California jug wines.

Fuck it, no.

He walked the few feet from his desk to the office window and stared down for a while at the crew boning out beef on the conveyor belt, on their feet fifty weeks a year in a forty-degree climate while he sat on his ass in a heated office. He went back to the swivel chair, watched Marie absently scratch the inside of her thigh, and considered the other side of the coin.

First, he could get pinched on this deal and bring an abrupt end to a fairly decent middle-class life. Elaine down the tubes, too. Second: What did it mean in his relationship with Adam?

If the deal blew up he himself might do a few years. He was old enough to do the time without destroying his life and old enough so there wouldn't be swarms of crazed convicts out to gang-rape him.

And Elaine could visit once a week, talking to him across a table.

If they didn't ship him too far upstate?

They could cover it with Elaine's parents; Nat and Rose were out of it enough to believe he had cheated a little on his taxes and been persecuted by the government. He would get a lot more reading done, work out regularly, be off alcohol completely, and come out none the worse for it.

And what of the boss wherever Elaine took the bookkeeping job she would have to take? Would he expect her to drop on him like a trapeze artist heading for the net?

He would pull a decent assignment for the couple of years: the library, an office job, at the very worst in the meat section of the kitchen, a slot where you could do a hundred favors and get them back in return. And the upstate hacks weren't about to beat up on a soft-spoken, middle-class white guy trying to do his own time. Softball in the warm weather, chess all year long. Not a picnic but certainly doable time.

But would Elaine then want *to go down like a trapeze artist after a year or so of Vito gone and her living alone hand to mouth, knocked for a loop in her middle age?*

It occurred to him that a couple of years might seem like doable time while he sat here in his own office but would it seem so doable once he was locked up? If he was worried now about Elaine with some new boss, how would he feel lying on a cot in the dark hundreds of miles upstate? He remembered his two weeks in the Tombs twenty-five years ago, after sentencing, waiting to be shipped upstate, on a tier of twelve cells that were opened from eight to four every day, the dozen prisoners free to pace the eighty-foot-long by six-foot-wide caged corridor that ran the length of their cell block. They played checkers or chess or sat on the floor, propped against the bars, and lied to one another about the scores they had made on the streets. A wild nineteen-year-old Spanish kid from the Bronx, Joe Loco, war counselor for the Penguins, one of the half-dozen highly organized New York gangs of the era, looking at twenty to life for killing a rival with a baseball bat in an East Harlem poolroom, had lain sprawled out on the floor away from everyone, his skinny little neck propped against the bars of his own cell. Vito was expecting a visit from Elaine, whom he had met a year earlier and was about to marry just before he was arrested. When she didn't show and Vito was pacing up and down the narrow cage, someone had asked what was wrong.

"My girl was supposed to be here," he had answered and continued pacing.

Joe Loco had smiled up at him, his eyes glassy from drugs smuggled into him by one of the hacks, and said in an exaggerated Spanish accent, "Relax, man, she's just out sucking and fucking with one of your friends."

Vito had stared at him for perhaps five seconds, then stomped his right heel down onto the Puerto Rican's nose, crushing the cartilage. He stomped once more, his heel landing on an eyebrow, then kicked out his front teeth with the toe of his shoe. He had stood back and watched the blood flow and pieces of teeth being spit onto the concrete floor as two Irish hacks rushed in and pulled him away, unnecessarily. They moved Loco out to another tier without filing a report—one of the hacks had later given Vito a pack of cigarettes and nodded his approval. "You'll get by upstate," he had said, "but you had time for six more good kicks to his head before we got you—we weren't rushing—and when you're upstate keep stomping until you're dragged off. It's all these fucking animals understand." The hack had been so pleased by Vito's performance that he had pulled him off the tier later that evening to a tiny guard's room and given him a cold can of beer along with some fatherly advice, after learning that Vito had never done time.

"They'll ship you to Coxsackie or Auburn. Attica if you're

really unlucky. Dannemora, God help you, if the people assigning you really fuck up." He had shaken his head sadly and said, "Which happens," then punched open another can of beer for himself. He carried a little church key in his jacket pocket, and judging by his belly used it ten or twelve times each shift.

"Auburn or Coxsackie you'll do okay, considering the job you did on that little psychopath today. Attica, you've got a problem. You listen carefully, you're getting advice I give out maybe twice a year. You're young and you're a good-looking boy. If it's Attica, get hold of adhesive tape and steel blades—buy them for cigarettes, steal them, just *get* them. Before you leave your cell each morning tape the sharpened blades to your wrists so they stick out the length of your hand. Wear them everywhere: on the yard, in the showers—especially in the showers—in the mess hall. They mostly disappear under your sleeves all day. Believe me, the guards up there will see them and they won't bother you about it a bit; they know without the knives you've had it. *With* them you're still in trouble. And I mean trouble—eighteen or twenty lifers'll line up on you. You let it happen once and it'll happen every week of your whole stretch there."

Vito's stomach had gone cold and the hack had seen it in his face.

"You'll come out of there with an asshole the size of the Holland Tunnel," he had said, then punched two holes in another can of beer for himself.

They had sat quietly for a bit, Vito frightened for the first time since his arrest, knowing that wherever he was sent it wouldn't be easy time. After a while the guard had said, "If by some absolute freak you wind up in Dannemora, I don't know what to tell you. Attica's a boy-scout camp next to it. You get to Dannemora and you're in one huge psychopathic ward disguised as a prison. End up there and you look carefully for the meanest, rottenest, ugliest son of a bitch on the yard, and make no mistake about who you pick, then ask him if you can be his girlfriend and every night he fucks you give him a big hug and a soul kiss and a thank you. Knives taped to your wrists in Dannemora won't count, they'll chew them up."

They had finished their beers and the hack had walked Vito back to his cell after the lights were out. He had levered open the cell door from just outside the tier, clanked it open with a steel on steel bang in the silence, escorted Vito to it, then without changing his friendly attitude had said, "Good night, kid," and when Vito turned around had given him the hardest kick in the ass that Vito had ever got. It caught him at the base of the spine and half crippled him for two days, raising a lump the size of a handball that felt like a malignant tumor.

"Wise up, you asshole," he had said as Vito writhed on the concrete cell floor. "Stay out of these prisons. They're built for fucking psychopaths, not for nice-looking young boys named McMullen."

He had clanked shut the cell door and left Vito in the darkness, both hands holding the fast-rising lump, his back arched with pain into a tight curve. He had never seen the hack again. Thank God he had been shipped to Auburn. And during the twenty-seven months he had done he had remembered sometimes as he lay on a bunk in the dark what the hack had said, and vaguely wished that it had been Jessie who had kicked his ass for him instead of a stranger.

If he did join Jessie and Adam would Adam, years from now, wish that Vito had kicked him in the ass instead? There was a fair chance that he would. If he didn't join them and things somehow went sour because of it, would Adam hate him for not having come along? There was a fair chance that he would. Vito recognized a situation familiar to him since Adam had become a teenager; Vito would be wrong no matter what he did.

He walked again to the window that overlooked the shop floor. The men on the conveyor belt continued to bone at a steady pace. Behind them, bundled in his white coat, Benny Torres packed cartons on the stainless-steel table set against the far wall. Vito felt his face flush with anger at Torres' betrayal, then thought for a moment of the irony in his being angry with Torres for stealing while he stood trying to decide whether to go off stealing with Adam and Jessie.

Adam would go with or without him and there was no way for Vito to stop him. He ought to make the decision based upon his own interests. Did he want to risk his neck for a third of a million, tax free? Or, as Jessie had said the other day up in Doheny's, did he want to be safe and sit in one of his walk-in boxes for the rest of his life, where he would never do time, never get hit by a car, never even catch skin cancer from too much sun. He was, in fact, looking down into a big walk-in box right now, where his crew worked. It felt a lot like he *was* doing time, and doing it without a shot at a third of a million. There was no opportunity stretched out before him here. Somehow, the long conveyor belt seemed to typify his plight; constant, steady motion that never really went anywhere. Just the idea of a score, a big one, gave him a feeling of lightness that he hadn't experienced in years. He would continue to consider it for the rest of the day but only because it would get his blood moving and distract him from the reality of the meat shop—his mind was already made up.

CHAPTER VI

JESSIE CALLED VITO AND ADAM ON MONDAY NIGHT AND CHANGED THEIR MEETING FOR THE NEXT DAY from the back room of the Starlight Tavern to Gramercy Park.

"The television says it'll be a perfect spring day," he told Vito. "Let's make it for cocktail hour. I'll bring along a shaker of drinks and we can have our meet on one of those nice little benches and take the air like gentlemen."

When Vito pointed out that the park was private Jessie snorted and said, "Leave that to the big kids why don't you, and meet me at the Twentieth Street gate at five."

It was the perfect spring day predicted by Jessie's television. Young lawyers, accountants, stockbrokers, male and female, walked the few blocks from subway to apartment with jackets open, briefcases swinging comfortably at their sides. Everyone's pace slowed to a stroll as they passed the park.

Vito arrived precisely on time. Adam had been there for five minutes. "He'll keep us waiting a little bit," Vito said. "Your grandfather has a fine sense of the dramatic."

"Have you ever been in here?" Adam asked.

"No. I've passed it and looked in a thousand times. Look at it—like a little English park from nineteen hundred."

Adam took a few steps backward on the bluestone sidewalk for a full view of the block-long, cast-iron fence and the main gate, wide and bulky enough so that a smaller man-sized gate was designed into the fence beside it. The vertical iron spears, set close enough together so that even a small child could not crawl through them, were so thickly coated with years' worth of black enamel that the definition of the casting was blurred. The top, pointed end of each spear stood a foot or more above

Adam's head. Behind the massive fence graveled walks led in four directions from the center, where a life-size statue faced downtown. A variety of trees, planted before automobiles had polluted the air, had grown to heights that no tree ever planted again in the city would reach. Along the walks were benches, miniature by public park standards, with cast-iron ends and thick coatings of green paint. The entire square-block enclosure was being used only by two old ladies who shared a bench on the west walk and a uniformed black nursemaid several benches from them, reading a paperback while she rocked a baby carriage with her foot. A dozen squirrels moved around purposefully on errands or chased one another out of territorial boundaries invisible to Adam.

"It's a little storybook park," Vito said. "Privately owned. You need a key to get in."

"Who gets them?" Adam asked.

Vito indicated the homes surrounding them. "People who live directly on the park. Each one gets a key."

"How do we get in?"

Vito shrugged. "We're leaving that to the big kids."

They stood quietly a few feet apart, backs against the fence, their faces tilted up slightly to catch what they could of the mild, late-afternoon sun. Before them, the few pedestrians and cars along the six-block stretch of Irving Place that ends abruptly at Fourteenth Street moved at a pace more suited to a horse-and-buggy era.

Vito broke the silence. "There used to be a pretty little nursery school a couple of blocks down," he said. "We almost sent you there instead of Jack and Jill. You don't remember going for the interview?"

Adam stared at him for a moment before speaking. "I was *interviewed* for nursery school?"

"You don't remember?"

"No. What the hell did they ask me?"

"The usual stuff. What games you liked to play. Did you watch television? Did you know your ABCs?"

"And of course I knew my ABCs," Adam said.

"You read part of a *New York Times* editorial and you missed exactly five words." Vito couldn't keep the pride out of his voice. "It had to do with the United Nations. The principal was in shock."

"Spare me the rest," Adam said. "They offered me a scholarship."

Vito smiled. "For openers. I think I could have extorted a thousand a semester out of the school to let them get their hands on you."

They stood quietly again, long enough for Adam to think they had dropped the subject of nursery school.

"Your mother wasn't enthused," Vito said. "She preferred Jack and Jill. I always thought this place had more to offer. They only took gifted kids."

"Pop, gifted is a bullshit word. Unless you're talking about a music school or something. Every class I was ever in was for *the gifted*. Most of them were just very smart kids who were also being pushed very hard. That doesn't make you gifted."

"You were, Adam. You *are*, I should say."

Adam felt his anger rising.

"Let's drop it, Pop. This isn't the time or the place."

"It's the perfect time and the perfect place," Vito said. He tried to modulate his voice, knowing that neither he nor Adam seemed ever to be angry with one another, only with one another's anger. They used anger as bidders at an auction use money—each new escalation triggered the other to up the stakes.

"I'm standing on a fine spring day beside my twenty-three-year-old son waiting for my father so the three of us can plan a robbery. The thought keeps occurring to me, Adam, that even though I was raised the way I was, I ought to take a cab to Bellevue and turn myself in for observation."

"You don't have to be here," Adam said evenly.

"*You* don't have to be here is the real point." Vito paused, then spoke more softly. "Your mother and I had such hopes for you, Adam. We had enormous hopes."

Adam shrugged. "Nobody's hopes work out, Pop. I'm half your age and I already know that."

They fell silent again, each wishing the other would continue on the soft note that had been struck. A young woman jogged past them, dressed in shorts and a blue sweat shirt, long-legged, with full breasts bobbing comfortably and a head of shining red hair tied back into a temporary ponytail. She was lovely, and their heads turned slowly in perfect synchronization to follow her for a bit. When she rounded the corner at the east end of the park they caught one another's eyes and smiled simultaneously, without saying anything. As Vito began to speak, Jessie came into view, moving leisurely toward them on the sunny side of Irving Place.

He wore a lightweight poplin jacket, expensive slacks tailored without pleats or cuffs, and a pair of delicate imported shoes with small gold buckles. From the neck down he could have passed for a thirty-year-old, moving on the balls of his feet like an athlete in training. He carried an attaché case that Vito guessed contained the cocktails Jessie had referred to yesterday.

"I'll bet there's a little alligator crawling across your chest," Vito said and reached to pull open Jessie's jacket.

Jessie moved away.

"Let's get serious here," he said. He turned to Adam. "Try to keep your old man on the track, Adam, or he'll have us all playing ringalevio in the park."

He took a brass key from his pocket and opened the gate. Adam looked at it closely. It was the most unusual key he had ever seen, with several small knobs projecting out at odd angles.

"It's a bitch to duplicate," Jessie said as they stepped into the park. "I think this one was made with a wax casting or something. And the pricks change it every couple of years. You'd think they were protecting a pile of gold instead of an acre of lawn."

They sat on a bench along the east walk, Adam and Vito settling into the tranquillity of the place while Jessie watched their reaction appreciatively, a man showing off his private garden, planted and tended with his own hands over a period of many years.

"Nice, no?" he asked, and set the attaché case on his lap. He twisted it so that the top was out of their line of vision while he set the three digits of the combination.

"We're all going to work together but we're not allowed to see his briefcase combination," Vito said to Adam. "You'll get used to Jessie's style."

"Habit," Jessie said, and opened the case.

A fresh package of nested, airline-style disposable glasses lay next to an unopened quart of Seagram's V.O. and a plastic bag of ice cubes that had been in the case for perhaps ten minutes. He tore open the package and poured each drink over two ice cubes, then tossed a cube to a nearby squirrel, who pulled back each time he touched his nose to it but kept returning, unwilling to give up the possibility that it was edible. They touched the plastic glasses and Jessie said, "Glass clinks a lot nicer but it's a pain in the ass when you're traveling." He raised his drink and added solemnly, "To the McMullens."

Each of them sipped his drink. Jessie sat back and surveyed the park, intent upon them enjoying the atmosphere.

"Pastoral," he said. "That's what they call this kind of place. Pastoral."

Adam looked slightly surprised. "That's a perfect word for it."

Jessie nodded his acceptance of a deserved compliment. "Lousy grammar doesn't mean a lousy vocabulary," he said. "You should remember that."

"How the hell did you come by the key?" Vito asked.

Jessie smiled.

"It set me back a hundred and a half," he said, "but it's worth every penny of it—like paying for membership in a good private club."

"It's legitimate?" Vito asked.

Jessie frowned and shook his head, no, patiently.

"The only legitimate keys go to these assholes around here who can afford two thousand a month rent. Old Jim Neary from Forty-seventh Street was a relief doorman in that big white building. He found some hotshot to duplicate them for him and he's sold keys to half of Hell's Kitchen. I was in here last week and it looked like someone had trucked in a couple of stoops full of beer drinkers straight from Tenth Avenue."

"When he runs through the West Side guys, he might have

to sell to blacks," Adam said. "The NAACP hears about this and they'll haul him into court for discrimination."

Jessie shook his head very seriously. "At least six guys have warned him—'If we see a nigger in our park we'll break your ass.' Neary knows better."

"Nobody chases you?" Vito asked.

Jessie laughed.

"There's a stooped-over guard hobbles around the place who should have retired five years ago. Biggest muscle in his body is his Adam's apple. He asked Butch Spillane for some identification and Butch told the guy if he was ever bothered again he'd pour gasoline on him and light him up. The old guy keeps his distance ever since."

They sipped their drinks and relaxed, waiting for Jessie to start talking business, but he seemed in no hurry.

"We should catch up on a little family talk," he said. "This family doesn't get together often enough."

"You really think that's a problem?" Vito asked. "It's only been six or seven years."

"That's my point. We don't get together often enough."

"Well, there's nothing like a good robbery to bring a family close."

Jessie looked to Adam to share his exasperation.

"Your father's always been a fucking wisenheimer. Started when he was about three. Does he do that to you, too?"

Adam nodded, then squeezed Vito's knee to cut short any comment and said, "But not much anymore. Probably less than I do it to him."

Vito remained silent.

"Meeting called to order," Jessie said, and rapped three times on the bench. "Adam's got the floor."

The park greenery and the spring weather had mellowed each of them. Vito and Jessie sat back with their whiskeys and allowed Adam to explain things at his own pace.

"You might not know it, Jessie, but I went up to MIT as a physics major. I had big plans to spend six or seven years learning everything there was to know about it and then I was going to 'do physics,' as the pros say. Brilliant physics."

"You would have, too," Vito said. "You could still do it."

"Let him talk," Jessie said.

"I got up to MIT and discovered a whole new world. I had been around really sharp students in high school, but most of them were drones. The bunch at MIT were so intellectually advanced you'd swear they had been dropped into the middle of Kendall Square from another planet. This was the absolute cream, skimmed as fine as possible. It was like living with a whole tribe of prodigies."

He looked at Vito.

"These were the *real* intellectually gifted that you were talking about before, Pop. Guys who spent twenty hours a day talking or listening, never cracked a book, then got A's across the board anyway. Nobody ever seemed to sleep but nobody ever seemed to study either. There was a tremendous energy level around the place. In the middle of it all the very best LSD east of California was being manufactured by a couple of eighteen-year-olds in their spare time. One of my classmates, Jed Sheckley, graduated high school at fifteen and had no patience for college so he hung out for a year and became what used to be called a phone freak, guys who would play really heavy games with the phone company, breaking security codes, the whole works. For the hell of it. Jed became one of the best, along with a guy from Berkeley called Captain Crunch. It bored him after a year so he started hacking computer programs. He formed his own software company and ran it for four years, then sold it to IBM for five million bucks when he was twenty and decided to go to college. He started at MIT when I did. Wanted to do molecular biology. That's what *everyone* was up in Cambridge for. The Whitehead Institute was molecular biology heaven. Sheckley told me to 'Get the hell out of physics. You can't do it without getting your hands on an accelerator and the damn things cost a few hundred million to build. You'll end up with a hundred other guys on an experimental team. Molecular biology you can still do yourself. A high quality centrifuge and a gel box and you can win a Nobel Prize in your kitchen.'

"He was right. I switched after a semester. Hell, you couldn't be around Kendall Square without catching molecular biology fever. The school got me some work on what they call UROP—the undergraduate research opportunities program. I spent a couple of hours a day working as a lab assistant for a doctoral candidate who was trying to show that viruses could cause cancer in mammals. They had proved it in birds and now they're up to trying to prove it in humans, but proving it in mammals was very hot at the time. There are hundreds of projects like that going on all the time, most of them funded by the National Institutes of Health. I did dog work: running gels, growing up bugs, making solutions.

"Anyway, the research was being done by Jimmy Chin. An absolutely brilliant young guy even by Cambridge standards."

"A Chink," Jessie said to Vito. "You believe it?"

"He was born on Mott Street," Adam said. "We got a little bit friendly because both of us were from Manhattan. We used to sit up late sometimes over a gallon of wine and a joint and talk molecular biology. I learned more from him than from most of my classes."

Jessie reached across and added whiskey to Adam's glass.

"Anyway, after I left MIT and started knocking around California, we sent each other postcards once or twice. Jimmy got his doctorate and left MIT. He became director of research for one of those little companies formed by hotshot scientific types and venture capitalists to exploit recombinant DNA technology. He got a profit-sharing deal that will make him filthy rich if they ever really connect."

"I've barely followed that stuff in the newspapers," Vito said. "Where is the big money in DNA?"

Jessie interrupted Adam's reply. "Gene splicing," he said. "You should try to keep current, for Christ's sake. Pretty soon they'll be breeding cows that give a thousand gallons of milk every day, chickens who weigh more than you or me. They're going to brew up crap that'll cure cancer."

"Nobody really knows what's going to happen," Adam said, "but the possibilities look limitless. The guys in it first are just hoping to be the Bell Telephones and the IBM's twenty years from now."

Jessie tried to hit a pigeon with an ice cube, and said, "The hell with thousand-gallon cows, Adam. Tell the Chink to work on a species of pigeon that never takes a crap and who'll walk around New York all day eating up the dog shit on the streets, then go back at night to sleep over in Jersey. We could get five hundred apiece for the little fuckers."

"Go on," Vito said to Adam.

"Well, Jimmy Chin was in touch with me just before I left California. He picked up the price of a first-class round-trip ticket for me to Boston. It was supposed to be for an interview—which I figured was off the wall; companies don't fly people like me first class no matter how much potential they might think is there. But I came in. And it turned out not to be an interview. It was to see if I could put him onto the right people for a job he needed done."

"Why you?" Vito asked.

"Why not him?" Jessie asked. "You heard what Adam said—this Chink isn't pressing shirts for a living, he's got his doctoral from MIT. Sounds to me like he knew just what he was doing when he hit on Adam. Thank God he did, for all of us."

"Out of the blue, Adam? He just had a hunch that you might know a thief or two?"

"What the hell's the difference?" Jessie asked.

Adam faced Vito and motioned with his hand for him to cease.

"Hold up, Pop."

"It's a fair..."

"Yes, it is. It's a fair question. But it's a bullshit tone of voice."

Jessie started to interject a comment but Adam cut him short.

"Stay out of this, Jessie, all right? It's between me and him."

Adam's voice was strong, but just short of having the sharp edge that would have aggravated both Vito and Jessie.

"Look, Pop," he said, "we're sitting here talking about going together on a deal. If you really can't hack it, say so and let's call it quits. Otherwise, while we're on this we forget the father and son stuff."

There was a long silence that Jessie broke.

"That's why they took this kid into MIT on a full scholarship."

Adam and Vito remained silent while Vito deliberated with himself. He leaned across Jessie for the bottle and splashed some V.O. into his glass.

"You've got a point, Adam," he said.

Adam responded to Vito's quieter tone by dropping his voice even lower and sitting back on the bench. Both Jessie and Vito were more attentive to what he said than they had ever been in his life, and Adam felt his chest tighten—they were listening to him as an adult. He wondered whether he could maintain the spell. Even Jessie, who treated him so differently than Vito did, was, for the very first time, doing it without a trace of condescension. The same touch of loneliness that he had felt yesterday in Christine's apartment started to engulf him but he fought it off successfully. The squirrels and a small flock of pigeons landing nearby seemed to freeze for an instant, as did his father and grandfather. The beige walls of the nursery school principal's office, covered with drawings, were suddenly clear in his mind—was he truly remembering it or inventing it on the spot? He wanted to say, "Relax, Pop. I'm not who you planned for me to be. Let me be who I am," but knew that he and Vito would then fall comfortably back into a familiar exchange after which nothing would be different. He fought the temptation and instead spoke in a tone that didn't invite a fight.

"You want to know why Jimmy Chin asked me, I'll tell you. Straight out. But we're opening a can of worms. You want it opened, Pop?"

Vito thought about it. Wanting not to, he glanced toward Jessie for guidance.

"I don't push in where I'm not wanted," Jessie said. He fished an ice cube from his drink and tossed it onto the gravel in front of a squirrel who was studying them from the armrest of an opposite bench, then looked into Vito's eyes without challenging him. "But if you're not too old or too pissed off to take a little fatherly advice, if there's a can of worms sitting between you and your son—open the goddamn thing up."

Vito said to Adam, "He's right, let's open it up."

Jessie offered to walk around the park for a few minutes and leave them alone. The surprise in both their eyes and the upward tilt of their heads toward him as he stood up brought out the similarities in their features—their frowns and the slight opening of their mouths gave each of them the same touch of näiveté over the same strong bone structure. Jessie smiled at them with enjoyment without saying why.

"Stay, as far as I'm concerned," Adam said, and Vito nodded his agreement. Jessie sat again and edged himself back out of Adam's vision.

"The reason Jimmy Chin picked me is because while I was at MIT I was the campus drug dealer, Pop—there's one at every college in the country.

"The second worm to come crawling out is that I fit into the role perfectly because I had been dealing since I was fifteen."

"Jesus Christ," Vito said.

"I started dealing grass when I was in Bronx High School of Science, and there's not much competition there. Lots of smokers, but everybody scared to deal it. When I went off to MIT I had just shy of ten thousand dollars in my bottom dresser drawer. There's money to be made in dealing, even half ounces of grass. I got busted at a concert in Jersey City when I was fifteen, peddling loose joints in the stands. I lucked out—the two cops took four hundred joints and a couple of hundred bucks off me, and while the little guy held my arms the other one gave me two punches in the gut that made me vomit all over myself. They left me curled up on the dirt under the stands. He told me if he ever saw me in Jersey City again he'd break every bone in my body and book me for resisting arrest. It was twenty minutes before I could get on my hands and knees to crawl. They didn't leave me carfare."

"It didn't scare you enough to quit?" Vito asked.

"It scared me enough to stay out of Jersey City."

"For Christ's sake, Vito," Jessie said. "Did you ever know a thief got scared off by a warning? It's why people finally figured out that capital punishment's not a deterrent."

"I don't necessarily see Adam as a thief."

"Well then you're necessarily wrong," Jessie said. "He's a McMullen, born and bred."

He raised his glass toward Adam and took a sip.

"Let me finish my rap," Adam said. "The years after I left MIT, I kept dealing drugs in Berkeley."

"But you never sold heroin," Jessie interrupted, then nodded his head approvingly when Adam said no.

"I finally stopped. My name was in too many people's phone books, the local narcs knew who I was, and it was only a matter of time before I took a fall. So if you're worried about me being corrupted, Pop, relax—I've been making money illegally for the past eight years."

"You never got pinched in all that time?" Vito asked. "You're sure you didn't stop because you got pinched?"

"No."

"What's the big deal here?" Jessie asked.

"The big deal is that if he did get busted and if something goes wrong on this deal, then Adam isn't a first offender. They won't treat him like a nice middle-class kid who made his first mistake."

"Well, he never got busted and that's that," Jessie said. Adam nodded in agreement.

"You make any money all those years, Adam?" Vito asked.

"I made a lot of money sometimes." He smiled. "Man, I spent it just as fast. I knew how to use it when I had it."

Jessie raised his glass again.

"I told you he was a McMullen. Born and bred."

They were interrupted by the approach of the old guard, who was obviously about to object to the liquor. Jessie lifted the bottle as he would a club and said, "Take a fucking hike, Methuselah, or when this is empty I'll whack you on the head with it."

The old man kept going.

"The deal that Jimmy Chin has is straightforward," Adam said. "But if you want to really understand it I've got to give you a little background."

"Knowledge is power," Jessie said. "None of us here is in a hurry."

He poured fresh whiskeys and sat back, prepared to hear Adam out, his head tilted up to catch the sun.

"Most of the recombinant DNA work going on is either true

fundamental research or it's oriented toward medical applications. Very little of it goes into agriculture possibilities. Any payoffs on the plant stuff look to be a long way down the line, so the private companies don't put too much effort into it. They all keep a little something cooking off in a corner, though.

"There's an outfit in San Jose, forty or fifty miles south of San Francisco, Engineered Genetic Systems. E.G.S. It looks like they've just made a huge breakthrough, maybe ten *years* ahead of everyone else, in what's called atmospheric nitrogen fixation for cereal grain plants. The dollar potential is so big it's hard to put a number on."

"How does one group get that far out front?" Vito asked.

"Luck, mostly," Adam said. "It happens more often than you might think in research. You've got to know what you're doing, too, but it's like everything else—dumb luck's a big factor.

"Plants need nitrogen. Absolutely crucial. The nitrogen—N Two—is part of the chemical bond that links amino acids together in the chain that makes up a protein. And protein is what a plant synthesizes for growth. There's plenty of nitrogen in the air—N Two—but the plant can't use it in that form. Before the plant can absorb the nitrogen the nitrogen has to be what they call 'fixed.' It has to be converted to something like ammonia; N O Three.

"There are a few ways to get this fixed nitrogen to the roots of a plant. The most practical way is to dump tons of fertilizers that contain nitrogen onto the soil, which is exactly what farmers do. They spend billions—I mean *billions*—of dollars every year on fertilizers. If somebody could *invent* a plant that would somehow fix nitrogen directly from the air, it's worth God knows what. Especially if it's one of the grain plants: wheat, rice, oats.

"Well, people have been fooling with it for a while but now it looks like this E.G.S. outfit just made a quantum leap."

"How the hell does somebody *invent* a plant?" Jessie asked.

"Certain plants can get nitrogen from the air naturally, but in a roundabout way. The legumes—beans, peanuts, soybeans, some other stuff—there's a bacterium that infects their roots, Rhizobium, if you're interested. The bacteria act like a very efficient little fertilizer factory. That's what crop rotation is all about—plant some legumes in a field then next year plant a grain; the legumes leave behind ammonia in the soil that can be taken up by the grain, which doesn't have any bacteria factory working on its roots.

"So people have been working on engineering mutant strains of Rhizobium bacteria—enhancing it so it will be a lot more efficient. They could then grow it in fermentation tanks and just dump it on the soil. The problem is that you're really just working on an improved fertilizer.

"The second approach, which bypasses the bacteria completely so it's more attractive because it's more direct, is to isolate individual cells from plant tissue and grow them under lab conditions, then speed up the mutation rates and hope you come up with new strains of plants that do what you want them to do. It's still kind of roundabout though; you're really just telescoping nature by controlling the rate of mutation. To say it the way a mathematician would, 'It's not an elegant solution.'

"The potentially elegant solution—the most challenging approach—is to introduce foreign genes directly into plant cells. To actually engineer the plant. Invent a new one that'll behave the way you want it to. One possibility involves a bacterium—Klebsiella pneumoniae—which fixes nitrogen for itself. It has seventeen known genes that fix the nitrogen; they're called nif genes. People at the Max Planck Institute, at Cornell, at the Pasteur Institute, have all had some initial success with taking these seventeen nif genes and implanting them into yeasts. The yeast cells took the nif genes but then still couldn't fix nitrogen, which just proved to everyone that the whole business is a lot more complex than meets the eye. And that's where things stood, until recently.

"Suddenly E.G.S. seems to have a breakthrough. No one knows why, but they seem to have gotten the yeasts to not only accept the nif genes but to get them expressed. The yeast is actually behaving as though the nif genes are its own. It's fixing nitrogen. Which means it's worth a fortune, and it's sitting in some low security lab in San Jose. My Chinese friend and his associates in Cambridge will pay a round, even, million dollars for the test tubes of the actual recombinant plasmids plus a logbook that goes along with it. They need a team of competent burglars and one of the burglars has to know enough to poke around the lab and locate the right stuff to steal. That's us, Pop."

The three of them sat quietly for a bit, then Adam asked, "What do you think?"

An expression of contentment came over Jessie's face. He closed his eyes and said dreamily, "A million-dollar jar of germs in a low-security building. That's my pension sitting out there in California."

"What do you think, Pop?" Adam said.

Vito smiled.

"After listening to you talk about nitrogen fixation and watching your face light up when you described the molecular biology scene at MIT, I think..."

"We're not here to discuss my career," Adam said. "You coming in on this, or not?"

After a moment or so of silence Jessie asked, "You entertaining any other three-hundred-thousand-dollar offers?"

Vito looked from his father to his son and said, "That's true." He held his empty glass toward Jessie.

"It's not the *QE Two,*" he said, "but buy the bench a drink, Jessie. We ought to have a good-luck toast."

"Get rid of your ice cubes," Jessie told them as he tossed his own away. "A score like this calls for nice, straight shots."

He poured a half inch of whiskey for each of them and raised his glass.

"To a smooth, easy piece of work," he said.

They touched glasses and tossed down the shots.

CHAPTER VII

ONLY A HANDFUL OF PEOPLE HAD EVER VISITED JESSIE'S APARTMENT DURING THE TWENTY-TWO YEARS he had lived there. It was on Forty-seventh Street, just west of Ninth Avenue, the upper reaches of Hell's Kitchen, which had once been nearly solid Irish but was now, as Jessie put it, "Mixed," which meant that Puerto Ricans had moved in. The Puerto Ricans had been entrenched there for two decades, barely noticed by the hard-core Irish remaining until the past five years.

"The neighborhood can't be too Irish for me," Jessie had recently answered an acquaintance from Staten Island who had asked whether it was still livable, but he hadn't meant it truly; his half Indian blood and a streak of perversity kept him from identifying completely with the Irish—until some outsider like this Wasp from Staten Island challenged his allegiance.

The Irish remaining were the toughest of a tough lot, distilled from eighty years' worth of longshoremen, sandhogs, priests, politicians, cops, and killers; the softer ones who had fled the neighborhood became the tough guys of wherever they moved.

Jessie occupied a third-floor walk-up in a five-story tenement built before the turn of the century that had been meant to house working-class poor even when it was new. He had never been one to entertain in his house, even when Vito was small and Louisa was still alive. His social life had always been conducted in poolrooms until they all but disappeared, local bars until closing time, then, over coffee and Danish at an all-night diner or a Bickford's. There, at several tables pushed together, eight or ten knockaround guys would swap stories until daylight. Night people, whose shoes were always shined to a patent leather gloss; bookmakers, number runners, bouncers, boxmen, steerers, a generous sprinkling of hard-core career thieves, everyone "in action," pinkie ring and gold watchband guys who dressed even more expensively and reached for a tab even more quickly than usual when they were broke. There were dozens of these people Jessie had known quite well over the years whose homes he had never been in, nor had they been in his.

Jessie's building consisted of railroad flats left unaltered over the years, two long, narrow apartments to a floor, each running the full length of the building, with a single, pull-chain toilet per floor shared by two families, its narrow door opening onto the public hall. Jessie could enter his apartment through the front door and walk directly into the living room, which overlooked the street, or use the rear door, which opened directly into the kitchen, a large room at the very rear of the building which housed a huge double sink that, with drainboard removed and a flat disc of rubber set over the drain, served as a bathtub. Within the apartment, three tiny bedrooms separated the living room and the kitchen. To go from one end of the apartment to the other Jessie had to pass consecutively through each of the three minuscule bedrooms or, conceivably, use the public hall. The bedrooms, because they were windowless, would have been illegal had they been constructed in the twentieth century.

The toilet in the hall would have been illegal also. Jessie shared it with the Garritys, a family with whom he had clashed early on. Tension had developed at first because Mrs. Garrity's father, Gerald Heffernan, had come to live with them when he retired after forty-five years as a low-level supervisor in the post office. As an unofficial fringe benefit Heffernan had, every working day of his life, spent an hour and a half each morning sitting on a post office toilet, where, pants bunched around his ankles, he would digest every word of the *Daily News* and the *Mirror*, then nap for the remaining time. Retired, his bowels could not readjust to a shorter time on the bowl. He spent his hour and a half each day in the shared, hallway toilet, the habits of forty-five years so ingrained that he still smuggled in the newspapers under his shirt.

Jessie had suffered silently for months but remained on speaking terms with the Garritys until one of their six sons, a ten-year-old who had been named Goo-Goo while still in the dresser drawer that served as a crib and who, even as an adult would be known on the West Side only as Goo-Goo Garrity, had let half an orange Popsicle fall from its stick to the floor near Jessie's door. When told to clean it up Goo-Goo had wriggled past Jessie and shouted up from the landing below, "Go fuck yourself, McMullen, and the squaw you came from, too," then continued running down the stairs. Peter Garrity, a helper for the Ballantine brewery, had answered Jessie's insistent knocking with half a snootful, barefooted and bare-chested. The area between his chin and his belt had the proportions of one of the beer barrels he spent his days wrestling off trucks and down into bar cellars. When Jessie had described what happened, Garrity had belched, laughed, and said, "McMullen, why don't you take my kid's advice?" at which point Jessie smashed down with his heel hard enough to break several of the small bones in Garrity's left instep, then swung a waist-high, roundhouse right directly into his bellybutton. As Jessie described it to a local bartender an hour later, "Garrity went down like melted butter." Jessie had tugged him by his hair across the narrow hallway to the orange puddle. Sitting on Garrity's back, he rubbed his nose in it for a long time, hard enough to leave bits of skin on the worn hardwood floor, then lifted Garrity's head in his hands and gave it a few vertical thumps until the popsicle puddle turned to a deep red—all this with Gerald Heffernan, five wide-eyed little Garritys, and the missus squeezed into their doorway as an audience.

Since that time, twenty-one years ago, the two neighbors had been unwilling to share even a common roll of toilet paper, as others in the building did—each person who used the cramped toilet on the third floor carried his own roll of paper in and out, including the tribes of Garrity relatives who came to drink and sometimes brawl with one another. None of them ever brawled with Jessie.

He would have had few visitors anyway, but it had been made even more difficult by having to tell whoever got up to use the john that if they required toilet paper there was a roll on the kitchen table. In addition, the apartment generally looked "like the Collier brothers should live here," as Vito had once pointed out while he literally climbed through the center rooms toward the roll of toilet paper in the kitchen. Jessie had called from the living room for Vito to bring his own roll next time if he was so out of shape that he couldn't climb. When Adam had visited recently he asked pleasantly whether Jessie sublet on weekends to Hunter Thompson. Jessie hadn't asked who that was.

He used two of the three bedrooms for storage, and little but kitchen garbage had been thrown out of the apartment in twenty-two years. Anything that was conceivably mendable, "might come in handy someday." Jessie carried in his head a precise inventory of every item in the place, but could never locate the few things that did, in fact, suddenly become handy. The inventory ranged from the innards of countless lamps to a small tank of helium at two thousand psi that he had rolled off the tailgate of a truck and onto his shoulders, mostly on a whim, while the driver and his helper ate lunch in a diner on Tenth Avenue. The tank had simply *looked* valuable. He also, from time to time, bought quantities of swag that were particular bargains and stored them in the apartment. He had, last year, jammed in a gross of fully assembled, six-foot-high floor fans, warranties and instructions dangling from each one, picked up for twenty dollars apiece from, "A couple of up-and-coming incompetent hijackers who thought they were taking off a trailer load of furs." He had moved the fans over a two-month period for an average of eighty dollars each, meanwhile sweating out July and August on the couch amidst his forest of fans because the house current wouldn't handle one of the huge machines and his television at the same time.

Margie, his thirty-four-year-old girlfriend, had been invited into the house for the first time only three months ago, and they had been dating for a year now. He had spent a few days "getting the place neat," but even with that she had surveyed the darkness beyond the living room, slowed her gum chewing nearly to a halt, then intoned in a pure Bronx accent, "Jesus. So this is what life on the reservation was like." Jessie, aware that she knew he had never been near a reservation, had come off the couch to give her a good kick in the ass, then realizing that he was shoeless, stopped—the kick wouldn't do a bit of damage, it would only be symbolic. A minute later, when he told her how close she had come to being kicked and that only his lack of shoes had stopped him, she had taunted him a bit, knowing that Jessie was from a generation in which his girlfriend might be free to curse, but sexual references ought to be made only by men or whores. She had sqeezed his big toe appraisingly with her fingers, with the pressure she might have applied to a ripe plum, and said, "It's too bad you stopped, Jess. I haven't had anything good in my ass for a long time." He had gone off to the kitchen for a fresh bottle of whiskey, using the public hallway rather than climb through the bedrooms.

He waited now for Margie, due at six o'clock. It was Wednesday, one of the two nights a week that she didn't waitress at The Lamplighter, an Upper East Side restaurant whose typical customer had been a patron for thirty years. Jessie, who had eaten there once, maintained that the biggest danger in the place was being run down by an aluminum walker. He sat and thought about where they should eat, when the phone rang. It was Dermot O'Doul's youngest son, Adrian, telling Jessie that Dermot, just two months shy of eighty, had keeled off a barstool at his local pub in Brooklyn at ten o'clock yesterday morning, dead. With all the excitement Jessie was one of the people overlooked until now. Dermot was being waked at Neary's in Park Slope and Adrian thought it would be a poor wake indeed without Jessie McMullen present.

Margie showed up at the living-room entrance fifteen minutes late, holding a pocket-size package of tissues. "In case I have to take a leak," she said, and motioned toward the bedrooms. "I don't want to rip a brand-new pair of panty hose groping through that tunnel for a roll of toilet paper."

"Any panty hose destroyed in this world is a favor to humanity," Jessie said. "A chastity belt is sexier than a pair of panty hose."

She pulled up the front of her skirt slowly, high enough to show bands of white thigh above the tops of black, sheer stockings, just where the metal eyelets of a garter belt clasped the nylon. She winked at him and said, "I agree with you," then smoothed her skirt into place.

When he mentioned the wake she answered quickly, without anger. "I'm not spending my night off at a wake in Brooklyn for someone I never even met. When I buried my four-year-old daughter I swore the next funeral I go to is my own."

He couldn't persuade her. He whisked the dust from his dark blue suit and spent a few minutes snapping a professional's cotton cloth across his shoes, putting as much effort into the backs as the fronts, sorry that shoeshine boys had pretty much gone out with the poolrooms. When his shoes gleamed he clipped his fingernails, cleaned them, then shaped them with a file.

He and Margie were due to meet Adam and a girlfriend of Margie's at Doheny's at six-thirty. Jessie decided to pick up Adam and bring him along to the wake.

"Young people aren't exposed enough to rituals anymore," he said. "Besides, I could use some company."

He offered Margie the use of the apartment. She and her girlfriend were welcome to watch television. She raised her eyebrows and surveyed the living room.

"Maybe we'll figure out something else to do," she said.

"Suit yourself," Jessie said.

He hurried out to pick up Adam, prepared to intimidate the first cabdriver he hailed into taking them to Brooklyn.

Adam had never been to an open-casket wake. For the first few minutes he stared, from a distance, at the made-up body lying at table height, but then he accustomed himself to it and looked over the crowd. It appeared to be anything but the poor wake that Adrian O'Doul had feared. Close to a hundred people were present, the average age somewhere near seventy. Other than Adam, Dermot's five sons and their friends were the young contingent and they were in their forties. Dermot's cronies, people from Jessie's generation, were in control and were running it the way they thought it should be run.

"For sure it'll pick up a little steam," Jessie whispered to Adam.

"How do you know?"

"Watch the digger over there. The one decked out in the mortician's pinstripes, with the vest. That's Michael Neary. You see the way he's circulating? Nervous as a cat. Neary smells it coming and he's been through thousands of Irish wakes."

Adam watched Neary, who repeatedly turned down offers from flasks and confided to people, "Ah, it's not like it was years ago. And perhaps we're all poorer for it. Back when we laid them out in our own parlors, we could bring a bit of cheer to a sad occasion. Now that we're not waking people from our own homes there's so much more *propriety* that's required." He wagged his head, saddened at the loss of the good old days, but he would then place his hands on the shoulders of whichever two people were flanking him and point out that, "There's something to be said for things now, too. It's done now with *propriety*."

By nine o'clock Adam could barely hear himself think, he only heard voices—people recounting tales of Dermot's bootlegging days in the twenties.

"Half the stories are lies," Jessie said, "but at a party like this everybody's just as happy with a lie as with the truth."

No one was bothering now to slip the flasks back into their pockets between drinks. Neary stood beside Adam and Jessie, surveying the room and actually wringing his hands together at chest level.

"You look like some old fag about to be mugged," Jessie said. "What's wrong?"

"The flasks are about dry, Jessie," Neary said. "There'll be a damned hat come out any minute now."

Five minutes later Adam nudged Jessie and pointed.

"Neary knows his wakes, all right," he said.

An upside-down gray fedora with a prominent "Dobbs" label was circulating from hand to hand, already brimming with bills. A little old man with a thick brogue moved beside it, his eyes on the money.

"For a bit of Jameson's Irish," he said to Adam, "before the liquor stores close. We don't want to have to break a window."

Jessie told Adam to hold his money and threw in a twenty for the two of them.

The old man squinted into the hat and said, "Jesus. A double sawbuck."

He peered up at Jessie.

"Ha, I might of known. Is that Jessie McMullen? It must be thirty years."

"Hello, Hugh," Jessie said. "Close enough to thirty. I don't remember the last time exactly but it must have been the West Side and you must have either pinched me or shook me down."

Jessie turned to Adam.

"Hughie, here, retired from the force with a cellar full of coffee cans packed tight with hundreds. Every bill the man ever put up on a bar—and those were few and far between—smelled from Maxwell House Coffee."

Hugh laughed.

"When I was on the job," he said to Adam, "we used to tell new guys assigned to the Borough Office, 'Leave some coffee grounds in the bottom of your can, it helps preserve the currency.'"

"My grandson, Adam McMullen," Jessie said. "This is Hugh Nolan."

They shook hands.

"Your grandpa can't remember whether I pinched him or shook him down the last time we met," Nolan said. "It was both. I collared him for running numbers and after he was booked I sold him back his work."

"He did, now that I remember," Jessie said to Adam. "But he waited till I walked out of the bar. He made the pinch on the sidewalk. Saved the owner a ten-day suspension on his license."

"It was some Greek owned the place," Nolan said. "Even

so, I would've been marked lousy all over the West Side if I'd closed him up. The job was different in those days, Adam. We behaved like human beings."

He studied Adam.

"You're Vito's son?"

"You know Vito?" Adam asked.

"Hell, I knew your old man when he was in a baby carriage. Your grandpa here used to keep his policy slips in the carriage next to Vito. Say hello to him for me. You come from good stock, young man."

He pushed through the crowd and said over his shoulder, "I better keep my eye on that hat."

"Just your eye, Hughie," Jessie called. "Not your fingers."

Nolan laughed.

"Old habits die hard," he said.

"Nolan wasn't the worst cop in the world," Jessie said. "He was one of the ones would pinch a crap game but ask if anyone owed any time. On parole. If you did he'd tell you to beat it before he called a paddy wagon."

During the next half hour Adam was introduced to a dozen people who were pleased to meet him and who sent their best to Vito. They ranged in age from forty-five to eighty-five. There was a warmth and a sense of structure and continuity that caused Adam to wonder why his father had never maintained ties to this group. One of Dermot's nephews, Phillip, who had been a classmate of Vito's in grammar school, sent his best to Vito then led Adam and Jessie out of the room quietly and took them down the carpeted hall to an unused suite. In it were a hundred or so suits hanging on two garment-center, wheeled pipe racks.

"Yves St. Laurent," he said. "Eight hundred a pop in your better stores. These fell off a truck so I'm letting them go for a deuce apiece."

He surveyed Adam quickly from head to toe.

"You look like a forty-two. They're on the left side of that rack."

"Phillip's been my tailor for years," Jessie told Adam. "Last

Christmas he had a beautiful assortment of cashmere coats."

"The returns killed me," Phillip said. "You can't fit people properly for coats on a moment's notice and except for a wake or a wedding I'm usually rushed. I work out of bars or diners. With one eye over my shoulder."

Neither Adam nor Jessie saw anything they wanted. They went back to the wake. A while later the liquor buying party returned. Their entrance caused Neary's eyes to widen, the first husky buyer wheeling a hand truck with two cases of whiskey on it. Following the hand truck was a flatbed dolly, four old men crouched over it, inching it along, "As though they're loading up the *Enola Gay*," Jessie said. Their suit jackets had been laid onto the dolly for cushioning, on top of which rode a shiny, aluminum keg of Budweiser, sweating in the humidity, chocked into place with numerous six-packs of Guinness stout. A dozen local barflies formed a procession behind the keg, shuffling two abreast with their heads bowed and their hands folded under their bellies, regulars at the bar where the keg had been purchased who had suddenly remembered knowing Dermot O'Doul.

"A wonderful old man," one of them said within earshot of Jessie. "None of us could go home tonight without paying our respects."

Jessie whispered to Adam, "Wonderful old man. You can tell he didn't know him very well. Dermot would cut your heart out and peddle it for dog meat if he could see a hundred bucks in it."

When the crowd spotted the beverages a cheer went up. Neary cringed. There were two other wakes running down the hall. Jessie nudged Adam and pointed out Dermot's wife, the bereaved widow. Judging by her gait she hadn't turned down any of the flasks offered her.

"Ah, Michael," she said to Neary and wiped away a tear that Adam couldn't see. "I swear old Dermot just smiled when they cheered."

She walked over and patted Dermot's forehead, then, with her son the priest supporting one arm and her son the battalion chief in Fire supporting the other, old Mrs. O'Doul threaded her way through the crowd on a beeline toward the hand truck of Jameson's. While two mourners began tapping the keg, four others went off to find a proper table to set it on. Apparently, the only suitable stand in the building was an open casket set on a wheeled table in the display room. Adam watched them return with it, barreling the casket down the hallway like old-time firemen pulling a wagon, Tommy Hicks out front, his face flushed, shouting "Gangway!" They wheeled the casket next to the head of Dermot's to form a tee, then hoisted the keg up and into the padded, satin-lined box.

"Fits like a fooking glove," Hicks said as he tested its stability.

Mrs. O'Doul exhaled a long "Ahhh," then pointed out that the scouting party had selected the identical model casket for the keg that she had picked for Dermot.

"Like two twins," she said. "Perfectly matched."

The coincidence touched her enough to bring tears to her eyes.

Michael Neary, observing it all from a position close to Jessie and Adam, shrugged and said to Jessie, "The hell with it, it's hopeless. I've been dragging my ass to AA meetings for sixteen months and nine days and I've had a little bust-out bar down on Fourth Avenue picked out all this time. A sweet little place perfect for tying on a two-day jag when I was ready. Well, screw it, Jessie. If I don't hop off the wagon now there'll only be a brawl. Damned if I ever thought that after a year and a half I'd bust out in my own funeral parlor."

He drew himself a beer and filled a second paper cup with Jameson's then stood for a few moments looking from one cup to the other.

"Jesus," Jessie said to him, "you look like a six-year-old with a chocolate cone in one hand and a vanilla in the other, both melting fast."

Neary drank half a cup of the Jameson's in a slow appreciative way then emptied the cup of beer in two long swallows. He closed his eyes for a few moments, then opened them and quietly considered the scene, a cup in each hand, a line of beer foam above his upper lip. He leaned closer to Jessie and Adam and confided, "I have to admit, Jess, that smooth as the

Jameson's is, it slides down even easier with a good cold brew chasing it along its way."

Neary finished his cup of whiskey then put his pinkies into the corners of his mouth and gave forth a piercing whistle. Everyone looked to him.

"We're supposed to close in a little bit," he announced. "But it would be a travesty to have a ten-thirty last call at Dermot O'Doul's wake. Closing time is extended!"

A cheer went up and several couples began dancing. Flashbulbs started going off and Jessie explained to Adam that people wanted Polaroids of Dermot to send off to friends who couldn't make it. Lefty Callahan, who had driven in from Albany, prepared to snap his Polaroid. After studying the corpse he complimented Neary on the makeup.

"A fine piece of work, Neary. I've seen Dermot emptying wall safes and he never looked this happy."

Lefty took the rosary beads out of Dermot's hands and replaced them with an empty Guinness bottle, set so the lip of the bottle rested on Dermot's chin.

"That's a hundred percent better," he said.

Neary started to object but Mrs. O'Doul stopped him.

"It's the way Dermot would like to be remembered," she said, then her lips quivered and she broke down for a bit before she could explain further.

"It was Guinness Dermot was drinking when he fell from that damned barstool."

Lefty, about to snap his picture, stopped suddenly and said, "Damn it. I can't get him full face without losing the keg in the background. And the keg sets Dermot off nice."

He reached over and tugged on Neary's sleeve.

"Give his head a little twist to the left, Michael," Lefty said.

"The hell I will. There's hours of work have gone into Dermot. He stays the way he is."

They stared at one another for a few moments then Lefty surveyed the people around him and complained loudly, "A fucking artist we're dealing with here!"

He reached into the coffin and used his hands as a chiropractor might to snap Dermot's head to the side. Mrs. O'Doul screamed, "Careful of the poor man's neck, you clot," and poked a gnarled little fist into Lefty's eye. Her blow coincided with Neary's, his a looping overhand right that broke Lefty's upper plate and sent him sprawling back against the beer keg, which toppled from its satin-lined nest and broke two of Frankie Fogarty's toes. Fogarty, who was a bit senile, burst out crying. He sat on the rug with tears running down his cheeks and never even rubbed his toes, just kept repeating, "There won't be a beer fit to draw from it for an hour and a half." After a few minutes he rose and hobbled through the crowd toward the six-packs of Guinness.

Jessie poured cups of Jameson's for himself and Adam and said, "I told you things would pick up a little steam."

By midnight word had spread through Park Slope that Michael Neary was running the first honest-to-goodness wake in years and it seemed that anyone who had ever hoisted a drink with Dermot drifted in. Several good-natured, one-punch fights ensued that were broken up quickly, and a small group of mourners propped up Dermot, who still clutched his bottle of Guinness, into a sitting position so that he would, "Seem more like a part of the proceedings." Mrs. O'Doul's voice rose above the general hubbub, complaining that Dermot's older sister, Dolly, who had just turned ninety-one last week, wouldn't get to see her beloved brother.

"Her last chance," she wailed. "And poor Dolly closer to Dermot than she was to anyone in the world but her twin brother, Sean."

"Jesus," Jessie said to Adam. "Dermot's older brother, Sean. It's like a voice from the distant past. He's been gone forty years. Got shot in a liquor store holdup on Broadway and Seventy-fourth Street."

"Did they catch the guys who shot him?" Adam asked.

"The cops shot him for Christ's sake," Jessie said. "Sean O'Doul didn't work in liquor stores, he held them up."

"Why isn't Dolly here?" Adam asked. "The ninety-one-year-old. In this crowd she'd be the belle of the ball."

"Dolly's in a fourth-floor walk-up on Forty-eighth Street. The past six years she's been too sick to be taken out. The woman's been legally blind for twenty years now—diabetes. Took all her toes, too, and three of her fingers, plus she's got half a dozen other ailments that have kicked the shit out of most of her other organs. There's a young Jewish resident from Roosevelt comes to her house once a week, told the Polack super who shops for her, 'She's a living miracle. Maybe the Irish are on to something,' then he lifted a near-empty quart bottle of Fleischmann's off the night table and said, 'You actually consume this drink?'

"'Rarely more than a pint a day now,' Dolly told him, 'and never a drop before noon,' then she polished off the half a day's ration left in the bottle in one long swig to wash down some pills he had just handed her."

Jessie winked at Adam and asked, "You in the mood for some fun?"

"Sure."

Jessie shouted to the O'Doul boys, who were taking photographs of Dermot to take to Dolly, "Adrian, with poor Dolly's eyes what they are a couple of Polaroids are a poor substitute indeed for Dolly getting to touch Dermot herself."

"You're right, Jessie," Adrian shouted back. "But there's no way to get her here."

"You know what they say, Adrian," Jessie called out loudly enough to attract attention. "If the mountain can't come to Mohammed..."

There was a long silence, broken by Lefty Callahan, who hollered through his busted upper plate, "A goddamned stroke of genius!"

"It's illegal!" Neary screamed. "You're not traipsing him around the city in one of my hearses!"

Old Mrs. O'Doul spread her arms and appealed to the crowd to give poor old Dermot a final tour of the old neighborhood.

As Neary started to protest again, Ray Kelleher shouted at him, "You've got a regular little mortician's mentality, Neary! Since the day you graduated undertakers' school everything with you is doom and gloom."

"It's not *legal*," Neary said. "The Board of Health..."

"Talk about a travesty," Kelleher shouted. "To worry about

some narrow legality at the wake of Dermot O'Doul."

He ran over to the coffin and threw his arm around the shoulders of the seated Dermot so that they were cheek to cheek.

"Fuck Neary and his hearse," he shouted to the crowd. "I've got my station wagon outside."

A cheer went up, after which six volunteer pallbearers pushed forward and carried the casket out the front door. They flattened Dermot out again before sliding the casket into Kelleher's station wagon, which became the lead vehicle in a procession of some fifty cars driven by totally drunk drivers. Since what was already being called "Dermot's Last Tour" had been Jessie's idea, he and Adam were seated in the makeshift hearse beside Kelleher, who drove. Mrs. O'Doul, seated in the rear in the narrow space alongside Dermot's coffin, nipped at a bottle of Guinness and began talking to her husband as they crossed the Manhattan Bridge.

"Wouldn't sit in a nice safe booth, would you—had to be perched up on a barstool like some eighteen-year-old steeplejack. At your age."

Adam half turned and with a sidelong glance watched her punch the coffin lightly several times, then cry her only heavy tears of the night. The crying turned into long, low sobs for a while, then she lay down beside the coffin and slept.

The first accident occurred on the west side of Canal Street, a fender-bender that held up the procession for no more than five minutes. When the New Jersey driver demanded to see a license Nutsy Noonan whacked him. The driver hurried off.

The second problem arose on Eighth Avenue in Chelsea. An immigrant Russian cabdriver who, as Noonan pointed out, "Can't have forty bucks' worth of damage on this fucking wreck!" began demanding a sobriety test for Tommy Archer. When he refused to be quiet, everyone lost patience and let the air out of his four tires while dozens of Puerto Ricans on the sidewalk cheered, for no apparent reason other than admiration for a group of people who could act decisively under pressure. As the air hissed during its escape, Michael Neary, who had joined the procession at the last minute, took the Russian by the collar and screamed into his face, "This is a wake, you heathen bastard! Behave with a little propriety!"

A pair of young cops, obviously street-wise for their age, stood talking to one another nonchalantly a half block away, twirling their clubs expertly by the thongs and rocking on their heels as though all was well on their beat. When several mourners began pounding on the trunk of the cab to get at the spare, the Russian decided to leave. He drove off on his rims, very slowly.

The cortege traveled north again and arrived at Forty-eighth and Ninth Avenue at about one o'clock. They double-parked until there were no spaces left, then used the sidewalks wherever there was access. Hugh Nolan appeared again, Dobbs fedora in hand, announcing that the liquor supply had grown dangerously low during the long ride from Brooklyn. The shaken-up beer keg, abandoned in Park Slope, was replaced by two fresh ones from McPartland's, which were set onto the lowered tailgate of Kelleher's station wagon; Dermot's casket had been removed and set onto the stoop of his sister Dolly's building for an alfresco viewing by old friends and neighbors. The Polish super hung some droplights out of the first-floor windows to illuminate the casket while several mourners opened it and propped Dermot back up into a sitting position. He had the bottle of Guinness clutched in his hands, "As tight as he ever did when he was alive," according to his son Adrian.

Jessie called several teenagers out of the crowd of Puerto Ricans who had gathered as observers at a respectable distance. He held out a twenty-dollar bill.

"You kids must have some Police Department sawhorses stashed in one of these cellars," he said. "The world can't have changed that much."

"Now you talking," one of them said, and pocketed the twenty. "We close this fucking street up, man."

As he hurried off with his friends Adam heard him say, "These old Irish dudes know how to party. You got to give them that." Five minutes later the block from Ninth to Tenth avenues was cordoned off.

"Reminds me of the end of the war," Jessie said to Adam. "We used to have block parties. There was always a nice feeling about them. Like there is now."

"Was my father at them?" Adam asked.

"Everybody was at them. He was probably keeping out of sight, though. Hell, your old man was only seven or eight years old then. The little kids that age spent their time ducking everybody so they could steal beer and scheme up enough change to buy loosies. In those days, at something like a block party, a seven-year-old would get whacked in the back of the head a dozen times a night just for being within reach of an adult."

"What were loosies?" Adam asked.

"Loose cigarettes. Every candy store kept an open pack of cigarettes that you could buy loose for a penny apiece."

"No choice of brand?" Adam said.

"You took what was open. And during the war you were glad to get anything. Wings, Spuds, all sorts of crap."

Adam would have to ask Vito about it, when Vito was in the right mood, and see whether his father remembered those years with as much affection as Jessie obviously did. He doubted it.

A viewing line formed. One by one, people would climb the four steps of the stoop to stand silently for a few moments and pay their last respects to the seated Dermot O'Doul who, under the glare of the harsh droplights that dangled just a few feet above his head, looked like a well-dressed drunk sleeping one off with a bottle of Guinness in his hands. Three of Dermot's sons, the priest, the bartender, and the manager at Met Life climbed the four flights to their Aunt Dolly's apartment. She was sober enough to stop them from carrying her down the stairs.

"You're each of you damned lucky if you manage to get yourselves down these steps with no broken bones," she said. "Bring him up here. God knows I'd hate to see poor Dermot dropped but if he is there'll be no damage done."

The O'Doul boys called up four husky young men to carry the casket up to Dolly. Adam was their third pick. Unfortunately, the staircase was too narrow for the box plus the pallbearers. They tried sliding it up, two men tugging in front,Adam and another behind, pushing. It got jammed in catty-corner at the first floor turn. They stood back and studied the situation, sweating enough to send down for fresh pitchers of beer while they took a breather.

"He was always a stubborn son of a bitch," Mickey Lawlor said. "You'd think he might have changed since they stuck him in that box."

Lawlor, who had been a moving man for years, chugalugged half a pitcher of beer, wiped his mouth, and made a decision.

"He comes out of the box," he announced. "We'll save a lot of weight and there'll be more room to negotiate him up without all that extra bulk."

Francis Reynolds agreed. "Good thinking, Mickey. It'll be a lot nicer for Dolly, too, seeing him more like he was, instead of shoehorned into this sardine can."

They opened the casket and hoisted O'Doul out. He went up easy, head first, Adam grasping an ankle. Mickey said while he had hold of Dermot's shoulder, "I wish half the fucking couches I moved in my lifetime were this stiff. Makes the carrying easy."

Dolly was in the doorway. After she peered at Dermot nose to nose she gave his cheek an affectionate little pat and told them to put him on the couch.

"I couldn't count the nights Dermot slept there when he had a bit of trouble and was keeping out of sight for a while," she said.

Adam left an hour or so later, the block party still in progress, Dermot O'Doul still stretched out on the threadbare couch of his sister Dolly. Jessie was sitting on a stoop with half a dozen cronies, beer in hand, swapping stories, when Adam said good night. On his way to the East Side in a cab that moved fast through the deserted, early-morning streets, Adam thought again of the pleasure he had felt when Adrian O'Doul had tapped him on the shoulder and said, "Adam. That's a nice broad pair of shoulders you've got. Give those three a hand getting my father upstairs."

The matter-of-fact tone implied that Adrian had known Adam since he was born, rather than having met him only hours earlier. After five years on the road, and his teenage years before that spent with middle-class Manhattan kids, Adam had felt suddenly like a member of a huge, extended, Hell's Kitchen family. It was a nice feeling.

CHAPTER VIII

VITO STRETCHED THE SKIN OF HIS NECK TIGHT AND ENJOYED THE FIRST LONG STROKE OF A NEW RAzor cutting a swath from his Adam's apple up to his chin. The five or six pints of Neapolitan blood coursing through his body should have created a heavy, dark beard, he thought, but his facial hair had always been wispy and was now turning gray to boot. Both Jessie and Adam had to shave more frequently than he; another group of genes that seemed to have skipped a generation and emerged intact in Adam. He wondered whether Jessie had somehow managed to hold back from him certain characteristics and instead present them, undiluted, to Adam.

The front door slammed shut and he listened to the sounds of Elaine emptying the bags delivered from Zookie's Deli and setting the table for their late morning Sunday breakfast. He finished shaving, patted on some Witch Hazel, and got to the table as Elaine managed to coax the final slice of lox onto a small platter. He tore off a tiny piece and tasted it.

"Novy. It's tasteless."

"You don't need salt at your age, Vito."

He smeared a thick layer of cream cheese onto half a bagel and laid a slice of lox on it.

"You've been reading the medical advice column in *Family Circle*. My blood pressure is one twenty on eighty," he said and knocked on the tabletop.

"Because I give you Novy every Sunday. It could be two hundred over ninety if I brought home belly lox."

He bit off a mouthful of the bagel and let the cream cheese, the lox, and the still-warm dough compete with one another on his palate, then washed it all down with a long draft of ice-cold Heineken that Elaine had poured for him. She listened to him exhale.

"Sex or food, it's a real toss-up for you, huh?" she asked.

He shook his head, no.

"The food started gaining about my fortieth birthday. It keeps widening its lead every year."

He flipped through the folded sections of *The Times* that she had brought in and pulled out the magazine for himself and the book review for Elaine. It was their regular Sunday morning ritual. He turned the pages but paid no attention to them; he had decided upon this as an ideal time to lay the groundwork for getting off to California for a week. Elaine was accustomed to his making a trip once or twice a year to visit packinghouses in Texas and Oklahoma. He would claim to be on one of those tours and he would take some trouble to deceive her. She expected a call every day when he was away but she never had occasion to call him. He would call each day from California and claim to be elsewhere. For insurance, he would tell her which Holiday Inn he could be reached at the following day in case of an emergency and he would take the trouble to book a reservation, then simply not show. If Elaine did try to reach him for some reason, she would find that he was expected in as a late arrival. His not arriving could always be explained by a sudden change in his schedule. The whole scheme should run smoothly with just a little bit of effort.

"I might be going to Texas next week," he said, without looking up from the paper.

"Which means I should have your shirts out of the laundry."

"Right."

"How long?"

"Monday to Friday, I guess. I'd be surprised if it runs longer."

"I'll be lonely," she said, and pouted for a moment, then returned to her reading.

When they finished eating they moved to the living room where Elaine took the couch and Vito his chair. They read and swapped sections of *The Times* in a set sequence that had evolved over the years, their timing now so refined that each unconsciously hurried through sections that the other would want quickly.

"How come we go through the Sunday paper in twenty minutes when it used to take an hour?" Vito asked. He had been reduced to reading an article in the Outdoor column on how to tie dry flies for trout fishing.

"Because the daily *Times* added that third section every day." She said it without looking up. "It's like a little magazine. It covers all the stuff we used to get only on Sundays."

Vito looked across to the couch where, legs tucked under her ass as always, she was flipping through a special fashion supplement for women. She was right, he thought. It hadn't occurred to him. But why hadn't she ever commented on it? It was the kind of minor observation that Elaine had made to herself at some point but would never think of mentioning except as an answer to his question.

She wet her forefinger on her tongue before turning each page, unaware that he was watching. Elaine shared her thoughts openly—if he initiated the exchange. If not, she was comfortably self-contained, going about her business, devoting a fair portion of each week to patrolling the department stores where she would check out new products with the cosmetic saleswoman and look over whatever was new on the racks—"Keeping current," she called it—then, over dinner, relating some funny incident or even commenting about a particularly good TV movie she might have seen after he had gone to bed the night before. But ideas or values or opinions? She expressed them freely in answer to his questions or comments but apparently felt no need to explore them with him. It was easy to forget that she had any ideas or values. He wondered which was the bigger factor in her silence, the sense of security she seemed to have about her ideas or the belief that at this point in their life the two of them pretty much agreed on everything fundamental. They did, he thought, except for something as fundamental as his risking a little jail time for a third of a million dollars. And taking their son along on the score. Actually, it was the other way around; Adam was taking him along on the score. He wondered whether, if things went bad, Elaine would pay much attention to the distinction.

As he studied her it occurred to him that her hair must be graying, at least a little. There was no way to tell, since she had it colored to a light auburn every month. Even she would have no idea. He suddenly felt guilty for lying to her about his trip to Texas. Oddly, he seemed to feel no guilt about the much bigger, unspoken lie: the burglary itself. It was her easy acceptance of his statement that he would be in Texas for a week that caused his guilt, he thought, for Elaine had never been naive. The reason she was so easily deceived was that she trusted him so implicitly at this point in their life. Then again, perhaps he seemed to feel no guilt about the burglary because if he once let his real feelings about it surface they would be too intense for him to handle.

She finished the fashion supplement and dropped it to the floor. He picked it up and began browsing through it.

"What are they showing this year?" he asked. "What's new in the dynamic world of fashion?"

"Strong punk influence right now."

"Between reading about it, then buying the makeup, then actually applying the stuff, Elaine . . . you put quite a bit of effort into the whole operation."

"You unhappy with the results, Vito?"

"Not for a minute."

"Well, that's what it takes. It's maintenance. A lot of time goes into maintenance. If you're really upset with the time and money it takes, I could put all those jars and tubes into the garbage and go for the scrubbed, natural look. Turn in my high heels for those running shoes that half the women in Manhattan are wearing and devote my days to volunteer work at one of the hospitals on the East Side."

"Let's not rush into anything too hastily," he said.

He moved quickly through the fur coats and outerwear, then found himself flipping pages more leisurely when he reached the lingerie ads.

"This is interesting," he said. "Maidenform has a new front-opening bra. You don't see them advertised much." He looked over the model, who stood in high heels and held her fur coat open among a group of polar bears, bearded arctic explorers, and fake Eskimos. "The woman they have doing their ads now doesn't look bad."

"I notice you've gotten pretty consistent on saying woman instead of girl."

"I keep current, too," Vito said.

They were quiet for a while. Irwin, their twelve-year-old parakeet, began mumbling unintelligibly from his cage in the corner.

"You've been on that page a long time," Elaine said.

He turned it nonchalantly.

"Means you're horny," she said in an even voice.

"Me?" he shook his head, no.

She stood up and yawned, accompanying it with a long, sensuous stretch, on tiptoes, her arms straightened toward the ceiling, until the lavender terry-cloth housecoat opened enough to reveal the deep cleft of her breasts.

"You're horny, Vito," she said. "You just don't know it yet. I spotted it the way you bit into the cream cheese and lox sandwich. I'm going into the bathroom to freshen up. Why don't you pull down the blinds and check out a few more of the lingerie ads? You'll come to your senses."

She walked the length of the living room clutching the terry cloth taut around her hips and waist, then turned before disappearing into the alcove that led to the bathroom.

"Maybe you want to put on a little music?" she asked.

"Which one of us is horny here, Elaine?"

"You. It's definitely you."

He studied her for a bit then nodded his head as though reaching an important conclusion.

"That purple housecoat cries out for a pair of high heels," he said.

"It's lavender. But I'll dig something up." She closed the housecoat demurely. "A little punk influence on the makeup, maybe? Just to keep current?"

He stood up to close the blinds.

"Sounds fine," he said. "How about some soft jazz? Mulligan, or Yusef Lateef?"

She winced. "Maybe you could locate some hard rock, Vito?"

He nodded, and pulled the blinds closed, then called out to her, "Elaine—you're sure I'm the one who's horny here?"

She called back through the closed bathroom door, "Definitely."

After a half hour of intense sex they lay on the living-room rug, a few feet apart, his hand on her open palm. "Now's the time for some soft jazz," she had said and he had put on Lateef with the volume low. Vito put his right hand over his heart to estimate his pulse rate.

"I'll bet we had it up past one forty," she said. "If we had decided to make love instead of screwing, you would have missed twenty minutes of aerobic conditioning."

They lay quietly for a while listening to the music and exploring one another's fingers absently.

"What would you do for sex if I were gone for a couple of years?" Vito asked.

She turned her head toward him in surprise, then patted his hand gently.

"There's a kid at the vegetable counter in Grand Union—in his late twenties—big, good-looking, and he's got a nice way about him. He's mad about me. That's the big thing now: younger man, older woman."

"Serious. What would you do?"

"Are you planning to join the navy, Vito? What do you mean, serious?"

"It's a hypothetical case. Supposing, God forbid, I got put in prison for two or three years. What would you do for sex?"

"I don't deal in hypothetical cases."

"Come on, Elaine, it's an interesting question."

"Well, if God forbid you were in some hospital for a couple of years I suppose I'd mail away for a big kit of assorted vibrators. They seem to be making a selection now where you might have trouble winning me back when you got home."

She rolled over on her side to face him. "But jail, Vito? At this point in our life for you to do something that might put you in prison? I'd start with that big kid at the vegetable counter then work my way through dairy, meats, fish, groceries, and mail you details of how great each one was. What the hell made an idea like being in prison pop into your head?"

"I was speaking hypothetically."

The record ended and he turned it over, then lay down beside her again and stared at the ceiling. The apartment was overdue for painting but he didn't want to go for the fifteen hundred it would cost to have it done right. He was entitled to a free paint job by the landlord's contractor, it was more than three years since their last one, but Elaine refused to let "that schmearer come in here and slap on what he calls white paint. His white is what the navy uses on battleships."

The apartment was comfortable for the two of them; a standard, New York, L-shaped living room, a decent-sized bathroom, a second, tiny bedroom that Adam had used years ago and that was now called the study, which neither of them entered very often, a windowless kitchen, and a tiny bathroom with a ventilator that didn't ventilate. If there were a second bathroom the place would be actually luxurious for their needs. The couch and chairs needed reupholstering, but they had been quality pieces to begin with so they carried the threadbare fabric pretty well. The first-rate Takiz rug on which they now lay naked aged imperceptibly and, if anything, looked better each year. Elaine had bought it the day Adam entered kindergarten, when Vito had hit his number, five ninety three, for twenty dollars straight. She had spent the whole ten thousand on the rug. Now it saved the entire living room from being shabby.

"Have you been overreaching on your tax evasion schemes, Vito?" she asked.

His instinct was to complain that first Jessie and now she was accusing him of tax evasion, but he wasn't supposed to have seen Jessie recently so he kept quiet.

"What tax evasion schemes? I'm a legitimate businessman."

"I thought you were in the wholesale meat business?"

She squeezed his hand to attract his attention.

"What's this hypothetical story about two or three years in jail, Vito?"

"Just what I said. Hypothetical."

"Since when do you deal in hypotheses?"

He raced through some possible answers that might divert her and decided that not responding was safest.

"I'm serious," she said. "You can steal all the undeclared cash you like and I'm not about to moralize. But there's a line that you know not to go over. There's a point where they really *will* lock you up. And you know where that point is."

She reached over and ran her hand through his hair; something she had done often twenty years ago.

"I couldn't take you being away now, Vito. I mean that. When we were kids it was different. The twenty-three months of visiting through plate glass or sitting with a wide table between us was tolerable. It was either going to make it or break it for us and it made it, but I couldn't do it now. There's no *excuse* for it now."

She kissed him quickly and tenderly, then rolled closer so that her upper body was on top of him, her breasts pressed against his chest. She cradled his head in her arms.

"And what in *hell* could we tell Adam? That his father is a criminal?"

He had told Elaine that he needed to go into the shop for a few hours to catch up on paperwork. Instead, he drove through the weekend traffic of the Bowery to Canal Street, found a meter just as he was about to pull into a lot, then stood at the open window of Dave's luncheonette and drank an egg cream before making the rounds of the industrial hardware stores where he would buy gear for the burglary. The egg cream was made with the same brand-name ingredients used when he was a kid but the taste wasn't there.

He watched the bustle of humanity around him. Chinatown's inhabitants apparently had gotten the message to "Go West" and the Chinese had bulged out along Canal Street, occupying the street-level stores and stands before taking over the floors above. These were no more the Chinese of his youth than the soda in his hand was the egg cream of his youth. These were the aggressive Hong Kong immigrants, legal and illegal, kung-fu film audiences who were not about to apologize when they bumped against him. The odors that reached his nostrils over the rim of the paper cup were distinctly Asian; not just the exhaust fumes of food being seared in oil, but ginger and soy intermingled with the strong smell of fresh fish from nearby stands where only an infrequent Caucasian customer asked to have the heads chopped off. The few heads that were removed were not thrown into the garbage. They were sold to old, scrawny Chinese women who knew value. Vito noticed that despite the enormous volume of food being sold there was very little garbage. An ecologist's dream, these people, if only they would handle the very little garbage that did accumulate with more care; much of it found its way to the gutter beside the curb, leaving trails across the sidewalk. The scene lacked only a nice little herd of pigs, he thought, who could graze along Canal Street, heads down, licking up the sixteenth-inch carpet of protein that stretched toward the Hudson River. He set down his empty cup, sorry now that he had consumed that many calories for something with so little taste.

Canal Street west of Broadway was crowded with young people seeking bargains in what were now called recycled clothes, plus artists from SoHo rooting out surplus odds and ends from bins that occupied half the width of the sidewalk.

Vito was surprised at the ease with which he reverted to the burglar he had been thirty years ago. For the first half hour, as he selected three top-of-the-line industrial flashlights, a pair of cutters with four-foot-long handles, and a set of cold chisels, he felt as though he were mimicking the teenage Vito McMullen he had known in the nineteen fifties, a skinny kid with a neighborhood reputation for a pair of balls the size of coconuts. The teenage Vito didn't appear in his memory as a younger version of himself. Instead, he was someone Vito had known years ago, a different person with whom Vito happened to share an identical set of childhood experiences along with the same name. It was how he always thought of his younger self when he looked back to his teenage years, and the dissociation was most intense when he thought back to his time in prison. Now, as he continued to select tools, for the first time in recent memory he was thinking of the teenage Vito McMullen as being himself, thirty years younger. He was no longer selecting the proper tools because he had once observed a young burglar select the proper tools. He *was* the young burglar, grown older. They were one and the same person. He had long ago forgotten how much skill he had brought to the task of breaking into a place that someone had set up with the express purpose of keeping people like him out, and the sense of accomplishment when he finally sat hours later with their money or valuables spread before him on his kitchen table.

He bought half a dozen hardened round punches that would go through a door lock neatly with one sharp blow, a plastic-tipped, weighted mallet, a heavy-duty saber saw with an assortment of blades, a three-quarter horse variable speed drill, and a fifty-foot industrial extension cord whose grounding plug he would later snip off. He carried everything to the trunk of his Caddy and fed three quarters into the meter, then bought a short and a long pry bar, fifty feet of two-thousand-pound-test nylon rope, a small block and tackle, and three large tool cases which would house everything comfortably. At an electronics supermarket near Sixth Avenue he found a digital multimeter, some miniature alligator clips that worked off spring plungers, and flexible magnetic strips that could be cut to size with scissors.

He spent nearly eight hundred dollars; an overkill, he thought, but remembered back to a July night when he was seventeen and working on the final inner door of an importer's warehouse in Red Hook, Brooklyn, with Peewee Grogan, who was only inches away from being a midget. Peewee was known as the only guy in Hell's Kitchen who could hit you with an overhand right to the balls. He had a reputation in the neighborhood for being able to slip through a sewer grating if he had to. In the alley beside the factory Peewee had stripped to a bathing suit, Vito had smeared him from head to toe with a thick coating of Vaseline, then Peewee had squirmed twelve feet through a tiny exhaust duct into the warehouse and opened the door from the inside, smiling happily with thumb upraised as he bled from dozens of long gashes inflicted by the points of sheet metal screws. Behind the inner metal door was a truckload of French perfume that Vito had presold to Terry Shorts for five thousand dollars. They worked on the door for three hours; a four-foot pry bar, which they didn't have, would have opened it in minutes. They jimmied at the door, then beat on it, then cursed it, then improvised a half-dozen tools; the job called for a four-foot pry bar. They went home empty-handed, Peewee looking as though he had just been paroled from a medieval torture chamber. Vito had never gone on another burglary without more tools than were needed.

He hadn't thought of Peewee Grogan in years. He hadn't thought about himself as a young burglar in years. Now, with the dangers safely behind him, the ability to recall his adolescence so vividly was enjoyable. Vito had burgled alone whenever possible; it was one reason for his neighborhood reputation of nerviness. Most of the up-and-coming teenage thieves needed company in a silent, dark apartment. He recalled going alone into a five-story building on Horatio Street when he was sixteen and finding a third-floor apartment door with only a snap lock on it. After ringing the bell for a while he opened the lock with a celluloid strip, entered quickly and closed the door behind him, then tiptoed across to the bedroom and peered in at the unmade bed until he was certain the place was deserted. He started to cross the bedroom, still on tiptoes; the next order of business was to open a window for access to the fire escape in case the tenants came home. Halfway across the parquet wood floor while still too far from a window that might stick or be locked, he heard a key turn in the door lock. He moved instinctively to get under the bed, the only burrow available. For some reason he slid in on his back; thinking about it later he seemed more in control that way, less like an animal run to earth who flattens himself, face in the ground, light blocked out, hoping that the hunters above might be unwilling to plunge a spear or knife into his back. He regretted his choice of position for three interminable hours. The bottom of the box spring was so close to the floor that it touched most of his body, he had to keep his head to one side because the spring would crush his face if he kept it upturned. He lay silently, inhaling dust and lint from the mattress, terrified of having to cough or sniffle. The husband went to bed immediately, sitting on the bed while he undressed. Vito slid to the other side and studied the thick, bare ankles just a few feet away. The man was a heavyweight. The wife watched Milton Berle for an hour while the husband, whose tossing and turning squeezed Vito's head and chest every half minute, tried to fall asleep in the ninety-degree humidity. When she finally got into bed Vito's left leg had gone numb with pins and needles. He waited, hearing their breathing and his own heartbeat. Each time he was about to leave he forced himself to wait longer, knowing that the half hour he thought had passed was probably more like ten minutes. Finally he slid out lengthwise, exiting at the foot of the bed to be as far as possible from their heads. He moved very slowly through the dark room, then inhaled deeply for the first time in hours when he reached the living room. After gently disengaging the safety chain and opening the door silently, his enormous sense of relief at being out of danger already ebbed; now he felt that after what he had been through he would hate himself for days if he left empty-handed. He was standing on a three by five foot Persian rug that he had noticed when he entered. He rolled it up and carried it under his arm down the stairway and home. Terry Shorts claimed the next day that it was a Belgian imitation and refused to give him more than twenty dollars for it.

When Vito's purchases were safely stored in the trunk of the Caddy he fed three more quarters into the meter and bought another hour, then walked a few blocks up Greene Street where he found a place that would serve a hamburger at the bar. It was a fifty- or sixty-year-old restaurant refurbished SoHo style, with a wall of floor-to-ceiling windows and too many hanging plants. He sipped a Scotch on the rocks and looked over the restaurant. It was busy—if this was anything like a typical day the account was worth two or three hundred pounds of chuck a week. The workers, the manager, and those customers being treated as regulars were all about Adam's age. He wondered what Adam had done with himself this afternoon, while Vito had been selecting burglar tools with as much expertise as any thief other than the top-level jewel guys would have brought to the task. He had put together a first-rate kit. It crossed his mind that Adam ought to consider himself lucky to be going on a job with someone as experienced as he. Perhaps that would be his defense with Elaine if she somehow found out about the caper; that Adam was lucky to be accompanied on a score by a father-grandfather team who between them had about eighty years of experience thieving. He would have to be sure there wasn't a kitchen knife within reach when he told her.

She had raised the subject of Adam earlier in the day while they held hands unconsciously in the afterglow of sex, blinds still drawn so that the living room was dim, Billie Holiday singing softly on the stereo.

"What do you think Adam's going to do?" she asked.

"About what?"

"School. Work."

Vito shrugged. "It's a waste if that kid doesn't go back to school."

"Have you told him that?"

"I mentioned it a few times."

"It might be worth more than just a mention, Vito. Your idea of hitting Adam on the head really hard is to drop a hint that usually gets lost completely."

Vito wanted to change the subject.

"I've brought it up with him three or four times," she said, "but any advice I give gets written off as a Jewish mother syndrome."

"For one thing, I'm happy to have him back after five years of doing God knows what," Vito said. "I don't want to drive him away by sounding like a parent."

"You *are* a parent."

"He's twenty-three, Elaine."

"It used to be, 'He's fifteen, Elaine,' and you wouldn't ask what he was doing or where he was going or who he was with. And I went along with that madness. My God, Vito, do you remember us sitting in that living room while Adam got dressed to go out on a Friday night? Both of us wondering where but afraid to start a fight with him. 'Will you be late, Adam?' is the most you would ask when he reached the door and you got a yes or a no and neither one meant anything—he came home when he felt like it. It was bizarre, Vito. Do you remember how we'd find out where he might be?"

Vito didn't acknowledge the question but he did remember, and looking back on it now it was bizarre. Adam had his own telephone in his room and a recorder for messages. The minute Adam was out the door Vito and Elaine would hurry to their kitchen telephone and dial Adam's number, then each of them would press an ear to the receiver to hear his message, coming from twelve feet away, which invariably had a hard-rock record playing in the background and might go, "Hey—it's about seven o'clock Friday and I'll be at CBGB's till two or three. Leave a number and I'll get back." They would hang up before the beep.

"It was a hell of a way to find out where our fifteen-year-old son was and what time he'd be home," Elaine said.

Vito nodded.

"And you're repeating it now, Vito."

"I'm not repeating it now. He's twenty-three. You can't make up for mistakes we made years ago by treating him now like he's a teenager."

"You don't have to. Just treat him as though he's your son instead of your father."

He would argue with her on that—with no great conviction—if he wasn't planning a robbery with Adam. They were quiet for a bit, and Vito hoped that she wouldn't raise the question of what Adam had been doing for the past five years while he was "finding himself." They had generally avoided talking about it; if either one brought it up the other would play it down, and whoever brought it up was happy to have it played down. During the whole five years they had never dealt head-on with their unspoken fears. Now that she was voicing her concern about Adam, Vito worried that she would accuse herself and him of years of parental neglect.

Instead, she broke the silence by asking, "What was your father's call all about last week? At the Seder."

Vito looked puzzled.

"Adam talked to him," he said. "He said Jessie wanted to wish everyone a Happy Passover."

"Come on, Vito. Jessie wouldn't know the difference between Passover and a Hare Krishna holiday. And when we drove back we didn't drop Adam off at his place—the two of you got rid of me first so you could talk. Adam's been enamored of Jessie since he was five years old. I think there's something fishy here and I think you sense it as well as I do. And I'm scared that you'll bury your head in the sand the way you always have sooner than deal with it."

"Jessie's call was to say, 'Happy Passover,'" Vito said. "Nothing more or less."

"You're telling me to mind my business, Vito. That it's just among you boys."

"No, I'm not."

"Well I'm making dinner next Sunday to celebrate Adam being back. I'd like to meet his girlfriend anyway. And I'm asking Jessie."

"Fine with me," Vito said.

"I want you to watch them, Vito. Please. And if you smell anything funny going on please hit Adam on the head with it. Don't ignore it. Promise?"

"I promise," he said.

He realized that had she brought all this up in the first few minutes after they had spent themselves sexually, while they clutched hands tightly, he might easily have confided everything to her. Even now it was tempting. Until he reminded himself that Jessie and Adam would likely go ahead with the scheme anyway and maybe never talk to him again.

"I'm worried about him, Vito." Her voice was softer.

He wanted to say, "So am I," but couldn't.

"Whatever values we ever gave Adam were a bit screwy."

"How?"

"Vito, you forged a birth certificate for him when he was thirteen so he could get a part-time job at Burger King."

"He wanted to work. And we encouraged it. Doesn't sound so awful to me."

"Forging a birth certificate is not a healthy example to set for a teenager," she said. "We never concentrated on giving Adam a set of values."

"I think you're wrong," Vito said, knowing she was right. He had never instilled values in Adam because he was unsure of what they should be. He had avoided passing on, at least consciously, the "grab it before the other guy does" philosophy with which Jessie had raised him, yet had been unable to impress on Adam a solid, middle-class value system of honesty; he didn't really believe in it. And so he had skirted the entire question of doing what a father should—teaching his son a set of moral values by which to live. And Elaine knew it, of course. Judging by the sadness in her voice now she was also aware of her own complicity in it, something Vito had realized for years. She, beneath a veneer of middle-class morality, was also a nonbeliever; it was why coming from Nat and Rose's solidly grounded household she had made the unlikely choice of Vito as a husband and had stuck by him through the two years of prison time. Now she would claim that it was her youth and that she had sensed in him the potential to grow but, in fact, she would have suffocated in a marriage to some substantial Bronx boy who was able to fit into society as a full-fledged member rather than observe it with the outsider mentality of Vito. Elaine was an outsider, too.

"He's enamored of Jessie," she said, thinking aloud. "He always has been. And that's scary."

"Jessie's got some good qualities, too."

"Jessie's a thief. You spent two years in prison and it wasn't in spite of what your father taught you it was *because* of it. And Adam is enamored of him and of his whole upside-down value system."

Her instincts, Vito thought, were right on the money. As usual. He looked her over in the dimly lit room as Billie finished the middle eight bars of "I Can't Get Started," and Lester Young his solo. Elaine lay on the couch, her makeup smeared in places from their mild debauchery, the beginning of a double chin visible because her head was tucked down against her chest. The sexy lustiness he had felt earlier was dissipated now. Beside him was a forty-four-year-old mother worried about their son and sad that things hadn't worked out better, that together they had made so many mistakes with Adam, that it had gone by so quickly and that they hadn't treated Adam's upbringing more *seriously*. They had been unfair to him, from some form of unintentional neglect, and both of them knew it, too late. Vito wanted to put his arm around her shoulders and press her head against his chest. He wished that he could share with her his own dilemma—that Adam would go ahead with or without him and that it was too late now to undo what he must have done for the past twenty years: unconsciously pass on to Adam Jessie's attitudes and values. Including Jessie's most fundamental value, that Vito secretly shared—that there were a lot worse things in the world than being a thief.

CHAPTER IX

EASTER SUNDAY DAWNED WITH CLEAR SKIES AND A STRONG SUN, THEN IMPROVED EACH HOUR UNTIL by midafternoon the temperature reached the low seventies and a light southerly breeze could be felt along the avenues. The day was perfect for Elaine's late afternoon dinner. There was no religious significance attached; Vito had recognized from the start of their marriage that Catholicism had no more meaning for him than any other set of beliefs. Adam could be raised as a Jew providing it wasn't shoved down the kid's throat—if Elaine and her parents wanted to influence Adam, that was fine, so long as Adam had the final say. It was Vito's determination that Adam have a voice in things that had brought on the argument over a *bris*.

Nat and Rose had neither spoken to Vito nor entered his apartment until Elaine became pregnant, then Nat had approached Vito for a serious talk.

"I'm Elaine's father," Nat had said without offering his hand. His tone of voice implied that he expected Vito to extend his sympathy. The old man sat on the edge of the couch and managed an indulgent smile when Vito offered him a soft drink.

"I'm not allowed to eat here," Nat said. "I'm a religious man."

He got down to business. Vito guessed that he had rehearsed his pitch for several days. If it was a boy there would have to be a *bris*. His tone made it clear that this was as inevitable as the rising of the sun next morning. Nat was simply here to clarify *why* there would be a *bris*, not to gain Vito's approval. Without a *bris* the child would not be a Jew. It would take only a few minutes, "A little snip," Nat said, done by a *mohel* and done properly—a doctor had nowhere the experience of a *mohel*.

Vito had said, no. The baby would be circumcised by a doctor, without a religious ceremony. Nat suggested that Vito talk to someone who understood what was at stake and yet could give an unbiased opinion: his rabbi at Congregation Young Israel. "A young man. Very up to date. Even if he is Orthodox."

Vito, a somewhat uncertain twenty-four-year-old, had relented to the extent of contacting a Reform rabbi. He had felt very magnanimous about doing it until Nat later said, "Reform? You might as well have talked to a priest." The young rabbi, a recent graduate of Union Theological Seminary who wore imported Italian loafers and tinted eyeglasses, sat with Vito on a sofa in a large office of the Stephen Wise Free Synagogue on West Sixty-eighth Street, reluctant to become involved but pressured by Vito to give an opinion. He eventually asked whether Vito intended to make the child aware of his Jewish heritage.

"There are some five thousand years of culture there that you don't want to simply throw on the ash heap, Mr. McMullen."

When Vito answered that he had no intention of raising a half-Jewish child who didn't know he was half-Jewish, the young rabbi shrugged, lowered his voice unnecessarily, and said, "Between us, then, what does it matter who does the circumcision? Having the end of your penis cut by a *mohel* doesn't make a Jew."

Adam had been operated on by the doctor. Thirteen years later he had decided to be Bar-Mitzvahed and since then Elaine had been comfortable enough to allow in the house some small recognition of Christmas or to have a dinner that happened to fall on Easter Sunday with no fear that it would be misinterpreted.

Margie had convinced Jessie to walk across the park to Vito's house. She was surprised when he agreed; he hated going more than a few blocks on foot and would stand on a cold, windy corner whistling at taxis for half an hour to avoid a ten-minute walk. He was pleased enough now, though, dressed in his Easter best: a blue, pinstriped suit with the tiny American flag screwed through the lapel that Jessie had worn since the Vietnam protests of the sixties, a white-on-white shirt, "medium starched," with French cuffs and a pointed collar, and an old-fashioned, pearl-gray fedora cocked just slightly to one side. His hair had been trimmed perhaps a sixteenth of an inch the day before.

"Like years ago," he had said when Margie complimented him. "Everyone dressed on Easter Sunday. That's when people had their heads screwed on straight and knew how to behave instead of this shit where everybody lets it 'all hang out' and nobody knows which way is up, for Christ's sake."

He took Margie's hand in his and steered her off the path and across the Sheep Meadow.

"So you think things were better in the old days?" she asked.

"Mostly. Not a hundred percent but mostly they were better."

"What was worse?"

"Dentists. Used to hurt like hell to go to a dentist. No more." He thought for a bit. "Couple of other things. I can't think of them just now."

"And what was better?" she asked.

"People. You never heard all this, me, me, me shit. There were codes. Even tough guys, they tipped their hat and stood up when they met a woman. It was a nicer world to live in."

"And that's it?" she asked. "Tough guys tipped their hats so life was nicer?"

"You know what I mean," Jessie said.

He thought for a few moments then said, "You know what's really changed? And not for the better. How people see the world. My whole generation, we knew that life could be tough. You took the good with the bad and you knew there would be some bad along the way. Now, anything goes wrong, somebody's to blame. Somebody's got to pay you for a bad break. I was just reading in the paper about a malpractice suit against some fancy, uptown surgeon, a guy almost sixty years old, operating for maybe thirty years. Specializes in this very tricky hand surgery where they're tying stuff together under microscopes. He had done something like ten thousand of these operations without a complaint. On this one the knife slipped or something and the guy on the table lost the use of three fingers for good. Jury awarded him something like a million bucks, based on the future earnings he'll lose, pain and anguish and whatnot. They found this doctor guilty of malpractice because he made a mistake."

"He isn't?" Margie asked.

"Once in thirty years? Sounds like they ought to give him a medal," Jessie said. "He wasn't drunk. He wasn't out partying the night before. He didn't have some kid filling in for him on the sly. He didn't cheat on his medical board exams. This wasn't the third or the tenth or the fifteenth time it happened. For the first time in ten thousand operations something went wrong. Not through negligence. And not through incompetence—this guy is first rate. The dice came up wrong for this patient is what happened. Tough break, no doubt about it, but life has some tough breaks in store for all of us. How the hell do you call that malpractice? One in ten thousand is just in the *nature* of things.

"And you see it all around you. A guy busts a leg, he sues everybody in sight and people kind of agree that *somebody's* got to pay him. Life now is supposed to be so sweet that there are no more bum breaks. I liked it better the old way, when sometimes a guy just shrugged his shoulders and said, 'That's life.'"

They walked quietly for a bit. On the east side of the Sheep Meadow a dozen advertising agency types in their early thirties played a serious game of two-hand touch football.

"Did you ever play football?" she asked.

"Yeah, when my polo pony was a little under the weather. Who the hell had time for sports? If anything, boxing would have been my game. I never did much of it with gloves on but when I did I was good. But I doubt that I threw a football twice in my life."

They paused to watch the next play, holding hands unconsciously. The balding quarterback was dressed in running pants and an old Rutgers Junior Varsity sweat shirt. He bent his knees and jerked his head from side to side several times as he called a series of numbers then, "Hut, hut, hut."

"Yo-yo's been watching too much television," Jessie said.

An explosion of overly dramatic grunts from the other copywriters and stockbrokers as they made body contact carried through the crisp air to Jessie and Margie. It was a deep-pass play, broken up beautifully by a skinny defensive end wearing a Cornell sweat shirt. His teammates congratulated him with shouts and hugs.

"They pat each other's asses a lot, these college guys," Jessie said. "Makes you wonder."

"It might be a gay league," Margie said.

"The gays are all playing in the pros these days. No, it's just an asshole game, football. Paramilitary shit. All of them getting their rocks off on organization, physical courage, discipline. Mainly discipline. It's a perfect sport for training people how to march off later in a marine uniform and get killed with a smile on their face for whatever pile of horseshit is being shoveled up by the rich and the powerful that year."

They walked on slowly, watching the next play over their shoulders.

"I remember I had to stop Vito from signing up for a high-school football team," Jessie said. He shook his head, genuinely puzzled at much of Vito's behavior. "Before that it was the Cub Scouts. Some crap about learning to build a one-match fire. It was no picnic raising that kid. Football. The fucking Cub Scouts. He had a lot of tendencies in those directions."

"Are we going to hit it off?" she asked.

"You and Vito? Yeah, he's okay. I get on him a lot because of the father-son thing. If he was just somebody I hung out with in a corner saloon I'd think he was fine."

"And is he somebody you'd hang out with?"

Jessie smiled. He wasn't sure.

"I'd drink with him, that's for sure. Hang *out*? It's hard to say. He's a little down the middle for me. Vito put in a couple of years upstate when he was a kid. A bullshit burglary charge. The judge should've sentenced him for stupidity. Well, you can come away from that with something that's not so terrible. Something that stays with you the rest of your life. The way you hear people my age talk about a hitch they did in the Navy fifty years ago. The trouble is it took most of the starch out of him. The guy is forty-seven years old for Christ sake and he's pissing his life away in some icebox down on Fourteenth Street."

Jessie groped for a way to explain himself.

"He's backed off on life is what he's done. After his mother died I sat down and really thought about how to raise him. I wanted to do the right thing. Hell, I wasn't a real family man and there I am with a seven-year-old on my hands. I was running a book for Buster Reardon up in the garment center at the time and getting my fingers into anything else that came along and I sure as hell knew that I couldn't open up any doors down on Wall Street for Vito. The situation I was in, there was no way the kid was going to become a hot candidate for Harvard or Yale. If I raised him a hundred percent legitimate, which I could've done, bang him on the head every time he got out of line and encourage the nuns and brothers to kick him in the ass a couple of times a day—which they would have loved—well, if I did all that he'd wind up in a solid job with the phone company or Con Ed. That's a fucking sentence. You go into one of those jobs at age eighteen it's like someone just banged down a gavel and gave you forty to life. When Vito was a kid the Catholic schools were like subcontractors for Con Ed and Bell Telephone—they sent them eighteen-year-olds like Fisher sent bodies to G.M. That the kids could spell and knew their multiplication tables wasn't the crucial thing, either. They were nice and docile. People who would sit in a dingy green room downtown, get underpaid every week, be nice to customers, never take a sick day and never be late, and never even *dream* of a union or of telling a boss to shove it. And do it till age sixty-five. Till their shoulders drooped and they didn't give a shit anymore that the seat of their pants were shiny. What those nuns and brothers did, where the parents backed them up, was to make kids feel so shitty about themselves that they were perfect employees for the phone company or the electric company.

"Well, whatever I did wrong, Margie, no one can accuse me of feeding my kid into either one of those penitentiaries. I figured the one thing I could teach Vito that mattered was how to reach out and grab life by the balls. Instead he ended up like almost everybody else—tiptoeing around half the time looking over his shoulder and worrying about the eight thousand terrible things that can hit you out of the blue."

They walked quietly for a bit while Jessie continued to think. As they neared Fifth Avenue he shook his head from side to side, bewildered still by his son's attitude toward life.

"He hit a number years ago," Jessie said. "Had a double sawbuck on it straight. A *double sawbuck*. Ten thousand he walked away with. You'd swear he just came from a funeral. Why? He tells me, 'Pop, I learned a long time ago to never get too happy. The minute you're convinced that life is treating you well and you relax, you're on top of things, you get whacked with something terrible. There's a man with an ax follows each of us around waiting for us to *really* begin enjoying life—then whack! Something really terrible happens. And the terrible things that can happen in life are a hell of a lot more intense than the good things. Your joys never match your sorrows,' he said."

Jessie shook his head again.

"Now is that a hell of a way to go through life?"

Margie wasn't sure.

"Did he explain it any further?"

"Yeah," Jessie said. "He said that you could break the bank at Vegas for a couple of million and that as big a moment as that is in life it's nothing compared to having someone you love die. I guess it has to do with losing his mother when he was seven."

Jessie studied her face as they walked, waiting for her to agree with him about Vito's foolishness. Instead, she weighed it.

"Your son Vito is right," she said. "The joys never match the sorrows. I learned that when I lost my daughter."

"Hell of a way to go through life," Jessie said, and shook his head.

He took her forearm and steered her in a diagonal jaywalk across Fifth Avenue.

Vito slid the table leaf from its storage place under the bed, used a torn undershirt from Elaine's supply of rags to wipe away several years' worth of dust, then aligned it in the dining table as Elaine finished ironing a tablecloth. The intercom buzzed and the doorman said that a Mr. McMullen was on his way up.

"It's either Adam or Jessie," Vito said to Elaine.

When the chimes rang twice in a peppy, offbeat cadence they knew it was Jessie. He kissed Elaine on the cheek and mumbled, "Long time," then introduced Margie to them as, "An old friend of mine." Vito went into the kitchen to mix Bloody Marys while Jessie and Margie moved into the living room. Elaine followed them, after lingering long enough to whisper to Vito, "The only way those two can be old friends is if Jessie was her baby-sitter."

Vito omitted the vodka from Elaine's drink—she had warned him that it was too early in the day for her—then added it to his own, deciding that it wasn't too early for him. Adam arrived with Christine before Vito had finished mixing the drinks. Vito shook her hand and kissed Adam on the cheek, then returned to the kitchen while Adam introduced Christine as an "old friend." Vito thought that for them to be old friends Christine would have to have been Adam's baby-sitter.

As soon as Christine was seated, Jessie tugged Adam's arm and led him to the kitchen where they watched Vito fill glasses from a pitcher, then garnish each drink with a stalk of celery. Jessie covered his glass with his hand as Vito was about to put in the celery.

"I know we're on the smart Upper East Side, Vito, but let's save my celery for one of the girls and double up on the booze instead."

Vito topped off Jessie's glass with another shot of vodka then delivered the drinks to the women. As he handed Elaine the Virgin Mary he knew from the way her eyes widened just a bit that she would have plenty to say later about Christine and Margie, who were now comparing the shortcomings of their respective health clubs while Elaine leaned toward them, her eyebrows raised attentively, her mind, Vito knew, far off. Vito was meeting both women for the first time. He knew from

Adam that Christine was thirty-six, two years older than Margie. Looking at their faces he would have guessed at a much greater age difference; Christine perhaps forty and Margie thirty. Watching the way they held themselves, he thought that he would soon be guessing Christine's age at fifty. Her face was what his mother-in-law would call *farbisseneh*: pinched and unforgiving. She used little makeup, old-time school-marm style, Vito thought, but her looks weren't good enough to carry it off. Her lips were too thin and premature crow's-feet were starting to form at the corners of her eyes. Vito was certain that her clothes, especially the sensible shoes, would be described by Elaine later as, "The Scarsdale matron special from Bergdorf's." Her hands were even bonier than the rest of her, so bony that Vito found them unpleasant to look at. He wondered—did she ever slip her hand into Adam's when they walked, as Elaine sometimes slipped her hand into his? What the hell was there for Adam to hold on to?

Margie was another story, he thought, certainly on a physical level. She was good to look at and obviously knew how to dress and make up. Her eyes were pale blue and she used a shade of mascara that enhanced them perfectly. She caught him studying her and smiled quickly—nothing *farbisseneh* on that face, Vito thought.

He returned to the kitchen, where Jessie handed him an empty Bloody Mary glass.

"Could I please get a bona fide drink? Tomato juice is what they feed old house cats whose bladders are fucked up."

Vito slid open the cabinet door above the sink, which held two dozen bottles of various liquors and wines. "Help yourself," he said.

Jessie chose from the rear row, a dusty bottle of Armagnac that retailed for sixty dollars, checking first that the bottle held enough to make it worth his while to get started, then pouring a healthy measure into a rock glass. He did not return the bottle to the cabinet.

"May as well keep this near at hand. You familiar with it, Adam? French brandy, and prime."

Adam studied the label and shook his head, no.

"If it's not from Colombia, and you don't smoke it or sniff it, he's not likely to know it," Vito said.

Adam ignored him.

"And maybe you want a snifter?" Vito asked Jessie. "It's a pity to waste something that good in a glass meant for whiskey."

Jessie waved away the suggestion.

"Your old man gets a little carried away," he said to Adam. "This stuff is nice but it's not in a league where you're supposed to lower your voice when you talk about it."

Vito nodded at Adam. "I'm sure it's what your grandfather drinks every day over on Tenth Avenue. It's your average longshoreman's after-work drink. Elevator mechanics are big on it, too. Six, seven dollars a pop, the kind of company your grandfather keeps can't resist it."

"I don't hang out with longshoremen or elevator mechanics. Though God knows there's nothing wrong with them. And I've had a couple of good runs in my life—nice, flush periods like when I bought the *QE Two* a drink. Believe me, what I was ordering aboard that ship makes this stuff look like something you hand out to cops and postmen at Christmastime."

He reached out and touched his glass against Vito's, then Adam's, then held it slightly aloft.

"But, a salud. Swill or no swill let's drink to the success of our venture."

The three of them drank. Vito was, for a change, amused with Jessie rather than angry. He smiled at Adam.

"Only your grandfather gets his hands on the back shelf of my liquor supply, helps himself to a sixty-dollar bottle of booze, and after two minutes of conversation the stuff somehow becomes known as swill."

"I call 'em like I see 'em," Jessie said, and smacked his lips. "Now, let's cut out the petty sniping and get down to business. How did your meeting up in Boston go?"

Both Jessie and Vito knew that Adam had brought a hundred-thousand-dollar cash advance back from Boston. He hadn't wanted to hide it in Christine's apartment. Vito had wanted to store it in his safe on Fourteenth Street but Jessie had disagreed.

"We'll be taking fifty of it with us to San Jose," he had said, then explained to Adam, "Say twenty or so for expenses and thirty in the tool kit. Something goes wrong on a score like this you can sometimes buy your way out on the spot. Means leaving fifty back here for a week or more. A safe is an invitation to a thief and this city is teeming with thieves. Unless it's a fancy bank safe, a safe's the worst place in the world to stash money."

He had argued for the safety of his cluttered apartment. Adam had agreed with him and had taken a cab from LaGuardia directly to Jessie's house to drop off the nylon athlete's bag of hundred-dollar bills.

Now, while Adam brought Vito up to date, Jessie finished off the Armagnac, pouring and sipping between admiring nods at Adam's handling of the Boston meeting.

"And the balance?" Vito asked.

"If and when we deliver," Adam said, "it's cash on the spot."

"*When* we deliver," Jessie said. "Not *if*. *When*."

"You're working with an enthusiast," Vito said to Adam. "Your grandfather never considers failure as a possible alternative."

"Fucking right I don't. Not with three McMullens on the case. I didn't raise you to walk around stepping on your dong, and from the way this kid's carried himself so far you've managed to pass on a little bit of my wisdom anyway."

Vito raised his glass in a silent thanks for the compliment and noticed that Adam flushed slightly with pleasure.

They agreed to fly to California on Tuesday and meanwhile to, "Join the girls for a while," as Jessie said to Adam.

Elaine served a rare roast beef with boiled potatoes and fresh peas and carrots. Vito had encouraged her to "Make something with a little pizzazz. You only cook a few times a year anymore and you're going to do an everyday dish like roast beef? Put in a couple of hours over the stove."

She had looked him over the way a fourth-grade schoolteacher might, her raised eyebrows and nearly imperceptible head-shaking serving as a clear message that he was, in fact, a hopeless child, unaware still of the ways of adults.

"The last great meal of my career, Vito, is somewhere safely behind me," she said, and covered the potato pot with a clang that was final, but skewed the lid a bit so that steam could escape. He shifted the cover to give another quarter inch of opening and she quickly moved it back to the position she had chosen, then informed him of a decision she had obviously come to a long time ago and now chose to reveal.

"When this building goes co-op and if we buy the apartment, this kitchen will make a superb second bathroom. I've already figured out just where the Jacuzzi will fit. I figure we'll convert the entrance to the apartment into a Dutch door with a nice little interior counter on the bottom half so that the nights we don't eat out in restaurants we can have takeout delivered comfortably. I've given up cooking, kiddo, and it's time we both faced that fact."

They had stared at one another for a bit, both in a good mood, a touch of sexuality creeping into the atmosphere, then she had broken the silence.

"Maybe you'd like to taste the gravy and correct the seasoning?"

Vito had called upon his Neapolitan genes for a pose of male superiority.

"I'm sure it's perfect," he had said, and left the kitchen with dignity.

The meal proceeded smoothly. Christine picked up a lull in the conversation by asking whether anyone had read the lengthy article in last week's *Times* about genital herpes. Everyone paused in their eating, then shook their heads or mumbled, no.

"It's terrific news for herpes people," she said. "It looks like a cure is just over the horizon."

"Well, geez—that's great news," Jessie said earnestly. "The herpes people must be partying today."

Christine rambled on for a bit as they ate, about the relationship of herpes to chicken pox, that they estimated nearly thirty million sufferers in the United States, and that it had been demonstrated that kissing someone with cold sores then performing oral sex could infect a partner.

Adam fidgeted a bit. Jessie asked Christine, "You're really into this herpes thing, huh? Without getting too personal... any special reason?"

He turned to Adam. "You might want to stay alert here, Adam."

"My ex-roommate, *God,* she had a case. When it was active it drove her right up the wall. She said the *burning*..."

Adam asked, "Maybe we could change the subject, Christine? I mean, you're not totally committed to a herpes discussion, are you?"

She shrugged, and Adam realized that his father's heavy-handed Bloody Marys had got to her.

"Good idea," Margie said. "Let's get onto something more cheerful. Who saw the article about the betting pool among nurses and orderlies in one of the hospitals in Vegas?"

No one had.

"In the intensive-care unit. All three shifts would pool five dollars each on one patient who was obviously terminal. It would amount to a few hundred bucks. Then each player would pick an exact time. Whoever came closest to when the patient died won the pool. The DA's office is investigating it now."

Vito asked how they had been found out.

"For sure, somebody ratted," Jessie said.

Margie confirmed it. "A nurse complained to the prosecutor's office."

"It's nice to think that there are still people with a little morality," Elaine said. "Even in Las Vegas. How did she hear of it?"

"She," Jessie pointed out to Adam.

"She had been in it from the start," Margie said. "Her gripe was that the orderly responsible for maintaining the respirators was winning constantly."

They discussed it for a while. Everyone found it repulsive and claimed they would want no part of it. Vito, though, pointed out that it was not all that surprising, it was a natural outgrowth of hospital work; a butcher quickly learned to not see a dead animal in front of him but rather a carcass, and, similarly, nurses and orderlies had to inure themselves to patient suffering and death or they couldn't perform their work. Sooner or later betting on the time of death would seem perfectly natural.

Christine felt that while the betting seemed callous it certainly wasn't criminal if everyone continued to provide the best possible care for the patient being bet on.

"How the hell could the pool winner enjoy spending his money?" Adam asked.

"Money's money," Christine said. "My best friend has made herself very wealthy in the past few years. She has no trouble enjoying her money. Her parents and some of her friends tell her it's awful but I just wish I had her opportunity. She works in administration at Sloan-Kettering, so when someone is referred for diagnosis or treatment she knows their prognosis immediately. Well, if any of them with less than a thirty percent chance of pulling through—the cancers they really can't do much for—if they also live in Manhattan then Gertrude passes it on to her partner, Harry, who checks them out. A lot of these people live in buildings that have gone co-op or condo and they haven't bought. You can go into those buildings and buy occupied apartments at the insider's price. The problem is that the tenant occupying it is likely to stay there for ten or twenty years. But *here*—Gertrude and Harry snap up an apartment that's going to be vacant in less than a year. At which point they roughly double their investment.

"And sometimes they get lucky. Would you believe a two-bedroom southern exposure on a high floor in Kips Bay that they closed a deal on just last Thursday with an advanced lung tumor? They'll net a hundred and fifty thousand and Gertrude says there's no way they won't flip that apartment within four months. The two of them own more than a dozen prime Manhattan apartments, and every tenant is terminal."

There was a silence during which Christine seemed to expect admiring head shakes for Gertrude's savvy. It occurred to Adam that she had misjudged his family badly. Because he had said they were thieves she thought Jessie and Vito would admire Gertrude and Harry as sharp operators.

"This Gertrude," Jessie said. "Your best friend. Is she the one with the burning herpes every time she takes a leak?"

"No. That was my ex-roommate."

"That's too bad," Jessie said. "You know, I'm not easily frightened but if I was Gertrude or Harry I'd be scared to death. I really believe that God's got a sense of humor. And if God wanted to play a first-rate practical joke on Gertrude and Harry, what do you think it would be?"

"They aren't hastening anyone's death," Christine said. "The apartments would revert to the original building owners. What's the difference who turns the profit?"

"They're mucking around in other people's misery is what they're doing," Jessie said. "It's like saying that grave robbing's okay because the person is dead anyway so what's the difference."

"What *is* the difference?" Christine asked. "Logically."

"Things ain't always logical," Jessie said. "It's like everything else in life, there are thieves... and there are *thieves*. Your friends don't even qualify as thieves. They're grabbers. Parasites. They're immoral. The fact that what they're doing is legal makes it even worse; at least if it was illegal they'd be putting their necks out, but they're not even doing that."

Elaine laughed, harshly, Vito thought.

"I happen to agree that Gertrude and Harry sound terrible but listen to your grandfather, Adam. Somehow, breaking the law outright would make them more moral."

"It would," Jessie said. "Like most people, Elaine, you confuse legality with morality."

"No, Jessie," Elaine said. "Like *most* people—and thank goodness most people feel this way or we would all be living in total anarchy—like most people, I recognize that in a reasonably just society..."

"If you ever run across a reasonably just society, be sure to call me," Jessie said. "You know, Elaine, you're a nice, middle-class girl. Maybe..."

"You left out Jewish," she said.

"Irrelevant to my case. What I was going to say is..."

"What case? I thought we were discussing something, not trying a case."

A sense of tension came over the table, fueled by Jessie's obvious impatience. Elaine tried again to draw Adam into the discussion.

"What do you say, Adam?" she asked. "Do you agree with your paternal grandfather that there are no reasonably just societies? Which, not too surprisingly, leads to the convenient philosophy that morality has nothing to do with legality, so you can go through life doing as you please."

Adam, who needed time to compose an answer, repeated, "My paternal grandfather?"

"Yeah," Jessie said. "He's the defendant in this case." He asked Elaine, "Does the witness have to answer yes or no, or can we bend the rules a little and let him explain his answer?"

She waited for Adam to reply, against her will beginning to be angry with him for not siding quickly with her. She knew that her real anger with Adam was not only his admiration for Jessie but even more, his failure to exploit his own potential. She was behaving unfairly here; a special family dinner with two outsiders present was not the setting at which to force Adam into a choice between Jessie and her. But recognizing her own unfairness simply fed her anger; how could anyone fight Jessie fairly?

Margie broke the silence, with a teasing tone good natured enough so that Jessie would have to answer lightly.

"I never knew you had a *philosophy* on life, Jessie."

"I don't," he said. "It's what I started to say a few minutes ago, when my well-brought-up, middle-class daughter-in-law wouldn't let me get a word in edgewise." He turned to Elaine. "Middle-class people might have a philosophy of life. Thank God, I've never been middle class. I just live by certain codes. It comes from my Indian heritage."

"Native American," Adam said.

Jessie nodded. "Native American."

Elaine could have eased off—Vito would point that out to her after everyone was gone—but she chose not to.

"You still haven't answered, Adam," she said. "You're a young man of the world. You've been out there traveling for five hard years. Do morality and legality have anything to do with each other?"

"I think I liked the herpes conversation better," he said. "But if you're going to pin me down then I don't think there's an absolute answer. I think it depends upon your point of view."

It angered Elaine more.

"That's the result of MIT's training to think rigorously? You hedge? You either agree with your grandfather or you don't, Adam. And if you do you shouldn't be ashamed to say so."

"I thought we invited people here to eat, Elaine," Vito said gently.

She knew that he was right but she felt betrayed. Vito knew of her fears for Adam and knew that sides had been formed here. Even if she had created the sides, unfairly, Vito should have joined her. She stared at Adam stubbornly.

"Well?"

Jessie interrupted.

"He already answered you, Elaine. It depends upon your point of view, he said. I agree with him a hundred percent."

He nodded his agreement to Adam, then said to Elaine, "The trouble with using legality as a measure is that you wind up being friends with people like Gertrude and Harry while you're busy avoiding some flat-out thief who happens to be a decent guy."

"How in the world can a thief be a decent guy?" Elaine asked. "Believe it or not, Jessie, this isn't some nice middle-class aversion to something a little bit out of the mainstream. But someone who simply steals from another person cannot be described as a decent guy."

Jessie shook his head in disagreement.

"You just happen to pick honesty as the important thing in life, Elaine. There's nothing sacred about it. Some of us think loyalty is more important."

"Loyalty to what?"

"To who, not what. To a tight circle. To the people you're related to, mainly. You pick out who you're going to be loyal to no matter what happens and you stick with it. You'll die before you'll turn on those people."

Elaine looked across at Adam who listened to Jessie with an expression of open admiration, and asked, "Exactly who gets into your charmed circle, Jessie? Just relatives?"

"No. A couple of old friends, too. Only a couple, though. Everyone at this table, for instance."

He looked to Christine. "You're not included. No insult meant, Christine, but I'd be lying if I counted you in. I don't know you long enough."

Elaine stared at Adam. "And you should tell her, Adam, that your grandpa never lies."

Adam answered her softly. "As far as I know, Mom, he doesn't."

She had asked Adam to take a stand and he had. She excused herself and went into the bathroom. Jessie put his napkin on the table and said to Vito, "We're going to run."

Vito nodded.

"Margie and me will buy you a drink," Jessie said to Adam and Christine. "There must be one decent bar someplace on the East Side."

They agreed quickly and left before Elaine returned.

Vito and Elaine sat quietly at the table, which held the remains of a meal not quite fully eaten. Her anger had dissipated and now she was mildly depressed.

"You should have given me some support," Elaine said. "You're right—it was the wrong time and place and I behaved badly but you still should have given me some support. There's too much at stake to worry about social amenities."

He was tempted to say that she was asking for the kind of loyalty above honesty that Jessie had been championing earlier but he let it go.

"You're trying to do the impossible, Elaine. Adam's an adult. Beyond our control. He is who he is. Attacking Jessie's moral system isn't going to ring some bell in Adam's head and somehow change his way of thinking."

Elaine sensed that Vito was right but was not about to say

so. The time to have challenged Jessie's value system was ten years ago, when Adam was in junior high school and would sometimes play hookey to walk across the park and visit Jessie, who would show him off to a select few in neighborhood bars as, "My grandson, Adam McMullen." Adam would hang out with Jessie for the afternoon, drinking Cokes, playing the jukebox and bowling machines, on especially lucky days transported out to Shea Stadium to watch the Mets from a perfectly situated corporate box along the first- or third-base line. Jessie had a deal worked out with an old-time usher whereby he paid a few dollars for a box going unused that day. Transportation to and from Shea was via stretch limo. A small local service was owned by a Greek with whom Jessie occasionally moved swag goods—on off-hours Jessie got a car at a rock bottom price. Adam loved it. The limo was, in many ways, more fun than the game itself. He would turn on the little television set, Coke in hand, while Jessie, beside him, sipped at a V.O. from the built-in bar as they moved in air-conditioned isolation along the Long Island Expressway and sometimes looked out through the tinted windows at people riding in ordinary cars.

"Remember, Adam, it only costs a hundred percent more to go first class," Jessie would say, whiskey glass raised. "What you're looking at out there in those Fords and Chevies is the hoi polloi of America. Good people, Adam. Salt of the earth. But it's worth whatever it costs to maintain a little distance. There's always an element of riffraff mixed in, ready to spoil your day."

Elaine and Vito had found out about it years later, when Adam was about to go off to MIT, at the point in his life where admitting childish wrongdoings to his parents helped establish him as an adult. They learned that Jessie had coached Adam on the kind of sick note to forge for school. It always gave a brief explanation then added that, since Adam had visited the doctor, a doctor's note was available if the school system required it.

"Keeps them off balance," Jessie had told Adam. "And if by some crazy chance they ask for a doctor's note, tell me. I can cover that base."

Elaine had been furious, more so because Vito, resigned to Jessie's ways, had smiled and shook his head slowly as Adam told the story. Nat and Rose, throughout Adam's childhood, had never missed sending a birthday card—five-dollar bill enclosed—a graduation card, a Chanukah card. They had called to check his condition every time he had a cold. Adam, in his teens, while playing hookey to run over to the West Side, would never think of calling them, no less visiting them. Jessie had not even shown up at Columbia Presbyterian when Adam's tonsils had been taken out, although Adam had hemorrhaged for hours because of a vitamin K deficiency. Jessie had taken an interest in Adam only when there was a payoff involved—at age thirteen or so when Adam would respond to his blandishments. And it had worked. To this day Adam thought that Jessie McMullen was terrific.

"You didn't get any hint that he's up to something with Jessie?" Elaine asked.

"Did you?" Vito asked.

Although he recognized what a trivial point it was, Vito found it easier to respond with a question than to lie outright. Her absolute inability to consider that he, Vito, might be part of Jessie's scheme emphasized for him just how aberrant his position was. He looked at Elaine, who sipped lukewarm coffee, deep in thought, obviously unhappy with the outcome of the day.

"You should try to spend a little more time with him, Vito," she said. "Even if it means breaking away from work a bit or even postponing this Texas trip. It might neutralize Jessie's influence a little."

He nodded absently and pretended to be absorbed in a magazine.

CHAPTER X

ADAM DROVE THE RENTED CHEVY SLOWLY ALONG THE ALAMEDA, CONCENTRATING ON THE ROAD while Jessie, beside him, and Vito, in the backseat, looked out for a suitable motel.

"Something nice," Jessie had decreed, "but big enough so we don't stand out like sore thumbs."

He saw what he wanted set behind a row of towering palm trees a few blocks east of Santa Clara University: the San Jose Chalet, two stories high with a red tile roof, a heated swimming pool, and featuring Wayne at the piano bar of the Chez Martine Lounge nightly from seven P.M. A bulletin board in the lobby listed the week's meetings and conferences; groups from Technicon, National Semiconductor, and Machine Intelligence, Inc. On Thursdays there was a lingerie fashion show in the lounge during lunch. The desk clerk shifted a reservation and gave them three adjoining rooms on the second floor overlooking the pool. They carried a small suitcase of clothing apiece, left the tools locked in the trunk of the car, and agreed to meet at the bar after unpacking and washing up.

Adam ran the shower on full hot with the door closed until the bathroom was filled with steam, then lowered the water temperature until he was mildly uncomfortable and stood beneath the hard stream of water for a long time before turning it off. He wrapped a bath towel around his waist, opened the door that led from his room to the small terrace, and stood in the open doorway to dry off in the mid-seventies California air. In the pool below a solitary figure swam laps at a steady, slow pace, using a graceful crawl stroke. He propelled himself through the water with a strong kick and no wasted arm motions, the side of his head emerging just enough to breath comfortably. Adam envied him. He had always wanted to swim well, but moved clumsily, gasping after a few minutes, unable to relax properly even in shallow water. The swimmer completed his laps and hoisted himself out of the pool at the far end. Adam realized that it was Jessie. He smiled with pleasure and was about to call down, then remained silent instead and admired Jessie's physique and carriage as he walked barefoot across the concrete, running his fingers through his hair until it lay back flat. His grandfather moved with an athletic assurance in or out of the water that was rare even in a twenty-year-old. It was Jessie's half-Indian blood, Adam decided, and wished that more of it had shown up in his own bearing.

They took a table in the lounge, not too near Wayne, who played an overly complicated rendition of the "Yellow Rose of Texas" to a lone salesman from Houston. Jessie had decided that the main bar was a "phony"; it curved into setbacks several times along its length.

"Serious drinking bars have to be dead straight. Once they curve or form a U, where everybody's facing each other, you know it's a bullshit bar," he said. "That goes for those marble-top jobs, too. Real drinking—the bar's got to be wood."

The seating captain introduced them to their cocktail waitress, Norma, who looked to be in her mid-fifties even under the dim, lavender lights. She was short and dumpy, fifteen pounds overweight with a pronounced double chin, outfitted in a low-cut, black, French-maid costume with white ruffled bloomers that puffed out enough for Jessie to comment in a low voice as she left their table, "They've got that poor old broad in diapers for Christ sake."

After three rounds of drinks they went into the Escoffier Room to eat: steaks served with a choice of a potato baked in aluminum foil or french fries.

Jessie asked the twenty-year-old waitress, whose name tag said VAL, whether the french fries were fresh or frozen. She smiled at him for a few moments—"Like I was a rube who just flew in from Des Moines," Jessie said later—then she explained patiently, "Sir, *all* french fries are frozen."

Jessie said, "What do you mean all french fries are frozen? What about *fresh* french fries?"

She smiled again.

"Sir, french fries are frozen food. Like ice cream. They don't come any other way."

Jessie studied her for a bit, as he would a photograph of a native in *National Geographic*, then said, "Tell me, Val, if you were to peel a potato—you know, get rid of the skin? The brown covering. Then slice the potato up and drop the pieces into nice hot oil . . . now wouldn't you come out with fresh french fries?"

She caught Adam's eye briefly and gave an expression of hopelessness at the old man's confusion, then spoke to Jessie gently.

"No, sir, you wouldn't. They're not made from real potatoes. It's a frozen food."

"Gimme the baked potato," Jessie said.

When she left the table he shook his head sorrowfully.

"That kid was raised in one of these nice suburban houses with a couple of cars in the driveway and she'll never know that she had a deprived childhood."

They decided to go to bed early and look over the laboratory the following day.

The building was close to San Jose Airport. Both Jessie and Vito were in California for the first time and they studied the streets as Adam drove toward the laboratory. Jessie first commented that, "Christ, it's got no color compared to New York—everything's just *green*," then asked whether Californians ate anything other than Shakey's Pizza and Jack in the Box.

"The ones I knew ate a lot of brown rice," Adam answered.

He spotted the lab on their left and slowed as they passed it for the first time. It was a two-story cinder-block building, unfenced, with parking spaces for perhaps a hundred cars behind, after which a portion of a recently working apricot orchard had been left standing on the rear of the property. A row of huge eucalyptus trees, their barks hanging in shreds as though they had just weathered a hurricane, had been preserved when the land was cleared. They bordered one side of the parking lot. The roads were such that Adam was able to encircle the place without losing sight of the building, which, they saw, formed a U that enclosed a garden measuring perhaps two hundred feet square. A row of soft drink and candy vending machines were set beneath the eave of the building that formed the base of the U. In front of the machines, forming a wide passageway for people using them, was an ivy-covered redwood trellis built high enough to obscure the machines from the view of anyone in the garden. There were a few dozen round picnic tables with striped umbrellas at which employees could eat lunch.

"Cold Shakey's Pizza, for sure," Jessie commented absently, then pointed out how lush the vegetation was.

"Anything'll grow here," Adam said. "We're in the Santa Clara Valley, one of the most fertile spots on earth. Between the climate and the soil it produces some of the best Mediterranean fruit in the world. Apricots, prunes, grapes, all the hard-to-grow, expensive stuff. It was all solid orchards until twenty-five years ago when they just bulldozed the trees for all these little tract-house developments. Goddamn shame."

They circled the place four times; there was no way anyone might take notice. Jessie and Vito took turns studying it through binoculars. They agreed that other than an alarm system and whatever all-night guards were employed, the security looked to be pretty loose. Vito suggested that they leave the scene for a few hours and return at noon to see what went on during the lunch hour.

They drove around downtown San Jose, getting a feel for the main streets and where the entrances were for the several freeways that crisscrossed the city. On Bascom Avenue a police car stopped beside them at a red light. The driver was a female in her mid-twenties, likely Mexican-American.

"If we do run into any trouble, I hope it's with one of the girls," Jessie said. "That guy next to her looks like he came up through the Hitler Youth Corps."

"California cops are all like that," Adam said. "You don't fuck with them. The woman's probably just as bad."

Jessie shook his head.

"Ridiculous," he said. "Where the hell is this country heading? I know a kid your age, Adam, Jimmy O'Toole, just started tending bar on the West Side after a couple of years as a wire lather. Stands six-two or -three and must wear a size eighteen collar. When I ask him which shifts he's going to be behind the stick he groans and says, 'They got me working nights, damn it. Screws up my whole love life. My girlfriend's a fireman and she's on a day shift.'

"Took me thirty seconds to figure it out; my first reaction was to protect my dick. Then I realize he means a real *girl*. He told me one of the guys he used to wire-lathe with is dating a cop. The whole thing is out of kilter.

"Me and Margie watched two cops last month at a table next to us in a Chinese restaurant on Ninth Avenue. Both of them in uniform. A young, good-looking guy maybe Adam's age looked more like a movie actor than a cop, and a sergeant, a forty-year-old tough broad with a face like the witch in *The Wizard of Oz*. They were taking a dinner break, and she ordered herself a martini and asked him if he wanted one. What he wanted was a beer but she pushed him until he ordered a nice, stiff martini. Made sure he drank it, too; she was looking to loosen him up. Two apiece, they had, and old hatchet face would say something in a low voice and squeeze the top of his hand on the table. This tall, handsome kid laughed like hell at whatever the sergeant said and squeezed right back on her wrinkly, liver-spotted old hand. You could see she was going to screw him before the night was out and if he didn't get it up and deliver the goods he'd soon be walking a beat in the ass end of the Bronx. Even Margie got disgusted watching him. 'Look at the little whore,' she told me. 'No shame at all. He's playing up to her for whatever he can get. *And* he's wearing a marriage band.'

"You can bet your ass that the tail end of that shift he wasn't out protecting senior citizens like myself from the muggers prowling Manhattan like a pack of wild beasts. He was burying his head in this tough old sergeant's snatch is what he was doing, and doing it on city time, too."

Jessie sighed as the police car pulled ahead of them. "At least these California cops take a little pride."

"The SS took a lot of pride, too, Jessie," Adam said. "Every picture I ever saw of them, their uniforms are impeccable."

Jessie waved away the comment with his hand.

"Don't let yourself fall for that left-wing crap, Adam. A little law and order and patriotism is good for people. Makes a nicer society to live in. And for people like us it don't matter anyway—whatever little rules they make, we know better than to piss away our life worrying about them. It's for the average people that it counts—they need a good strong set of rules to follow. Makes it better for all of us."

There were no surprises at lunchtime. About a hundred employees ate at the outdoor tables, perhaps half of them from brown bags, the others from disposable dishes bought from a stainless-steel truck that pulled in a few minutes before twelve. Eight or ten cars left the lot.

"The big shots," Jessie said. "Off to scoff up a tax-deductible lunch courtesy of the blue-collar workers of America. If they're heading for the Chez Martine Lounge I hope the management there put a fresh diaper on old Norma."

They parked on the shoulder of the little-traveled road, taking advantage of a slight elevation to look down into the interior garden through field glasses. The employees returned to work at a quarter to one and the McMullens headed back to the motel for lunch and a swim. They would return before four o'clock to watch how things were set up for the nighttime, then again at midnight. It was the routine from four in the afternoon until eight in the morning that really mattered.

There was no second shift. Fourteen workers and supervisors stayed late, the last two of them leaving together just before nine P.M. A single security guard from a private service worked the four-to-midnight shift and was relieved by a tall, black guard who worked from midnight to eight. Neither guard seemed to make any regular set of rounds. Vito and Jessie agreed that they likely spent time in front of a small television set or dozed for most of the night.

"Those guards aren't doing shit," Jessie pointed out. "The work ethic is long since gone. Everybody's just looking for a free ride these days."

They checked out the building for three consecutive nights, stopping at their vantage point several times between midnight and eight. Jessie and Vito agreed that just before three A.M. was the best time to go in; the guard would be relaxed by then and they would have several hours of darkness in which to work. Over drinks at a table in the motel lounge Jessie had said to Adam, "You have any thoughts about any of this, talk up. Don't be bashful, Adam, it won't carry you too far in life."

Adam had shrugged, and said, "Everything I hear makes sense."

Vito, hearing it, wondered for the hundredth time whether the whole caper made any sense, but he dismissed it. It looked as easy as anything he had ever pulled off and the payoff was big enough to "Make him well," as the meat market expression had it.

They worked out the details in Jessie's room, while he and Vito drank at a slow pace. Both of them had held down their drinking since boarding the airplane in New York. Jessie and Vito agreed quickly on things, Adam noticed; two pros who had crawled through plenty of dark windows in the wee hours of the morning. Vito had sketched out a rough map of the place. They would go in about three next Wednesday morning, leaving the car parked on the shoulder from which they had studied the place. A note under the windshield wiper saying they were out of gas and would be back in the morning ought to take care of any patrol car that might cruise by.

"Let's not forget to gas up and check the radiator and battery terminals," Jessie said, and Vito nodded.

The tools would be taken in one trip, each of them carrying two bags through the rectangularly planted apricot trees, then, "Nice and brisk across the parking lot, hugging that line of big trees that look like they're on their last legs," Jessie said, looking at Adam. "Even in the most fertile valley on earth."

"Eucalyptus all look like that," Adam said. "Those are healthy trees."

The idea was to move fast into the central garden area where they couldn't be seen from anywhere but the little-traveled road that offered a vista of the garden. They would move immediately behind the trellis that masked the row of vending machines where they could catch their breath and relax, completely hidden from anyone not in the building itself. Vito would be responsible for disarming the alarm on the window—Jessie yielded quickly with the comment that, "Vito's more up to date. There weren't many of the goddamned things around when I was cracking cribs."

Once they were inside it would be Adam's show. "It's up to you to locate the right pile of germs," Jessie said. A discussion of what to do about the guard ensued. For the first time Jessie and Vito disagreed.

Vito wanted to enter silently, creep about their business while the guard napped or watched television, then, "Go on our way without disturbing anyone. There's a ten-to-one shot he'll never know we're in there. We can come and go with no fuss."

"And if he does stumble onto us?" Jessie asked.

"Then we do what we have to do. Tie him up and finish the work."

Jessie spoke with exaggerated patience. "Except that if he hears something he's not going to come at us with a nightstick, he's going to have his big ugly gun in his hand while he practices how to say perpetrator for the six o'clock news just like the real cops do. The only way we get to tie him up then, Vito, is to shoot him first and hope that the shot doesn't kill him and hope that he doesn't get to shoot one of us and hope that somebody driving by doesn't hear the shots and hope that we've already located the stuff while we're doing this O.K. Corral routine in a dark hallway 'cause otherwise we leave empty-handed. It's ridiculous. Even if you're right that it's ten to one the guard don't tumble, if God forbid he does, then it's almost a sure thing we leave a dead body behind—him, or one of us."

"And your scheme?" Vito asked.

"Take him out of commission when we go in. We're the ones with the cannons out and ski masks on our heads while he's watching some rerun of 'I Love Lucy.' The masks and the guns will scare the living shit out of him. We tie him up—and it'll be easy to tie him, Vito, since this way he'll be all in one piece—and we go home with our swag."

They couldn't agree. Jessie finally said, "He's in this, too," and turned for an opinion to Adam, who got up and paced the room slowly, pretending that he was just beginning to ponder the question. In fact, his mind had been racing during the few minutes that Jessie and Vito had argued about the guard. The thought of carrying guns had never occurred to him—he realized now that his father and grandfather from the first had taken it so for granted that there had been no need even to mention it. The thought of really hurting or maybe killing the tall, black, midnight-to-eight guard whom they had watched through binoculars upset Adam more than it frightened him. The ski masks they had packed brought home to him even more than did the guns how real the potential for violence was.

He had formulated for himself a moral code. It was important to him that he live by it, and physically hurting someone violated the code. Stealing did not, and because of it he had thought himself as much a thief as his grandfather and perhaps even more a thief than his father. Now he realized that his father, when he discussed a criminal way of life, assumed an entirely different level of commitment than Adam did. "You can't be half a thief," Vito had once said, and Adam had not understood it. Now, pacing slowly among the Formica furniture and reproductions of bland paintings of San Francisco Bay in an anonymous motel room that reminded him of every room in which a buy had gone down during his hashish dealing days, he decided that his father had been right. Yet instead of feeling some delayed admiration for Vito for having known something that he didn't, he felt instead disappointed in his father; if Vito had known the chances of someone being killed were the table stakes for entry into this deal, then how had Vito been able to go along with it? Why, for that matter, had Vito not put up a much stronger fight against Adam's going into it? He realized that Vito's concern for him from the beginning had only been whether Adam was endangering himself with a potential jail term; the moral implications had never really been there. Also, Vito had weakened on taking out the guard early only because a shoot-out would likely result in their leaving empty-handed.

Adam had wanted his father in on this burglary—Vito knew his stuff and as an added benefit their partnership promised to put them on an equal footing when it was over—but he hadn't expected that Vito's commitment would be so total. Nor had he expected to see revealed an unknown facet of his father's character that he didn't especially like. He felt no disappointment with Jessie's attitudes, and it occurred to him that he had never held Jessie to the same standard of morality that he did Vito. Vito's moral ambivalence, which had come through to Adam throughout his childhood, had, surprisingly, caused Adam to hope that beneath the uncertainty his father had some strong set of ethics.

He thought for a moment of saying exactly what was on his mind but dismissed it quickly. The robbery was going to happen. It had all gone too far. He stopped pacing.

"For my taste," Adam said, "Jessie's way sounds better. There's less chance of anyone being hurt."

Vito shrugged. He was actually inclined toward Jessie's approach anyway and had resisted it mainly out of the perversity that Jessie always brought out in him. Adam studied them as they returned to their little map. His father had been raised a thief, and Jessie seemed to have been born one. He, Adam, had assumed for years that he, too, was a thief, part of a family of thieves. The notion had always appealed to him. Now, sitting within arm's length of his father and grandfather, he felt alienated from them. If they had considered that the guard might be killed and then dismissed it he would not have felt so left out. Instead the two of them brought to the planning such a shared, deep-rooted acceptance of a possible death that Adam suddenly felt he had perhaps understood nothing all this time and had deceived himself into thinking that he wasn't the outsider of the three. He had forgotten that Vito and Jessie went back a long way, years before he was born. For the first time since leaving New York his chest seemed to become hollow with a familiar feeling of loneliness and isolation.

They went on a dry run that night.

"We better spend a little time right in that garden and give a peek through some windows," Vito had said. "I want to be sure that when we waltz in there with our arms full of tools there are no big surprises."

Jessie had agreed, and now Adam pulled off the road onto the wide shoulder. Jessie and Vito wore dark pants and tee shirts. They emptied their pockets onto the floor of the car and told Adam to return at exactly four A.M. It was now five to three. He drove off slowly and in his rearview mirror watched them cross the road.

They walked casually until they were far enough away from the macadam to have no excuse for being where they were, then Vito took the lead, moving quickly, Jessie about ten feet behind. Vito called over his shoulder, "Holler if you have trouble keeping up." Jessie answered, "Fuck you," and maintained the ten-foot separation. They moved at a fast walker's pace through the knee-high grass of a wide aisle between two rows of apricot trees then doglegged to their left as they emerged from the grove and hugged the line of eucalyptus trees. They reached a corner of the building and entered into the open, U shaped garden area along a brick walkway. Vito reached the shelter of the trellis and squatted, Indian style, breathing heavily, in front of a Pepsi machine. Jessie was beside him a second later. They caught their breath. After a while Jessie said, "We're sitting pretty. Let's have a look."

"Let's just sit quiet for five more minutes," Vito whispered. He checked the second hand on his watch. "We're in a nice safe spot and the easy mistake now is to move too fast. Let's relax and get our pulse down to normal and make sure we're thinking straight."

Jessie hesitated, then nodded, yes, and lowered himself into a sitting position, legs outstretched. Vito listened to Jessie's breathing, which, by his watch, continued heavily for a few minutes after his own had returned to normal. They sat silently with elbows nearly touching in the sanctuary of the sheltered alley between the vending machines and the trellis, sharing the danger of being discovered in the dark and sharing the warmth of working as a two-man team in a strange, hostile setting. For the first time in years neither of them wanted to pick at the other.

Adam drove to the Futura Bowl, Forty-four Lanes, Open All Night, which he had noticed a few days earlier. It included a coffee shop. A half-dozen lanes were being used by a league of women who, Adam learned from the waitress, worked the production line on the four-to-midnight shift at a local electronics plant. They bowled intensely at a near semiprofessional level.

He took a booth and had a fried egg sandwich with a glass of milk, then sipped at a cup of coffee and fantasized about his life after he had his share of the robbery money—three hundred and twenty-five thousand dollars after expenses. Tax free. He would go on a long vacation first and spend the odd twenty-five thousand. A few months down in Cozumel, Mexico, where he would learn to scuba dive, something he had always wanted to do, and learn to sail a small boat. Half a day at each activity, with a good teacher, intensely, the way the women outside bowled, then a few hours each night overlooking the beach from an old-fashioned hotel room with a ceiling fan, reading the best books he could find on the theory of each sport. A few solid months of working hard at two specific skills from the time he woke up until he went to sleep, with no breaks in between. The diving frightened him a bit and he was determined to dive because of it. After Mexico another six or eight weeks to visit Nepal, where he would see what he could of the culture. Lots of books again and time spent at learning something rather than simply relaxing.

Adam had never got to Nepal. Three years ago he had spent six weeks in India along with a brilliant dropout from Cal Tech trying to put together a deal to smuggle eighty pounds of hash oil into the States. It had never come off. After a week in a good hotel in New Delhi they had gone up to Bandipura in the lush Vale of Kashmir to stay with a Hindu furniture merchant in his walled-in, three-hundred-year-old estate. On their second night the man had gone to a wall safe, quickly dialed the combination, then withdrew an LP album.

"Do you like the Beatles?" he asked.

When they nodded, yes, he set it carefully on a cheap phonograph and played each side of "Sergeant Pepper" while the three of them sat silently and listened as though it were a Beethoven symphony. When it was over the Indian exhaled a long sigh of appreciation and returned it to the wall safe. He played it once a week during their stay. He later tried to cheat them of their money and the hash oil deal fell through. Adam had wanted then to spend some time in Nepal but it would have meant dipping into business capital—funds set aside for buying hashish. He decided to put off the visit for a time in the future when he was flush.

Now the future was about to arrive. After Nepal he would have to formulate some kind of longer-range plan. School occurred to him from time to time; MIT would readmit him happily and he often found himself wanting to go much deeper into molecular biology. Or maybe not return to school at all but rather use his money to buy some type of business and try to amass a really significant bundle. Living somewhere in Marin County with five thousand dollars worth of stereo equipment and driving a Porsche held an appeal for him. He would worry about long-range plans after his two or three months of vacationing; at least his vacation plans were firm. The only conceivable hitch in them that nagged just below the surface of his fantasy was whether doing all of it alone would get to him. There were times he enjoyed being by himself but he knew from experience that at other times he grew lonely and depressed. He wished there were someone in his life at the moment with whom he wanted to share his vacation. It was not Christine; he wouldn't want her along even if it hadn't ended between them. He knew that the breakup had been caused mainly by her recognition that she could not convince him to go to Lebanon, but there had been other things as well. The Easter Sunday dinner at his parents' house had certainly fueled it. Her open admiration for Gertrude, who was growing rich from terminal cancer opportunities, had given him pause, and Jessie's disdain for her when they were drinking together after the meal had also influenced him. His parents' disapproval of her had hastened the breakup, too. Oddly enough, while he wanted to be independent he also valued their approval.

Now he decided to put off dealing with that part of his plans. A vacation would come later. They had to get through the robbery first and get through it clean, without getting caught and without hurting anyone. He finished his coffee and left a dollar for the waitress.

Vito checked the alarm on the windows and saw that it was a simple system meant to discourage teenage vandals or junkies looking to swipe a few typewriters. The windows were Andersen casements, insulated glass set into wood, the glass taped with foil and a proximity switch at the top that would interrupt the alarm circuit if the window was opened. The hinges were mounted on the exterior, each of them fastened to the window frame with five exposed screws that could be removed in a few minutes.

"These windows may be great for saving energy," Vito whispered, "but they're a thief's dream."

It would take him ten minutes to bore through the top of the wood frame quietly with a two-inch bit in a brace, then snake a strip of magnetic tape into the proximity switch gap. That would take the window out of the alarm circuit. After removing the hinges he could coax out the entire window in its frame comfortably with a pry bar. The only possible noise would come when the gear assembly on the opener pulled apart and that would be so minimal that just the noise from the air-conditioning ducts would certainly smother it unless someone were in the same room.

"We'll be inside in twenty minutes, tops," he told Jessie. "Let's find out where the guard is."

They traversed the three walls of the building that bordered the garden, both of them in a severe crouch to keep their heads just below the window line, pausing wherever a window was lit for Vito to peek in. Each proved to be a room where a light had been left on inadvertently.

"This is nice," Jessie said. "Means these guards don't even make rounds or they'd be shutting the lights off."

"But we still don't know where the son of a bitch is," Vito said.

He checked his watched. Nearly half an hour had passed since Adam had dropped them off.

"Well, we better find out where this guard coops, or drools into the centerfold of *Penthouse*, or whatever the hell he finds to do for eight hours," Jessie said. "If we don't know where this *yahn* is when we go in, we're fucked." He shook his head in the semidarkness. "How the hell does someone *work* at a job like that for thirty of forty years?"

"Next item is to check out the outside perimeter," Vito said. "The way it's built, every room looks out or into the courtyard. Unless the guy's sitting in a corridor we've got to spot him on the next circuit."

Jessie agreed. "You sit and relax," he said. "I'll cover it all in twenty minutes."

Vito reached out and grasped Jessie's forearm lightly.

"Pop, don't take this wrong, but I'm the one who ought to make this circuit. I've got twenty-five years on you."

To his surprise, Jessie did not even begin to misinterpret it. He nodded, and said, "Watch yourself out there; anybody driving past can see you."

Vito located the guard in one of the offices along the front of the building. He peeked through the window into the nearly dark room and saw the tall black man in blue shirt-sleeves, the top buttons undone, sitting in a leather armchair. The dim light came from the screen of a fourteen-inch portable Sony tuned to a black-and-white movie. The room was set up as a rest place, with one wall devoted to kitchen cabinets, a sink, a refrigerator, and several Mr. Coffee machines. A sofa and two chairs occupied the opposite wall. The guard had set his Sony on the counter, rabbit ears extended, and sat across from it, shoeless, with his feet propped on a glass-topped coffee table. On an end table beside him was a half-filled ashtray and a can of Coors. Vito studied him for a bit from a safe vantage point; the guard was closer to the window than was the television set and so he was turned slightly toward the interior wall of the room. It was the gun that Vito needed to locate and finally he made it out, in its holster, belt attached, lying on the salt-and-pepper industrial carpet a few feet away from the chair. The door to the room was fully open. The whole setup was ideal, if they found it to be the same on the night of the burglary. Vito wanted to look heavenward and mouth the words, "Thank you," but decided to do it only after they had left the place next week with their plasmids in hand.

CHAPTER XI

THE ENTIRE PIECE OF WORK LOOKED TO BE SO SIMPLE THAT JESSIE AND VITO HAD CELEBRATED IN THE MOtel lounge. It was their first night of relaxed drinking since arriving in California. Adam indulged himself a bit, too, though he made no attempt to keep up. They had four idle days before the break-in and Jessie had become adamant that they, "Not spend another night in this hick town. This is like doing time." He had pressed for a quick side trip to L.A., which he had never seen. "We can relax and behave like the McMullens are supposed to on some of the front money," he said.

Neither Adam nor Vito had been eager to visit L.A., but neither were they pleased at the prospect of four dull days in San Jose. They had given in quickly and the three of them had set out early the next morning on the five-hour drive.

Now they were checked into the Beverly Wilshire, Adam and Vito on separate floors of the new building, both overlooking the pool, and Jessie in the only other available room, a junior suite at two-sixty a day. They had been told at the front desk that the hotel was overbooked, then Jessie said to Adam, "Pay attention here. You've got to know how to travel," and went off to find the assistant manager. He introduced himself with a handshake, leaving two folded hundreds in the assistant's palm, who then checked the computer screen and discovered the open rooms. Jessie had suggested matching coins for the suite but Vito and Adam had told him to take it. It pleased him. On the door was an engraved brass nameplate: THE MANUEL J. HERNANDEZ, JR., SUITE. When Adam wondered aloud who Manuel J. Hernandez might have been, Jessie speculated, "Some Mexican porter who put fifty years of his life into keeping these hallways clean then croaked of a heart attack unclogging a toilet in this very room. A fast man with a plunger, Manuel; that's what it should say on his nameplate."

Each of them had unpacked and showered then met in the lobby. Vito had been inclined to take a leisurely drive over into the Valley, which he had often heard referred to by acquaintances or talk show hosts and was curious to see at firsthand. Jessie had turned both thumbs down and groaned in the lobby of the Wilshire.

"The Valley? What the hell can be in the Valley, eight thousand cows moping around bumping into each other? Let's stroll up Rodeo Drive and see how the filthy rich live."

Adam had agreed and after a few blocks they stopped off at the Cafe Rodeo. The place was crowded but light and airy, the single interior wall of exposed brick with inset arched mirrors, the bar a square set into the center; not a serious drinking bar, but Jessie was willing to hang out for a while to "check out the locals." They pulled up stools and waited for the bartender to finish a conversation with a waiter at the service section beside them.

"He got killed Monday night on the Hollywood Freeway," the bartender said, and shook his head with a sense of life's injustice. "Poor guy had fifty-nine lousy miles on a brand-new Mercedes."

"Fifty-nine miles," the waiter said sadly.

A pretty waitress in her mid-twenties waiting to place an order asked, "What sign was he?"

"Aries," the bartender said.

She cringed. "Oh, God. He must have been completely out of his mind. He got on a freeway last Monday night? Do you have any *idea* what the charts looked like for an Aries last Monday? My roommate is an Aries and he wouldn't budge from the apartment for twenty-four hours. I had to send out for food; he knew enough to not even dial the telephone. I'll tell you, those really bad days on the chart are when you're glad to have a VCR in the house."

Jessie rapped out a tattoo on the bar with his knuckles several times and the bartender turned. Jessie smiled at him.

"When you people are through reading each other's palms over there, maybe we could get a drink?"

The bartender, a tall, fit, thirty-year-old with blond hair that likely came from years spent on a surfboard, reddened for a moment then leaned forward with the aggressiveness of a jock who had gone through high school and college as a minor campus hero. Vito, already mildly amused, noticed that he actually squinted at Jessie while he spoke in an artificially low voice.

"You interrupted my conversation, *sir*. I find that just a little bit rude and I don't permit rudeness at my bar. I believe you owe me an apology." He leaned even closer. "*After* which I'll be happy to serve you a drink."

"You an Aries?" Jessie asked.

"August four. That's *Leo*, mister."

Jessie leaned closer, but on his elbows so that his total relaxation was obvious.

"First thing you want to do, Leo, is get a good pair of sunglasses to correct that squint seems to be giving you such a problem. Then you ought to check out the chart for Leo today. It's a first-class fucking disaster. You could run into a Mack truck, a steamroller, God knows what. You could get totaled out like your friend's Mercedes and you'd only have what—twenty-seven, twenty-eight years on you? Today, Leo, you should've stayed home in front of your VCR jerking off to an X movie. Now pour me a V.O. on the rocks, see what my partners want, and let's all make believe we just walked in the bar."

The bartender had run through his intimidation routine. It hadn't worked and now he wanted to back off but also wanted to save face.

"I'll just have a beer, please," Vito said nicely.

The bartender hesitated for a decent interval then nodded magnanimously. "One beer," he said and turned to Adam, who said, "Me, too."

He served them both before asking Jessie, "Yours was?"

"V.O. on the rocks."

After pouring it the bartender found something to do at the

far end. The McMullens sat for nearly an hour, pleased to be in one another's company and comfortable enough to remain silent for periods of time while they watched the activity of the indoor-outdoor restaurant that felt so different from anything back in New York. Even the snatches of overheard conversation from passing customers were different; current California wisdom for any occasion seemed to be summed up as, "Hey, what goes around comes around."

After a short time Vito commented that, "Living here you'd feel like you were spending fifty-two weeks a year on vacation. The whole atmosphere's a lot like a Caribbean resort hotel."

Adam agreed. "Berkeley seems different at first but underneath you get the same feeling. The name of the game in California is total comfort; you're not supposed to struggle for anything. You don't wait on lines, you don't get squashed in subways, you never fight the weather, and you can arrange your life so you go weeks at a time without laying your eyes on a poor person. Total comfort. And when they get it they don't understand why they're not happy. They confuse comfort with happiness."

"Let's not get too heavy here," Jessie said. "You take people like you find them when you're traveling."

They occasionally drew one another's attention to a particularly outstanding example of the type that Jessie described as having walked into a Beverly Hills men's store and asked the salesman to, "Make me look like the mannequin in the window." When they left the restaurant Jessie put a five under his glass for the bartender, who Vito expected would avoid a thank-you by pretending not to notice. Instead the bartender nodded amiably, thanked Jessie, and told them to have a nice day, which reminded Adam of a Berkeley health food clerk who had once told him sweetly to have a nice life. Outside, Vito expressed his surprise at the bartender's friendliness. Jessie shrugged and said, "He was all right. Lot of kids like that, no one ever told them not to behave like an asshole. Once you straighten them out they're okay."

• • •

They drove into downtown Hollywood and parked the car, then walked for a while along Hollywood Boulevard, eyes downcast, reading the names of movie stars on brass plates set into the sidewalk. Jessie continued to enjoy his sudden recollection of old-timers long after Adam and Vito had become bored. Vito finally claimed that his legs were giving out, though they felt fine. He did it reluctantly; for the first time in his memory he was deriving enjoyment from his father's pleasure. They drove back toward the hotel along Santa Monica. Jessie noticed a beer joint while they were stopped at a light and said, "Let's broaden ourselves a little. That's what travel is for. We'll just have a couple of quick ones and see what the down-to-earth people do for fun around here."

Adam pulled into the small parking lot that the bar shared with a dry cleaner and a taco stand. As they walked toward the side door of the bar they passed close to a lanky forty-five-year-old in genuine cowboy clothes. He leaned against a large, overflowing garbage hopper, one leg bent at the knee so that his foot was propped against the side of the hopper in a classic Western pose. He had the foul look of someone who had been sleeping on park benches for weeks, his hat badly stained and his boots broken down. Vito expected to be asked for a handout but the cowboy just watched them pass.

They entered the Lucky Star Beer Bar and Jessie said softly, "Jesus Christ."

"Just remember," Vito said, "you've got to take people like you find them when you travel. We're here to broaden ourselves."

The place catered to displaced Southwestern floaters: ex-oilfield workers and ranch hands who had driven pickups rather than ridden horses but who still maintained a romantic vision of themselves as America's last cadre of the totally self-sufficient, despite the Social Security card in each of their wallets. There was a pool table, just shy of regulation size, and a jukebox that Adam stopped to check out. It played only country and western. The pool table was being used by two younger guys. The bar was a long, straight, serious drinking bar, at the far end of which three cowboy types sat silently, each a few barstools apart, working slowly on the beers set before them. They had the look of the cowboy leaning against the garbage hopper outside. The near end of the bar, where the McMullens sat, was empty but for some dollar bills and change that must have belonged to the pool players.

"Lucky on draft, Lone Star in bottles," the bartender said. They ordered bottles, which were set out without glasses. The bartender, as tired and run-down as the three silent customers, propped himself against the register, looking as though he wanted to be on the other side of the bar. The only life came from the two pool players. The shooter would let out a high-pitched whoop if he pocketed anything more difficult than a hanger.

Hung on the back bar was a large pen-and-ink drawing done by someone with a flair for poster art. It was a woman standing, her legs too long and her breasts too high and firm for their size, cheesecake style, wearing only a cowboy hat and boots, mesh stockings and a garter belt, and a holster with a pistol. The heel of one hand rested on the pistol tensely, ready to draw. Next to the poster was a framed oil painting of a nude who sat unnaturally on the edge of an unmade bed, her legs facing straight out but with her knees clasped together demurely, the bed surrounded by red velvet drapes. She seemed meant to be at least part Mexican, with deeply bronzed skin, high cheekbones on a chubby face, and lips set in the pouting innocence of a Cupid. A wide gold armband that seemed uncomfortably tight encircled one of her biceps. The artist had captured in her eyes the resentment of a long-term prisoner. She looked to be about fifteen, her breasts smaller than those of the cowgirl in the garter belt but, like them, too firm. Vito was puzzled by what seemed to be hundreds of tiny punctures on the breasts of both women, not part of the picture, clustered toward the nipples. After a minute he noticed a single dart on the back bar beneath the painting, apparently available to any drinker who became bored with the pool table. Jessie's attention was obviously caught by the tiny punctures and his eyes widened when he saw the dart.

"Please don't ask the management about that dart," Vito said.

"Do you *believe* this?" Jessie asked.

"Let's have one fast beer and get out of here, Jessie. You say anything and it'll turn into a first-rate mess. We'll wind up getting pinched."

"But that's fucking disgusting," Jessie said.

"I agree. But we're in California to do a piece of work. It's not your mission in life to straighten out the world."

"That's what's *wrong* with the world is that people have stopped trying to straighten it out," Jessie said. "Hitler should have been straightened out right off the bat. Someone ought to just whack out Fidel Castro and Yasir Arafat and get them assholes out of the picture. And somebody's got to start grabbing the kids in sneakers who snatch gold chains off people in the subways and start kicking their fucking teeth in on the platform before the cops get there." His voice rose a bit. "Jesus, Vito, your goddamn problem is you're *complacent*, like everybody else."

Vito felt his recent, warm feelings about Jessie evaporating. He turned to Adam.

"Do you believe this? I'm getting a lecture on social responsibility from Jessie McMullen, avowed thief and proud of it. Does this make sense, Adam?"

Adam thought for a few moments then said, "On the one hand, someone *should* have stopped Hitler." He looked at Jessie. "On the other hand, Jessie, are we here for lectures on morality or are we in L.A. for a pleasant three-day break?"

Jessie accepted the criticism from Adam as he always did, with good grace.

"How come your son always makes sense even when you don't?" he said, and squeezed Vito's neck affectionately. It was an unusual gesture for Jessie and at the same time that Vito welcomed it, he felt, guiltily, a resentment that Adam was able to say things to Jessie that he, Vito, could not.

The pool players finished their game and walked toward their place at the bar near the McMullens. They stopped at the jukebox. Vito tightened now that he had a closer look at them. They were just what the doctor would order for Jessie's present mood: one a burly roustabout, his partner a big cowboy, each in their mid-thirties, each with the beginning of a beer belly, several rotted front teeth, and tattoos on their forearms. From their horsing around over which songs to play Vito knew they would remain loud at the bar, which would suit Jessie perfectly. In later explanations they would become, "A couple of big-mouth mutts looking for trouble," which would justify Jessie's hitting them. Their rotted front teeth would tempt him even further; Jessie had a long expounded maxim that, "When a guy's over thirty and he still don't take care of his teeth he's a fucking lowlife." Also, neither one looked to be a pushover; each was a big, rough-and-ready young guy, someone you thought twice about tackling even if you were a tough guy. Those were the only opponents Jessie thought worth taking on. He often said that people his own size or smaller were no fun to whip, only the really big guys were satisfying. The fact that there were two of them would sweeten it up further for him, as would their Western accents. From Jessie's early few years of riding the rails and boxing in mining camps he knew how tough country boys like these could be, yet decades of living in the tenements of Hell's Kitchen had biased him. He sincerely believed the words of the song about New York that if "You can make it there, you'll make it anywhere," and had adopted the provincial standard of any working-class neighborhood in the five boroughs that anyone from outside the city was somewhat inferior.

Jessie hadn't noticed them yet.

"Let's get out of here," Vito said. "The place is a dump."

Jessie seemed amenable but insisted on using the men's room first. He walked to the rear of the place.

"Your grandpa's spoiling for a fight," Vito said.

"Why?"

Vito shrugged. "Might have to do with the phase of the moon for all I know. The need to belt somebody comes over Jessie regularly, kind of like a bitch comes into heat."

"Can we get him out of here?"

"I'm trying."

"What if we can't? What the hell do we do?"

Vito's tone was resigned.

"Watch his back for him is all, in case one of these hoboes at the bar jump in. Otherwise, your best bet is to watch him, you never have." He smiled. "And Jessie in action *is* sweet to watch."

Adam was surprised at his father's ability to enjoy Jessie's craziness—he had never seen it before—and impressed with how cool he was about the ability of the two of them to watch Jessie's back. It occurred to him that in a bar fight Vito was a lot better than he had ever suspected and he was grateful to his father for working from the basic assumption that he, Adam, was up to it. He wasn't a fighter, and the thought that he might soon be in the middle of the real thing caused his stomach to tighten. A few seconds later he realized that Vito knew that about him, by his gentle tone of voice when he said, "Adam, if this gets bad, get a beer bottle in your hand and use it. Even big tough guys can't compete with it. And swing it hard. With something in your hand the only way to lose a bar fight is to worry about hurting the other guy. Watch your grandpa and you'll see the real secret is to hit like a mule—it's the guy who considers things who gets hurt."

Vito saw Jessie approaching as the pool players left the jukebox to stand at their stools beside Adam. Jessie was within earshot as one of them said, "Double or nothing. Winner has to hit a nipple." He called to the bartender, "Tommy, reach me the dart."

This would do it, Vito knew. He visualized Jessie standing at a Tenth Avenue bar weeks from now, saying, "I hit this hick a shot he'll never forget," and demonstrating a short, straight right punctuated with a "Bing!" at the impact point. One of his cronies would point out, "Ah, Jessie, the fooker deserved it. Throwin' darts at a woman's breasts. Jesus Christ, it gives me the shivers," and the shivers would be warded off with a round of drinks—Jessie's on the house.

Jessie stopped behind them as the roustabout leaned forward, aimed carefully, and threw the dart at the cowgirl's left breast. He hit her on the lower rib cage.

"Why the hell would anyone want to throw a dart at a girl's tit?" Jessie asked.

The two of them turned, still smiling, unaware that Jessie was boiling inside.

"What's the problem, Pop?" the thrower asked.

"Just curious why anyone would want to do that. What are you two, a couple of serial murderers roam the highways around here raping twelve-year-olds?"

Their smiles disappeared but Jessie's age kept them from throwing punches. The dart thrower reddened.

"Hey listen, Pop..."

Jessie interrupted him with a smile.

"That's the second time you called me pop, Tex. Hell, I got around a lot when I was young but I doubt that I'm your father. Who knows, though. You carry a picture of your mother on you? Maybe I'll remember her—I must've fucked half the whores in Texas."

It took a few moments to register, then the dart thrower threw the roundhouse right that Jessie was waiting for patiently. He moved under it easily, stepping into the second opponent as Vito knew he would. "When there's two of them," Jessie had always taught Vito, "you hit the partner first. He's just standing there flat-footed, waiting to get in a free punch." It's what Jessie did now, using his momentum to swing a low, right-hand body punch, both his feet coming off the floor as though he were delivering a single practice shot into a heavy bag. He landed in the center of the cowboy's beer belly and the cowboy crumpled. The dart thrower had regained his balance and threw a left hook that Jessie slipped in a professional way, with just a half-turn of his head that took all the impact out of the punch, then he swung his own tight, short, left hook, pivoting from the knees to put his full weight into it as always. It landed square on the roustabout's ear and left him standing, but off balance. Jessie drove his straight right, head and shoulders following his fist by inches, the punch he loved to land because it did the most damage for him. The roustabout went straight back, taking quick little steps on his heels in an attempt to stay upright, across fifteen feet of floor until he hit the jukebox. He tried to stand but his knees wobbled, then gave out. He sat on the floor, dazed, as Jessie approached. The cowboy was on his hands and knees at the bar beside Vito, groaning and trying to vomit while the three hoboes watched impassively. Vito worried only about the bartender, who certainly had a bat handy.

"You make any moves," Vito threatened, "and I'll whack you with this bottle."

The bartender shrugged.

"Hey, mister, I don't give a rat's ass. Your buddy fell in love with this cowgirl he can take her fucking picture home with him for all I care. I'm tired of handing out that damn dart all day anyway."

Jessie stood above the roustabout and motioned for him to get up.

"Stand up and get hit like a man or I'll kick you in the belly," he said.

It struck Adam that Jessie would have been happy had someone made him go to a neutral corner. The roustabout probed at the bridge of his nose, which had obviously been broken by the straight right punch, then rose and put his hands up. Jessie motioned him forward with outstretched, open hands. After a moment he tried to bull his way into Jessie, but did it with too much caution. Jessie dropped his left shoulder in a feint that caused his opponent's hands to drop nearly a foot and Jessie came through with another straight right, this one landing flush in the mouth. The roustabout went down again against the jukebox and sat with no intention of getting up, spitting out blood and teeth. Jessie pointed a finger at him and said, "Now maybe you'll get your rotten teeth fixed, you fucking lowlife." He walked toward the door and motioned for Vito and Adam to come along. As he left the bar, Vito heard one of the hoboes say, "I seen a lot of bar fights over women but this is the first one I ever seen over a damn picture of a woman."

The McMullens ate dinner at the Brown Derby then returned to the hotel, where Vito and Jessie decided on a few drinks at the Il Padrino bar. Adam bought the new issue of *Rolling Stone* and said that if he couldn't read himself to sleep he might join them later.

"My guess is we'll still be here," Jessie said.

He and Vito found space about halfway down the bar and ordered a round of drinks.

"That fight took ten years off you," Vito said. "You look like a man who's just had a monkey gland transplant."

Jessie flexed the fingers of his right hand several times and examined the knuckles.

"A nice scrap once in a while is good for the constitution," he said. "Gets a little adrenaline pumping. It's what's lacking in your life."

"Am I about to get some sound advice on how to conduct my life, Jessie?"

"That's what fathers are for."

Vito smiled and raised his glass in a silent toast.

"I'm serious," Jessie said. "You could use a little excitement here and there. The last couple of days you've got a little bounce in your step that hasn't been there for years."

Vito shrugged.

"California air," he said, but it occurred to him that he had felt lighter on his feet ever since buying the tools on Canal Street.

"California air, my ass," Jessie said. "The air in this town could kill a horse if he breathes deep enough. What you overlook, Vito, and it surprises me coming from a bright guy like yourself, is that a real thief—a *thief's* thief—isn't just in it for the money. He'd go on a score every once in a while if there was only fifty bucks sitting in a safe. It's a way of life, Vito."

He indicated the hotel bar and lounge with a sweep of his arm.

"And not a bad way of life, huh? A week ago you were cutting up cows on Fourteenth Street with nothing to look forward to. Today you've got the dice in your hand in a high-stakes crap game. And the McMullens are on a roll, Vito. I can feel it."

Vito touched his glass to Jessie's.

"From your lips to God's ears, as my mother-in-law would say."

They sipped their drinks and sat quietly. After a few minutes Vito noticed two glamorous brunettes in their late twenties at a nearby table. Both of the women smiled pleasantly when they saw him looking over. Jessie had picked up on them, too. He nodded a greeting.

"Nice," he said to Vito.

"Nice? You've got to get off Tenth Avenue more often. They're hookers."

Jessie looked them over appreciatively.

"That's a vulgar way to refer to a woman, Vito. I never brought you up like that."

"Are you going to sit here and tell me they're *not* hookers?"

Jessie shrugged. "Who are we to judge? They look like they might accept gifts, but sometimes that's just part of a warm personality."

He picked up his drink, walked over to their table, and introduced himself. They smiled and invited him to join them. He settled into a comfortable armchair and motioned to Vito, who, after a few minutes, signed the bar check and carried his drink to the table.

Margo and Denise looked even better close up. Both had come to L.A. seven or eight years earlier to break into movies, Margo from Shreveport, Louisiana, where she had won a local beauty contest and gone on to place second in state championships, Denise from Battle Creek—"At the confluence of the Kalamazoo and Battle Creek rivers"—also a local beauty pageant winner and one of Michigan's finest baton twirlers. Neither had yet landed a speaking part though they had appeared in a dozen movies and done some modeling. Denise was proud to have been a guest at Hef's mansion four years ago, and Margo, as a background player in a street crowd in her last film, had survived the editing to get five seconds on screen only a few heads away from Paul Newman.

Jessie raised his glass.

"Here's to us watching the two of you accepting Oscars before long. Remember to thank all the little people who contributed so much."

Denise asked, "Are you guys staying at the hotel?"

"We're here for a few days," Vito said.

"Do you get to California often?"

Before Vito could answer Jessie said, "As my friend Vito here says, not often enough. We're big fans of the earthquake state." He turned to Vito. "You're out here what, four times a year, Vito?"

Vito nodded.

"I get out a little more often," Jessie said.

"And you always stay at the Wilshire?" Margo asked.

"It's a home away from home for me," Jessie said. "I maintain a small suite here. Nothing pretentious, just comfortable."

"The Manuel J. Hernandez, Jr., Suite," Vito said. "Manuel, Jr., was a fast man with a plunger."

Both women stared attentively at whoever was talking and laughed wherever it seemed appropriate, without hearing much of anything. Jessie seemed to favor Margo. Denise picked up on it quickly and concentrated on Vito, who decided he would rather listen than talk. An only child, her parents had pushed her into baton twirling when she was four years old and most of her summers until she entered Kellogg Community College were spent at camps that scheduled three to four hours a day of twirling practice. As a teenager she had traveled to twenty-seven states to compete. When her parents' family room in a suburb of Battle Creek was finally so overcrowded with trophies and medals that there was no room for the television set, her dad had built an addition onto the house, sixteen feet by twelve, that he called the trophy room. She had given up twirling after competing in the national championships; there was no place further to go.

"What the hell did you *think* about those thousands of hours you were twirling?" Vito asked.

"You just concentrate," Denise said. "The whole secret of twirling is concentration and total dedication. After that it's just your natural talent. Dad says you're born with it or you're not."

Jessie, overhearing her, said, "Baton twirling? I've always felt they should make it an Olympic event."

"What for?" Vito said. "It's the kind of thing the Chinese would dominate in no time."

Denise disagreed.

"There's no *way* anybody's going to beat your American girl at twirling a baton. It's just kind of genetic."

"Did you watch the rowing in the last Olympics?" Jessie asked. "A friend of mine competed against the Finn. Charlie Murphy. He placed second."

Margo remembered the event.

"Murphy came so *close*," she said.

Vito knew Murphy slightly. A thirty-five-year-old bartender in the West Village, he had a rowing machine in his Chelsea tenement on which he worked out daily to the sound track of *Ben Hur*. On the night of the Olympic rowing event Murphy had called in sick so he could, "Go up against the Finn." He set his television in front of his machine, amplified *Ben Hur* just short of drowning out the crack of the starting pistol, then pulled for dear life, his perspiration pouring onto the carpet.

"When you know it's four more years for another shot, you row your heart out," Murphy said. "I gave the son of a bitch a run for his money. He only took me by a boat's length."

Jessie asked Denise what it was like at Hef's place.

"It was four years ago," she said, "but I don't expect it's changed much. Hef didn't strike me as a man whose values would just shift every few years; he seemed real steady and sure of himself. If you think about it, just that he smokes a pipe says a lot about his character."

"Jesus, you're right," Jessie said. "I just never made the connection, Hef and his pipe."

"We were introduced, right near the pool. He's real down to earth and quiet, doesn't put on any airs or try to act like a big shot. He just circulates around in his bathrobe and pajamas wanting everyone to be comfortable."

"What the hell does he do, take naps all day long?" Jessie asked.

Denise laughed.

"No. I think the bathrobe is just Hef's way of putting people at ease. You really choke up a little when you know you're going to meet him, it's kind of like being introduced to the president. Or Robert Redford."

"Who took you there?" Vito asked.

"A girlfriend. She had almost made the centerfold a few years before."

"I take it you never made the centerfold?" Jessie asked.

She smiled, a smile that Jessie guessed she had learned to use as a young girl when she placed second in a twirling competition.

"Thank God," Jessie said. "Years ago I could sit in a barbershop and enjoy looking over the centerfolds. The last few years they look like illustrations for a medical textbook. Those pictures are enough to turn you off the color pink for the rest of your life."

Denise retained her smile.

"I don't see anything to be ashamed of, showing the human body. Hef always says that it's the wholesome, girl-next-door look he wants."

"Well," Jessie said, "I'm all for catching a good long peek of the wholesome girl next door if she's got her flimsy little panties on or a pair of stockings. But if she's totally naked, looking like she expects her gynecologist to come through the door any minute, I'd rather she kept her shades down."

"Jessie here is from the old school," Vito said. "Who'd you meet at Hef's?"

"Stars," Jessie said. "Give us the names of stars."

"There were a few," Denise said. "But one thing you learn in the entertainment business is to never reveal names. My agent told me from the beginning that discretion is the byword in Hollywood."

"Our lips are sealed," Jessie said. "Give us a little juicy gossip. Inside stuff. You know, the *real* Hollywood that we never get to read about back East."

Denise wouldn't budge; her agent had obviously made an impression with his warning about discretion. She had little gossip to relate; she had been at the mansion on Super Bowl Sunday and the men had been absorbed in front of the forty-inch projection TV set, gambling heavily on the game. One of them, unnamed but, "He had a big part in *Godfather One*," was such a serious gambler that in the fourth quarter, when his fifty thousand dollars placed earlier with bookies and another twenty thousands put down in threes and twos at varying odds against his fellow guests at Hef's was obviously lost, he became so desperate for action that during time-outs when the cameraman selected someone in the audience on whom to home in with a long-lens shot, the *Godfather One* actor would call out, "I'll lay two thousand against ten that the next face he picks up on is black." He lost three of those bets consecutively, to "an actor whose name I can't mention, but he's *super* handsome and gets five million a picture."

"Franchot Tone," Jessie guessed.

Denise was puzzled, but maintained the professional attitude that she and Margo had gone with from the beginning; don't question or upset the johns.

"Divulge *names*," Jessie said. "That's the reason I travel to Hollywood so often, for *names*. It's my stock-in-trade at fancy Park Avenue dinner parties or the bar at P. J. Clarke's. The people I hang out with *hunger* for names."

Vito knew that at most Jessie might recognize the names of three current movie actors: Burt Reynolds, Al Pacino, and Clint Eastwood. After that he was lost, unless one mentioned Clark Gable or Roland Gilbert. But his overly done, intense interest in movie-star gossip had the desired effect on Denise. She knew in her heart that people back East hungered for inside stories and it gave her a feeling of importance to be in possession of the information and yet unwilling, for ethical reasons, to reveal it. She lifted her head upright and refused to name names. Vito noticed, as her head lifted and her back straightened, that her breasts were sensational.

Margo described the excitement of three days as a background extra within touching distance of Paul Newman.

"Even though he's kind of short, you know, sort of not very tall, those eyes are just so..." She searched for the proper word.

"Piercing," Vito volunteered.

"That's *it*, piercing. That's exactly what they are. It just gives you the shivers, even if you're in the biz and you're not, you know, star struck."

Jessie shook his head with disappointment.

"Paul Newman. Who would've believed it. For years they had me fooled with Alan Ladd. A real tough guy—took a hell of a beating off William Bendix and stood up, too, never rattled—and years later I find out they had him standing on orange crates half his career when he really should've been working for the Ringling Brothers. Now Newman. What the hell makes these dwarfs go into the movies?"

"Paul Newman isn't a *dwarf*," Margo said.

Jessie waved away her objection.

"The cat's out of the bag," he said. "But trust us, we're souls of discretion."

As he searched for the cocktail waitress a sudden thought seemed to come to him.

"I'm not sure I want another drink here," he said. He turned to Margo.

"Look, if you don't have a prior engagement I'd love to give you a tour of the Manuel J. Hernandez, Jr., Suite then maybe take my shoes off and relax with a drink and some nice feminine company for a couple of hours. I'm sure my friend Vito would enjoy doing the same thing with your friend." He turned to Denise. "Maybe you could show him a little fancy baton work, it's a once-in-a-lifetime opportunity for him."

He addressed the two of them.

"But we're both going to be too tired to drive you home, so the only way we'll consider it is if you girls are willing to accept cab fare."

He raised his hand to ward off a possible rejection.

"I know it may appear a bit gross—I'm sure Hef would put a couple of stretch limos at your disposal—but we'd rather give you the cash for a cab."

He hesitated, then said, "I understand they're outrageously expensive in L.A."

Margo nodded her assent.

"I figured two hundred ought to cover it," Jessie said.

Margo pursed her lips, then said, "That's about right for the meter but it would mean leaving the driver without a tip. Two-fifty would cover all the expenses."

"Jesus Christ," Jessie said. "No one wants to leave some hardworking refugee from Bangladesh tipless right here in the capital of American opportunity. Two-fifty sounds great."

Denise avoided Vito's eyes while Jessie motioned to the waitress for a check. Margo, after a few moments of thought, pointed out to Jessie and Vito, "You realize we'll need separate cabs. We don't live near each other."

Jessie squeezed her neck affectionately, as he had squeezed Vito's neck earlier in the Lucky Star Beer Bar, and said, "That was understood from the get-go. Even if you two were rooming together we wouldn't want you cramped up in a single taxi. This isn't Des Moines. Separate cabs, of course."

Vito told Jessie to run off with Margo, he and Denise would have another drink. While Denise went to the ladies' room he sat alone at the table. He was uncertain about taking her up to his room but didn't mind consuming more of her time while he decided; he would pay her in any event. Time was money for Denise—the girl was working. Hookers had never held any appeal for him and on the two occasions in his life he had tried them it hadn't worked out well. He brought to even a one-night stand a need to feel desirable; not loved, or even liked necessarily, but wanted, at least on a purely sexual level. The exchange of money ruined that for him, and if Denise did, in fact, find him attractive and happened to be in the mood for sex he would never believe it. He might easily take her to the room and after half an hour or so roll over and say, "It was a good try but let's call it quits, Denise." Even if it did work out he would very likely be sorry when it was over, wondering why, after six years of not cheating on Elaine he had handed two hundred and fifty bucks to a woman who couldn't seem to distinguish Hugh Hefner from the president of the United States. Elaine actually shopped for bargains in clothes and cosmetics, saving twenties here and tens there, putting a lot of effort into reducing their budget by two hundred and fifty dollars. The best thing to do here was to pay her and say good night.

On the other hand...

The woman was an absolute knockout, her face what one visualized when someone talked of a Hollywood starlet. And even as a third-rate centerfold possibility her body wasn't going to be a big disappointment when she undressed.

And she probably needed the money.

Although he intended to pay her anyway.

But if he was paying her anyway then his concern for Elaine's tens and twenties was meaningless. As a matter of fact, to give Denise the two-fifty in return for nothing was *really* throwing money down the drain; Elaine would have every right to be truly outraged if she found out he had done that.

And, paying or not paying, true desire on the part of Denise or not, there was no long line of twenty-eight-year-old splendid female specimens hot on the trail of the forty-seven-year-old Vito McMullen, wholesale butcher. Nor did he expect there to be in the future. This was a unique opportunity.

He remembered Jessie's advice to him as a teenager: "Vito, keep one thing in mind with women. You'll never hear an old man bitching about what a bad lay someone was, but you'll meet a lot of guys drunk at a bar crying about some gal they could have fucked and didn't fifty years ago. The truth is, there's no such thing as a bad piece of ass; some are just better than others. The only ones you'll ever regret are the ones you pass up."

Probably good counsel, Vito thought.

He was still undecided, though leaning heavily toward receiving some sort of value for his two hundred and fifty, when he looked up and made his decision. Denise was approaching the table, still twenty feet away. She had redone her makeup and walked with a trace of the old baton twirler in her, erect, each step just a hint shorter than normal but enough to open up the six-inch slits on the sides of her skirt. When she saw him watching her she flashed him a smile that he guessed she had flashed at hundreds of twirling judges, yet it was ninety percent genuine. The woman was still not disillusioned with life. The smile decided him. He would ask her up to the room after offering her cab fare home if she really wasn't in the mood to join him, and take her acceptance, if it came, as proof that she wasn't just with him for the money. She would be free to go if she chose and if she chose not to then he ought to accept it as proof of his attraction; forty-seven-year-old butcher or not. There was such a thing as being paranoiac and Denise seemed an honest enough young lady.

They walked across the cobbled driveway that separated the two wings of the hotel, then into the marble lobby of the new wing.

"I'm glad your friend went for Margo," she said, and squeezed Vito's arm.

He said, "Me, too," and hoped that she didn't feel obliged to run through a litany of soothing hooker clichés on the way to the room.

The elevator door opened and Adam stood directly before them. He stepped out and nodded, completely surprised, as was Vito. After a moment Vito said, "Denise, this is Adam. Adam, Denise."

They stood silently, then Adam said, "I was going to have a drink with you and Jessie. He still there?"

"Jessie left. Come on, I'll have a drink with you."

"No, I'll catch up with you later. Nice meeting you, Denise."

He walked across the lobby, a bit stiffly, Vito thought. On the elevator Denise said nothing. Running into Adam had ruined it for Vito. While he could go on a burglary with his son, he couldn't get laid in a hotel room with his son waiting downstairs. He wasn't sure that made any sense. He knew, though, that now he would lead Denise to the privacy of his room where he would say he suddenly felt sick and give her the two-fifty along with best wishes for success in the movie business. She wouldn't be heartbroken and he would console himself over his lost opportunity with a centerfold contender by deciding she might well have herpes—the thought had run through his mind earlier. He wanted to get back to the bar quickly, where he would take an easygoing, man-to-man approach with Adam, who, having had ten minutes to consider the situation, would shrug and say something like, "Hey, I'm a big kid, Pop." Vito knew, though, that Adam would feel better not having sat for an hour waiting for his father, just upstairs, to finish cheating on his mother.

CHAPTER XII

ADAM DROVE CAREFULLY ALONG ALAMEDA TOWARD THE LAB. BESIDE HIM, VITO CONFIRMED TO Jessie, item by item, that he had filled the tank, checked the coolant level, cleaned and tightened the battery terminals, put a pressure gauge on the spare, tested the jack, and checked that every light was working. After that no one spoke until they reached their parking spot on the road behind the laboratory.

It was five minutes to three when Adam turned off the ignition. He took a deep breath and wondered why his heart beat so fast; half a dozen times in his life he had walked across airports carrying a suitcase with enough grass or acid in it to put him away for years and had never been as nervous as he was now. It was knowing the guard was in there and that they would have to deal with him, he decided. Had it been a simple burglary he wouldn't be nearly as nervous. Perhaps it had been a mistake to go along with Jessie's scheme of taking out the guard immediately. Vito may have been right; slip through the caper quietly and go with the ninety percent chance that they would never have to confront an underpaid, armed man most likely raised in an Oakland ghetto who might grasp an opportunity to be a hero. It seemed a little late to discuss it now, Adam thought. He taped the out-of-gas note to the inside of the windshield and stepped onto the graveled shoulder of the road.

Jessie had said a week ago that they had gotten a break; there would be a waxing moon which meant very little light on them when they crossed the open spaces. Adam looked up and saw it as he stood beside the car, a slender crescent low in the sky, just above the outline of the Santa Cruz Mountains. They locked the car and moved quickly into the partial cover of the apricot orchard, each of them carrying two cases of tools. Vito led through the row of trees, with Adam about fifteen feet behind him and Jessie following. They stopped and squatted for a few moments when they reached the edge of the parking lot, then moved out quickly, close to the line of eucalyptus trees. When they reached the building they continued on in a crouch to pass under the windows. A car engine revved somewhere on the road in front of the building then faded out into the night.

At the vending machines they sat on the ground behind the shelter of the trellis and caught their breath. Jessie was puffing audibly. Vito checked his watch and motioned with his hand for them to relax for five minutes. They sat silently, waiting for their pulse rates to subside.

Vito motioned when five minutes had passed. Adam had expected the wait to seem interminable, instead it flew by. He only noticed that even in the warm California air his thighs and buttocks grew cold against the brick walkway. He wondered about his father's and grandfather's pulse rates—he guessed that his own had picked up speed. Vito distributed the three black ski masks. After each of them had adjusted the eye and mouth holes properly Adam looked at Jessie and Vito and wondered whether he himself looked as intimidating. Nearly certain that he must—the masks were identical and he was as big as Vito or Jessie—he still doubted it; some emotion that he knew was irrational told him that an adversary would sense through the black wool that he was the indecisive member of the trio.

Jessie and Adam remained seated while Vito moved away quickly. He would confirm that the guard was in the room where he had last seen him—if not, make a methodical check until he had located him—then return to disarm the alarm system. Adam breathed deeply and consciously relaxed his body, yoga style, while he searched the sky for either of the dippers, the only constellations he could recognize. A light breeze moved the leaves of the apricot trees in the distance and caused the eucalyptus, out of sight from Adam's vantage point, to rustle. Adam wished the breeze would reach into the deep shelter of the U; he could feel the first trickles of perspiration crawling down under the mask.

Jessie reached across and touched his forearm.

"We're going to walk through this caper, Adam," he whispered. "What the crew of the *QE Two* used to call a piece of cake. At your age I was on a lot tougher numbers and saw nothing out of them but a Swiss cheese sandwich. You're starting at the top."

"That's America for you," Adam whispered. "If each generation can't do better than the last then what the hell did all those immigrants come over for?"

Jessie pinched his cheek lightly through the mask and whispered affectionately, "Don't be a fucking wise guy, Adam. You've got a touch of your old man in you."

After a bit he added, "And only one of my parents came over; my mother was already here. It was her land them greedy immigrants were robbing."

"And ever since you've done your best to even it up for her," Adam whispered.

"Whatever little bit I can," Jessie said and smiled, though through the mouth hole of the mask it appeared as the grotesque expression of a gargoyle.

"You'll be fine," he whispered, and squeezed Adam's arm.

Vito returned quickly. The guard was where he had been nearly a week ago.

"He looks like he hasn't moved," Vito said. "Except this time the gun is sitting in its holster on top of the TV."

He set to work quickly, tightening a two-inch bit into a brace and boring through the top of the wood casement window, just a few inches above the two halves of the alarm proximity switch. It took nearly ten minutes to break through. While Jessie returned the brace and bit to the tool bag, Vito took out a device he had rigged up back in the hotel room: a length of thin magnetic strip bought on Canal Street, cut to just under two inches and epoxied to a long piece of stiff but malleable wire. The wire returned on itself in a sharp, one-hundred-and-eighty-degree bend. When the strip was fed into the room through the hole, Vito could, with a long pair of pincers inserted beside the wire, bend and manipulate it until the magnet was at the proper height to be pulled gently into the narrow opening between the proximity switch halves.

He worked with the pincers for another five minutes before the magnetic strip was positioned properly, then he withdrew the pincers and removed from the tool kit a long, slender Teflon rod and a tube of glue. He squeezed several drops of the glue onto the Teflon rod, quickly passed it through the hole, transferred the glue onto the top of the magnetic strip, then pulled the strip into position between the proximity switch halves and applied upward pressure with the wire. He held it in place, waiting for the glue to set.

"How long will that take to stick?" Adam asked.

"About a minute," Vito said. "It's Crazy Glue."

Jessie nodded his head in admiration and said, "Just like in the TV commercials. Your old man's no dope."

"What are you gluing it to?" Adam asked Vito.

"The top part of the proximity switch. The bottom part's nothing but a magnet that keeps the switch closed. If you open the window and pull away the magnetic part the switch opens the circuit and all hell breaks loose. Once my little magnet's cemented safely in place we can open that window wide and the switch never knows the difference."

After a few minutes Vito let go of the wire. The magnetic strip held in place against the switch.

"Jesus," Jessie said. "Imagine the money we could knock down giving a TV testimonial for Crazy Glue. Fuck that guy in a football helmet stuck to the top of the goalpost."

Vito tightened a Phillips head attachment into the end of a Yankee screwdriver, set it on reverse, and removed the hinge screws methodically. He wrapped a cloth around the end of a pry bar then tapped it silently into the opening at the bottom of the window frame near the opener and pushed hard against the fulcrum of the sill. The gear assembly of the opener broke loose with a soft metallic screech. With a second pry bar he levered out the hinged side of the window, then pulled it firmly with his hands. The two locking mechanisms along the center post gave way easily. He set the window, in its frame, against the building and stood back for a moment. Before them was a clear opening into the building, eighteen inches wide by four feet high.

"We could go through that wearing tails and top hats and not get dirty," Jessie whispered.

Vito went in first and motioned for Adam to pass through the main bag of tools, those they would most likely need. The other bags and boxes were left on the walkway; if they were needed they would be brought in. Adam entered next, then Jessie. They stood for a few moments, Vito using a flashlight, and got their bearings.

They were in a small office that had obviously been designed for one low-level executive but was now divided into two work spaces, both of them too cramped for comfort.

Jessie looked around.

"So this is what the *Wall Street Journal* calls a rapidly expanding company in the rapidly expanding field of genetic engineering, right here in rapidly expanding Silicon Valley. Who the hell works in this office, a couple of sardines?"

"Each of us knows what he's doing?" Vito asked.

They said, yes. Vito opened the door, took a left into the dark corridor, and moved slowly but surely, counting the number of office doors on his right as he went along. Jessie followed him closely, Adam just behind. They had decided early on that Adam wouldn't carry a gun, after only a few minutes of argument during which Adam had remained neutral. Jessie had wanted him to be armed; first because "Three guns'll scare the shine half again as much as two," and second because, "You're doing what you always do, Vito—treating my grandson like a second-class citizen. I remember what it was like at his age and you seem to have forgot. You go out to do a piece of work with a couple of guys who are packing and you're not allowed to and later on you feel that you didn't really contribute your share. Like you got brought along on a half a freebie."

Vito had been adamant, as he had been adamant about nothing else—if Adam carried a gun, even if Adam wanted to carry a gun—he, Vito, would bow out then and there. He had stood in the motel room and pointed his forefinger at Adam while he raised his voice to Jessie.

"You, and this kid, may *think* that he knows what he's getting into here but you're both wrong. He's never *done* it, Jessie. He's never stood in that situation and wanted to shit his pants because he knew he was facing a ton of time if the asshole on the other side of the room decides to be gung ho. He does *not* carry a piece. No, no, no!"

"If things go sour, ain't he better off with something in his hand?" Jessie had shouted.

"No! 'Cause if there's got to be some Wild West shit, it's you or me is going to do the shooting, Jessie. I am *not* going to have this kid going through life knowing he tried to kill somebody, or worse, did it. No!"

"You carried them when you were younger than him. Did you ever have to use it?"

"Yes!" Vito had shouted. "Yes! I never talked about it and I'm not going into details now, but yes I *did* pull a trigger. It was just dumb luck that the guy didn't die. And I don't feel good about it. I'll be damned before I see Adam carry that load through his life."

There had been a long silence, then Jessie had asked Adam, "Can you live with going in there empty-handed?"

Adam had replied with relief and a feeling of gratitude for his father that he hoped didn't show, "I guess I'll have to."

He was now unarmed. Vito and Jessie had pistols in their hands. Thirty-eights; both of them agreed they were scarier than a smaller caliber and scaring the guard was most of the battle. Vito motioned for them to stop; just ahead was the open door of the room in which the guard was presumably still watching his program. The dim light from the television set illuminated the dark vinyl tiles of the corridor. The sound became clear; Adam recognized it as a rerun of Sargeant Bilko, a program he had rarely been allowed to watch as a ten-year-old because it came on past his bedtime. They moved to within a few feet of the door, hugging the wall, then Vito motioned for them to go into their previously rehearsed routine. He positioned himself very close to the door, back to the wall, Jessie shoulder to shoulder beside him, both watching Adam who used his right arm, forefinger extended, to call beats as an orchestra conductor would; he chopped the air silently and mouthed, "One," then again with, "Two," then in cadence, "Three," and Vito pivoted his body into the room, gun extended, Jessie on his heels.

"Freeze!" Vito said, and moved toward the television set to take the guard's gun out of harm's way, Jessie pointing his own gun at the couch, clutched at eye level in the standard, two-handed FBI grip, Adam following in order to show a third ski-masked burglar and up the odds another notch against the guard making a foolish move. The guard wasn't there. Nor was his gun. The McMullens looked at one another, each of their facial expressions hidden from the other two beneath a ski mask.

After nearly half a minute of standing still and looking at one another—it seemed to Adam that his father and grandfather were silently blaming each other for the problem but he couldn't be certain because of the ski masks—Jessie spoke softly.

"He's probably off taking a leak."

"And he took along his gun?" Vito asked. "For what?"

"Let's think this out," Jessie said, with as much a hint of alarm as Adam had ever heard in his voice. "The guy might just be a diligent worker—he's not supposed to leave his gun behind."

"Or he might have heard us come in and he's off phoning the cops," Vito said. "And sitting around a corner in that hallway now hoping for us to walk out so he can blow us away."

"Let's sit tight and wait for him," Jessie said. "He's going to come back here for sure and we take him. What else can we do?"

"We could get the hell out of here," Vito said.

"If he called the cops, you think we'll make the car?"

Vito thought for a moment. "No."

Jessie shrugged.

"Then we wait," he said. "And hope. There ain't much choice."

After a moment Vito nodded and they moved against the wall near the door, Vito in the first position, Jessie next, Adam third, pressed against an end table in the corner of the room, his shoulder touching a lamp shade. They waited, Vito and Jessie with guns in hand.

Adam tried to breathe softly and regularly. He thought that this outright criminal business of burglaries and stickups seemed to have one thing in common with drug dealing and smuggling; nothing ever went smoothly. The Indian furniture dealer in Kashmir who played the Beatles had tried to swindle him out of his money. A suitcase filled with sixty pounds of compressed Colombian marijuana had simply failed to appear at the luggage conveyor at Kennedy on a run he had once made from Miami to New York. Later he learned to never put that much weight into a piece of especially nondescript luggage with a combination lock on a run from Miami; there was so much grass being moved out of Florida that airline baggage handlers would grab off that kind of suitcase just because it was so likely to contain drugs.

Four out of five drug deals went bad. The salvation was that the one in five that worked made up for them, and more. He would have to ask his father later whether four out of five criminal scores went bad, too.

Vito turned suddenly and said to Adam, "You were the last one out of the office we came in through. Did you close the door behind you?"

Adam thought for a few moments.

"I think so."

"Don't think so," Vito said. "Either you're sure you did or you're sure you didn't or you don't know."

Adam thought he had pulled the door closed but couldn't be certain.

"If the guard's in the north wing of the building he has to pass that office on his way back here," Vito said. "If the door's open it's all over."

"I'm not sure," Adam said.

Jessie thought for only a few moments then said to Vito, "We've got to make a move."

Adam's lack of a gun now presented a problem. The ideal thing would be for Vito to prowl through one wing, hoping to take the guard by surprise, Jessie prowl the opposite wing, and Adam wait in the room just in case the guard had left the building for a six-pack or would somehow miss Vito and Jessie. But Adam had no gun.

"So let him take one," Jessie said. "I brought along an extra."

He withdrew a thirty-eight from a shoulder holster under his Windbreaker and offered it to Adam, holding it delicately by the handle between his thumb and forefinger so that the barrel dangled harmlessly toward the floor. Adam could sense that beneath the ski mask his father's face must be red.

"No," Vito said.

Jessie shrugged.

"You're his dad. But it sure as hell wouldn't hurt our chances here if he was holding something."

They stood silently. Jessie proffered the gun to Adam and said to Vito, "It's your choice."

Vito wet his lips, his tongue a quick-moving streak of red accentuated by the black mask.

Adam didn't want the gun. He clenched his teeth and hoped to hear in his father's voice the same adamant tone he had heard earlier in the hotel room: that under no circumstances would he permit his son to carry a gun. Adam knew that if the time came when he ought to use it, he wouldn't. The damned thing scared him and he would never be able to put his finger against the trigger, no less pull it. He wanted to hear his father say that he would sooner walk off the caper even now than let his son carry a pistol, that they would have to take their chances and make do with Adam unarmed, that Adam was in over his head here.

"It's up to you, Adam," Vito said.

Vito's tone was neutral. Less than neutral, Adam thought; he sensed that his father wanted him to say, yes.

Adam took the thirty-eight from Jessie, his index finger wrapped tightly around the handle with his other fingers, away from the trigger.

"Who does what?" he asked.

As he said it the guard stepped into the room.

The guard's mouth opened wide and he sucked in a loud breath. His gun, in its holster, dangled near the floor from its belt, which the guard held in his right hand. He started to pull it up instinctively. Before it rose even a few inches Vito stomped down on the holster with his left foot and pinned it to the floor. He pressed the barrel of his gun hard against the guard's mouth.

"Put your fucking hands up or I'll kill you," Vito said evenly.

The guard raised his hands and drew in another deep, audible breath, loud enough to drown out Adam's own intake of air.

Vito and Jessie tied his hands behind his back with quarter-inch nylon cord that Vito had brought along and slipped a black eye mask meant for troubled sleepers over his eyes, then put him on the floor in a fetal position and tied his ankles together. From the ankle tie Jessie ran a length of rope behind his back and looped it around his neck, just snug enough so that any attempt to straighten his legs would choke him. Vito lifted the telephone handset, stepped back several paces until the cord was taut, then jerked it firmly and pulled the cord from its box on the baseboard. He tossed the handset nonchalantly into the corridor. Jessie knelt beside the guard and stretched a long piece of gaffer's tape across his mouth, then ran the tape around his neck and mouth three times. He patted it firmly in place and asked the guard, "You breathing all right?"

The guard grunted an affirmative, "Uh-huh." Adam, keeping his distance from the guard, thought that they had made everything too tight—the ankle to neck tie, the hand tie, and the tape across his mouth. Even the black eye mask looked constricting, although he knew the elastic band must be comfortable if people were meant to sleep with it. Jessie, moving on his knees, circled the guard, his forefinger tracing an outline of the guard's fetal position on the carpet, letting his arm brush the man's body so his action would be understood. When he completed his circuit he lowered his head and spoke in the guard's ear.

"Listen to me. I just traced an outline with chalk of your sorry black body just the way it's laying on this rug. Like the cops do when people get shot on the sidewalk. When we come back to this room if there's even a little piece of you out of these chalk lines then that piece gets blown away by my dumdum bullets. You understand?"

The guard nodded his head, very gently; the rope from his neck to his ankles was snug. Just before they left the room Adam returned the gun to Jessie and said, "I guess I won't need this."

Vito led them out, Jessie following, Adam next.

After a few minutes they saw that the west wing, the bottom of the building U, consisted only of administrative offices. They moved quickly into the north wing, Adam in command now, reading names or designations on the doors and skipping most of them, occasionally opening a door to peer into a small laboratory, then moving on quickly. After fifteen minutes they had exhausted every office and lab and moved into the south wing. The third door had two nameplates pasted on it, one above the other, black plastic strips with simple letters cut into them; Dr. Gregory Kravalski and Dr. Sha Wu. Beneath them was a stenciled notice: RESTRICTED.

"This is it," Adam said. "Kravalski and Sha Wu are running the Nif project."

The door was locked, the first one they had come across. Vito studied it.

"What's the problem?" Jessie asked.

"No problem. I can jimmy this open in ten seconds. The question is whether they got this door bugged or not."

"We better assume they do," Jessie said.

"That's just what I'm doing. There's too much at stake here to just hold our breath and hope bells don't go off while we pry the son of a bitch open. There's a nice, safe way to do this and it won't add on more than a lousy ten minutes."

He sent Adam for a tool chest. "The big one," he said, and went into the unlocked office adjacent to the one they wanted to enter. When Adam returned, Vito opened the toolbox, took out a circular saw, and had Adam plug it in.

"What are we doing?" Adam asked.

"Going through to where we want to get," Vito said and knocked on the wall. "This is just a partition, two by four studs with maybe half-inch Sheetrock. People alarm windows and doors, put in high security locks, but you can walk through the walls of most rooms in five minutes."

He set the blade depth for a bit more than half an inch and cut a square into the wall, about eighteen inches on a side, close to the floor, then with a hammer smashed the square of Sheetrock into pieces which tore away easily. A stud was nearly in the center of his cut. He used the saw again to enlarge the width of the opening to the next stud then increased its height. After tearing down more wallboard he had an opening on his side of the partition about fourteen inches wide by four feet high.

"Now we hope I'm not coming out against a goddamn bookcase or something," Vito said, and used the hammer and his foot to smash through the opposite Sheetrock until there was a clear opening through which they could fit. Nothing was in their way.

"It's messy," Vito said, "but it sure goes easy."

He brushed plaster dust from his pants then pushed his body sideways into the other office. Adam and Jessie followed while Vito used a flashlight to find the wall switch. He turned on the lights and the three of them stood for a bit to look over the office. Vito pointed to a proximity switch on the top of the office door.

"They got it bugged, okay," he said.

Jessie shook his head in disappointment at having been proven right once again about his fellow man. He said to Adam,

"Sneaky bastards. And your mother accuses me of being a cynic."

Vito ignored him.

"It's your show now, Adam," he said. "As your grandfather here would say, 'Find us the right jar full of germs.'"

CHAPTER XIII

ADAM TRIED THE DESK DRAWERS FIRST. THEY WERE LOCKED. VITO PRIED THEM OPEN QUICKLY, THEN walked to the opposite side of the room to be out of the way and sat on a slate-top lab bench, his legs dangling. He unconsciously rubbed the insides of his running shoes against one another softly, as he had rubbed his sneakers when he was a teenager sitting on concrete parapets in playgrounds on the West Side. After a minute Jessie left to watch over the guard.

The room was perhaps twenty feet square, with lab benches running the length of one wall, another bench set up as an island down the center, and, on the wall through which they had entered, a refrigerator, a storage cabinet, a desk, and a four-drawer file cabinet. The opening that Vito had kicked through had fallen next to the desk along an empty stretch of wall. The lab was lit with fluorescents set into the ceiling above clear plastic diffuser sheets.

Adam found the logbook he wanted in the top desk drawer and flipped through it as Vito watched him. After a few minutes Adam's interest deepened and he lowered himself into the desk chair without looking up from the page and read for a while. It seemed to Vito that he was completely absorbed in the notes. Perhaps ten minutes later Jessie entered the room through the opening in the wall only a few feet from Adam, without distracting him from the logbook.

"How's the professor doing?" Jessie asked Vito.

"Looks from here like he knows what he's doing," Vito said.

They waited patiently for Adam to finish reading. He crossed his legs and read more intently. Another five minutes passed in silence, then Adam turned the logbook facedown on the desk and opened the small refrigerator.

"You figure out what we're looking for?" Jessie asked, and peered over Adam's shoulder.

Adam nodded.

The top shelf of the refrigerator held half a dozen large navel oranges and what looked like a tuna on rye wrapped tightly in Saran. From the center shelf Adam removed a rack of small test tubes, each of them corked and labeled, which he set on the desk to compare the carefully written letters and numbers on each label with the logbook. He selected eight test tubes, placed the others back in the refrigerator, then taped a paper towel around each of the eight tubes that he wanted and clustered them together. While he squeezed them together gently in his hands he had Jessie wrap tape around the whole assembly until the tubes formed a single unit that would fit into a jacket pocket snugly. Jessie held onto the test tubes and asked, "That's the whole story?"

"We got it," Adam said. "Let's get out."

Vito was surprised. He had worked a lot harder in his life on burglaries that netted nothing. This, he thought, was a pleasant change.

While the guard thought they were in the building he would continue to lie still, and so they moved along the corridor and through the window opening quietly, then hurried across the large inner courtyard, stopping briefly at the end of the building to check the roads before traversing the empty parking lot along the line of eucalyptus trees. Halfway through the apricot grove, just a few hundred feet from the car, Adam, bringing up the rear, called ahead to Jessie and Vito. They waited until he caught up.

"Did either of you put the logbook into one of the tool chests?"

Jessie shrugged.

"I never even saw it."

Vito said, "I didn't touch it. That was your end, Adam."

"Shit," Adam said. "I left it back there. I think on the desk."

"Fuck it," Jessie said. "We got the germs."

Adam set down the two tool cases.

"The deal is for the plasmids *and* the logbook. We need it."

"You stay," Vito said. "I'll go back for it."

Adam bristled.

"I can get it. You just said that's my end, Pop."

He turned and hurried back toward the building before Vito could say more. Vito sat on one of the toolboxes and clenched his fists.

"Why does *nothing* ever go nice and smooth?" he asked.

"Who ever said the world was meant to run nice and smooth?" Jessie asked. "Let's get these tools in the car—we can do it in two quick trips while he's gone."

"I'll wait here," Vito said. "I'm nervous about Adam."

Jessie groaned loudly and lifted two tool cases.

"Why don't you go be nervous on somebody's else's score, Vito. You can't do him a bit of good sitting here. Let's get the tools in the car and be all set to roll when Adam gets back."

Vito considered it for just a few seconds, then picked up two tool cases and followed Jessie toward the car, his heart beating fast. It had speeded up the moment Adam had turned and hurried back to the laboratory.

Adam entered the window opening carefully, crossed the tiny office, and held his breath as he stepped into the corridor. He glanced to his left, toward the room where the guard, he hoped, was still tied harmlessly in his fetal position on the floor and still, he hoped, breathing regularly. He ignored an impulse to walk down and look in on him and moved instead to his right, toward Kravalski and Wu's lab. He entered the adjacent lab, used the flashlight in his pocket to find his way to the opening in the wall, and slid through. He crossed the lab and flipped on the wall switch. Alone in the room, he was suddenly frightened, thinking that someone might be lurking in the silent offices, then he reminded himself that he was the bad guy lurking in the building. The logbook was on the desk. He forced himself to stop for a few moments to be sure he had everything he should and surveyed the lab carefully, as he would a motel room before checking out, then, satisfied, opened the office door and closed it softly behind him. He moved quickly down the corridor. At the doorway to the office through which he had entered, he stopped; the condition of the guard worried him. Another minute taken to be sure the man wasn't choking to death couldn't hurt. He hurried to the room where the guard was tied.

The man seemed not to have moved an inch out of the imaginary chalk outline drawn by Jessie. Adam kneeled beside him.

"You breathing okay?"

It startled the guard, who, after a moment, grunted affirmatively, "Uh-huh."

"We'll only be another half hour," Adam said. "Hang on and relax."

He patted the black man's shoulder and walked out of the room, calmer now. As he approached his exit to the outside world a vision of himself flashed across his mind: his leaving the laboratory a minute ago through the door instead of through the wall opening. He had done it unthinkingly—he had left through the door. And that door was bugged. He brought himself up short; no alarm had gone off. And relaxed again for a moment as he continued to walk, then remembered his father's comment in the lab as he pointed up at the proximity switch. "Those little bastards will do you in every time if you're not careful. The internal bugs. And half the times those are the silent ones. They trip in the local station house and at Holmes and you don't even know you set the son of a bitch off."

He broke into a jog, then, when the enormity of it hit him, into a run for his exit hole.

As he neared the eucalyptus trees he saw the first flashing red lights on a police car moving fast parallel to him, running without a siren. They swerved off onto the grassy area between the trees and the road, obviously wanting to get to the rear of the building. He veered to his left, crouched just a bit; to get lower to the ground would slow him up too much. He was no longer moving on a direct line toward Jessie and Vito but with a bit of luck the cops wouldn't see him if they were concentrating on the building. The sensible thing was to drop to the ground and lie flat until the cops entered the building, then move out to the road. He didn't have the nerve to do it. The apricot trees were only another hundred feet. They would give him cover. A few feet into the grove the police car spotlight illuminated a wide area around him; they had spotted him. He looked over his shoulder and saw the car moving directly toward him now, the headlights, the high beams, the spotlight, and the roof flashers lighting up the trees around him more intensely than daylight. He ran fully erect through the knee-high grass between two rows of trees. The car was suddenly just behind him, slowed up so as not to run him over. From only twenty feet or so he heard a cop say calmly through an amplified speaker, "Stop now or I'll put a bullet in your back!" He started to dodge to his right, toward where Jessie and Vito would be waiting, then realized he was going to be caught. To run any farther would only mean being caught close enough to the car so that Jessie and Vito would likely be taken too. He stopped suddenly and raised his arms in the air even before the cops ordered him to. As he felt a pair of hands from behind move down his chest and stomach to the insides of his legs he realized that he was still clutching the logbook in his hands.

"Who's with you?" the cop asked insistently.

Adam thought for a moment, then said, "Two of them. They're still in the building."

Vito, behind the wheel, engine running but the car lights out, had seen the flashing red in the rearview mirror.

"Cops!" he said, and he and Jessie turned to watch through the rear window. The police car had swerved off the road before its headlights had picked up their car. Vito had started to leave the car but Jessie had caught his arm.

"Sit still! You can't do anything out there. Just be ready to gun this thing if the kid makes it."

The words had infuriated Vito: "If the kid makes it." They had sat and watched the chase, then saw, deep in the grove of apricot trees, the silhouette of Adam, hands raised.

"My God," Vito said. He repeated it several times, until Jessie pinched his forearm, hard enough to raise a bruise that would last for days, and said, "Glide out of here, Vito. Nice and easy. No lights. There's nothing we can do." After a few moments Vito drove slowly, then picked up speed and turned on his headlights when they were several blocks away. At a full stop sign he wasn't certain for a bit that he could continue driving. He wanted to lay his forehead on the steering wheel and cry. He shook his head slowly and said, "My God."

CHAPTER XIV

ADAM REFUSED TO SAY ANYTHING OTHER THAN TO GIVE HIS NAME, HIS ADDRESS, REquest a lawyer, and remind first the cops and then the deputy DA that he was acting precisely within the rights they had carefully recited to him after searching the building for his accomplices. He repeated perhaps a hundred times that his name was Adam McQuade, he was homeless, and he was expecting a lawyer soon. They cajoled him with promises of leniency, then threatened him with fifteen or twenty years in Folsom Prison, where a horde of Hell's Angels would rape him nightly. A husky, sympathetic detective came in alone around ten A.M., tousled his hair, and informed him sorrowfully that the guard had suffered a heart attack and was now in intensive care. He would likely die before noon. That was murder and his chance to save his skin was to cooperate immediately.

"You look like a decent kid," the detective had said. "I have a boy just about your age. How old are you, Adam? Nineteen? Twenty?"

"My name is Adam McQuade, I'm homeless, and I'm waiting for my lawyer to get here. And you're jeopardizing your whole case here by pressing me. If you want me to talk a little then bring in another five or six cops plus the DA so all of you will have to perjure yourselves that my rights weren't violated."

"Go fuck yourself," the detective had said as he left the room. "When you're sitting around on a raw asshole for twenty years up in Folsom you'll wish you had taken some fatherly advice."

Adam sat alone in a holding cell and wished he had taken some fatherly advice given a month or so ago: stay away from crime—they put you in prison for it. He also wished that Vito had pressed harder and longer with the advice; he, Adam, was only twenty-three. How had his father not realized that he was still a kid in so many ways?

Jessie and Vito left the San Jose Chalet and checked into a quiet motel in Los Gatos, a manicured little town that bordered San Jose on the west, in the foothills of the Santa Cruz Mountains. They pulled off Route Seventeen into a deserted parking area at a small irrigation reservoir and dropped the boxes of tools into it. Jessie worried about the condition of the plasmids; Adam had said nothing about storing them.

"They had them in an icebox," Jessie said. "For all we know this shit could go sour on us if it stays warm too long."

It seemed to Vito that Jessie was worried a lot more about keeping the plasmids intact than about keeping Adam intact.

When they were settled into the Los Gatos motel Jessie got through to Ray Garvey, his lawyer in New York.

"Adam got pinched out in California on some kind of bogus burglary rap," he said. Vito sat sprawled in a chair, sipping a Scotch and listening, wondering how soon Elaine would have to be told. Not too long, for sure.

"I'm calling from New York," Jessie said, "but I can't give you a number to reach me at. Don't ask more. We need a good California criminal lawyer who can handle a case in San Jose. He's got to be a class act. You hire him on your responsibility; I got money in my pocket and I'll get it to you in the next day or so. I'm going to call you back in an hour. I need help here, Ray."

Jessie dipped into the bottle of Scotch then propped two pillows against the headboard of his bed and made himself so comfortable that it antagonized Vito.

"What the hell are we going to *do*?" Vito said.

"We're going to not panic is what we're going to do. We relax a little bit and don't make stupid moves. You taught me that while we were waiting outside the window on this score. First order of business is to get a lawyer in to Adam.

"Then?"

"Then we find out the lay of the land. Adam might get lucky here. The authorities could decide to treat the whole thing as a juvenile prank."

Vito came out of his chair and stood above Jessie, who was stretched out on the bed, his legs crossed at the ankles.

"Juvenile prank!? What the hell is the matter with you? We left a guard tied up on the floor back there with a gag stuffed in his mouth. We took him over with pistols. There's test tubes missing that some Chinaman in Boston is ready to lay out a million bucks for, so the stuff must be worth plenty to the people we robbed it from. Adam got nailed wearing a ski mask. A fucking *ski mask*! That's the sign of a pretty serious thief. Is he supposed to say he was out trick or treating, Jessie? How the hell is any DA going to treat this as a juvenile prank?"

Jessie sipped his drink.

"Vito, till we know what the score is it won't do any good to think of the worst. When a lawyer talks to the DA we'll know how much hot water Adam's in. But the kid could luck out. Believe me. The criminal justice system in this country is a fucking mess. I know, I been in and out of it a lot more than you have. There's ten thousand cracks in it that people fall through all the time. Thank God. Now Adam may *not* get lucky, but you never know. Let's wait and see and not panic. Let's deal with the reality."

"Why do you keep saying that *Adam* may get lucky? That we don't know how much hot water *Adam's* in? Why ain't you saying *us*, Jessie?"

"For Christ's sake don't start picking on me for my English. I've been saying, Adam, because he's the one sitting in the can."

Vito poured himself another drink.

"Just remember, Jessie, anything we can do to take the weight off my son—and your grandson—we're going to do. *Anything*."

"Well of course we are, for Christ's sake. You talking to me about loyalty is just a little bit ridiculous, Vito. I taught you whatever you know about it. And Adam. We already went into our pockets to get the kid a lawyer, didn't we?"

"Going into our pocket's not what I'm talking about, Jessie."

Jessie chose not to answer. He topped off his own drink instead.

They met with the lawyer late in the day over cocktails at The Oaks, a low-lit bar and restaurant in Palo Alto just a few blocks from the Stanford University campus. The furnishings were comfortable in the way that Vito now associated with California—roomy armchairs and plenty of space between tables—but without the tackiness of San Jose; whatever looked like wood was, in fact, wood. The waitresses wore uniforms rather than costumes and there was no music.

Michele Dempsey, the thirty-five-year-old San Francisco lawyer hired by Garvey, was a Stanford Law School graduate and had edited the *Law Review*. She mentioned it a few minutes after shaking hands.

Jessie had been upset when Garvey had called back with the name, Michele Dempsey.

"You mean, Michael," Jessie had said.

"Michele."

"Ray, don't tell me you got my grandson some fucking San Francisco lawyer is going to give him AIDS."

"Jessie, you wanted a real class-act criminal lawyer. You got one. It happens to be a woman."

Jessie had hung up and shaken his head at Vito.

"How the hell is anyone supposed to stay sane in America in the nineteen eighties? Things just change too fast."

Now, Vito was pleased when Michele Dempsey ordered a Perrier.

On the brief ride from Los Gatos, Jessie, halfway over his fear of a woman, had worried about the lawyer being Irish.

"You never know," he had said. "She might be a drinker. That's not what Adam needs here."

"It's not what *we* need here."

Jessie hadn't answered.

Dempsey squeezed her wedge of lime into the Perrier.

"It's going to be expensive," she said.

Jessie banged Vito's knee under the table and said, "We're not rich people."

"Then you might want to look for a lawyer more suited to your pocketbook," she said.

Jessie shook his head.

"We're not crying poverty. All I'm saying is that this is family money we're spending. Money I've managed to squirrel away after fifty years of hard work."

He extended his hands across the table, palms up, to show her some imaginary calluses.

"We're not a couple of Cubans with a ton of drug money to throw around, that's all I'm saying."

"I don't know much about Cuban drug dealers, Mr. McMullen. They all seem to be in Miami or New York. None of them get arrested in California, unfortunately."

Vito ignored the next few knee taps from Jessie asking silence.

"You saw Adam this afternoon," he said. "Could we drop the subject of money for a little bit and hear how he is and what the case looks like?"

"No," she said, "we can't. My talent is in winning freedom for criminals who by and large deserve to spend the rest of their lives behind a double set of bars. Most people in prison, with a few exceptions, belong there. If I wasn't rich enough to live in a very secure building on Nob Hill and send my kids to expensive private schools, I might not be willing to get so many of my guilty clients back on the streets. But we work on an adversary system of justice in this country so I'm morally bound to fight just as hard for my guilty clients as I am for the occasional innocent."

Vito interrupted her.

"It sounds like you picked the wrong line of work."

She shook her head, no, the tired pro who sees a tough job through, and incidentally grows rich in the process.

"No. The system works better than most people think, if you want to live in a society where you can walk around without looking over your shoulder the way you would in Russia or

China or fifty other countries where the government screws you at will. The American people actually set John De Lorean free after watching him buy cocaine on videotape and I say—thank God. So the people I set free are mostly reprehensible specimens of human beings but that's my role in an adversary system. The ones I handle, though, aren't public defender cases. They have money, generally dirty and ill-gotten. The only charity work I do—and I do some—is for people I'm convinced are either innocent or who even though they're guilty are being fucked over royally by our ambitious prosecutors climbing up their ladders. There are more of those cases than I care to take on. The others—I want to be paid. It's almost a moral obligation to take away as much of their ill-gotten gains as possible. Which is why even at the age of thirty-five I still occasionally have what my male counterparts would call a wet dream—that the Cubans have relocated to San Francisco."

She watched Jessie fidget at the wet dream reference, then turned to Vito and said, "With all due respect, Mr. McMullen, your son doesn't strike me as one of my charity cases. He's neither innocent nor is he being fucked over by the system. The kid is as guilty as hell and if I can get him back on the streets—and I might just be able to do that—then I want to be well paid. So the discussion of my fee before we talk about anything else is totally appropriate."

They sat quietly for a bit and digested her pitch. Jessie broke the silence.

"What's it going to run?"

She nodded.

"I bill you for time. Mine, any lawyers on my staff, a couple of minority paralegals, a couple of secretaries. Office time for lawyers is going to run you a hundred an hour. My office time runs one-fifty. My court time—and no one but me will ever be in the courtroom—my court time will cost you fifteen hundred a day."

Jessie whistled through his teeth.

"That's where my talent runs rampant, Mr. McMullen, and I charge accordingly. Next to Melvin Belli I'm a bargain. Depending on how the case shapes up, whether we strike a deal or not or whether we go to trial, you're looking at a low of thirty-five or forty thousand and it could run nicely to a hundred."

She dipped into her glass and resqueezed the spent lime.

"Exclusive of appeals," she added. "And if we're into a trial that begins to look hopeless we'll be waiting for a guilty verdict and orchestrating the whole thing toward an appeal. A real possibility, I might add."

"And the appeal?" Jessie asked.

She shrugged. "Another forty or fifty."

They finished their drinks and Jessie motioned to the waitress for another round.

Vito and Jessie confirmed that they could handle the bill, which Dempsey warned, as they clinked glasses, would be pay as you go. She then told them of her meeting with Adam.

"He lied about his name, which is no big deal. They'll be getting back a report from the Bureau of Criminal Investigation on his prints just about now and since he has an arrest his name is going to come up."

Vito tightened his hand on the table and said, "What arrest?" He turned to Jessie. "Did you know about any arrest?"

Jessie said no. Vito knew by the way he said it that he was being truthful.

"He got busted on a drug charge in Berkeley a few years ago," she said. "Very heavy, too. Federal. It involved a few hundred thousand dollars' worth of LSD and a machine to tab it. Of course the U.S. attorney and the local papers applied their favorite method of accounting and translated it to the usual 'street value' of untold millions. The judge threw it out the next day because the dopey cops running it behaved as though it was still nineteen fifty. They had no probable cause—their screw-ups just went on and on. They may have set a record for violating the most constitutional rights on a single case. It ought to be put in textbooks. I knew of it at the time because the lawyer who handled it is a friend of mine. Adam went back a month or so later and had it all expunged."

"What's that going to mean for this case?" Vito asked.

"If it was thrown out and expunged, what the hell can it mean?" Jessie said.

"They mean—*sort* of expunged," she said. "The prosecution is free to take it into account here and he won't be treated as a first offender. Which would give us a hell of a stronger hand to play, incidentally. Adam McMullen has had his 'one bite of the apple,' as the prosecutors are going to tell me when this record kicks out of the B.C.I. computer. And they're free to do that and the judge is going to take it into account in sentencing."

"Jesus Christ," Jessie said.

"You never knew about the arrest?" she asked Vito.

"No. He was living in Berkeley and we were in New York."

"Well, your son seems to have a pair of balls for his age, Mr. McMullen. Most middle-class druggies scream for their parents after the first night in jail. He's behaving now the way he did then—stand up criminal style. His values may be misdirected though, if you don't mind me saying so."

"My grandson's not middle class and never has been," Jessie said.

"You make the words, 'middle class,' sound the way most people speak of homosexuals," she said.

Jessie chewed on a taco chip.

"Maybe we better not get off on this subject, counselor."

Dempsey smiled.

"You're probably right," she said.

"I've already talked for twenty minutes with the deputy DA handling it," Dempsey said. "They're anxious as hell to make a deal. That's a big plus for us. Taking this thing to trial would be like holding Adam's hand and jumping off the Golden Gate Bridge together. Hoping to find a soft spot in the water. The DA's office has already met with some of the directors from Engineered Genetic Systems. At six in the morning. That also looks like a big plus for us. They want their plasmids back and they want to know where the stuff was headed for and they want the two people who were with Adam. If Adam's willing to deliver those three things for them, they're talking about minimum jail time for him. Like seven or eight months and another five years' parole and probation. Mind you, that's what they're offering for openers. They'll go for zero jail time at the drop of a hat. Your son will walk. With three years' probation. They want their plasmids and they want the buyer. They want the accomplices for good measure. They aren't looking to put Adam on the cross and I believe them. My impression is that they're treating those stolen plasmids the way they would have treated a stolen set of the Wright brothers' original drawings if they had known how the aviation industry was going to develop."

"They want to make a rat out of him," Jessie said.

Dempsey's voice took on some emotion for the first time.

"Hey, mister," she said, "he's *your* grandson."

"What if Adam doesn't go for it?" Vito asked. "Suppose he just holds out, gives up no one, and doesn't know where the plasmids are?"

He stared hard at Jessie, wanting him to hear the answer clearly.

"They're going to crucify him," Dempsey said. "And they will. You cannot stand in front of a district attorney and a judge in the United States of America and say, 'Fuck you.' They won't tolerate it. Not when they've got the goods on you. Just to begin with they'll stack up a maximum burglary count and an assault—Adam didn't carry a gun but his partners did, and that means the law can treat him, if they choose to, as though he carried one of the guns. Let me tell you a little about sentencing out here. The judge goes by the report he gets from the county adult probation officer. The probation officer actually fills in the preprinted menu. One side of it consists of factors in aggravation; those are the possible negatives for Adam. Did the crime require sophistication and planning, for example. The answer in this case is, yes, and that's going to hurt him. Did Adam play an active or passive role in it? Well, he didn't carry a gun and that's a plus, but he was in the laboratory, not sitting in a car, and he was caught carrying the logbook—not so good."

"Is there another side to this probation menu?" Jessie asked.

"Factors in mitigation. Mainly, that's his cooperation and remorse. That's what will be the disaster for him. At any rate, based upon the report the judge has three sentencing choices for a given crime: light, medium, or heavy. In Adam's case, if he doesn't cooperate, the judge will go for the heavy sentence. Both of the charges I'm talking about rate as much as fourteen years and they'll whack him with consecutive sentences, which the judge is free to do. 'Fuck you, kiddo,' is what the judge will be saying when he bangs his little gavel down a couple of times. I will appeal the consecutive sentences since both charges stem from the same crime but I wouldn't hold my breath until it was overturned. Your son, Mr. McMullen, and your grandson, Mr. McMullen, *if* he behaves perfectly in prison and applies himself diligently in the library and tutoring his fellow cons with remedial reading problems, could be out in about fifteen years. A few years shy of his fortieth birthday. With his whole life in front of him, of course. And only on parole until he's fifty-five."

She took another of Jessie's cigarettes and asked Vito, "How old are *you*?"

Vito looked across at Jessie, who avoided his eyes by concentrating on his drink.

She left them ten minutes later, after a warning that bail would be set so high that it would be impossible.

"Adam claims to be homeless so the DA will point out that he has no roots in the community. They're all going to want him sitting in jail anyway—their game now is maximum pressure."

She grabbed the check and placed an American Express gold card on top of it in the plastic tray. Jessie picked up the card and examined it—with an eye toward the difficulty of forging one, Vito guessed—and asked, "Are these things as powerful as they claim?"

"I don't know how people get through life without it," she said.

Jessie pointed at the check.

"This is a surprise," he said. "Every lawyer I ever met reaches for checks in slow motion. Maybe I should've been dealing with girls all these years."

Dempsey shrugged.

"It'll find its way into your first bill," she said. "With about fifty percent office overhead tacked on."

While the waitress was writing it up Vito said to Dempsey, "You never asked anything about Adam's family background or schooling—doesn't that usually matter to a court?"

"If your son had stolen a convertible and gone out joyriding it might matter. It's not going to mean much on these charges."

After a moment she added, "And to be very candid, Mr. McMullen, Ray Garvey mentioned to me on the phone not to pursue Adam's family background. He didn't feel it would be a productive line for me to follow as a defense."

She walked away from the table with a brief wave, her carriage that of a woman who was fit, who played squash or tennis on a regular basis. She dressed sensibly and carried a worn leather attaché case, a person devoted as much to her work as to her career, with enough self-confidence to simply meet her profession's minimum requirements in terms of appearance.

"Another fucking leech lawyer," Jessie said, and sipped his drink. "This time a broad instead of a guy."

They waited until they were back in the motel room to discuss it.

"I don't like your attitude on this whole thing, Jessie. You're hedging."

"Nobody's hedging. I'm just not running around like a chicken with its head cut off. Before we give ourselves up to Walter Winchell or whoever's doing that kind of thing these days we've got to get in and talk to Adam tomorrow. Let's hear what's happening straight from the horse's mouth."

"And if it's just what Dempsey says—and it will be, Jessie—then we turn ourselves, the test tubes, and the Chinaman in?"

Jessie paced the room several times.

"Maybe after we do it you'd like for us to take a couple of cyanide pills, too, Vito? You know—as a final gesture to show where our hearts are."

Vito stood and blocked Jessie's pacing. He put his forefinger close to Jessie's nose and said, "Old man—before this is over I will shove a cyanide pill down your fucking wrinkled throat sooner than see Adam rotting inside a prison. Do you hear me—*old man*?"

Jessie's face set, just slightly, as it always did before he swung a punch. The skin on his forehead tightened just enough to smooth out the wrinkles and his eyes concentrated fully on Vito. After a moment he put his arms around Vito and hugged him hard, their cheeks pressed together. He patted Vito's back strongly several times—something he had done forty years earlier as an only parent on just a few occasions. Now, in his father's embrace, Vito remembered those few occasions and his anger with Jessie dissipated.

"What the hell are we going to *do*, Jessie?" he asked. "I won't be able to live, with my son sitting in a prison."

Jessie pinched his cheek lightly.

"We don't panic, Vito. They're offering a deal that's just for openers—you heard that leech Dempsey say so. They might strike a deal just to get the germs back. Maybe we got to toss the Chink in, too. If we have to, we have to. Let's talk to Adam, talk again to Dempsey, talk to Ray Garvey, and then we do whatever we got to do. Adam's my grandson, too, Vito, and I'm not going to watch him do fifteen years."

"*Any* time, Jessie. I don't want to only hear about fifteen years. I want to hear you say Adam isn't going to do *any* time."

"We'll talk to him tomorrow," Jessie said. "You jump ahead of yourself too much, Vito. It's a real problem you've got."

Vito slept poorly and was fully awake long before he wanted to be. Jessie had called the day before and found that they could not get in to visit Adam until one o'clock. Vito showered for a long time then turned the television to a game show and stared at it stupidly, his thoughts alternating between Adam and Elaine, first hoping that the holding jail was not a zoo, then feeling his stomach tighten even more at the thought of breaking the news to Elaine. Sooner or later she would have to be told. She still believed he was off on a business tour of packinghouses in Texas and Oklahoma. He had called her every day, pretending to be tired and under pressure from suppliers, cranky at the traveling and daily meetings with dull Southwesterners who squeezed him to the wall financially while they extolled the virtues of ultraconservative politics and told jokes about blacks that usually began, "Did you hear about Rastus driving his big, new, white Cadillac down Main Street?" Elaine had swallowed the story whole.

Refreshed from the shower and a shave he thought that Jessie might not be far wrong on one point; rushing into the DA's office was not the way to handle it. They should work through Dempsey to strike a clear deal with the prosecutors and extract whatever concessions they could. So long as the jail time for Adam—even short time—didn't become a bargaining chip. That was the point on which he and Jessie were going to disagree and Vito was not going to give an inch on it.

Jessie wanted to drive. He circled several times around the jail and the Civic Center without finding a restaurant that served liquor, and so they drove for five more minutes into downtown San Jose, where Jessie pointed out that St. James Street could give the Bowery a run for its money.

They parked just before noon and entered a place decorated with imitation antiques to resemble an English pub. Both of them had several whiskeys then ordered the French dip sandwich at the bar. They drank draft ales with the sandwiches.

"They told you one o'clock?" Vito asked.

Jessie nodded, his mouth full.

"Then we ought to move right along," Vito said. "It's a quarter of, and there's probably a pile of horseshit to go through to get in."

Jessie finished his sandwich, then spoke softly and sincerely.

"Look, I been thinking a lot about all this, okay? As far as turning ourselves in, you may be jumping a little too quick for my taste, but then again I might be getting a little bit selfish, too. I don't know. I want to do the right thing here. But Vito, believe me, Adam's not going to want us to rush into the DA's office with the stuff and climb up onto a couple of crosses so he can walk. Believe me, Vito, I know him, too. And from what he told Dempsey and what he told the cops, the kid's going to want us to deliver the stuff to the Chink and stash his end of the money while he takes a chance on a court trial and doing a couple of years."

Vito started to object but Jessie quieted him.

"Let me finish. I ain't taking his side on this, Vito. But that's what he's going to want. I can smell it. And I'm not as quick as you to tell him, 'You don't know your ass from a hole in the ground, kid, I'm deciding your life for you here.' But I don't want to influence him either. If he takes the attitude I think he's going to take I'm leaving it in your hands to talk him out of it. I don't want to be in the middle and I don't want to catch myself taking his side and trying to talk you into something. Neutral, Vito. That's my position and I go with what you two decide."

"And what if Adam and me don't agree, Jessie? What do you do then?" Vito asked. "Because if he wants to do even six months of jail time I'm not going along with it."

Jessie shrugged.

"Push comes to shove, Vito, I'll go with whatever you want."

Vito squeezed Jessie's forearm.

"But hear the kid out, Vito. Hear him out. And do it without me there for a while. Just the two of you."

"What do you mean?"

"You spend the first hour with Adam alone. Do your talking, take your best shot with him. Convince the kid. Without me there in the middle. Visiting's from one to two-thirty. I'll come up at two o'clock sharp and the three of us can continue the conversation. But I don't want to be accused later of encouraging him or anything else. You two have your private talk. I think it's fairer that way."

Vito thought for a few moments, then said, "You're right, Jessie, it is fairer. Thanks."

He hurried off and told Jessie not to arrive before two; he wanted his full hour alone with Adam.

The exterior of the jail was unlike any that Vito had ever seen, a two-story, up-to-date building that in New York would have been one of the more attractive public schools. He was relieved that Adam looked well and that the jail seemed decent.

They argued in low voices for half of their scheduled hour about what was to be done. Adam had thought it out carefully.

"Even without the log Jimmy Chin will go for the million," Adam said. "You can see by the way they're acting, the stuff's worth five times that. Me being in a position to rat him out is going to be an extra incentive, too. If we go for a hundred thousand on this court case it still leaves us nine hundred to whack up. Where the hell am I ever going to get my hands on three hundred thousand, Pop? Or you? Or Jessie? If they hit me with even four years, I'll be out in two. That's a hundred and fifty thousand a year take-home pay."

"Nothing's *worth* two years in prison, Adam. *Nothing*. Least of all money. And you won't do two years, they'll make you do *fifteen* years. The best fifteen years of your life. That's more like twenty thousand a year, if you're dumb enough to think you can figure it that way. You can take the New York City sanitation test and make that kind of money."

"They won't give me heavy time, Pop. Don't you see this fucking leech lawyer is saying that so we'll make a deal and she nails us for maybe forty thou without fighting a case?"

Vito forced himself to keep his voice low.

"Christ, but you sound like Jessie!" he said, then realized that Adam sounded *too much* like Jessie. It was the word "leech." Jessie had used it last night.

Vito held his breath for a moment, then asked, "Has Jessie managed to talk to you somehow?"

Adam didn't respond for a bit, then nodded his head.

"We talked on the phone this morning. For twenty minutes, half in code—they must have them tapped. We figured you'd argue this way, Pop. The truth is, you'll blow the chance of a lifetime for the three of us. And if you want the cold, hard truth it's because you don't have enough confidence in me to think I can do two years. *You* did it when you were about my age. Jessie's done it. Well, I can too, for this kind of money."

Vito stood up.

"It's not going to happen this way, Adam. Whether you like it or not."

"Don't go running into the DA," Adam said. "You've got

nothing to deal with. Jessie's on his way East right now with those eight test tubes."

Adam smiled, in a way that reminded Vito of John Wayne in countless movies; the absurdly macho, "that's life," man-to-man smile of someone about to do his duty because he's a better man than those around him.

"Hell, Pop," Adam said, "I'm going to make you rich in spite of yourself."

CHAPTER XV

VITO LANDED AT KENNEDY JUST BEFORE SEVEN IN THE MORNING, EXHAUSTED. HE HAD CAUGHT the ten P.M. redeye from San Francisco but had not even tried to nap on the plane, instead reviewing what had to be done. Shooting Jessie—shooting to kill him—had been paramount in his plans from the moment he walked out of the jailhouse in San Jose. About the time the plane crossed the Continental Divide, Vito had realized that he couldn't really do it. He had then begun to think more clearly.

The district attorney, according to Dempsey, first and foremost wanted the stolen material; turning in Jessie and himself without the plasmids in hand would gain nothing for Adam. Vito's first order of business was to get hold of the test tubes. Jessie would almost certainly have them in his possession for at least the next few days—more likely a week. The California authorities' attitude had established the real worth of the stuff; Jessie would now run true to form and squeeze the Chinaman for every extra cent he could. No one had ever accused Jessie McMullen of selling cheap. He would begin negotiations at two or three times the original price, pressing hard but never hard enough to endanger the deal, hinting that the Chinaman and his backers now risked exposure, always bargaining from the underlying position that whatever he could extract over the million dollar mark was "found money." Money that needn't be shared with his partners since he had "wrung out the Chink" on his own. Jessie looked out for number one.

Vito wanted to berate the young Pakistani cabdriver for weaving too fast between lanes on the way into the city, for the jarring, atonal, Eastern music coming from his portable tape deck, and for the cloying atmosphere created by some rare form of incense burning in a tiny dish mounted far forward on top of the dashboard. As they drove through the Midtown Tunnel he had fantasized tipping the driver only a dollar and saying, "Welcome to America, Muhammed. It is *still* the land of opportunity if you're willing to break your ass but it's a tough environment where money talks and you've got to deliver the goods to get paid. So here's a dollar because you're running a rotten cab. Clean up your act and stop poisoning passengers with shit incense, shit music, and shit driving."

Had the driver been alone, as the law required, Vito might have done it. Instead he had given him seven dollars on the twenty-three-dollar call. Muhammed was not alone. His dark, skinny wife was beside him, wrapped in a faded red sari and nursing a six-month-old boy who, as Muhammed explained over his shoulder while they tailgated a *New York Post* truck down Lexington Avenue, was "An American citizen. *Born* here. A family must be together so Shabana and our son travel with me for the twelve hours each day." He had laughed a bit and moved his head from side to side to the strange music. A happy man.

Vito checked into a sixty-five-dollar room in the Chelsea Hotel. He would call Elaine late in the afternoon and claim to be stuck in Tulsa for another few days. The desk clerk, seated in the middle of a mess behind a narrow opening that reminded Vito of a small-town post office, offered a bargain.

"Pay in advance for six days and you get the seventh free."

Vito hoped to have his hands on the test tubes and be back in California in much less than a week. He paid for two nights. The aged bellman who accompanied him, for reasons known only to himself, wore a Russian-style fur hat. The rest of his uniform seemed to have come from several different thrift shops. When they entered the tiny elevator the bellman ordered Vito to, "Push eight," then stood silently while they ascended. Above the panel of buttons was a framed, full-page color ad, likely cut from Sunday's *New York Times*. In it, the toothy Leona Helmsley, resplendent in a diamond tiara and a gold lamé gown stood with outstretched arms beneath a crystal chandelier in the lobby of the Helmsley Palace. The caption read, "The Queen Stands Guard." A cartoonist's balloon from her mouth had been added with ball-point pen that said, "Welcome to the Chelsea Hotel."

As they walked through the labyrinth of hallways on the eighth floor the bellman said, "You've picked one of New York's best neighborhoods, you know. If you don't want to leave the hotel you can send out for food. Ring me downstairs, I'll bring it up. You've got two terrific pizza stands, a deli, a doughnut shop. Even Chinese takeout. All two minutes away."

Vito tipped him two dollars and wondered whether anyone ever chose to eat dinner in the room. The peeling paint and the weak light bulb gave it the look of a place someone checked into to commit suicide. He stood for a few minutes at the window, which faced onto Twenty-second Street, and looked downtown over the jumble of low roofs and water tanks and thought again about where Jessie might have the stuff hidden. The possibilities were limited. Jessie was concerned about keeping it cold and he wouldn't be adding ice to a cooler twice a day. He would have it in a refrigerator, more than likely Margie's. Vito would start there. At the Easter Sunday dinner she had mentioned living in Brooklyn. He checked with information and found a listing for an M. Considine on Eighth Avenue in Park Slope. That would be her. He remembered that she waitressed on a night shift, which meant she ought to be leaving her apartment in the late afternoon.

Vito showered, tried unsuccessfully to relax, instead sat at the long, empty bar of the El Quixote restaurant, which had an entrance off the hotel lobby, and sipped his way through three Scotches while he studied an eighty-foot-long mural of the Don attacking windmills while Sancho Panza looked on. At two o'clock he walked out onto Twenty-third Street and over to Seventh Avenue. A few blocks downtown he found an industrial supply store where he bought a short length of one-inch iron pipe. He put it under his jacket and hailed a cab.

The driver used West Street, circled the Battery, and crossed the Brooklyn Bridge. Vito looked out to his right through the spider web of wires onto the broad expanse of New York Bay in bright daylight, the sun reflecting off the choppy water. The East River might well have been pure. Below him a tug pulled a line of three barges upriver. Far behind it was the outline of the Statue of Liberty. The entire scene bespoke expansiveness and freedom, an entryway to the open sea. The colossal, copper statue that seemed to have grown out of the water, poised delicately and beckoning a welcome, made him think for a moment of Muhammed and his family riding in their taxi, and then of Adam, locked up in a six-by-ten cage in San Jose.

He had the driver pass Margie's building and drop him at the corner, then he walked the few hundred feet back to it, a four-story attached walk-up in the middle of the block. The bells in the tiny vestibule showed four tenants, Considine on the top floor. He walked back another block to an open corner phone diagonally across from the emergency entrance of Methodist Hospital and dialed her number. She answered after a few rings and Vito managed a Puerto Rican accent: "Cheet—wrong number," he mumbled, and hung up, then hurried back to the building.

He used a credit card to open the inner door of the vestibule and moved quickly up the carpeted steps to the top-floor landing. Hers was the only door. It was equipped with a standard peephole at eye level. Vito sat on the top step which put him just a few feet from the door and settled himself for a wait. He took the length of pipe from under his jacket. If Margie was alone in the apartment he would have no problem; when she opened the door to leave he would push his way in easily. If Jessie was in the apartment with her, which was likely, Vito would need the pipe. He couldn't shoot his father but he would have no trouble splitting open his forehead. Maybe twice. His throat constricted with anger and hurt as he brooded upon the depth of Jessie's betrayal. He tightened his grip on the pipe and tapped it several times into his open palm, unable to decide whether he hoped Jessie was or was not in the apartment.

• • •

He sat for nearly half an hour. Several times children entered and left apartments below. Vito heard them bound up the steps two at a time and call to one another in the stairwell. He realized that he enjoyed the sounds of city kids around him but never got to hear them—very few children lived in his Upper East Side apartment building. Although he was waiting for it, the brief sound of the safety chain being opened on Margie's door startled him. He stood up and pressed himself against the wall, pipe in hand, as the dead bolt clicked. The door pulled open. He stepped out quickly and pivoted, the pipe cocked just above shoulder level, his left hand a foot or so in front of his face to push whoever was in the doorway back into the apartment. It was Margie. She pulled back and opened her mouth to scream but stopped when she saw that it was Vito.

"Is Jessie here?" he asked quickly, his open hand inches from her face.

"No."

"Tell me if he is or it'll turn into a fucking mess."

"I'm alone," she said.

They both relaxed a bit. Vito closed the door with his foot.

"You don't seem so surprised," he said.

She made a little motion with her hands that signified acceptance.

"I try to take life as it comes," she said.

"Jessie told you I might show up?"

She stared noncommittally for a few moments then nodded, yes.

"He tell you what for?" Vito asked.

"No. He said the two of you had a falling-out and..."

"A falling-out? That son of a bitch called it a *falling-out*?!"

"Those were his words."

She looked at the pipe that Vito, unconsciously, still held cocked behind his ear.

"I take it he understated the case," she said.

He lowered the pipe.

"What else did he say?"

"That you'd likely be a little riled up."

He nodded at her several times.

"Well, I *am* riled up. Our pal Jessie called that shot right."

They faced one another quietly, just a few feet apart, in the beginning of the narrow hallway that ran the length of her apartment. She volunteered nothing further but there was no hostility in her expression.

"What the hell did he say you should do if I showed up?" Vito asked.

"I'm supposed to tell you he's out of town. Which he is. And that you came to the wrong place."

"Did he say I'd be looking for something?"

"No."

"Well I am. And I think it might be here."

She extended her arm toward the long hallway.

"Be my guest, Vito. Just don't mess the place up, please."

He went into the kitchen and opened the refrigerator. There was very little in it. Margie followed him and watched silently as he removed a can of coffee, a container of milk, and a jar of jam, the only packages large enough to hold the cluster of test tubes. It occurred to him that Jessie might have separated the tubes. He cut through a bar of margarine and probed jars of ketchup and mustard with a knife, then emptied the milk into several glasses which he poured back into the container when he saw that it held no tubes. He spilled the coffee onto a paper napkin then replaced it in the can. The jar of jam held nothing but jam.

"Don't tell me the two of you are into drugs," she said.

Vito sat at the kitchen table. He shook his head with fatigue.

"I've about run out of steam," he said. "I knew finding the stuff here was a long shot but I had my hopes up."

"What is it you're looking for, Vito?" she asked.

"You really don't know?"

"You think it would be like your father to tell me?"

He shook his head, no.

"Sit down," he said. "I'll tell you what I'm looking for. And why."

• • •

He gave her the highlights, omitting the specific nature of the goods and their value. He included Adam's situation, Jessie's behavior, and what he, Vito, hoped to accomplish. She seemed at first bewildered then incredulous.

"I don't believe you."

"You think I'm lying?" Vito said.

"No, you're not lying. I don't believe your behavior. Yours, or Jessie's. I've been around thieves, it's how I came upon your father. I lived for three years with one of the better counterfeiters on the East Coast. I've dated holdup guys and one jewel thief. I know the score, Vito, I'm a knockaround girl. You and Jessie want to rob, go ahead. But I've been around Adam a few times. Your son's not a criminal, he's a nice kid. You should thank God he's as nice as he is. How the hell could the two of you take him along?"

Vito shrugged, then shook his head from side to side in an acknowledgment of guilt. He avoided looking into her face.

"If your father was here," she said, "I'd crack his goddamned head open with that pipe."

"That's why I brought it," Vito said.

"You're damn near as bad, Vito," she said. "Your only saving grace is that you're willing to do something for your son now."

She let another minute pass in silence, then said, "You're serious about turning yourself in if you have to?"

"Without the stuff it's meaningless. But with the stuff—if they would cut Adam loose by me turning myself in, then, yeah. I'd turn myself in."

She stood up.

"Well, I'm not going to be part of that kid doing ten or fifteen years," she said. "Come on."

She led him down the long hallway to her bedroom, where she knelt and pulled from the bottom of the closet a picnic cooler chest. In it Vito found the cluster of test tubes surrounded by cans of Scotch-Ice; cans that after refreezing would refrigerate the cooler for ten to twelve hours if left undisturbed.

"I've been keeping this crap cold—whatever it is," she said.

"Jessie's up in New England somewhere. He told me you were trying to screw him out of his end of a deal."

Vito wanted to kiss her.

"Tell him that I smacked you around," he said.

"I'll tell him he should cut his stinking wrists. That's what I'll tell him. Get that kid out of jail, Vito. I can take care of myself."

CHAPTER XVI

IT WAS NINE P.M. WHEN VITO WALKED THROUGH THE GATE AT SAN FRANCISCO AIRPORT, tired. Dempsey was there, alert and carefully groomed, looking as though her day was just starting. Vito had called her from New York, explained that he had the plasmids—no questions to be asked—and told her to strike the best possible bargain with the DA. They walked across the concourse slowly.

"The deal's even better than I had hoped for," Dempsey said.

Vito smiled.

"If my father was here he'd say you were pumping up your fee."

"It'll be big enough without any pumping. I'm just letting you know that first of all I earned it and secondly that your son—for whom I happen to have developed a bit of affection—got very lucky here."

The DA had agreed to forget about Adam's accomplices and his buyer if the plasmids were brought in. Every last cc of the stuff. In return Adam would be sentenced to five years, of which ninety days would be jail time, the remainder to be served as a special parole term.

"They want five years hanging over his head," she said. "In case a drop or two from those test tubes accidentally got held back."

Engineered Genetic Systems was far ahead of any competition in this development program and were only months away from going to market with it. If a sudden breakthrough was announced by anyone in the field within the next year, Adam would be slammed back in on some trumped-up parole violation and made to serve out the full term in prison.

"What if someone makes a legitimate breakthrough six months from now?" Vito asked.

"Pray that no one does. The prosecutors are not about to be fucked over here. The DA also said, and believe me he *meant* it, that if they get screwed here and have to put Adam away for the five years he'll do the toughest jail time that can be done in California. The tiers in Quentin or Folsom they call psycho blocks. They're for mass murderers, mutilators, cultists who go in for human sacrifice with a knife, people doing three consecutive ninety-nine-year bits before they're eligible for parole. It's kind of tough to make those guys toe the line in prison. So they give them a block of their own where they can work things out pretty much their own way."

"The judge decides where Adam does his time?" Vito asked.

"No. At the sentencing the judge actually commits the prisoner to the custody of the director of corrections. Everyone sentenced in California gets shipped first to the medical facility at Vacaville. The staff there gives them a physical and batteries of psychological tests then selects the appropriate facility for each prisoner. It's a very up-to-date, enlightened system. In theory. But Santa Clara County isn't a backwater; there are ninety-five deputy DAs in the office, so the DA carries some real clout in the state. If he wants to screw Adam he'll call in some credit cards at Vacaville.

"Your son will go onto a psycho block. That's where the DA promised he would toss Adam McMullen," Dempsey said. "And make no mistake—he'll do it."

"And where will Adam do the ninety days?" Vito asked.

"They won't ship him anywhere for just three months. He'll do the time in the Santa Clara County Jail. It's not an Air Force base but it's a nicely supervised little jail."

"What are the chances they'll screw Adam anyway?" Vito asked. "After you give them this."

"Absolutely none," Dempsey said. "That I guarantee. Prosecutors don't work that way. They'll abide by this agreement to the letter. *If* every drop taken out of that lab is returned to them."

She stopped as they approached the terminal exit.

"You *did* bring every last drop," she said.

Vito nodded, yes, and hoped that his devious father hadn't skimmed a bit off the top of each test tube.

Dempsey dropped Vito off at a Holiday Inn five minutes from the airport, called the district attorney at home, then continued down to San Jose. Vito expected to hear from her in the morning. He turned the thermostat to seventy-five and stripped, letting his clothes fall into a heap on the carpeted floor. Being naked always put him into a deeper sleep. He sprawled face-down diagonally across the king-sized bed, exhausted but feeling for the first time since Adam's capture as though a tight girdle had been cut loose from his chest. Listening to the hum of the fan blowing out warm air from a vent close to the ceiling, he breathed deeply in the darkness for a few minutes, the side of his face floating on a soft, oversized pillow. He felt at peace. His mind drifted into a series of comforting, disconnected visions that meant he was about to sleep. He was back again years ago fucking Marie on the overhead conveyor among sides of beef in the refrigerated room, her warm, strong thighs encircling his body and her face just a few feet from his, radiating a uniquely sexual combination of joy and discomfort as he walked along locked into her, his arms wrapped around her waist, fingers spread wide and pressed deeply into her buttocks, ignoring the forty-degree temperature; he was warm now, in his slowed-down, twilight memory. Elaine suddenly replaced Marie and he observed himself press his face against her breastbone and suck softly as she pressed her breasts inward and rolled them gently against the sides of his face.

He could manage telling Elaine that Adam would do ninety days of jail time. Five years of jail time and he would have wanted to swallow a bottle of sleeping pills sooner than tell her. Now it would almost be easy.

He fell into a deep sleep.

Someone's clenched fist pounding on the door woke him. He sat up in bed, sensed that it was not yet dawn, and after a few seconds spent orienting himself became convinced that there were cops in the corridors, the DA standing behind them. The screwing he had feared was coming true. Adam had been thrown to the wolves and he, Vito, was about to be thrown in with him, either through Michele Dempsey's complicity or weakness. Vito picked up his shorts from the top of the pile and pulled them on, then unlocked and opened the door, keeping his hands at chest level; he didn't want an overly anxious San Jose cop blasting a hole in his stomach.

It was Dempsey, alone. Her face was red with anger.

"Water," she said. "You gave me eight test tubes of ordinary tap water."

Vito had paced the length of the room several times, bewildered, while Dempsey studied him from an armchair. After a few minutes he had pulled on his pants then scooped cold water onto his face until he was fully awake. Now he sat on the edge of the bed while Dempsey waited silently for him to think things through. He resisted the impulse to think out loud.

His first thought was that Jessie had screwed him beautifully. The real stuff was safely hidden away and Jessie had bought himself the time he needed. Margie might well have been in on the swindle, although he doubted it. He couldn't imagine her being that good an actress nor could he imagine Jessie trusting a woman.

His second thought was that Michele Dempsey might have screwed him beautifully. She could have easily substituted water for a very valuable commodity. To have stolen the plasmids from Jessie only to have them stolen in turn by a "leech lawyer" would be absolutely ironic. Vito doubted it, though. As money-oriented and worldly-wise as Dempsey was, she had an underlying quality of integrity about her. And her anger here was real.

As he looked past Dempsey to the drapes that covered the motel room window his mind wandered and he visualized Jessie, Adam, and himself leaving through the laboratory window, each carrying a tool box, Jessie holding the plasmids. What if the cluster of test tubes they took from the lab refrigerator had contained only water? He nearly shivered, involuntarily, with the certainty that he had hit on the truth.

"What if the stuff I gave you *is* what Adam stole?" he asked Dempsey. "Maybe there was nothing but water in the lab."

Her face registered neither surprise nor doubt.

"How?" she asked.

"He must have had a buyer lined up. That's what everyone's assuming and it's the only thing that makes sense. Suppose the buyer was sent by E.G.S. What if the big breakthrough they've been touting to stockholders is really nowhere in sight? Maybe they don't have a goddamn thing near completion and a nice burglary gets them off the hook—now they can't quite duplicate it—whatever. Suppose Adam was nothing but a dupe and he happened to get caught."

She sat impassively and considered it. Vito expected a small, cynical laugh. Instead, she spoke evenly.

"My first reaction, Mr. McMullen, is that you're crazy. Or grasping at straws. Considering it just a little further, though—I've seen half a dozen schemes that were more farfetched. Do I think that's what happened? No. Is it possible? Yes. It's my experience that when very big stakes are involved anything is possible."

"What can we do?" Vito asked.

"Nothing at all. If that *is* what happened, then it worked. Your son, unfortunately, is holding the bag."

CHAPTER XVII

ADAM REFUSED TO SEE HIM. VITO STOOD AT A METAL DESK AND ARGUED WITH A TIRED jailer nearing retirement who finally said, "Mister, we can keep them under lock and key, we can turn their lights out at ten o'clock, we can strip-search them when we decide to, but we can't force them to visit with people they don't want to see. Father or no father. They got rights, too, you know. The courts tell us so about once a month. They got so many rights you wonder who's got the better deal, the prisoners or the guards. Because we're all doing the time together when you think about it."

Vito then brought in Michele Dempsey. She met with Adam and implored him to visit with his father but he wouldn't do it.

"He knows you turned over the goods," she said. "And he says that you broke the code." She shook her head in genuine wonder. "You've raised a son who has at best a *peculiar* moral system."

After a day Vito saw that it was hopeless and left California, crossing the continent for the fourth time in two weeks. He would confront Jessie, if Jessie could be found, and hope that he still had the stuff. And hope that it hadn't all been water to begin with. Meanwhile, he would have to tell Elaine; better that she learn of it from him than from the Santa Clara Probation Office, which would be starting a background check soon.

He arrived in New York tired and defeated. And depressed at the thought of facing up to Elaine. He didn't call ahead, simply taxied in, said hello to the doorman, rode upstairs alone in the elevator, and unlocked his apartment door just before midnight.

Elaine had just finished watching the eleven o'clock news. She came off the couch as Vito called out, "Hello," hurried across the living room, and embraced him with a long kiss. She wore her favorite lounging robe, a lavender terry-cloth that reached her ankles, the nap worn threadbare at the seat and elbows, the vestige of a wine stain faintly visible on the front. Five years earlier, late one night when they were both a little drunk and in a playful mood, Vito had reached across the coffee table in an attempt to undo the then new robe that she, feigning inattention, had carefully allowed to fall half open during the past ten minutes. He knocked over half a glass of Barolo that splattered onto the robe and the rug.

"Sex maniacs should only drink white wine," she had said, and after first giving him what was supposed to be an inadvertent flash of bare breasts had hurried to the kitchen and back to save the rug with a dose of white wine first, then a heaping pile of salt. It had worked, and after the white wine had neutralized the red and the salt had sucked the resulting solution from the rug—she had said distinctly, suck, rather than absorb—he had finally spread the robe open and encouraged her gently with his hands onto the floor while he whispered into her ear, "I can *hear* that salt sucking up the wine."

"Me, too," Elaine had said. "Sexy sound."

Now she kissed him intensely and after half a minute of a warm, welcoming embrace her kiss slowly became sexually charged. She worked her tongue into his mouth and moved it aggressively in a way that he couldn't remember her doing, some forgotten technique of their lovemaking that had surfaced because of his long absence. She wrapped her arms around his lower back and pulled him to her with the same aggressiveness that he couldn't place. He pressed against her, excited by the novelty of her embrace.

They relaxed a bit after a few minutes. She went in to straighten up the living room while he went into the kitchen for a drink, wondering whether to tell her immediately about Adam or see through the forty-five minute sex scene that was about to ensue. There would be something terribly dishonest about sharing sex with Elaine while he held back bad—not even bad but tragic—news about Adam. He would have his drink and tell her. He reached for the bottle of Scotch and discovered that it was on the second shelf up, where he never put it, rather than the first. When he opened the small freezer compartment of the refrigerator for ice cubes he nearly recoiled with surprise; a small, white soup bowl set in the middle of the freezer held half a dozen ice cubes from a tray broken open. Elaine would never dream of saving half a tray of ice cubes; she always left them in the tray to melt beside the sink. And the bottle of Scotch on the second shelf—Elaine couldn't even reach the second shelf without the step stool.

And her tongue exploring his mouth in such an unfamiliarly aggressive way while she pulled him against her.

He carried the soup bowl of welded ice cubes into the living room and held it out to her at arm's length as she straightened up from the floor with sections of the past few days of *The New York Times* in her hands.

"Who put these in my freezer?" he asked, and stared at her. "You didn't."

She focused on them more intently than she should have, then blushed deeply and avoided his eyes. He knew she was about to attempt a lie, at which she would fail wretchedly. Elaine had never been able to carry off an even tolerable, second-rate lie. She would turn red, avoid eye contact, and, if pressed with a forefinger under her chin to deal directly with Vito's doubts, smile. Smile. A vulnerable, nervous smile that he always thought of as some basic animal instinct passed down in the genes from two million years ago on the Serengeti Plain of Africa that said—"Don't hurt! I submit. I smile." Like a female great ape bending over in the tall grass beneath a blazing sun and presenting her ass to a dominant male who had just beaten a rival for mating rights.

She looked at him and smiled.

"Who the hell was in this house, Elaine? Don't lie. Someone put these ice cubes in the freezer and someone drank my Scotch and put it back on the wrong shelf."

She got set to cry.

"Don't cry," he said. "Just tell me the truth. Whoever did this also had his tongue in your mouth and played some games you haven't played in years. Just tell me who it was."

She cried for a few minutes.

He was hurt and angry mostly because Elaine had brought someone into their house. His first reaction was to want every detail. Who was he? What did he look like? Where did she meet him? When was he here? Exactly what had they done?

She was thinking clearly enough to resist blurting it all out in a show of repentance.

"Think about it for a few minutes, Vito. Why torture yourself with details?"

There was more than a kernel of truth in what she said, but it also occurred to him that her typical coolness under fire was pretty amazing. Thank God Jessie had never been exposed to it; she would likely have been invited along on the burglary. She told him that it was no one he knew nor had she known him; a good-looking sculptor in his early thirties who had hailed the same cab as she outside a Greene Street gallery late in the afternoon. They had shared a ride uptown during which she was surprised that a younger, handsome guy found her so attractive. They stopped for a drink, continued with dinner, then came to the apartment for a nightcap.

"Nightcap my ass," Vito said. "You came up here to get laid."

"It was a stupid thing to do," Elaine agreed. "I was lonely."

Vito knew from her tone that she considered using the apartment as the stupid thing. Her attitude seemed to be that bringing home her handsome young man was akin to bringing home some sort of sex toy. The toy in this case just happened to be made of real flesh and blood. What surprised Vito was how little deep jealousy he felt; it occurred to him that had he slept with the hooker in L.A. it would have represented about the same level of infidelity. It was the use of the house that every few minutes angered him. He wondered if they had used the bed but didn't bother to ask; she would say no even if they had. He also realized that his low-keyed attitude had a large component of selfishness in it; she was now on the defensive. Telling her about Adam would be much easier.

Elaine was subdued as she listened to the story of Adam, but it didn't last. When she got over the initial shock of his being in jail she sat down on the edge of the couch. Vito sat on a hassock, forearms on his knees, and leaned forward so he was just a few feet away from her. With as little hemming and hawing as he could manage he revealed his own and Jessie's role in it. Her eyes widened and she stared at him dumbly for what seemed to be several minutes, then sat back on the couch, drained, with an expression of utter amazement that caused Vito to remember how she had asked him to keep an eye on Jessie because she thought that Adam was being influenced by him. He knew that not a bit of her reaction was studied or exaggerated for effect. Her amazement turned slowly to a deep, bona fide anger, and the anger seemed to restore her energy. Vito set his face into an expression of pain and grief, truly felt, but he also hoped it would cement their alliance in the face of what he perceived, and wanted her to perceive, as a shared tragedy.

"You son of a bitch," she said, deliberately. "You *stupid, selfish...*" and couldn't find words.

"Don't go overboard, Elaine," he said. "I've made some mistakes here, but considering that you've just recently been fucking someone in our home you're not exactly perfect either."

"How *dare* you compare a few hours of stupid sex with someone I'll never see again with you ruining Adam's life!"

She came halfway off the couch and punched him. Pounded his mouth, actually, with the side of her clenched fist rather than her knuckles. He saw it coming and forced himself to hold his head still. She hit him just once then sat still and quivered intensely, her arms wrapped tightly beneath her breasts and her shoulders hunched forward, rigid in an effort to stop her body from shaking. Vito had never seen her so close to being out of control. The depth of her feeling made him pause; he always considered Elaine to be as strong as he was, though in fact he knew that her character included a vulnerable, little-girl quality that she kept hidden, partly because he never encouraged it—even more because he had always made it clear on some nonverbal level that he simply wouldn't tolerate it. Now he wished that it would surface. He could deal with Elaine the weak little girl. Elaine the weak little girl was who he *wanted* to deal with. He would comfort and support her, her head against his chest, and stop her quaking with a strong, male certainty and control over events that she would welcome.

The memory of Adam standing across the jailhouse table in his John Wayne stance, smiling crookedly and telling Vito that, "I'm going to make you rich, Pop," flashed into Vito's mind and he realized that the same sort of adolescent fantasy of omnipotence that had motivated Adam was now motivating him. The hell with it, he thought. Someone in a lifeboat has to take charge and the two of us and Adam are in a lifeboat. He reached forward to envelop her in his arms, hoping she would cry.

"Fuck you!" she said, and hit him again, this time getting her knuckles into his eyeball.

The little-girl quality that Vito had encouraged never surfaced. Instead Elaine's anger developed into a cold resolve that *something* was going to be done for her son and that whatever fate her husband might suffer was secondary.

"Jessie might still have the stuff," she said. "He's a devious, scheming old bastard. He could have planted that water at Margie's knowing you'd look there first. It's exactly his kind of thinking."

Vito agreed.

"Then turn the son of a bitch in," she said. "If he's got it, they'll find it."

"And if he doesn't? If he's already sold it? Or if the water Margie had was what we took out of the lab?"

She shrugged.

"Even without it, it can't possibly *hurt* Adam for a judge to see that he was led into this by an old criminal."

They sat quietly for a bit, then Vito said, "So I turn my old man in."

"Yes. You turn your old man in and you turn yourself in too, Vito. You stand in front of a judge and explain how a boy Adam's age could barely resist following his father and his grandfather into this madness. He wanted their approval."

Vito was silent again.

"If you don't, I will," she said.

"You may not believe this, Elaine, but giving myself up is the easy part. Jessie, as bad as he is, is my father. And I was raised from the first grade on, that you just *never* rat someone out."

She ignored him and looked in at the kitchen clock.

"It's about ten o'clock in California now," she said. "You can call your lady lawyer at home."

He paced the living room just a few times, hoping that Michele Dempsey hadn't stolen the stuff or that they hadn't been duped from the beginning into stealing test tubes of water or that Jessie hadn't already sold it. If Jessie did have the stuff in his refrigerator when the cops got there, then Adam would walk for sure and he, Vito, would likely walk, too. If the cops found nothing, all three of them would so some time, and Vito would feel a lot worse about turning in his father. Elaine stared at him with a silent hostile demand to make the call. He traversed the living room one last time then picked up the telephone.

CHAPTER XVIII

ELAINE STOOD ALONE IN THE CORRIDOR OUTSIDE THE COURTROOM. FOR THE THIRD time in the past hour she stepped into the adjacent parking lot and stared at the Santa Clara County Jail, only a few hundred feet from her, wondering just where in the small building Adam was. Vito, along with Michele Dempsey and the deputy district attorney handling the case, was in the judge's chambers where the plea-bargained deal was being consummated. After that Adam would be brought to the chambers—at his request, without his father present—where a final disposition of his case would be made. He had earlier refused Elaine's visit. She had hoped to see Adam when he was led from the jail to the chambers, but ten minutes ago she had learned from the court attendant that prisoners were delivered to court through a tunnel that connected the buildings.

She and Vito had arrived in San Jose the previous day and were met by Michele Dempsey, who then accompanied Vito to the DA's office where he formally surrendered. He had been booked, printed, and photographed, then brought to the Superior Criminal Court where he was arraigned and released on his own recognizance. Elaine and Vito had checked into a nearby motel, still not knowing whether the New York police had found Jessie. Dempsey had called their room later that night; Jessie had been arrested and the plasmids found in his refrigerator. He had already told the New York DA that he had no intention of "rolling over and playing dead," and would not waive extradition. Finding the plasmids had made all the difference in the deal that Dempsey cut with the DA—it allowed

Vito to walk away with only probation. Adam, too, in spite of his refusal to cooperate, would do no further jail time.

"I'll have to get up and testify against Jessie at his trial," Vito had said to Elaine when he hung up the phone. He had no stomach for it.

"Good," she had said from across the room, where, during the phone conversation, she had stood motionless at a window through which the only view was of half a dozen cars in the dark motel parking lot.

Now Elaine walked past the guard into the corridor of the courthouse. She regretted not having followed his advice an hour ago and walked the half block to the cafeteria he had pointed out. After a few minutes Vito came out of the courtroom, alone. Elaine tensed.

"No surprises," he said. "Exactly what they promised is what happened."

She exhaled a long, audible breath.

"Just probation?" she asked.

"Five years," Vito said.

"And the judge went right along with it?"

"I felt like I was at a mortgage closing," Vito said. "Everyone passing papers in triplicate back and forth, stamping and stapling. I could have been taking a nap. The judge never even looked up at me."

He was lying. The judge had read through Vito's deposition of the day before, then looked at him with practiced judicial disdain and said, "Your son seems to have been raised with the kind of paternal influences that we expect from fathers and grandfathers who distill whiskey far back in the hills and hollows of Kentucky." He had made a loud, guttural sound of disgust, as though he had just tasted something rancid, and said, "If it were not for the sentencing arrangement worked out by the prosecutor—which I'm going to abide by—I would put you away for five years. You're a sorry excuse for a father."

Vito wanted now to repeat it to Elaine—his saying it would help in a small way to bring them together. He could not. They stood silently in the corridor and waited, knowing that Adam was just about entering the judge's chambers and would, before too long, come out through the courtroom door.

Dempsey walked through the door first and held it for Adam, who hesitated when he saw his parents. He stood for a moment framed in the doorway, the perfect portrait of a recent graduate about to interview for a California banking position, healthy, handsome, and fit, dressed for his courtroom appearance in what Vito thought might well be captioned in a Brooks Brothers ad as "classic trial attire for the young offender": a single-breasted blue suit not quite expensive enough to stand out, with a button-down shirt and a British regimental tie. He wore deeply polished cordovan bluchers. Later, Vito learned that Michele Dempsey had brought him the outfit, when, without telling Adam, she presented Vito with a clothing bill that included a twelve-dollar pair of Argyle socks.

Adam turned to his right sharply and walked toward the building entrance. Elaine hurried after him while Dempsey walked across the corridor to Vito, who didn't move. He had decided earlier that Adam would likely talk to Elaine if she were alone. He was right. Adam stopped at the far end of the corridor and embraced his mother.

"Did it all go okay?" Vito asked Dempsey.

"Just the way it was supposed to," she said.

"Adam say anything to you?"

"He said, thanks."

"That's all?" Vito asked.

"He also asked about his grandfather. The judge told him that he was in custody in New York."

"Does he know it was me who turned Jessie in?"

"It's not a secret," Dempsey said. "He also knows it's the only reason he's walking out of here."

"You think it made any impression?"

She shook her head, no, and said, "Not right now. The first thing he said when we left the judge's chambers was that he wants to fly to New York to visit his grandpa." She shook her head in disbelief. "That's what he called him, his *grandpa*. The way he choked a little as he said it, if I hadn't met Jessie I'd think he was a twinkling old man with a weak heart in an AT&T commercial."

"What did you say?" Vito asked.

"I advised him to save his air fare. His grandpa will be here in San Jose before you know it."

"Will he?"

"Of course," she said. "I assume he's not a fool. They'll offer to plea-bargain to avoid a trial and extradition hearings. With the case they've got against him, he'll take it."

"The case being my testimony."

"Yes," she said, with no particular expression in her voice.

"What will they settle for?" Vito asked.

She shrugged.

"Depends on his record, who the judge is, who he uses as a lawyer. It..."

"It won't be you?"

"I'm representing you, and you're testifying against him. He'll need his own lawyer. What I was going to say about his deal is that they'll likely go for something around ten years. He'd be a fool not to take it."

"That's still like a life sentence at his age," Vito said.

"Please don't choke up and call him Pa," Dempsey said. "I might puke."

"He's my father," Vito said.

"Thank God he's not mine," Dempsey said, and extended her hand. "You'll get a final bill in a couple of days. I've already made my good-byes to Adam. It's been real, meeting the McMullens."

They shook hands and she took a few steps, then stopped to think for a moment. She walked back to him.

"I watched you listen to the judge tell you what he thought of you as a father. I probably ought to tell you... he said to Adam that his decision against cooperating to convict Jessie was deplorable. That Adam ought to walk out of here and thank his father for finally behaving like one."

"Thanks," Vito called out softly as she walked away. She acknowledged it with a nod over her shoulder.

He looked over at Elaine and Adam, who stood close to the wall of the corridor. She was talking and he listening. Adam's head was cocked and he leaned back slightly in the reserved posture of someone who really didn't want to hear what was being said yet wasn't angry with the person saying it. After a few more minutes he kissed his mother good-bye and hurried through the doors into the parking lot. Elaine approached Vito at a slow pace. She seemed exhausted.

"What did he say?" Vito asked.

She was close to tears but very much in control and clearly still blaming Vito for everything.

"He'll be in touch. That's how he ended the conversation—'I'll be in touch, Ma.' And he left."

Vito reached out to put his hand on her shoulder. She turned just slightly, as though it were inadvertent, but it caused him to retract his arm.

"He's staying out here," Elaine said. "He wants to be able to visit his grandpa."

"Did he mention me?" Vito asked.

"Yes. He said the day I bring your name up will be the last day I ever hear from him."

Vito nodded.

"That's what I figured."

Elaine was not lying; Adam had spoken those words to her. First, though, she had pointed out to him that Vito had done it for his sake. That it was the only time during the whole affair where Vito had acted like a father. Adam had considered it for a few moments, then, just before threatening to end his contact with her if Vito's name was ever mentioned again, he had looked into her eyes and shrugged. It was a very small acknowledgment of doubt that, had Vito known of it, would have lifted his spirits.

Standing beside Vito now, Elaine didn't tell him of the message she had picked up from the shrug. It would show her concern for Vito's feelings, and that would be a small first step toward bringing them closer. Her anger stopped her. She said nothing.

Vito looked out through the windows at the bright California day that was so inappropriate for his mood. Across the parking lot near the jailhouse entrance, Adam leaned against the side of a van, apparently waiting for a taxi that he would have called for from the lobby of the jail. The side of the van was painted with an elaborate mural of a beach scene in which a blond surfer rode in the perfect curl of a monstrous wave toward the observer. The scene formed a background for Adam that seemed meant to advertise his decision to remain in California. It brought home to Vito how far away from him Adam would be. Without a word to Elaine he hurried through the lobby doors and walked fast across the parking lot. Adam, when he noticed him approaching, did not move. He remained in his crooked posture, slouched a bit, his right shoulder against the van, his left hand on his thrust-out hip. Vito stopped a few feet in front of him and spread out his hands, palms up, in a gesture of vulnerability.

"God forbid, Adam," he said, "but either one of us could die tomorrow. Let's not let it happen while we're mad at each other."

Adam lifted his chin a bit and stared at him. Vito was sure that he was formulating a macho, John Wayne reply. Instead, tears welled up in Adam's eyes and his throat must have constricted; the words did not come easily. They were spoken at the risk of crying outright.

"You turned out to be a piece of shit," he said, then hurried away before he broke down.

Vito watched his forced, steady gait across the parking lot toward the road.

CHAPTER XIX

THE DAY WAS WARM ENOUGH FOR THE REAR DOORS OF THE VAN TO BE KEPT OPEN, SWUNG around and latched to the sides, a heavy steel grating pad-locked in place to lock up the four prisoners being transported through the Napa Valley toward San Quentin. The temperature was in the high seventies, in Jessie's mind unnatural for October; had he been on the streets of New York, where he wished he was, there would be a pleasant chill in the air and barely noticeable puffs of vapor would appear when he exhaled. During the months of plea bargaining he had rarely been outdoors, then, during his thirty days of tests and interviews at Vacaville for placement, he had, inexplicably, not wanted to be outdoors. Now, his left arm pressed lightly against the grating, he stared out at the seemingly endless vineyards and reflected that his vantage point at the rear of the van was perfectly appropriate for someone on his way to prison. Whatever he saw he had already passed. It was all behind him, rows of stubby grapevines, the occasional groups of stooped migrant workers, even the expanse of clear sky overhead—everything was already receding from his life by the time it became visible.

On the bench across from him, their knees almost touching his, sat two young Chicanos, one of them starting a ten-year bit on a second armed robbery conviction, the other a hard-working auto mechanic beginning a life sentence for stabbing to death a cousin with whom his wife had slept. They swayed in unison each time the van traveled over a wavy section of the two-lane blacktop. Beside Jessie was a thirty-five-year-old heavily tattooed Hell's Angel convicted on a second cocaine sale.

The four of them had ridden in silence, broken occasionally by low humming and foot tapping from the Hell's Angel. It had annoyed Jessie but he decided to let it pass and wait for something more substantial to complain about—the motorcyclist seemed mildly hyper and wouldn't be able to sit quietly through the entire ride. Sooner or later he would begin running off at the mouth.

After another half hour of intermittent humming the Angel turned to Jessie and said, "I hear your kid fucked you over, Pop. Tough way to start your time."

Jessie let a few seconds pass then looked straight ahead at the two Chicano kids and asked them in a gentle tone of voice, "Does it make sense to you that this guy should give a shit whether I start my time tough or easy?"

The Chicanos remained impassive. After a few moments the armed robber moved his eyes to watch the Hell's Angel's reaction.

The Angel laughed softly and shrugged his shoulders.

"Hey, no big deal," he said to Jessie. "Relax. We all got some long bits to do and I'm trying to pass the time of day. You know, a little friendly chitchat and bingo, your time is over before you know it. Half the people you're going to meet at Q. are there because someone ratted them out. All I'm saying is that knowing it was your own kid—it's got to hurt, you know? I'm like making an observation. Showing a little sympathy for my elders. It's a tough way to start your time."

Jessie turned to study his fellow prisoner, their faces just a few feet apart, then leaned even nearer to him and squinted, as though wanting to examine an interesting specimen at closer range.

"From what someone said up in Vacaville you ride around on a motorcycle or something?"

"I'm a biker. Oakland chapter of the Angels."

"A *biker*," Jessie said, trying out a new word in his vocabulary. "Tell me, kid, you going to be at Quentin for any length of time?"

"Unless somebody has a sudden change of heart it'll be ten years minimum."

"Well," Jessie said, "it's going to be my home for at least five years, which means we may be running across each other here and there. So it may be best if you understand things from the get-go. First off, how I do my time ain't your business. Second, I don't tolerate comments about my kid or other members of my family, all of who I hold sacred. Third, I think of people your age who ride around on motorcycles dressed like fucking lunatics and disturbing the peace as a pack of Nazis who need a good kicking around to straighten them out. Fourth, I happen to be just the guy to do the kicking and you are exactly the kind of scum bag I would love to go to work on. If in the next five years in the joint, starting *now*, you ever talk to me directly without starting off by saying, 'Excuse me, sir,' then I'll bust you up worse than if you took a spill on your little toy bicycle at sixty miles an hour."

The biker stared at him dumbly for a few moments then looked across at the two Chicanos and laughed heartily.

"Do you fucking *believe* this?" he asked.

They remained impassive.

He turned to Jessie, sure enough of himself to put his left hand onto Jessie's shoulder as he said, "Listen, McMullen..."

Because his seated position gave him no leverage for a solid punch, Jessie jabbed the end of his thumb into the Angel's eyeball then drove the back of his elbow hard to the diaphragm as he stood up. It took away every bit of the Angel's wind. Jessie stood above the seated figure and hit him methodically with a series of consecutive left and right hooks. During the long period of riding in silence while Jessie had waited patiently for the Angel to open his mouth, he had decided that he wanted to inflict a lot of damage, sufficient to require at least a short stay in the prison infirmary, with enough stitches to create gossip on the yard. It would be a good way to start his time.

After a minute or two he realized that while his mind had wandered, the Angel had lost consciousness. He reached down with his left hand and entwined his fingers into the Angel's hair to hold his head in place on the wood bench, then used his right fist as though he were mimicking a pile driver to smash up the Angel's face at a steady pace, working first across the eyebrows where the closeness of the bone would produce the easiest, deepest cuts, then onto the cheekbones, twisting his fist just slightly each time his knuckles landed. As the Angel's skin opened with each blow it crossed Jessie's mind that the man must have some Irish genes for him to cut so easily. Jessie had heard for years the theory of professional fight people that Irish fighters cut easily not because they were thin-skinned but because they lacked a certain layer of fat between the facial bones and the skin. He had never fully accepted it, sensing that the Irish would prefer a missing layer of fat to a thin skin.

As he began working on the Angel's nose he decided that later, in Quentin, it would be worthwhile to look into whether the man did have some Irish in him.

Jessie used three blows to knock out the Angel's front teeth, then stopped. From the way the teeth had broken he guessed that at least some of them had been bridgework. He released the handful of hair and allowed the limp body to slide completely off the bench onto the floor in the narrow aisle, then wiped his right hand dry on the Angel's State of California prison shirt.

The driver and the guard riding shotgun up front may well have heard the low-level thumping through the high, small grating behind their heads; if so they had chosen to ignore it. When they arrived at Quentin shortly, Jessie would shrug and say, "He fell," and if the fallen Angel later confirmed it, as he would have to so as not to be marked a rat, the prison authorities, like prison authorities in any state Jessie knew of, would be pleased to accept it. Unreported tales of prison violence were better than reported ones for everyone in the system.

Jessie sat down, breathing hard, then looked across at the Chicanos whose posture and facial expressions hadn't changed a bit. He let out a soft, "Whew!" and explained his shortness of breath by saying, "I'm not a kid anymore. You become a grandpa, like me, and you slow up."

They nodded silently.

After a bit Jessie asked, "You guys see what happened?"

The Chicano who was starting his second bit nodded and said softly but certainly, "Yeah. He fell."

CHAPTER XX

VITO PULLED THE SEVILLE INTO AN UNDERGROUND GARAGE ON KISSENA BOULEVARD, TOLD the attendant that he would be three or four hours, then walked up the ramp, on his way to Nat and Rose's new apartment for the first time. The neighborhood wasn't classy, he thought, but it was a far cry from Davidson Avenue in the heart of the Bronx jungle. He could finally attend their Seder without having to swap his Caddy for Julio's rusting Toyota and he didn't feel obliged to hug the curb as he walked toward their building. Elaine, now able to visit them every few weeks, had told Vito that this part of Flushing was an odd ethnic mix: a fair number of Jews, a sprinkling of blacks and Puerto Ricans, large numbers of Indians, and a recent heavy influx of Orientals—Chinese and Koreans—who were buying up commercial property along nearby Main Street as fast as they could. The streets could have been cleaner but the litter along the curbs struck Vito as the normal overflow of a crowded, working-class neighborhood rather than the deliberately dumped mounds of garbage that had blanketed the courtyard of Nat and Rose's Bronx apartment house. There wouldn't be rats scavenging the streets here nor would there be beer cans in the hallways. As he found the address and entered the brown brick, six-story building, the irony of attending the Seder here occurred to him; Nat and Rose had finally migrated from their hellhole in the Bronx only because of Adam's threat at last year's Seder—that he wouldn't go to another one on Davidson Avenue. Now they were ensconced safely in Flushing and Adam would not be at their first Seder here.

Adam had called Elaine every month or so for most of the

past year, careful to select a time when Vito would not be home. He never spoke for more than a few minutes. Elaine repeated for Vito whatever was said but never mentioned him to Adam, until two months ago. On the word, "father," Adam had hung up the phone. Elaine had not heard from him since.

Vito kissed Rose and commented that he had forgotten his paper cup for the wine. She pinched his cheek, then pointed to a tumbler set beside his plate that looked as though it had once held grape jelly.

"You can celebrate our first Seder in the new apartment with a full-size glass," she said.

Nat, already *davening*, looked up and mumbled a hello, then returned to his prayer book. Vito walked around the table to Elaine and bent to kiss her cheek.

"How's the traffic?" she asked.

"About the same as it would be in the Bronx, but here you don't drive in fear of getting a flat." He turned to Rose. "You going to give me a tour?"

"Where did we move?" she asked. "Park Avenue? Have a look around."

"Don't lose your way," Nat intoned without glancing up. "In these Flushing suites you need a map to get back to the dinner table."

Vito looked around. The apartment was immense by the standards of Nat and Rose, with a living room that easily measured twelve by twenty, a bedroom sufficiently larger than their last so that each piece of the massive, mahogany bedroom set bought on a layaway plan during their first three years of marriage seemed forlorn, and an eat-in kitchen that Rose commented was, "Too big. I don't know where anything is." The half dozen cheaply framed reproductions of Chagall had been hung with apparently no attention to spacing or their height off the floor.

"The super put them up," Rose said. "For five dollars. He's not cheap, this one. Everything is more expensive in Flushing."

"Irish," Nat said. "He's got a cellar full of kids down there."

"You're sure he's Irish?" Vito asked. "All those kids, he could also be Hasidic."

Nat shook his head, no. "Between Hasidim and Irish I can tell the difference."

The apartment was freshly painted with a white that reflected a pleasant bluish cast and the living-room floor was covered with a rich, beige, wall-to-wall carpet that Nat and Rose had allowed Elaine to buy them only after dozens of phone calls and endless repetitions that, "We're not people who take. We give." When they had finally relented and Rose agreed to accompany Elaine to ABC Carpet, Elaine had arrived there early and told the salesman, "When my mother arrives, whatever we look at, you quote the installed price at exactly half of what it really is. I'll mentally double it and you and I understand that the bill will be twice what you quote."

The salesman, who had been raised on Ocean Parkway in Brooklyn, had simply nodded and said, "They all get crazier as they get older. My brother is a big, successful TV producer. Knocks down a million or two a year—who knows how much. My parents are still on Ocean Parkway. When he finally convinced them to use his chauffeur-driven limo when they visit his little estate up in Larchmont, the only way they do it is for my father to ride up front with the chauffeur—people shouldn't think he's trying to be a big shot—and my parents insist on paying the tolls. 'The car would just sit anyway,' they tell my brother, 'except for the gas. But tolls come from your pocket.'"

Even with the half-price ruse, Elaine had spent a long time convincing Rose to accept the hundred percent wool beige.

Now Rose pointed at the carpet and asked Vito, "So how do you like your beautiful gift, darling?" then turned to Elaine and said, "Only your husband buys such a rich gift. Mrs. Koch's son-in-law gave them a vase when she moved from the Bronx and it's all I heard about for six months. A nice enough vase but really a nothing. I called her last week and told her I got hundred percent wool wall to *wall*. Almost six hundred dollars installed. I could tell by her voice she thought I was lying. She said it has to be acrylic—wool would cost twice that."

"Use it in good health, Rosie," Vito said. "Tell me, how long have you known her?"

"Close to forty-five years. We were neighbors on Davidson Avenue before Elaine was born."

"And you still call her Mrs. Koch? What does she call you?"

"Mrs. Ruden, what else? We were never really close friends. Just good neighbors."

Vito went to the bed, where he had deposited his coat and a brown paper bag. He brought the bag to Rose.

"Here. It's the first time I'm in your new home."

She took from the bag and placed on an end table a small box of coarse, Kosher salt, a box of matzoh, and a box of sugar, then thanked Vito and patted his cheek.

"Always, you know about things," she said. "The nice gestures that count. Now, if my grandson was here, life would be perfect."

"You'd find something else," Elaine said. "Young people go where they feel they can make the life they want for themselves. Adam likes California."

"What could be in California that's not in New York? I don't understand these young people."

"New York's the capital of the world," Nat said, between Hebrew phrases.

"California's got sunshine," Vito said.

Rose dismissed it with a wave of her hand.

"Not even so good for you from what I read in the newspapers. Skin cancer . . . wrinkles."

Elaine raised her hands defensively.

"Please don't torture us with any clippings. I've read them. You're suddenly supposed to wrap up like a mummy before going onto a beach."

Rose looked to Vito for support.

"A mother tries to be a mother, and . . ."

She let it trail off.

Nat set down his prayer book.

"Four thousand miles away," he said. "Gypsies go four thousand miles away. Normal people stay close to their families."

"It's not four thousand miles," Elaine said. "It's thirty-five hundred."

Nat shrugged.

"Call me *pisher* for five hundred miles. It's still further than Jews should travel."

The Seder went as it had in those earlier years during which Adam had not been present, the ceremony not cut short but progressing too quickly, with no youngest male to ask the questions and Nat's age apparent to all, including himself. He stumbled over the procedure sometimes, enough so that at one point even Vito was able to correct him: "Nat, the *karpas* should be passed and *davened* over before the bitter herbs."

Nat accepted it with his own rough form of gracefulness.

"A rebbe for a son-in-law, I wound up with," he said to Rose, with a touch of pride in his voice that he knew Vito would detect.

When Rose went to the front door to let in the angel Elijah, Vito commented that they could finally open the door unchained—there would be no *schvartzer* in sneakers waiting to mug them.

"I knew that was coming," Nat said. "Your material's getting stale."

Rose opened the door and gasped. Adam stood there, smiling, arms outstretched. He hugged Rose and said, "Grandma, I've been out here half an hour waiting for you to open the door for Elijah."

"Better than hitting the lottery," Nat said several times. It captured perfectly all of their feelings about Adam's arrival. When Adam shook Vito's hand their eyes met for just a few moments. It told Vito nothing. The mood became festive and Nat insisted on repeating one small portion of the ceremony—the asking of the questions. Adam said that he suspected any repetition was not orthodox.

"So then tonight we'll be Reform," Nat said, and handed Adam a white satin yarmulkah and a book.

Adam read aloud the sewn-in label before setting it on his head.

"The Bar Mitzvah of Owen Lapinsky, nineteen sixty-three," he said. "Who's Owen Lapinsky?"

Nat had been waiting for the question.

"Ha! Every Seder all of you read the *koppel* labels and get a big laugh because I don't know. Well this one I just dug out especially for you, Adam. This is not a stranger's *koppel* you're wearing. This was a young man we knew in the Bronx. Watched him from the time he was born. A personality that God made to give pleasure to anyone who's ever known him. A Little Leaguer, the only Jew to always bat fourth in the Fordham Road team. A potential Hank Greenberg. A little, stocky left-hander who knocked out home runs over the fence so often that he had free haircuts to last five years—his team was sponsored by Ralph's barbershop. A home run, a free haircut by Ralph's. A *boyla*, as we would say, who gave nothing but *Naches* to his parents. *Naches*, Adam—it means joy, pride, happiness . . . it means everything that a father or a mother dreams of from a child. This is all that Owen Lapinsky ever gave his parents. Now he's in his thirties and teaching—master's degree, NYU. He teaches the biggest problem kids there are in the school system, the ones with the disturbed emotions, the damaged brains, the physical handicaps. What nobody else will touch. The kids whose classroom gets put in the basement. Next to the boiler so no one should hear them. And he's so good that his supervisor, the principal, a black man, tells him, 'There's a place in heaven for you, Owen.'

"He's about the nicest young man we've ever watched being raised. And of all the *koppels* in my drawer I picked this one for you to wear because I hope some of it wears off on you, Adam. You should be the kind of man whose *koppel* you're wearing, then Grandma and me will have nothing but *naches* from you."

It was the longest statement he had ever made to his grandson. Nat, in an unusual gesture, raised his tiny cordial glass of sweet wine and toasted Adam.

"*L'chayim,*" he said.

"*L'chayim,*" Adam said, then added in a level voice, his one-ounce glass of wine outstretched, "I love you, Grandpa."

Nat nodded an acknowledgment, clinked glasses, and tossed off the Manischewitz like a merchant seaman ashore for the first night. Rose, as she touched her glass to Adam's, said, "A *master's,* Lapinsky, NYU."

After they had all sipped from their wineglasses Rose said to Adam, "I want you to know that Grandpa set aside that *koppel* early this morning. With his cataracts, took hours to read the label in every one. He boiled it down to two—Owen Lapinsky or Scott Zuckerbrot."

Nat scoffed.

"Between Zuckerbrot and Lapinsky was never a contest. A nice enough boy, Zuckerbrot. Also a master's. Columbia. Economics. But wasn't an athlete as well. Never played Little League. Lapinsky was an all-around."

"You set aside a yarmulkah, Nat?" Vito asked. "Knowing Adam was in California?"

Nat seemed surprised by the question.

"Why not? I thought he wouldn't be here? What, would my daughter and her husband raise a Gypsy?"

Through the rest of the evening Vito wondered what Adam's attitude would be toward him. It was difficult to gauge. Adam was friendly enough but he would behave that way in any event for his grandparents' benefit. They had no idea of a rift between Adam and Vito. Vito did sense, whenever his eyes met Adam's, a barrier. Perhaps, he decided as the evening progressed, less a barrier than a reserve. A desire to establish a subtle distance rather than a hard wall. Adam still carried in him some deep hurt, at the very least a sadness, which precluded his being warm and loving with Vito. Vito braced himself against the possibility that, after the Seder, Adam might walk away from him again as he had in the San Jose parking lot and fly off to California, having fulfilled the only purpose of his mission, to visit his old, fading grandparents.

• • •

They stood in the foyer for the yearly half-dozen rounds of good-byes and well wishes, Elaine weighted down with two shopping bags. In them were meats and kugels wrapped in crinkled foil with enough small punctures and rips from having been reused too often so that food aromas would fill the car, plus jars of liquids at least one of which would be screwed on with a crossed thread, causing it at some point on the journey home to leak and soak into the paper shopping bag until the bottom disintegrated. For some reason known only to herself Rose refused to use plastic shopping bags. Elaine, so pleased with Adam's presence, for the first time in Vito's memory did not berate Rose for loading her down with, "All this stuff that no one in their right mind needs unless they're trying to gain ten pounds." They made their good-byes with no bickering.

"You'll be in New York for a while?" Rose said to Adam and pinched his cheek hard. "No traipsing around the country like some kind of displaced person?"

Vito and Elaine each felt the other grow tense waiting for Adam's answer. Both tried not to show it.

"That's my Cherokee blood, Grandma," Adam said. "Cherokees are wanderers, like all the American Indians. But I'll be around for a little while, anyway. I'll come out next week if you want to cook."

"When don't I cook?" Rose asked.

Vito and Elaine carefully did not look at one another. Each felt the other's relief.

They rode down on the elevator silently, Elaine wanting to let the two men work things out for themselves if that was going to happen. Vito decided that he would put no pressure on Adam; Adam was the one who felt that he had been betrayed. Vito would, now that they were away from Nat and Rose and free to speak openly, let Adam break the silence and thus make his feelings known. Adam, when he entered the elevator, had decided the same thing.

Often during the last ten months Adam had put in eight hours of machining steel followed by a few hours of numbing, half-priced, "Happy Hour" drinking toward the end of which he would brood about his lost third of a million dollars. The drinking was followed by a solitary meal at a Taco Hut or Burger King, after which he would lie alone on the lumpy mattress of a San Francisco rooming house and remember the pain in his father's face when Adam had said, with such honest disappointment, "You turned out to be a piece of shit." Sometimes, loosened more by alcohol than he could handle, he had cried aloud at the memory and fallen asleep without undressing.

When they reached the sidewalk Elaine took the parking check from Vito and said that she wanted to hurry ahead. Vito and Adam walked beside one another, their steps slowing in unison until they were nearly standing still. Vito indicated the neighborhood with a sweep of his arm.

"Beats the Bronx, doesn't it?" he said.

"I don't know. I kind of miss those dead dogs on the street."

"You have a place to say?"

Adam nodded. "Yeah."

Vito braced himself for Adam's reaction to his next question.

"How's Jessie?" he asked.

Adam hesitated, then said very gently, "He's dead, Pop."

Adam had gone up to Quentin once every week during the six months that Jessie was there. Jessie had seen the prison dentist soon after he arrived to cure a longtime mild toothache that proved instead to be a tumor too far along to get. They operated, with very little hope of success, and their lack of hope proved to be well-founded. He had forbidden Adam to say anything to Vito until after he was cremated and Adam had abided by Jessie's demand.

"He died six days ago," Adam said.

"It went hard?" Vito asked.

Adam closed his eyes against the memory.

"It was cancer. And one of the rottenest kinds—jaw and neck. It's the first time I ever saw someone die of cancer." He shook his head. "Jessie looked like a dead warrior when he finally died. A skinny, naked warrior sprawled on the bed like a soldier on a battle field who fell in hand-to-hand combat. It was like one of the drawings in that kids' book of the *Iliad* you used to read to me in bed. Wouldn't take morphine—said if he wanted to be semiconscious he'd sooner tell them to pull the plug. The doctor hardly believed it. The day he died, when I got there, twenty minutes earlier a main artery in his neck where they had operated just opened up. The cancer had eaten into it enough so it just gave way. No morphine—nothing—and the doctor stitched it up while Jessie gritted his teeth and clenched the bed railings."

"Could he talk?" Vito asked.

"Not after the second operation. They did two. He could make some noises that I understood a lot of but mostly he used one of those Magic Slates that kids use."

They came to a standstill and leaned against the front fender of a car, as teenagers would.

Adam smiled wryly.

"He didn't give an inch, right to the very end. The day they told him he was going to die for sure he wrote me out a little note on the slate. I was ready for something pretty heavy. It said the good news was that his building wasn't going co-op—Christine's friend wouldn't make a nickel."

"Did my name ever come up?" Vito asked.

Adam smiled.

"Your initial. Between the writing and the grunting, he shortened everything he could. You became V."

"And what did he have to say, or write, about me?"

"He stayed pissed off at you until pretty near the end. Then he relented a little."

"And how do *you* feel about me these days, Adam?"

Adam considered the question, then said, "Well, let me put it this way, Pop. I'd really prefer not to deal with it right now. Why don't we let it work itself out at its own pace? My feelings are mixed, to be truthful, but I'm here."

Vito nodded.

"I brought back Jessie's ashes," Adam said. "He couldn't decide what he wanted done with them but he knew he wanted them carried to New York. A week before he died he wrote on his slate that it would be the only free airplane ride he'd ever get. I figured the two of us ought to do it together."

"Thanks, Adam," Vito said, and squeezed his neck gently.

They decided that the only appropriate site to scatter the ashes would be Hell's Kitchen. "The West Side," Adam said, and smiled. Somewhere in the Forties, on Tenth Avenue. They met the next day at ten A.M. sharp in the Market Diner on Eleventh Avenue, a place that Jessie had eaten in perhaps a thousand times. Both of them, without having discussed it, arrived in suit and tie, shoes shined to a high polish. They walked through the brisk, spring day to Tenth Avenue then uptown to the high Forties where Vito pointed out a five-story tenement.

"We lived in that building when my mother died," he said.

They climbed the narrow stairs to the roof, where, to protect against burglars, the door had a crash bar installed on it and a sign: EMERGENCY EXIT ONLY. ALARMED.

Vito laughed. "Seems fitting for Jessie, doesn't it?"

They stared at the sign for a few moments, then Vito said, "Let me go find the super. For ten bucks he'll be happy to shut it off and let us out there."

Adam stopped him.

"You think it's what Jessie would want, Pop?"

Vito laughed again.

"No. You got anything sharp enough to scratch away that wire insulation? I can jump it in a minute."

He used the edge of a key. They walked across to the edge of the roof and looked down on Tenth Avenue. Adam said that he was pleased there was a nice wind blowing.

"Dropping them down in still air wouldn't be very romantic, would it?"

Vito agreed.

They watched the street activity for a few minutes. There was, as always, a preponderance of taxis honking constantly as they weaved their way uptown through the heavy traffic. Several tractor trailers moved slowly, the hiss of their air brakes each time they paused loud enough to reach the rooftop. The sidewalks were crowded with pedestrians. Most were transients but when Adam studied the scene for a few minutes he realized there were dozens of neighborhood people—men who lounged in front of bars or women with shopping carts, who stopped for a while to talk to one another. He wondered if anyone on the sidewalks below had been at Dermot O'Doul's open-air wake.

Vito said, "There are a couple of hundred people in this neighborhood—some of them might be walking down there now—who Jessie would love to see get a big chunk of his ashes in their eye."

"Let's hope we get them all," Adam said.

Together, they held the small urn and shook it out, then stood silently for a few minutes staring downtown, where the ashes had blown and disappeared almost instantly. When Vito felt tears beginning to fill his eyes he motioned silently to Adam that he wanted to go.

"Okay, Pop," Adam said.

After a few moments he asked, "He was a tough guy to figure out, wasn't he?"

Vito nodded, yes.

Adam, looking genuinely puzzled said, "You know, a couple of days before he died I sat beside him on the bed and I asked him, 'Jessie, answer me something. Did you really *know* what you were going to do with the million when you got it from the Chink? I'm not asking whether you were going to set aside my share and my father's share or whether you weren't. Whether you were going to rob us, or not. All I'm asking was whether you really *knew* what you were going to do.'

"He looked at me for a while with those eyes that showed nothing but intense pain, then he scribbled a few pages worth on the slate; 'Grow up, Adam, and learn to figure that kind of question out for yourself.' I just kept staring at him and I asked, 'Grandpa, did you *know* what you were going to do? It means a lot to me.'

"The last thing he ever wrote on his slate was 'Adam, who the hell knows anything in life?'

"Well, he's dead and now he's buried, Pop. What do you say we find one of his West Side joints where there'll be people at the bar at ten-thirty in the morning and the two of us can have a couple of drinks together?"

Vito put his arm around Adam's shoulder. They walked across the roof slowly, with a sense of funereal dignity, toward the door with the deactivated alarm.

ABOUT THE AUTHOR

Vincent Patrick was born in the Bronx, New York, in 1935. He has held a broad range of jobs, from door-to-door Bible salesman to bartender, restaurant owner, teacher in a community college, and vice president of an engineering consulting firm. He also adapted his novel, *The Pope of Greenwich Village,* for the screen. He presently divides his time between New York City and Boiceville, New York.

THE LAIS OF MARIE DE FRANCE

BY
ROBERT W. HANNING

The Vision of History in Early Britain: from Gildas to Geoffrey of Monmouth

The Individual in Twelfth Century Romance

BY
JOAN M. FERRANTE

The Conflict of Love and Honor: The medieval Tristan legend in France, Germany, and Italy

(Translator.)
Guillaume d'Orange. *Four Twelfth Century Epics*

Editor with George Economou.
In Pursuit of Perfection: Courtly Love in Medieval Literature

Woman as Image in Medieval Literature, from the Twelfth Century to Dante

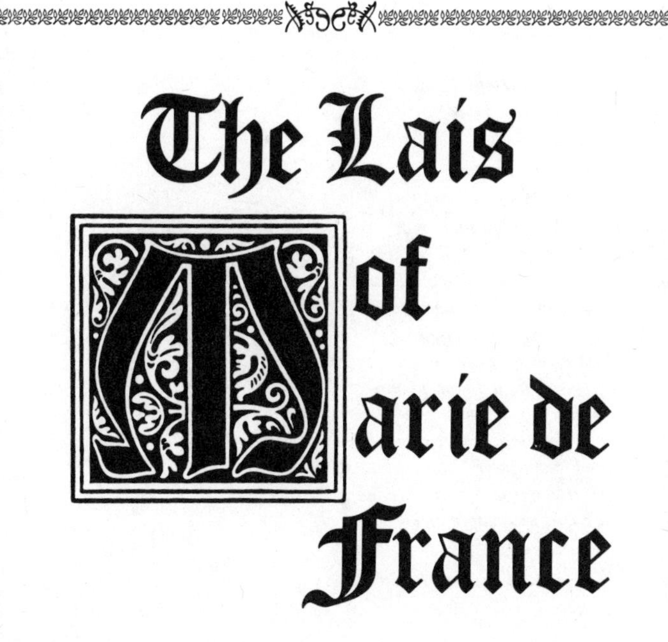

Translated,
with an introduction
and notes, by
ROBERT HANNING
& JOAN FERRANTE

Foreword by
JOHN FOWLES

E.P. DUTTON ❦ NEW YORK

For information contact:
E.P. Dutton, 2 Park Avenue,
New York, N.Y. 10016

Library of Congress Cataloging
in Publication Data

Marie de France, 12th cent.
The lais of Marie de France.

Bibliography: p.
Contents: Prologue.—
Guigemar.—Equitan.—Fresne.—
Bisclavret. [etc.]
I. Hanning, Robert W.
II. Ferrante, Joan M.
III. Title.
PQ1494.L3E5 1978
841'.1 78-8378
ISBN 0-525-14340-8

Published simultaneously in Canada
by Clarke, Irwin & Company
Limited,
Toronto and Vancouver

Designed by Barbara Huntley

10 9 8 7 6 5 4 3 2 1

First Edition

To
our
students

Contents

FOREWORD

MARIE DE FRANCE is the first woman novelist of our era. If I cannot quite simply call her the first woman novelist, that is only because I believe the writer of the *Odyssey* was also a woman. The great Greek story, woven as it is of questing, of false ambition and hostile fate, of selfish and unselfish love, of the relationships between men and women, stands grandparent to all subsequent fiction—and not least, through the intervening generation of the *Aeneid,* to Marie de France herself. Indeed I regard Marie's work as a strong retrospective argument for assuming a female mind behind the *Odyssey*. This is not the place to discuss the parallels in moral attitude, in sensibility and angle of vision, in the sophisticated embroidering of folk-theme, even in certain social problems common to twelfth century Northern Europe and the Greece of two thousand years earlier . . . although I recommend a reading of the two texts side by side to the curious. We shall never know who Homer, or the Homer of the *Odyssey,* was; but Marie was undeniably a woman. Hers is the first indisputably feminine view of the human comedy expressed through art.

The more fastidious may complain that I am abusing the term "novel" and extending it intolerably backward, especially since Marie, like Homer, wrote in verse. But to class writers by a mere historical hazard of outward form has long seemed to me an appallingly old-fashioned view of literature, as false as the pre-Linnaean classification of the natural world by fortuitous external correspondences . . . calling whales fish because they live in the sea, and so on. Virtually all Marie's importance, to say nothing of her charm, lies in her storytelling, her psychology, her morality, her highly individual use of her material—that is, it lies in her fictional powers, not her versifying ones. The latter are, I suspect, no more than competent in purely poetic terms. She is generally crisp and neat, but little more; and at times, at least to my ear, she can descend dangerously near to doggerel.

However, on that score it must be added at once that we know miserably little of a vital factor in the understanding of any writer: how he or she conceives the medium of transmission to the contemporary outside world. We must read Marie in cold print and silence, but it is quite possible that she would have seen herself, at least during the original composition, as providing matter for oral performance. We know that the Celtic *lais* she based her stories on were, in Bédier's phrase, "half sung, half spoken"; and Marie's verse is far less easy to dismiss if one includes a deliberately intended spoken function in the valuation. It works almost uniformly well, sometimes brilliantly, at a quasi-dramatic level; and we should also not forget the primordial other functions of verse both as a concentrator of wisdom and as a rudimentary mnemonic system.

Modern readers need therefore to bear in mind the possibility that what they are reading now is, so to speak, only the libretto. The art of the *diseuse* derives from early medieval public story-recitation and gives us a good clue to the now largely vanished skills of the professional oral narrator. One thing such skills tacitly excused the writer was the insertion of all those implicit stage directions about physical details and emotional reactions (adjectives and adverbs) that novelists have been increasingly obliged to employ since the invention of print and the consequent tyranny of an atomized, single-reader audience. Anyone who has tape-recorded and transcribed old people's reminiscences will know the problem here: how an amusing and vivid anecdote on the tape can seem oddly flat in the typewritten transcript. This is perhaps the hardest leap of the imagination that we have to make to appreciate Marie today—in simple, to read between her lines.

Fortunately things are much easier when it comes to the content behind the form and the style. Here we are unmistakably in the presence of a born and engagingly shrewd storyteller. Marie's method must, for the reason I have suggested, seem naïve to anyone coming fresh from the complex and elaborately realistic techniques of our own print-conditioned culture; but her actual themes are far less naïve than archetypal. The great majority of them are antique only in their outward setting and detail, while her characteristic obsession with the problems of sexuality and fidelity (identical bees —long-suffering Penelopes and marriage-wrecking Circes— buzzed in that old Greek bonnet, it may be noted) is nothing if not contemporary.

The Freudian and Jungian undertones of almost all her stories are obvious. One that has always particularly pleased me in that way is the erotic *Lanval*. It would be hard to imagine a more exact premonition of what Thomas Hardy, much later in European literary history, termed the "Well-Beloved"— the unattainable muse-figure that haunts every male novelist. *Eliduc* is a beautiful reworking of one of the oldest themes (and aging wives' nightmares) in all literature. The strange *Bisclavret* is about far more than a werewolf. Even the tiny and subtly ambiguous *Laüstic* might serve as label to a familiar enough syndrome, still today. Never mind the medieval image: we have all known of the not very daring *affaire* between two overromantic egos that ends up as a dead bird in a precious casket, more treasured for its failure than lamented for its lack of courage.

I should in any case like to suggest that Marie's surface naïvety—I would much rather call it economy—is misleading. The pen has one great advantage over the camera. It can leave out—in movie jargon, "lose"—far more easily, and leaving out is a key trick in all good prose fiction. A camera cannot photograph a voice, it has to show the face as well. And you can tell novelists quite as much by what they do not describe as by what they do—that is, by how well they use their art's exceptional facility for exclusion.

It is true that in Marie's age writers had infinitely less choice in terms of form and technique; but to assume that we have nothing to learn from them or to admire in what they did achieve with very limited means, and that they can therefore be dismissed as mere primitives, childish at worst and childlike at best, seems to me foolish—as foolish as to call the Ancient Greek architects primitive because they made no provision for heating ducts and elevator shafts. Personally I would award Marie—along with her contemporaries Chrétien de Troyes and Béroul—high praise for the elegance of some of her solutions to basic and in no way outdated problems of narrative technique, and especially in this matter of what she chooses to leave out. One of the oldest human chauvinisms has to do with time—that our own must be wiser than the rest. This may be true of science; it is very seldom true of art.

Marie also possesses an exquisite eye for the precise, poetic and colorful detail when it is needed. The editors justly praise her very marked gift for hitting on symbolic correlatives of action and personality. The same flair is seen in the characterizing touches, the moods and humors, the fragments of dialogue, that she gives her men and women. The result is that her stories remain both universal and particular—are as formal as tapestries at one moment, as natural as life the next. It is a gift, like her frequent dryness, that she shares with that other laborer on two inches of ivory, Jane Austen. Marie works very small, is very deft and concise; and the miracle is that she so often reaches far beyond her historically and formally restricted setting.

In this context I have one small complaint against the otherwise scrupulously exact translation of Joan Ferrante and Robert Hanning, and that is that they have elected not to carry over into their English version Marie's love of switching from the past tense into the narrative present. They are right, of course, in judging it a largely outmoded technique in modern English and a ubiquitous one in medieval French storytelling, in no way special to Marie. Yet it does for me seem emblematic of her greatest attraction—that ability to suddenly reach out across eight centuries, to be present again. I know of no other medieval writer, except perhaps Langland, who has ever had quite that effect on me, of being at certain moments nearer my own livingness than actual daily life itself. This is not a test that any academic critic would or could allow, yet I think most readers will know what I mean, and that there is no surer hallmark of genius in fiction. It is the one gift that all its greatest exponents share: the imagined present, however past, drowns the real present. The notion that time is linear and irreversible becomes the ultimate fiction; and the long-dead writer lives, not a hand's touch from your side.

If I must query that one decision of the editors, let me hasten to give them nothing but good marks for their care and scholarship in the presentation of the stories. One cannot easily enter such a remote language and world without skilled guidance, and that they have most fully provided. The language is in fact rather less remote than it may at first look; not too hard a "code" to crack for anyone with a reasonable knowledge of modern French and a little patience. Saying out loud will often solve when the eye is baffled; and the effort is worthwhile. There are twists and inflections and smiles in Marie's voice that not even the most painstaking and faithful translation, like this present one, can ever quite capture.

Now I must end. It is with a considerable envy of those who are about to meet this seductively humane and intelligent Frenchwoman for the first time. I have always associated her memory with one of Mallarmé's most famous lines, *Le vierge, le vivace, le bel aujourd'hui* . . . with that freshness, greenness, immediacy that has from the beginning distinguished the less coldly classical side of her country's art. Marie cannot be known in a day or a single reading; but once known, like a spring day in the Anjou of the royal family to which she may have belonged, she will not be forgotten.

Dorset, May 1978 —JOHN FOWLES

THE LAIS OF MARIE DE FRANCE

Sturges: "To read or interpret the text correctly is to enter into an erotic relationship with it. Love and interpretation are metaphors for each other." (p. 255)

"... if her lovers are like readers and her readers are like lovers, it is because these functions are analogous means of engaging another by inviting his participation in the creation of meaning through interpretation." (p. 264)

INTRODUCTION

MARIE DE FRANCE was perhaps the greatest woman author of the Middle Ages and certainly the creator of the finest medieval short fiction before Boccaccio and Chaucer. Her best work, the *Lais*—the collection of short romances and tales translated in this volume—is a major achievement of the first age of French literature and of the "Renaissance of the Twelfth Century," that remarkable efflorescence of Western European culture that signaled the end of the "Dark Ages" and the beginning of many ideas and institutions basic to modern civilization. One of the twelfth century's most significant innovations was its rediscovery of love as a literary subject—a subject that it depicted, anatomized, celebrated, and mocked in a series of masterpieces, almost all of which were written in lucid French verse. Among these pioneering love texts, which would soon be adapted and imitated in all the vernaculars of Europe, none better stands the test of time than Marie's *Lais*. The combination of variety, virtuosity, and economy of means that characterizes the twelve short stories of fulfilled or frustrated passion —the shortest of which, *Chevrefoil,* is but 118 lines long, while the longest, *Eliduc,* requires but 1,184—gives ample and constant evidence of Marie's mastery of plot, characterization, and diction, while the woman's point of view she brings to her material further distinguishes the *Lais* from the longer narratives of love and adventure composed by her male contemporaries, of whom the best known to modern readers is Chrétien de Troyes, the creator of Arthurian romance and the first chronicler of the love of Lancelot and Guinevere.

Unfortunately, we know practically nothing about this superb storyteller, except for her name, her extant works (in addition to the *Lais,* a collection of animal fables and the moral, supernatural tale, *St. Patrick's Purgatory*), the approximate period of her literary activities (1160?–1215?), and the fact, derived from her name and comments in her writings, that she was of French birth but wrote at or for the English court, which, as a result of the Norman Conquest, was French-speaking in her days. (See below for further information about Marie's activities and other works.) From the *Lais,* however, a comprehensive picture of Marie's artistic personality and predilections emerges, several facets of which deserve particular attention.

Perhaps the most recognizable "signature" of her work is the symbolic creature or artifact around which a *lai* is organized for maximum intensity and suggestiveness within the least possible narrative duration. The nightingale in *Laüstic,* the hazel tree wound about with honeysuckle in *Chevrefoil,* the hungry swan in *Milun*—all provide valuable insight into the nature of love in their respective narratives, insight that might otherwise require development through thousands of lines of poetry. Marie carefully places her symbols in the context of character revelation and tersely expressed dramatic irony, which prompts the reader to draw separate conclusions about the worth of the lovers and their love in a given *lai.* Accordingly, symbols and situations frequently parallel each other in two or more *lais,* yet the denouements, and the judgments we pass on their justice or injustice, will vary widely from one *lai* to another. The result of this process of "paired contrasts" is that, as we read on, our experience of each narrative is reinforced and complicated by resonances, often ironic, of its predecessors. What emerges is not a unified moral perspective on passion and its consequences: Marie's art avoids easy generalizations such as "married love is wrong, adultery right," or the reverse, but demonstrates instead that character, fortune, and the ability to seize and manipulate opportunities interact in any love relationship. Devotion, loyalty, ingenuity, which transcend marital ties or social norms, provide the grounds for our sympathies with or condemnation of any of Marie's lovers.

In addition to our involvement with the protagonists of the *Lais,* we respond constantly to the mastery with which Marie presents them. The deft touches of irony (as in the conclusion of *Equitan,* where the adulterous king, to avoid discovery, leaps into the vat of boiling water he has prepared in order to destroy his mistress's husband), or of homely sentiment (e.g., the description of the early-morning discovery of the abandoned infant heroine of *Le Fresne* by the porter of a monastery), remind us of the artist's complete control across the entire spectrum of narrative technique. Marie tells us in the *Prologue* to the *Lais* that she has undertaken the novel task of translating the body of love tales created by the Bretons, those famous exponents of the art of exotic storytelling. As there are no extant "Breton *lais*," we cannot substantiate Marie's claim or decide to what extent her plots may follow Breton originals. But it is clear from her use of classical Latin and contemporaneous French material that she was a well-educated and highly trained literary craftsman who wished to be recognized for her skills. She wrote as an expert on love and storytelling for the first large, sophisticated, and elite audience of medieval Europe—an audience that appreciated, as we can, the inventiveness as well as the charm and power of her love tales. In order to appreciate Marie's achievement fully, the modern reader should know something of the cultural milieu in which she worked.

The twelfth century in Western Europe saw a tremendous expansion of intellectual, social, and artistic activity; it was truly a cultural renaissance, responding to new political structures, social tensions, and economic advances that were only dimly foreshadowed during the early-medieval centuries. The expansion of urban life brought with it the rise of scholastic centers, which were usually attached to the cathedrals of important towns like Chartres and Paris. Training in grammar (or, as we should call it, literary analysis and philology), rhetoric, and dialectic or logic produced a new class of intellectuals who were technically clerics but were often only minimally involved with or controlled by ecclesiastical authority, unlike their early-medieval predecessors, who were almost all monks and deeply committed to a life of religious observance and obedience. Graduates of the twelfth-century schools were equipped for service at the burgeoning courts of France and England, where they formed a civil service and also found an outlet for their literary abilities. The rise of a courtly aristocracy at these same centers of political power gave the school-trained *clercs* an audience that was also new in medieval civilization. It comprised, in addition to the learned clerics themselves, the greater and lesser aristocracy of *chevaliers,* who fought for a living but also cultivated arts of nonlethal competition and personal refinement that were unknown to early-medieval warriors; and—most important, in the opinion of many scholars—it also included noblewomen, many of whom were involved in feudal politics and highly educated in religious and secular subjects, even though regular courses of advanced study in the schools were open only to men. (Among the many remarkable women of the twelfth century, besides Marie, special recognition is due to Eleanor of Aquitaine, heiress to a great duchy and successively wife to the kings of France and England; her daughter Marie, Countess of Champagne and patroness of Chrétien de Troyes; and Héloïse, mistress and later wife of Peter Abélard, well known throughout France for her brilliance, courage, and successful career as an abbess.) The fertile interaction of these groups gave birth to a vernacular literature in which learned interests, previously expressed exclusively in Latin, and themes of importance to a courtly elite in search of self-defining ideals mingled and cross-pollinated.

One of the themes explored in twelfth-century courtly narrative was the individual's recognition of a need for self-fulfillment and his or her struggle for the freedom to satisfy this need. The tension between the personal quest for perfection and one's social obligations was a recurring theme of courtly literature, and narrative and lyric poets alike used love as a symbol of the quintessentially private sphere of existence and desire. The nature and problems of love—for it was by no means always viewed as a positive force by Marie and her contemporaries—were explored in lyrics and in long and short narratives. Besides Marie's *Lais,* the latter group includes *contes,* short tales borrowed from the works of Ovid, the classical master of love and self-conscious art, whose influence was everywhere visible in the period. Among authors of longer chivalric romances, Chrétien de Troyes dominates the age, but Béroul and Thomas, authors of versions of the tragic love story of Tristan and Isolt, and Gautier d'Arras also excelled. All explored the problematic interrelationship of love and chivalry from many points of view, with an art that moved easily from quasi-symbolic representation to detached social comedy.

The narratives of the courtly poets were connoisseurs' literature: fanciful, ingenious tales that simultaneously amused their audience and challenged it to discover deeper meanings beneath the polished language and the idealized adventures. A long chivalric romance of Chrétien, for example, comprises a series of puzzles to be solved by aficionados of the genre: Why did the hero or heroine act in a particular, unexpected way at a particular moment? What vice or anti-courtly attitude does a villain represent? Unlike earlier medieval epics, in which heroic values are universally acknowledged even though cowardice or treachery may cause their subversion, twelfth-century courtly tales and romances usually portray the protagonist's gradual discovery of real values through love (one thinks of Marie's Guigemar, for whom love is wounding and healing, a cause of sorrow before it is a cause of joy), or the transformation of a delusory set of external appearances and relationships by the timely revelation of a hero or heroine's true identity (as is the case in *Le Fresne*). The line of European narrative fiction that uses the portrayal of love as a means for exploring the interaction of self and society, appearance and reality, descends continuously from the twelfth-century courtly narrative to the twentieth-century novel. Marie is thus one of the creators—the only woman among them—of a grand tradition that has shaped and defined our literary culture.

We know almost nothing about Marie herself, except that she was originally French and lived in the latter part of the twelfth century. It is not unusual to have virtually no information about medieval authors except what we can glean from their and others' works. There are none of the public records and reactions we take so for granted with modern writers—

no copyrights or publication dates, no standard editions, no critical reviews, no authors' memoirs or letters to establish the date or proper text of a work. More often than not, the best manuscripts we have are much later than the works themselves and have gone through several copyings; if there is more than one manuscript, they usually do not agree in all particulars. All of this means that we have to learn mainly by inference, to establish the text by judicious comparison and selection, and to deduce facts about the author from references in the work, from connections with the works of others (when there are obvious sources or influences), and, though much more rarely, from direct remarks by other writers, as in Gottfried's literary excursus in the *Tristan*.

All we know about Marie besides her name is her work: the *Lais*, the *Fables*, and *St. Patrick's Purgatory* (*L'Espurgatoire Saint Patrice*).[1] Marie names herself at the beginning of the first *lai*, at the end of the *Purgatory*, and at the end of the *Fables*, in the latter case rather assertively:

> Me numerai pur remembrance
> Marie ai nun, si sui de France.
> Put cel estre que clerc plusur
> prendreient sur eus mun labur,
> ne voil que sur li le die.
>
> I shall name myself so that it will be remembered;
> Marie is my name, I am of France.
> It may be that many clerks
> will take my labor on themselves.
> I don't want any of them to claim it.

"De France" means, presumably, that she was born in France, either the Continent as opposed to England or the Ile de France as opposed to Occitaine, probably not that she was of the royal house (as some have assumed).[2] Beyond that, she tells us only that she wrote the *Lais* for a "noble king" and the *Fables* for a Count William. The king is probably Henry II (ruled 1154–89).[3] Count William may be William Longsword (Guillaume Longespée), illegitimate son of Henry II, Count of Salisbury after about 1197, or William Marshall, Earl of Pembroke from 1199, or William of Gloucester, or, most likely of all, William of Mandeville,[4] Earl of Essex from 1167 (died 1189).

Marie herself is even more difficult to identify. She may be the illegitimate daughter of Geoffrey of Anjou—and hence a sister of Henry II—who became abbess of Shaftesbury around 1181 and died c. 1216, or the abbess of Reading, or Marie de Meulan, daughter of Count Waleran de Beaumont.[5] It seems unlikely that we shall ever really know who she was. All we can be sure of is that she frequented the court of Henry II and Eleanor, that she was probably a noblewoman (the circle in which she moved, the subjects that concerned her, and the level of her education make it extremely unlikely that she was not of noble birth—a lower-class laywoman would have had little opportunity for education). She was certainly educated, knowing, besides her native French, Latin, from which she translated the *Purgatory,* and English, from which she translated the *Fables*. But even her dates are difficult to determine. If we accept the chronological order of *Lais, Fables, Purgatory,*[6] we are still left with a wide range of years. The *Purgatory* was probably written after 1189 because it mentions a Saint Malachi (l. 2074), who was not canonized until 1189; it may have been done as late as 1208–15.[7] The *Lais* have been dated from 1155–70, by analogy with other literary works that seem to have influenced Marie: Wace's *Brut,* c. 1155, *Piramus et Tisbé,* 1155–60, and *Éneas,* c. 1160.[8] Several critics think that Chrétien knew Marie's *Prologue,* which she wrote after the *Lais,* by the time he wrote *Erec;*[9] if this is so, the *Lais* were probably written by 1170.

We can make such connections with other literary works, but they do not help us with the dating, since we cannot date the analogous works precisely. *Eliduc* was probably a source for Gautier d'Arras's *Ille et Galeron,* dated 1178–85.[10] Denis Piramus mentions Marie's *Lais* in his *Vie S. Edmund le Rei,* saying that they are popular among counts, barons, knights, and ladies (11.35–48); if Denis wrote between 1170 and 1180, as his editor, Kjellman, thinks, the *Lais* must have been written by then. Certainly Marie knew some version of the Tristan legend (she tells part of the story in the *Chevrefoil* and seems to use episodes in other *lais:* the procession of lovely ladies, each mistaken in turn for the heroine, in *Lanval;* the trap of stakes set for the lover in *Yonec;* the secret shrine of love in the woods in *Eliduc*); but whether she knew the Tristan poems that we have—Béroul, Thomas, or some earlier version—we cannot tell.[11] We can only say that Marie probably wrote the *Lais* between 1160 and 1199.[12]

She wrote them all in French, in octosyllabic couplets. For the *Lais,* she drew on Celtic tales, probably oral, and French sources, in some cases written. She seems to have known Ovid and contemporary versions of other classical material, like Wace's *Brut,* the *Roman de Thèbes,* and the *Roman d'Éneas,* as well as Arthurian tales and the Tristan story. The *Fables* draw on at least two versions of the *Romulus,* derived from a Latin version of Aesop; the *Roman de Renart* material; popular tales; and *fabliaux*. The *Purgatory* is a translation of a Latin text, *Tractatus de Purgatori sancti Patricii,* by the monk Henry of Saltrey.

Marie begins the *Fables,* as she does the *Lais,* with a conventional prologue that reveals her sense of moral obligation: those who know letters should give their attention to the books and words of philosophers, who wrote down moral precepts so that others might improve themselves. This didactic purpose is not absent from any of Marie's material. She has translated the *Fables,* she tells us in the epilogue, from English into French as Alfred had translated them from Latin into English, and as Aesop did from Greek into Latin (a popular belief). They are short tales with a moral lesson at the end, using, for the most part, animals as the principal actors, in the Aesopic tradition. The lessons are conventional: the dangers of greed and pride, the oppression of the weak by the strong, the superiority of a simple life over a luxurious one lived in servitude or terror—the *Lais* make many of the same points, but in a far more subtle way. Marie gives several of the *Fables* a feudal twist with the lessons she draws from them: xxvii, a man cannot have honor if he shames his lord, nor can a lord have honor if he shames his men; xix, those who choose bad lords are foolish, for by subjecting themselves to cruel and evil men they gain nothing but shame; lxii, a prince should not have a covetous or deceptive seneschal in his kingdom unless he wants to make him his lord. Some of these lessons are of interest in connection with a recurring theme in Marie's *Lais*—the journey to another land and a new life: ci, no one should put himself in the hands of one who would harm him: rather, he should go to another land; xxii, if you look for a better land, you never find one where you will be without fear or sorrow; lxxx, those who do ill in their own country and depart leave it to no purpose, because they will do the same wherever they go; it is their hearts they should change rather than their countries. This is, indeed, what several of Marie's heroes do.[13]

In *Saint Patrick's Purgatory,* the hero makes a spiritual journey to another land, from which he returns a better Christian. This work, which Marie translated from Latin, has a religious as well as a moral purpose: it was intended not only to help others to improve themselves, but also to teach them to fear and serve God. At the same time, although the subject is overtly otherworldly—the pains of purgatory and the joys of the earthly paradise as seen by an Irish knight—one cannot help, once again, making connections with the *Lais.* The journey through purgatory is described as if it were real, but the narrative is preceded by a comment that suggests it is actually a vision: many souls, we are told, leave their bodies temporarily, have visions or revelations, and then return; they see in the spirit what seems to be corporeal, and they only *seem* to feel the real pains (ll. 163ff.). (One wonders if this is what happens to those characters in the *Lais* who apparently have strange, otherworldly adventures—e.g., in *Guigemar, Lanval,* and *Yonec,* people are transported by magic by the will of those who desire them; it is perhaps only the spirit that goes, and yet the body seems to have the experience.) The Irish knight, after he has repented his sins, approaches purgatory through a deep hole in the earth, following a long, dark passage that finally opens onto a field, where he sees a beautiful house (cf. the tunnel through the hill, then the meadow, and finally the bird-knight's castle in *Yonec*). In the house, monks prepare the knight for the journey he is about to undertake, and for the temptations and torments of the devils he will encounter. He passes through them all—and they are described in graphic and grotesque detail—calling continually on God to defend him. Finally he crosses a bridge that leads to a land of light, where a religious procession welcomes him with joy; the Irish knight may expect to return to this place after he dies, and after he has actually experienced the torments he just witnessed. This paradise, where souls go when they are delivered from the pains of purgatory, is on this earth, in the East; here they will remain until the Last Judgment, when they will go to heaven. It may be the same sort of earthly paradise that Marie has in mind, in the *Lais,* as the homeland of the fairy in *Lanval,* or of the bird-knight in *Yonec*. Her heroes or heroines can experience the joy of such a place only briefly, only as momentary visions, in this life, but that is often enough to sustain them. Lanval alone chooses to relinquish this world and follow his love back to her otherworld; the lady in *Yonec* makes her way to such a land, but is not permitted to remain.

The *Lais* are the one work for which Marie does not claim a literary source. They are tales she has heard and put into rhyme: Celtic tales, which were originally transmitted by Breton minstrels, but whether Marie heard them in French or in Celtic is not altogether clear. She does give some of the names in "Bretan" (*Bisclavret,* l. 3; *Lanval,* l. 4; *Laüstic,* ll. 2–4), which suggests that she knows something of the language, but since she also gives the meaning of some names in English, we cannot assume on that basis that her direct source was Celtic. In any case, she makes it clear that she is the first to put these stories into rhyme, that is, into a conventional literary form, the octosyllabic couplet. She is not the first to render short narratives in verse (the Ovidian tales, *Narcissus* and *Piramus et Tisbé,* antedate the *Lais*), but she may be the first to do it with nonclassical material.

Courtly romances in Marie's period treat Celtic subjects in narrative poems, but they are much longer than Marie's *Lais.* The romances also differ from the *Lais* in that they are concerned with both love and chivalry, with the proper balance between a knight's responsibility to his society, his service to others, and the fulfillment of his own desires while Marie's primary concern is with the personal needs of the knight or—and this is unique in this literature—of the lady. In her *Lais,* the lovers often live in a hostile world—a court that rejects, a marriage that enslaves, social conventions that constrain—and love offers the only opportunity to escape that world; to free the mind, if not the body, from the world's oppression; to endure the pains. This is not to say that every *lai* presents a picture of an ideal love; several (*Equitan, Bisclavret, Laüstic, Chaitivel*) reveal the treachery or selfishness of imperfect love. In fact, as many critics have pointed out, the *Lais* offer a spectrum of love situations.[14] If one goes systematically through the collection, noting the aspect of love that Marie emphasizes in each, one ends with a fairly complete sense of her idea of love, as well as the strong impression that she conceived of the *lais* as complementary pieces.[15] We cannot be sure that the order we follow is the order Marie intended. It is, however, the order given in manuscript (H), which is the earliest extant manuscript, the only one that contains all twelve *Lais,* the one and widely accepted as the best available version; but H is mid-thirteenth-century, not contemporary, and therefore may not reflect the author's plan. Bearing this reservation about the order of the *Lais* in mind, we can nonetheless note obvious correspondences among them, opposing perspectives and variations on the same theme.

The message in the early *lais* seems fairly clear, but as we read further into the collection, and as they resonate more and more with each other, the moral line becomes more ambiguous, more complicated. The first two *lais* (Marie does tell us in so many words that she is beginning with *Guigemar*) offer a fairly straightforward contrast between fulfilling and destructive love. Guigemar is a good knight who lacks only love, which is symbolized by his wound; his lady, trapped in an unhappy marriage with a possessive old man, also lacks love. Guigemar's love frees and fulfills her, her love cures and fulfills him. Neither chivalry nor marriage can function properly without love (in *Milun,* Marie will show how chivalry can interfere with love and marriage). *Guigemar* focuses on the needs of the hero and on the bond between the lovers; there is no relationship, no trust to be broken, between the woman's husband and the hero, and the husband's claims on his wife are undercut by his treatment of her. The love is thus virtually without stain (if somewhat limited in comparison to what we see of love in the last *lais*), as the aid and sanction of supernatural forces suggest. In *Equitan,* the second *lai,* there *is* a bond between the two men (the husband and the lover) that is both personal and public—the husband is the lover's seneschal and serves him loyally, so the king's affair with his wife is at once self-indulgence and a betrayal of a public trust. The wife's moral position is not justified because of any mistreatment; indeed, it is vitiated by her husband's goodness and her possessiveness and ambition. There is no supernatural intervention; on the contrary, the machinations of the lovers are responsible for all that happens. One concludes that, important as love is in the fulfillment of the individual, it is not to be pursued at all costs. The different natures of these two loves—one necessary and true, and ultimately rewarded; the other self-indulgent and treacherous, and finally punished —are pointed up by the ease with which the first is acknowledged (a woman with a good sense of her own and her lover's worth, Guigemar says, need not be begged at length [ll. 513ff.]), while Equitan has to carry on a lengthy debate, filled with ironies, in order to persuade his lady to love him—as if the more words, the less feeling.[16]

Guigemar shows how necessary love is, and how real love can endure the proofs of suffering and separation; *Equitan* shows how a love that arises solely for pleasure, from self-indulgence rather than deep need, can lead to treachery and self-destruction. In the third *lai, Le Fresne,* a love that begins as simple pleasure and physical indulgence rises, through the woman's devotion, to self-sacrifice, which ultimately earns its reward. But in *Bisclavret,* the *lai* which follows *Le Fresne,* the woman cannot attain the degree of devotion her situation requires; instead, fearing for her own safety and unmoved by her husband's suffering, she betrays him and is punished for it. The devotion Fresne shows to her lover, despite his willingness to bow to social pressures and marry another woman, is eventually repaid, not simply by marriage to him, but by reunion with her parents and sister, and a recovery of her identity. Bisclavret's wife, who faces an equally demanding test, fails to pass it. She betrays her husband's love and trust, turns to another man, and incurs lasting shame for herself and her descendants. Bisclavret, like Fresne, lives many years in exile from his true self (Bisclavret as a werewolf, Fresne as a foundling); both had been rejected by women who failed in their family responsibilities, in the first case, that of a wife to her husband, and in the second, that of a mother to her child; both are protected in their defenseless states: Fresne by the abbess who takes her in, Bisclavret by his king, who rescues and sustains him. Marie has extended the scope of her attention to significant human relations beyond the pair of lovers (the family, and the court). The king in *Bisclavret* rewards the loyalty of a good vassal, whom he does not recognize but whose gesture of devotion he appreciates, in contrast to the king Equitan, who abused the loyalty of a faithful minister; in both *Bisclavret* and *Equitan,* the wronged husband is avenged on his wife and survives, a nice balance to the defeat or destruction of the unsympathetically treated husbands in *Guigemar, Yonec,* and *Milun.*

Indeed, Marie attempts to balance her presentations to a

remarkable degree. In the first four *lais,* she seems to be concerned with a sexual balance: a good pair of lovers in *Guigemar,* a bad pair in *Equitan,* a woman's devotion in *Le Fresne,* a man's endurance in *Bisclavret;* a deficient husband and a poor king in *Guigemar* and *Equitan,* a bad mother and treacherous wife in *Le Fresne* and *Bisclavret;* a wise and kind abbess in *Le Fresne,* a sensitive and wise counselor in *Bisclavret.* There is a similar balance in the next pair of *lais:* a knight caught in the trap of a society that refuses to recognize his worth (*Lanval*), a princess imprisoned by the possessive love of a father who will not allow her to marry (*Les Deus Amanz*); both are rescued by a love that is put to public trial, which turns out well in one case, sadly in the other. In both *lais,* there is a king hindered in his public duty by personal ties: in *Lanval,* by subservience to an immoral and vindictive wife, in *Les Deus Amanz,* by possessive attachment to a child.

Although, by subjecting it to public trials, Marie further extends the public aspect of the love in *Lanval* and *Les Deus Amanz* and thus continues the move outwards she made in *Le Fresne* and *Bisclavret* by introducing significant relationships outside the pair of lovers, she ultimately rejects the public setting: both Lanval and the girl in *Deus Amanz* leave their societies in order to follow their loves. Lanval exonerates himself before his court and retains his love because he is able to make a total commitment to that love, which had given him all that the world denied him—wealth, success, and joy—to the extent that he even leaves his world behind to follow it (her) to an unknown world. The girl in *Les Deus Amanz* is unwilling to leave her father and commit herself completely to her love, and therefore she loses her love. But her lover is also at fault: love inspired him with a feeling of unusual strength, with a belief that he could overcome any obstacle, but it also makes him so impatient and reckless that he refuses the help he needs, his strength fails, and he dies. He makes a total commitment in his effort to win the girl, but he refuses the aid she has provided, whereas Lanval graciously accepts all the fairy offers. Marie seems to be saying that one must not only serve love with total devotion, as in *Le Fresne,* but also be ready to receive what love gives.

The source of help in *Lanval* is supernatural, a fairy's powers; in *Les Deus Amanz,* it is the human knowledge and skill of the Salerno doctor (another woman). Marie alternates supernatural force with human ingenuity throughout the *lais;* the supernatural is usually positive or helpful to the lovers (as in *Guigemar* [I], *Lanval* [V], *Yonec* [VII]), while the human is usually treacherous or destructive (as in *Equitan* [II], *Les Deus Amanz* [VI], and *Laustic* [VIII]). Always maintaining her sense of balance, Marie reverses the situation in *Le Fresne* (III) and *Bisclavret* (IV).

There is another kind of alternation at work in *Lanval* and *Les Deus Amanz*—between a love that is taken seriously (*Lanval*) and a love that has comic or parodistic overtones (*Les Deus Amanz*). The same is true of the next pair: the love in *Yonec* is serious and tragic; the love in *Laustic* is superficial and frustrated. The former, however, is fruitful, while the latter issues only in a dead symbol. In both *Laustic* and *Les Deus Amanz* the lovers play at love; in *Les Deus Amanz,* they fail because they don't really understand the game, and in *Laustic,* they only go through the motions without real feeling.

Yonec and *Laustic* return to the love situation of the first *lais* in the collection, the triangle: as in *Guigemar,* there is an unhappy marriage in *Yonec,* with a lover coming magically from afar; in *Laustic,* as in *Equitan,* there is a self-indulgent affair in which the lover is bound by friendship to the husband. In this set of *lais,* however, the husband is a much more active figure and his action introduces considerable violence into the two stories. The lover in *Yonec,* who appears in the form of a bird, is killed in a vicious trap laid by the husband, who is himself killed, many years later, by the lover's son—violence begets violence; in *Laustic,* the bird, which symbolizes the love is killed viciously by the husband. In *Yonec,* the lover leaves a trail of blood which his lady follows; in *Laustic,* the bird's blood stains the lady's gown. In both *lais,* the husband is a hunter, a predator, and the lovers are his victims; and in both, it is the joy felt by the lady that makes her husband aware of her love and arouses his desire to destroy it. Marie is saying that love does not exist in a vacuum, that even a good love is vulnerable to the hostility of the world around it. In *Laustic,* however, the lady's joy is superficial, represented by the feigned delight in the nightingale's song; the love is nothing more than an exchange of gifts and words, and at the first threat of danger, the attack on the bird, both lovers give it up, relegating it to the symbol of the dead bird in an ornate coffin. Theirs is a stillborn love, with no issue, while the love in *Yonec,* though it ends tragically for the lover, does not die with him; the bird-knight is killed, but his child lives to avenge him. Thus, as in *Guigemar,* because the need for love is real and the love good, it cannot be completely destroyed by the hostile world. The world around the lovers seems to become more and more of an obstacle or a threat in these *lais;* but at the same time, the love, when it is good, lasts and is fruitful.

In *Milun,* the *lai* that follows *Yonec* and *Laustic* and is thematically linked to them by the motif of a bird (in this case a messenger of love), a child is also born of the love; he grows up not to avenge his father, but to meet him in combat, and to reunite him with his mother. The *lais* that present negative aspects of love do not extend over a long period of time, indicating perhaps that the situations they describe, of self-indulgent or superficial feeling, are static, while in the other *lais* the love is active and aids the individual to grow. The time span in the *lais* which present positive aspects of love seems, in contrast, to increase through the collection: in the first, *Guigemar,* we see a lover grow from an unfeeling adolescent to a loving adult; in *Le Fresne,* the heroine grows from a foundling to a loving woman; in *Yonec,* a child is born and grows up to avenge his father; in *Milun,* the child grows up to reunite his long-separated parents. Actually, in *Milun,* the peacefully resolved combat with the father indicates that the father has finally grown up. Chivalry must, as it were, defeat itself before love can function fully.

Milun, and the *lai* that follows it, *Chaitivel,* are both concerned with fighting for glory and the relation between chivalry and love, which is normally a romance subject, but not treated here as it would be in a romance. Marie does not seek a balance between chivalry and love, but shows instead how chivalry—when it means only the pursuit of worldly glory—interferes with love, seriously in *Milun,* humorously in *Chaitivel* (again that balance). In *Milun,* all the characters (father, mother, and son) are caught up in the pursuit of glory—glory is what first attracts the girl to the knight, what separates them, and what finally brings the father and the son together when both become rivals for the same reputation. It is only the son's compassion for his father's white hair that prevents serious tragedy; human feeling in the issue of the love finally defeats the desire for glory that had for so long stood in its way.

There is, however, another element at work in the *lai,* which counters the violence of fighting—the written word. When the lovers cannot be together, they correspond for twenty years. We are moving, here, toward a higher level of understanding between lovers, a communication of thought which serves when physical consummation is impossible (cf. Tristan and Isolt in *Chevrefoil*). That words are meant to replace physical force is underscored by the arrival of a letter announcing the death of the mother's husband just as the son prepares to go and kill him. The same opposition between words and arms is presented in *Chaitivel:* the four lovers attempt to win the lady's love by fighting, but they try too hard; three of them are killed and the fourth incapacitated. The lady, who glories in their devotion, attempts to comfort the remaining lover with her conversation, and assuages her own grief by composing a poem about it. The whole *lai* reveals the foolishness of literary conventions of love—indeed, both *lais, Milun* and *Chaitivel,* expose the futility of the romantic view of knightly service for love.

In the following *lai,* the *Chevrefoil,* unsatisfied love is again the inspiration for a poem, but in this case, the lover transcends his sorrow at the enforced separation by writing a *lai* that records the joy he experienced when the lovers were together. He transforms love to art in his *lai* as Marie does in hers. Tristan and Isolt are able to meet for only a brief moment—the rest of their life is bitter pain—but they manage to derive great joy from the words they exchange, which is all they can hope for in this life. In *Eliduc,* too, though the lovers by mutual consent renounce the world in order to give their lives to God, words remain their one point of contact; they send messages back and forth and offer prayers to God for each other, a higher form, perhaps, of the *lai* in which Tristan records his love, but not unrelated. In the last four *lais* of the collection, the word seems to replace supernatural forces and human ingenuity (which alternately dominated the earlier *lais*) as the symbol or expression of the love Marie is describing. The spirit of the love, freed from physical and worldly concerns, is conveyed by the characters' words, as it is by Marie's poetry. Magic symbolized their feelings, words express them. The ability to commit the feelings to words indicates a control, perhaps even a transcendence, of them.

The separation of the lovers in *Milun,* dictated by the demands of the world, of chivalry and marriage, lasts twenty years: in *Chaitivel,* the separation, forced by death and physical disability, is final; in *Chevrefoil,* the separation is caused by social pressures of the woman's marriage, as in *Milun,* but further complicated by Tristan's relation to her husband, and it is lifelong, broken only by brief encounters. The separation in the last *lai, Eliduc,* is brought about by renunciation. First the wife renounces her husband and her worldly life, and then the lovers renounce their marriage and the world; all three make their sacrifices in favor of a higher love. Paradoxically, however, their renunciation of the physical union and of the world draws them all closer together in a selfless love. This *lai,* which centers like so many others on a love triangle, resolves the problem in a unique way, by rearranging the three characters in three successive pairings, ending with the two women living together as sisters in a convent. This *lai,* which is the longest, also resolves various earlier themes: the knight wronged by his king, as in *Lanval,* is vindicated and restored; in exile he fights, not for his own glory, but to defend another king from attack; nature, not magic or human ingenuity, offers the means to revive the princess. At the same time, *Eliduc* presents complicated human situations, which cannot easily be resolved: we are not allowed the simple expedient of a vicious spouse to enable us to sympathize with the lovers; the two women, the devoted wife and the naïve girl, both command our sympathy. Even the knight, who is weak, indulgent, and sometimes violent in his pursuit of the new love, cannot simply be condemned—he is wrongly exiled, but serves both his own and his adopted lands well, and falls naturally enough into a relationship that offers him human comfort (something we have been taught to applaud in other *lais*). As in *Chevrefoil,* we are forced to acknowledge the demands and pressures of society, of knightly service and marriage, even when they conflict with love. Yet even here Marie does not insist on a total renunciation of human love—how could she when she has been at such pains to teach its values and show its positive effects?—but she does offer other possibilities when physical satisfaction is impossible: art and religious devotion.

In the course of the *lais,* Marie presents a realistic picture of human love despite, or perhaps partly by means of, the supernatural trappings.[17] Love offers joy, but never altogether without pain, and regardless of its strength, it cannot last forever. Note how often death intervenes, particularly in the later *lais: Les Deus Amanz, Yonec, Laustic, Chaitivel;* in *Equitan* the lovers also die, albeit deservedly; in *Chevrefoil* their death is forecast; and in *Lanval* and *Eliduc* they move into another life. Throughout the *lais,* the world—in the shape of jealous husbands, possessive fathers, selfish wives or mothers, ungrateful lords—seems hostile to the lovers. Often it imprisons them: the wives in *Guigemar* and *Yonec* in towers; the wife in *Laustic* in her house; the women in *Milun* and *Chevrefoil* in their marriages; the man in *Bisclavret* in his wolf form; the girl in *Eliduc* in a deathlike trance; the girl in *Les Deus Amanz* by the impossible task her father sets her suitors. The lovers are exiled, outcast, rejected: Guigemar, because of his wound, becomes a stranger in a foreign land; Fresne is rejected first by her mother, who abandons her to strangers, and later by her lover; Bisclavret as a werewolf is shut out of human society; the court ostracized Lanval and he, in turn, rejects it; the lover in *Yonec* is a stranger from another land, the lady an outsider in his; Milun exiles himself from his love in order to pursue glory; in *Chaitivel,* death permanently exiles three of the lovers; Tristan lives in permanent exile; Eliduc, banished by his king at the beginning of the *lai,* exiles himself from the world at the end.

Exile necessitates a journey to another land, sometimes another world, and Marie seems to imply that love *is* ultimately of another world.[18] It may sometimes bring freedom to those who are confined, as it does to the women in *Guigemar* and in *Yonec*—they are able to leave their towers without difficulty when they decide to follow their love—but it cannot survive being constrained within a small space, as in *Laustic*.[19] It must have some issue—if not a child, as in *Yonec* and *Milun,* then a symbol, such as the flowers in *Les Deus Amanz* or the enshrined bird in *Laustic,* which represent loves that, for different reasons, never fully lived; or poetry, whether the vain affirmation of the lady's triumph in *Chaitivel,* or the living recollection of real joy in *Chevrefoil.*

Marie develops her ideas not by direct statement but through symbols, by emphasizing small but significant details.[20] The genre she chose to write in, the *lai,* because it is so much shorter than the romance, the other available narrative form for similar subjects, necessitates the focus on details. The first clue she gives us to the meaning of a *lai* is often its title, about which she makes a considerable fuss, sometimes giving alternatives, as in *Chaitivel,* where the two names indicate two perspectives: the lady's (she wants to call it *Quatre Dols,* the *Four Sorrows,* to commemorate all her admirers), and the man's (he insists on *Chaitivel,* the *Unfortunate One,* meaning himself). The last *lai* also has two names; formerly *Eliduc,* it is now known as *Guildeluec and Gualadun:* that is, for Marie it is more the story of the two women than of the man. Sometimes a name makes an ironic comment on the story, as in *Equitan* and perhaps *Le Fresne* (Equitan lowers himself, improperly, to a position of equality with his seneschal by making love to the latter's wife and leaving the seneschal to run the kingdom; Fresne, the ash tree, suggests a whole range of nurture and abandonment—see the comments on the *lai,* p. 90.)[21] For some *lais,* Marie supplies the title in several languages, as though to point up the universality of the situation (*Bisclavret, Laustic, Chevrefoil*). In some cases, the name serves as a symbol of the love: Laustic is the nightingale, dead but richly preserved; in *Chevrefoil,* the honeysuckle evokes the two lives bound together; Yonec is the child born of the love. In *Les Deus Amanz,* as in *Chaitivel,* the lovers are not named, but Marie makes much of the names of the places where the story occurs, suggesting that the lovers are, in effect, dominated by the world around them, which eventually overwhelms them. Marie makes it a point to recall the name of each *lai,* usually at its end. She reminds us, both at the beginning and at the end of most of the *lais,* that they are stories she has heard and recast: that is, she never lets us forget that she is the intermediary between us and the material. It is not unusual for medieval writers to call attention to themselves and to the authority of their versions (cf. Gottfried in *Tristan,* Wolfram in *Parzival*), because for the most part they were dealing with material that existed in other versions, and they were anxious to have their audience appreciate what they had brought to it.

In addition to its title, the symbolic object that is central to the narrative is often an indication of a *lai*'s meaning. The knot and belt which the lovers exchange in *Guigemar* represent the deep feeling and constancy of their love, a commitment that will endure for having been so freely given. It is significant that they do not exchange the conventional token of constancy, a ring, for Marie often uses rings ironically: in *Equitan,* the lovers exchange this standard symbol of loyalty while plotting to betray two loyalties, one to a husband, the other to a vassal; in *Le Fresne,* the ring the mother bestows on her abandoned child is a reminder of the bond that she denied; in *Milun, Chaitivel,* and *Eliduc,* the ring is the first token of love, the first sign of attraction and interest, but, as it happens, not necessarily of lasting devotion; and in *Eliduc,* the man's acceptance of a ring constitutes a denial of his marriage bond. In *Yonec,* the dying lover gives his lady a ring with the power to make her husband forget what has happened—scarcely a symbol of loyalty, however sympathetic we may be to the love.

In three successive *lais,* birds offer a symbolic comment on a love relationship: in *Yonec,* the lover appears in the form of a hawk; in *Laustic,* a live nightingale stands for the lover (in the lady's excuse to her husband), the dead bird, a lifeless object in a rich shrine, stands for the love; in *Milun,* a starving swan is the messenger of love, carrying letters between the lovers for twenty years. In both *Yonec* and *Milun,* the bird symbol gives way to a child, who, in *Yonec,* is all that remains of the union; while in *Milun* the child becomes the agent that reunites the lovers. The love in *Laustic* lacked the substance—not the opportunity, for in Marie will creates opportunity—to bear fruit, so its lifeless symbol is fittingly worshiped as though it had value.

The honeysuckle, which winds itself around the hazel so that neither can exist alone, just as Tristan and Isolt are bound together by their love, is the dominant symbol of *Chevrefoil;* one wonders what connection there is between the hazel of the metaphor in *Chevrefoil* and the names of the twins, Ash and Hazel, in *Le Fresne.* Marie does not mention the love potion which plays such an important part in other versions of the Tristan story, but she does use a potion in *Les Deus*

Amanz, not to arouse love or passion but to strengthen the love that already exists, and to enable it both to meet the challenges it faces and to bear fruit; since it is never drunk by the hero, the only fruit it produces are the flowers that grow where it spilled. It is tempting to see this potion as a comment on the Tristan story, perhaps even as an anti-potion.

A final important symbol is the hunt, an activity at once opposed to and emblematic of the love quest. Guigemar's hunting results in a self-inflicted wound that only a woman—his future mistress—can cure; Equitan avoids his public responsibility by hunting in the forest and violates feudal loyalty by "hunting" his seneschal's wife. Bisclavret has a pivotal hunting scene with the hero as the prey, while in *Yonec* the husband sets a trap for the bird-knight by announcing his plans to go hunting, and then leaving spikes in the window to catch the lover. The medieval nobility's passion for hunting combined with the Ovidian connotations of the love hunt and the predatory aspect of selfish passion make the hunt a particularly effective symbol in the *lais.* The hunter may play the role of the jealous, possessive husband, with the hero, in the form of an animal, but a predatory one, as the prey.

Since we lack precise or complete information about Marie's dependence on and transformation of earlier narrative material, especially Celtic, we cannot accurately judge the extent of her influence on the creators of subsequent *lais* (i.e., short narratives about love and sometimes adventure, whether or not they are called *lais* by their authors). There are, however, many *lais* and romances whose direct debts to Marie have been widely accepted.[22] Nine of the *lais* are more or less closely translated into Old Norse in a thirteenth-century manuscript now in the library of the University of Uppsala, Sweden. In Middle English, there is a truncated translation of *Le Fresne,* and three versions of *Lanval,* two from the fourteenth century and, the best known, Thomas Chestre's *Launfal Miles,* from the fifteenth. The story of *Laustic* is retold in the late twelfth-century English poem *The Owl and the Nightingale,* in Alexander of Neckham's thirteenth-century *De naturis rerum* and in the fourteenth-century *Roman de Renart le contrefait,* which also contains a story apparently influenced by *Bisclavret.* We also see *Bisclavret*'s influence in the thirteenth-century *lai* of *Melion.*

The anonymous thirteenth-century *lais* of *Tyolet, Tydorel,* and *Guingamor,* attributed to Marie by early editors, all show Marie's influence, with *Guingamor* owing debts to *Guigemar* and *Lanval. Lanval* was especially popular; beside the Middle English versions already mentioned, its influence appears within longer poems in Middle High German and Italian. Other long narratives inspired by Marie's *lais* include Gautier d'Arras' *Ille et Galeron,* almost certainly based on *Eliduc,*[23] Hue de Roteland's *Ipomedon* (c. 1185), where brothers who are unknown to each other meet in chivalric combat and discover their kinship thanks to a ring given to one of them by their mother (cf. *Milun*) and Jean Renart's *Galeran de Bretagne* (c. 1230), based on *Le Fresne.* Several elements of the plot of *Partenopeu de Blois* (1180–1190?)—the white deer, the pilotless ship that takes the hero to his future mistress, their discovery after a period of secret love—recall *Guigemar,* but both versions may have a common source, now lost.

The greatest Middle English "Breton *lai,*" *Sir Orfeo,* is, according to its most recent editor, A. J. Bliss, a fourteenth-century translation of a lost French original; Bliss also argues for a common authorship of *Orfeo* and the Middle English translation of *Le Fresne* (*Lay le Freyne*).[24] Geoffrey Chaucer appears to have known *Sir Orfeo* and used its prologue for his version of a Breton *lai,* the Franklin's Tale.[25] Chaucer's interest in the problems created for a faithful wife by her husband's departure from home in quest of chivalric honor recalls the situation of *Milun,* but there exists no evidence to support a suggestion that he knew, directly or in translation, Marie's *lais.*

The influence of Marie's *lais* was by no means negligible in later medieval generations. A more recent debt to Marie may be noted in closing: John Fowles' collection of tales, *The Ebony Tower* (1974), is in part based on *Eliduc;* in a "personal note," the author pays tribute to Marie, speaks about her life and her art, and appends a translation of *Eliduc* into prose.[26]

The twelve *lais* are found in one mid-thirteenth-century manuscript (H), British Museum, Harley 978, in the order followed in this translation. Nine of the *lais,* in a different order, are preserved in a late-thirteenth-century manuscript (S), Bibliothèque nationale, nouv. acq. fr. 1104. Fragments or single *lais* appear in three other thirteenth- and fourteenth-century manuscripts: (P), Bibl. nat. fr. 2168; (C), British Museum Cott. Vesp. B XIV; (Q), Bibl. nat. fr. 24432. The Warnke edition (1900) follows (H) with additions from (S) and (P); Ewert (1947) and Rychner (1966) follow (H), and Rychner includes a few passages from (S). We have followed Ewert's text (H) in this translation, checked against Rychner.

Marie's language is quite simple, and therefore difficult to render in good literary English. There are few complex sentences and little use of the passive voice. Marie wrote in octosyllabic couplets, a form which cannot be reproduced in English without a distorting, singsong effect. We have, therefore, chosen the standard English expedient of free verse, giving the translation line by line (except for a few unavoidable transpositions) in order to catch something, however little, of the poetic quality of the original. Marie rarely names the characters in her tales and often refers to them by pronouns; where this creates confusion, we have substituted a noun or, when possible, a name. She often shifts from one scene to another with no indication other than "but" or "then"; the reader must be alert to such changes.

The translation remains close to the text, allowing for idiomatic differences between Middle French and modern English (e.g., *soz ciel* may be translated "on earth," rather than "beneath heaven"). Where Marie seems to give a word particular importance by repeating it, we repeat it in the translation. On the other hand, the stylistic device of paired synonyms, not uncommon in twelfth-century French poetry, we have respected only where it does not distort English usage. But words like *aventure,* which can mean "adventure," "chance," or "happening," are translated differently according to the context. *Chambre* is rendered as "chamber" or "room" depending on whether the reference seems to be formal or intimate. *Curteis* is usually translated as "courteous," although it carries the sense of "courtly." Where the verb tenses shift between past and present, as is common in medieval French texts, we have retained in accordance with English narrative usage a single tense throughout a passage. The titles of the *lais* are given in French with the English translation in parentheses, unless the title is a proper name.

We are especially indebted to Lawton P. G. Peckham for his generous and careful reading of the translations and his most helpful suggestions; any errors that may have crept in are the responsibility of the translators. We extend thanks as well to John Thaxton of E.P. Dutton for his interest in this translation, his suggestions for improving it, and his labors to bring it to early publication.

1. For the most reliable up-to-date information about Marie and her works, see E. J. Mickel, Jr., *Marie de France* (New York: Twayne, 1974).

2. E. Winkler identified her with Marie de Champagne, daughter of Louis VII and Eleanor, but this is not generally accepted. (For full reference, see bibliography.)

3. E. Levi argues for his son, Henri au Court Mantel, crowned in 1171, died 1183, but this identification has had little support from other scholars.

4. Strong arguments are made for William of Mandeville by Ahlström and Painter, which are accepted by Mickel, Brugger, and Rychner, e.g., that the clerks of the exchequer often referred to him simply as Count William, as Marie does in her dedication of the fables, while other nobles were named by their counties. Recently Antoinette Knapton suggested William of Warren, in a paper delivered at the Courtly Literature Society meeting, San Francisco, Dec. 27, 1975.

5. Fox, Ewert, and Wind, support the abbess of Shaftesbury; Levi opts for the abbess of Reading, Holmes and Whichard for Marie de Meulan, and Knapton for Marie de Boulogne, younger daughter of King Stephen of England, abbess of Ramsey, later married to Matieu of Flanders.

6. Both Ewert and Rychner, recent editors of the *Lais,* accept this order.

7. See Mickel, p. 17, on the later date.

8. Ewert and Illingworth date them 1155–70, Rychner, 1160–70.

9. Ewert, Illingworth and Rychner, in particular.

10. Fourrier dates *Ille* c. 1178; Mickel gives it a *terminus post quem* of 1185.

11. Béroul's poem may have been written in some form as early as 1165, but references in the extant version put it as late as 1191. If one dates Thomas

1160–65, Marie may have known his poem, as Hoepffner, Levi and Wind think; Martineau-Génieys thinks Thomas wrote after Marie and drew on her work.

12. Mickel notes that Lanval is mentioned in *Guillaume de Dole,* written c. 1200, and that Dol was no longer an archbishopric, as it is referred to in *Fresne,* after 1199, so the *lai* must have been written by then.

13. Mickel points to a number of similarities between the fables and the *lais,* in narrative methods, in the attitude towards reality, in feudal morality, p. 37.

14. See Spitzer, Mickel ("A Reconsideration"), and Damon, the latter for a psychological analysis of the *lais.*

15. See Frey.

16. For a similar phenomenon in Chrétien de Troyes, see W. T. H. Jackson, "Problems of Communication in the Romances of Chrétien de Troyes," *Medieval Literature and Folklore Studies: essays in honor of F. L. Utley,* ed. J. Mandel and B. A. Rosenberg (New Brunswick: Rutgers University Press, 1970), pp. 39–50.

17. See M. H. Ferguson, for an interesting study of Marie's use of folklore motifs and her twisting of the conventional story patterns in order to present the realistic view.

18. See H. S. Robertson, "Love and the Other World." Mickel notes that the courtly elite enclosed themselves in a world forbidden to the profane on the spiritual level, not unlike the other-world in Celtic myth, *Marie de France,* p. 64.

19. See Cotrell.

20. See Stevens.

21. See Mickel, "Marie de France's Use of Irony."

22. Much of this material on her influence is taken from Ewert's introduction and notes to his edition.

23. See P. Nykrog, "Two Creators of Narrative Form in Twelfth Century France: Gautier d'Arras—Chrétien de Troyes," *Speculum* 48 (1973), 258–76, for a discussion of Gautier's use of Marie's *lai.*

24. *Sir Orfeo,* ed. A. J. Bliss (Oxford University Press, 1954), pp. xxxif., xliv–xlvii.

25. See L. H. Loomis, "Chaucer and the Breton Lays of the Auchinleck MS," *Studies in Philology,* 38 (1941), 18–29.

26. John Fowles, *The Ebony Tower* (New York: New American Lib., repr. 1975), pp. 107–133.

Prologue

Whoever has received knowledge
and eloquence in speech from God
should not be silent or secretive
but demonstrate it willingly.
5 When a great good is widely heard of,
then, and only then, does it bloom,
and when that good is praised by many,
it has spread its blossoms.
The custom among the ancients—
10 as Priscian testifies—
was to speak quite obscurely
in the books they wrote,
so that those who were to come after
and study them
15 might gloss the letter
and supply its significance from their own wisdom.
Philosophers knew this,
they understood among themselves
that the more time they spent,
20 the more subtle their minds would become[1]
and the better they would know how to keep themselves
from whatever was to be avoided.
He who would guard himself from vice
should study and understand
25 and begin a weighty work
by which he might keep vice at a distance,
and free himself from great sorrow.
That's why I began to think
about composing some good stories
30 and translating from Latin to Romance;

1. In this reading we have followed Mickel's suggestion, to ignore the emendation of *trespassereit* and take the (H) reading *trespasserunt* ("The Unity and Significance of Marie's Prologue"). The other way, these lines would mean "the more time went by, the more difficult the sense became, and the more care they must take to find what might be overlooked."

but that was not to bring me fame:
too many others have done it.
Then I thought of the *lais* I'd heard.
I did not doubt, indeed I knew well,
35 that those who first began them[2]
and sent them forth
composed them in order to preserve
adventures they had heard.
I have heard many told;
40 and I don't want to neglect or forget them.
To put them into word[3] and rhyme
I've often stayed awake.

In your honor, noble King,
who are so brave and courteous,
45 repository of all joys
in whose heart all goodness takes root,
I undertook to assemble these *lais*
to compose and recount them in rhyme.
In my heart I thought and determined,
50 sire, that I would present them to you.
If it pleases you to receive them,
you will give me great joy;
I shall be happy forever.
Do not think me presumptuous
55 if I dare present them to you.
Now hear how they begin.

2. The order of the next four lines has been shifted; in the French ll. 37–38 precede ll. 35–36.

3. *Ditié* can be a moral saying or a song. It may refer to the *surplus*, the glossed meaning, what Robertson calls the doctrinal content, or to the fact that the *lais* were sung, cf. *Guigemar*, ll. 885–86.

Guigemar

Whoever deals with good material
feels pain if it's treated improperly.
Listen, my lords, to the words of Marie,
who does not forget her responsibilities when her turn comes.[1]

5 People should praise anyone
who wins admiring comments for herself.
But anywhere there is
a man or a woman of great worth,
people who envy their good fortune
10 often say evil things about them;
they want to ruin their reputations.
Thus they act like
vicious, cowardly dogs
who bite people treacherously.
15 I don't propose to give up because of that;
if spiteful critics or slanderers
wish to turn my accomplishments against me,
they have a right to their evil talk.
The tales—and I know they're true—
20 from which the Bretons made their *lais*
I'll now recount for you briefly;
and at the very beginning of this enterprise,
just the way it was written down,
I'll relate an adventure
25 that took place in Brittany,
in the old days.
At that time, Hoel ruled Brittany,
sometimes peacefully, sometimes at war.
The king had a vassal

1. The French *en sun tens* could also be rendered, "in her day"; Rychner opts for this sense, seeing in it an implied contrast between Marie as a modern writer and the ancient writers and sages referred to in the Prologue to the whole collection.

30 who was lord of Leonnais;
his name was Oridial
and he was on very intimate terms with his lord.
A worthy and valiant knight,
he had, by his wife, two children,
35 a son and a beautiful daughter.
The girl's name was Noguent;
they called the boy Guigemar.
There wasn't a more handsome youngster in the kingdom.
His mother had a wonderful love for him,
40 and his father a great devotion;
when he could bring himself to part with the boy,
his father sent him to serve the king.
The boy was intelligent and brave,
and made himself loved by all.
45 When his time of probation was at an end,
and he was mature in body and mind,
the king dubbed him knight,
giving him luxurious armor, which was exactly what he desired.
Guigemar left the court,
50 but not before dispensing many rich gifts.
He journeyed to Flanders to seek his fame;
there was always a war, or a battle raging there.
Neither in Lorraine nor in Burgundy,
in Anjou nor in Gascony,
55 could one find, in those days,
Guigemar's equal as a fine knight.
But in forming him nature had so badly erred
that he never gave any thought to love.
There wasn't a lady or a maid on earth,
60 no matter how noble, or how beautiful,
who wouldn't have willingly granted him her love,
had he asked her for it.
Many maids asked him,
but he wasn't interested in such things;
65 no one could discover in him
the slightest desire to love.

Therefore both friends and strangers
gave him up for lost.
At the height of his fame,
70 this baron, Guigemar, returned to his own land
to visit his father and his lord,
his good mother and his sister,
all of whom were most eager to see him.
Guigemar stayed with them,
75 I believe, an entire month.
Then he was seized by a desire to hunt;
that night he summoned his companions in arms,
his huntsmen, and his beaters;
next morning he set out for the woods
80 to indulge in the sport that gave him much pleasure.
They gathered in pursuit of a great stag;
the dogs were unleashed.
The hunters ran ahead
while the young man lingered behind;
85 a squire carried his bow,
his hunting knife, and his quiver.[2]
He wanted to fire some arrows, if he had the opportunity,
before he left that spot.
In the thickest part of a great bush
90 Guigemar saw a hind with a fawn;
a completely white beast,
with deer's antlers on her head.
Spurred by the barking of the dogs, she sprang into the open.
Guigemar took his bow and shot at her,
95 striking her in the breastbone.[3]
She fell at once,
but the arrow rebounded,
gave Guigemar such a wound—
it went through his thigh right into the horse's flank—

2. As practiced by the medieval aristocracy, the hunt proceeded according to precise, complicated rules that governed the actions of each participant.

3. "Breastbone": so Rychner glosses *esclot;* Ewert reads, "front hoof."

100 that he had to dismount.
He collapsed on the thick grass
beside the hind he'd struck.
The hind, wounded as she was,
suffered pain and groaned.
105 Then she spoke, in this fashion:
"Alas! I'm dying!
And you, vassal, who wounded me,
this be your destiny:
may you never get medicine for your wound!
110 Neither herb nor root,
neither physician nor potion,
will cure you
of that wound in your thigh,
until a woman heals you,
115 one who will suffer, out of love for you,
pain and grief
such as no woman ever suffered before.
And out of love for her, you'll suffer as much;
the affair will be a marvel
120 to lovers, past and present,
and to all those yet to come.
Now go away, leave me in peace!"
Guigemar was badly wounded;
what he had heard dismayed him.
125 He began to consider carefully
what land he might set out for
to have his wound healed.
He didn't want to remain there and die.
He knew, he reminded himself,
130 that he'd never seen a woman
to whom he wanted to offer his love,
nor one who could cure his pain.
He called his squire to him;
"Friend," he said, "go quickly!
135 Bring my companions back here;
I want to talk to them."

The squire rode off and Guigemar remained;
he complained bitterly to himself.
Making his shirt into a bandage,
140 he bound his wound tightly;
Then he mounted his horse and left that spot.
He was anxious to get far away;
he didn't want any of his men to come along,
who might interfere, or try to detain him.
145 Through the woods he followed
a grassy path, which led him
out into open country; there, at the edge of the plain,
he saw a cliff and a steep bank
overlooking a body of water below:
150 a bay that formed a harbor.
There was a solitary ship in the harbor;
Guigemar saw its sail.
It was fit and ready to go,
calked outside and in—
155 no one could discover a seam in its hull.
Every deck rail and peg
was solid ebony;
no gold under the sun could be worth more.
The sail was pure silk;
160 it would look beautiful when unfurled.
The knight was troubled;
he had never heard it said
anywhere in that region
that ships could land there.
165 He went down to the harbor
and, in great pain, boarded the ship.
He expected to discover men inside,
guarding the vessel,
but he saw no one, no one at all.
170 Amidships he found a bed
whose posts and frame

were wrought in the fashion of Solomon,[4]
of cypress and ivory,
with designs in inlaid gold.
175 The quilt on the bed was made
of silken cloth, woven with gold.
I don't know how to estimate the value of the other bedclothes,
but I'll tell you this much about the pillow:
whoever rested his head on it
180 would never have white hair.
The sable bedspread
was lined with Alexandrian silk.
Two candelabra of fine gold—
the lesser of the two worth a fortune—
185 were placed at the head of the cabin,
lighted tapers placed in them.
Guigemar, astonished by all this,
reclined on the bed
and rested; his wound hurt.
190 Then he rose and tried to leave the ship,
but he couldn't return to land.
The vessel was already on the high seas,
carrying him swiftly with it.
A good, gentle wind was blowing,
195 so turning back now was out of the question.
Guigemar was very upset; he didn't know what to do.
It's no wonder he was frightened,
especially as his wound was paining him a great deal.
Still, he had to see the adventure through.
200 He prayed to God to watch over him,
to use his power to bring him back to land,
and to protect him from death.

4. Rychner notes that this term referred during the Middle Ages to a certain type of inlaid work. There is, however, also a widely diffused medieval legend about a marvelous ship made by Solomon that intrudes into some versions of the story of the Grail, and moreover the description of the bed contains reminiscences of the biblical Song of Solomon (see Ewert's note).

He lay down on the bed, and fell asleep.
That day he'd survived the worst;
205 before sundown he would arrive
at the place where he'd be cured—
near an ancient city,
the capital of its realm.
The lord who ruled over that city
210 was a very aged man who had a wife,
a woman of high lineage,
noble, courteous, beautiful, intelligent;
he was extremely jealous,
which accorded with his nature.
215 (All old folk are jealous;
every one of them hates the thought of being cuckolded,
such is the perversity of age.)
The watch he kept over her was no joke.
The grove beneath the tower
220 was enclosed all around
with walls of green marble,
very high and thick.
There was only one entrance,
and it was guarded day and night.
225 On the other side, the sea enclosed it;
no one could enter, no one leave,
except by means of a boat,
as the castle might require it.
Inside the castle walls,
230 the lord had built a chamber—
none more beautiful anywhere—to keep his wife under guard—
At its entrance was a chapel.
The room was painted with images all around;
Venus the goddess of love
235 was skillfully depicted in the painting,
her nature and her traits were illustrated,
whereby men might learn how to behave in love,
and to serve love loyally.
Ovid's book, the one in which he instructs

240 lovers how to control their love,
was being thrown by Venus into a fire,
and she was excommunicating all those
who ever perused this book
or followed its teachings.[5]
245 That's where the wife was locked up.
Her husband had given her
a girl to serve her,
one who was noble and well educated—
she was his niece, the daughter of his sister.[6]
250 There was great affection between the two women.
She stayed with her mistress when he went off,
remaining with her until he returned.
No one else came there, man or woman,
nor could the wife leave the walls of the enclosure.
255 An old priest, hoary with age,
kept the gate key;
he'd lost his nether member
or he wouldn't have been trusted.
He said mass for her
260 and served her her food.
That same day, as soon as she rose from a nap,
the wife went into the grove;
she had slept after dinner,
and now she set out to amuse herself,
265 taking her maid with her.
Looking out to sea,
they saw the ship on the rising tide
come sailing into the harbor.
They could see nothing guiding it.
270 The lady started to flee—

5. The book in question is Ovid's *Remedia amoris* (Remedies for Love), a companion volume to the Roman poet's equally tongue-in-cheek *Ars amatoria*. E. J. Mickel notes the irony of this mural, presumably commissioned by the husband to encourage his wife to love him, but, as Marie describes it, predictive of the coming relationship between Guigemar and the young wife.

6. The French text is ambiguous as to whether the girl is the niece of the husband or the wife.

it's not surprising if she was afraid;
her face grew red from fear.
But the girl, who was wise
and more courageous,
275 comforted and reassured her,
and they went toward the water, fast as they could.
The damsel removed her cloak,
and boarded the beautiful ship.
She found no living thing
280 except the sleeping knight.
She saw how pale he was and thought him dead;
she stopped and looked at him.
Then she went back
quickly, and called her mistress,
285 told her what she'd found,
and lamented the dead man she'd seen.
The lady answered, "Let's go see him!
If he's dead, we'll bury him;
the priest will help us.
290 If I find that he's alive, he'll tell us all about this."
Without tarrying any longer, they returned together,
the lady first, then the girl.
When the lady entered the ship,
she stopped in front of the bed.
295 She examined the knight,
lamenting his beauty and fine body;
she was full of sorrow on his account,
and said it was a shame he'd died so young.
She put her hand on his breast,
300 and felt that it was warm, and his heart healthy,
beating beneath his ribs.
The knight, who was only asleep,
now woke up and saw her;
he was delighted, and greeted her—
305 he realized he'd come to land.
The lady, upset and weeping,
answered him politely

and asked him how
he got there, what country he came from,
310 if he'd been exiled because of war.
"My lady," he said, "not at all.
But if you'd like me to tell you
the truth, I'll do so;
I'll hide nothing from you.
315 I come from Brittany.
Today I went out hunting in the woods,
and shot a white hind;
the arrow rebounded,
giving me such a wound in the thigh
320 that I've given up hope of being cured.
The hind complained and spoke to me,
cursed me, swore
that I'd never be healed
except by a girl;
325 I don't know where she might be found.
When I heard my destiny,
I quickly left the woods:
I found this boat in a harbor,
and made a big mistake: I went on board.
330 The boat raced off to sea with me on it;
I don't know where I've arrived,
or what this city's called.
Beautiful one, I beg you, for God's sake,
please advise me!
335 I don't know where to go,
and I can't even steer this ship!"
She answered him, "My dear lord,
I'll be happy to advise you;
this is my husband's city,
340 and so is the region around it.
He is a rich man of high lineage,
but extremely old;
he's also terribly jealous.
On my word of honor,

345 he has locked me up in this stronghold.
There's only one entrance,
and an old priest guards the gate:
may God let him burn in hell!
I'm shut in here night and day.
350 I'd never dare
to leave except at his command,
when my lord asks for me.
Here I have my room and my chapel,
and this girl lives with me.
355 If it pleases you to stay here
until you're better able to travel,
we'll be happy to put you up,
we'll serve you willingly."
When he hears this,
360 Guigemar thanks the lady warmly,
and says he'll stay with her.
He rose from the bed;
with some difficulty they supported him,
and the lady brought him to her chamber.
365 The young man lay down
on the girl's bed,
behind a drape that was hung
across her room like a curtain.
They brought him water in a golden basin,
370 washed his thigh,
and with a fine, white silk cloth
they wiped the blood from his wound.
Then they bound it tightly.
They treated him very kindly.
375 When their evening meal came,
the girl left enough of hers
for the knight to have some;
he ate and drank quite well.
But now love struck him to the quick;
380 great strife was in his heart
because the lady had wounded him so badly

that he forgot his homeland.
His other wound no longer bothered him,
but he sighed with new anguish.
385 He begged the girl, who was assigned to take care of him,
to let him sleep.
She left him and went away,
since he had requested it,
returning to her mistress,
390 who was also feeling somewhat scorched
by the same fire Guigemar felt
igniting and consuming his heart.
The knight was alone now,
preoccupied and in distress.
395 He didn't yet know what was wrong,
but this much he could tell:
if the lady didn't cure him,
he was sure to die.
"Alas!" he said, "what shall I do?
400 I'll go to her and tell her
that she should have mercy and pity
on a poor, disconsolate wretch like me.
If she refuses my plea,
shows herself so proud and scornful,
405 then I'll have to die of grief,
languishing forever in this pain."
He sighed; but a little later
formed a new resolution,
and said to himself he'd have to keep suffering;
410 you have to endure what you can't change.
He lay awake all night,
sighing and in distress.
He turned over in his mind
her words and appearance,
415 the bright eyes, the fair mouth
whose sweetness had touched his heart.[7]

7. Reading *doucors* with MS (P), instead of Ewert's *dolur* from (H).

Under his breath he cried for mercy;
he almost called her his beloved.
If he only knew what she was feeling—
420 how love was torturing her—
I think he would have been very happy;
that little bit of consolation
would have diminished the pain
that drained him of his color.
425 If he was suffering from love of her,
she had nothing to gloat about, either.
Next morning, before dawn,
the lady arose.
She'd been awake all night, that was her complaint.
430 It was the fault of love, pressing her hard.
The damsel, who was with her,
noticed from the appearance of her lady
that she was in love
with the knight who was staying
435 in her chamber until he was healed;
but her mistress didn't know whether or not he loved her.
The lady went off to church
and the girl went off to the knight.
She sat down by the bed;
440 he spoke to her, saying,
"My dear friend, where has my lady gone?
Why did she rise so early?"
He paused, and sighed.
The girl spoke frankly:
445 "My lord," she said, "you're in love;
take care not to hide it too well!
The love you offer
may in fact be well received.
Anyone whom my lady chooses to love
450 certainly ought to think well of her.
This love would be suitable
if both of you were constant:

you're handsome and she's beautiful."
He answered the girl,
455 "I'm so in love with her
that if I don't get relief soon
I'll be in a very bad way.
Advise me, dear friend!
What should I do about my passion?"
460 The girl very sweetly
comforted the knight,
promised to help him
in every way she could;
she was very good-hearted and well bred.
465 When the lady had heard mass
she returned; she was anything but neglectful:
she wanted to know whether the man
whom she couldn't help loving
was awake or asleep.
470 The girl called her
and brought her to the knight;
now she'll have all the time she needs
to tell him what she's feeling,
for better or for worse.
475 He greeted her and she him;
they were both very scared now.
He didn't dare ask anything from her,
for he was a foreigner
and was afraid, if he told her what he felt,
480 she'd hate him for it, send him away.
But he who hides his sickness
can hardly be brought back to health;
love is a wound in the body,
and yet nothing appears on the outside.
485 It's a sickness that lasts a long time,
because it comes from nature.
Many people treat it lightly,
like these false courtiers
who have affairs everywhere they go,

490 then boast about their conquests;
that's not love but folly,
evil and lechery.
If you can find a loyal love,
you should love and serve it faithfully,
495 be at its command.
Guigemar was deeply in love;
he must either get help quickly
or live in misery.
So love inspires bravery in him:
500 he reveals his desires to the lady.
"Lady," he said, "I'm dying because of you;
my heart is full of anguish.
If you won't cure me,
I'll have to perish sooner or later.
505 I beg you to love me—
fair one, don't deny me!"
When she had heard him out,
she gave a fitting answer.
She laughed, and said, "My love,
510 I'd be ill advised to act too quickly
in granting your prayer.
I'm not accustomed to such a request."
"My lady," he replied, "for God's sake, have mercy!
Don't be annoyed if I speak like this to you.
515 It's appropriate for an inconstant woman
to make some one plead with her a long time
to enhance her worth; that way he won't think
she's used to such sport.
But a woman of good character,
520 sensible as well as virtuous,
if she finds a man to her liking,
oughtn't to treat him too disdainfully.
Rather she should love and enjoy him;
this way, before anyone knows or hears of it,
525 they'll have done a lot that's to their advantage.

Now, dear lady, let's end this discussion."
The lady realized he was telling the truth,
and immediately granted him
her love; then he kissed her.
530 From now on, Guigemar is at ease.
They lie down together and converse,
kissing and embracing often.
I hope they also enjoy whatever else
others do on such occasions.
535 It appears to me that Guigemar
stayed with her a year and a half.
Their life was full of pleasure.
But Fortune, who never forgets her duty,
turns her wheel suddenly,
540 raising one person up while casting another down;
and so it happened with the lovers,
because suddenly they were discovered.
One summer morning,
the lady was lying beside her young lover;
545 she kissed his mouth and eyes,
and said to him, "Dear, sweet love,
my heart tells me I'm going to lose you.
We're going to be found out.
If you die, I want to die, too,
550 but if you can escape,
you'll go find another love
while I stay here in misery."
"Lady," he said, "don't say such a thing!
I would never have any joy or peace
555 if I turned to another woman.
You needn't be afraid of that!"
"Beloved, I need your promise.
Give me your shirt;
I'll make a knot in the tail.
560 You have my leave to love the woman,
whoever she may be,

who will be able to undo it."
He gave her the shirt, and his promise;
she made the knot in such a way
565 that no woman could untie it
except with scissors or knife.
She gave him back the shirt,
and he took it on condition
that she should make a similar pledge to him,
570 by means of a belt
that she would wear next to her bare flesh,
tightened about her flanks.
Whoever could open the buckle
without breaking it or severing it from the belt,
575 would be the one he would urge her to love.
He kissed her, and left it at that.
That day they were discovered—
spied upon and found out
by an evil, cunning chamberlain,
580 sent by the husband.
He wanted to speak with the lady,
and couldn't get into her chamber;
he looked in a window and saw the lovers,
he went and told his lord.
585 When he heard about it,
the lord was sorrier than he'd ever been before.
He called for three of his henchmen
and straightaway went to the wife's chamber;
he had the door broken down.
590 Inside he found the knight.
He was so furious
that he gave orders to kill the stranger.
Guigemar got up,
not at all afraid.
595 He grabbed a wooden rod
on which clothes were usually hung,
and waited for his assailants.

Guigemar will make some of them suffer for this;
before they get close to him,
600 he'll have maimed them all.
The lord stared at him for a long time,
and finally asked him
who he was, where he came from,
how he'd gotten in there.
605 Guigemar told him how he'd come there
and how the lady had received him;
he told him all about the adventure
of the wounded hind,
about his wound and the ship;
610 now he is entirely in the other's power.
The lord replied that he didn't believe him,
but if it really was the way he had told it
and if he could find the ship,
he'd send Guigemar back out to sea.
615 If he survived, that would be a shame;
he'd be happier if Guigemar drowned.
When he had made this pledge,
they went together to the harbor,
and found the ship; they put Guigemar on it—
620 it will take him back to his own land.
The ship got under way without waiting.
The knight sighed and cried,
often lamenting his lady
and praying to almighty God
625 to grant him a quick death,
and never let him come to port
if he couldn't regain his mistress,
whom he desired more than his own life.
He persisted in his grief
630 until the ship came to the port
where he'd first found it;
he was now very near his native land.
He left the ship as quickly as he could.
A boy whom Guigemar had raised

635 came by, following a knight,
and leading a war-horse.
Guigemar recognized him and called to him;
the squire looked at him,
recognized his lord, dismounted,
640 and presented the charger to him.
Guigemar went off with him; all his friends
rejoiced that they had found him again.
He was highly honored in his land,
but through it all he was sad and distracted.
645 His friends wanted him to take a wife,
but he refused them altogether;
he'll never have to do with a woman,
for love or money,
if she can't untie
650 his knotted shirt without tearing it.
The news traveled throughout Brittany;
all the women and girls
came to try their luck,
but none could untie the knot.
655 Now I want to tell you about the lady
whom Guigemar loved so dearly.
On the advice of one of his barons,
her husband had her imprisoned
in a dark marble tower.
660 There she passed bad days, worse nights.
No one in the world could describe
the pain, the suffering,
the anguish and the grief,
that she endured in that tower.
665 She remained there two years and more, I believe,
without ever having a moment of pleasure.
Often, she mourned for her lover:
"Guigemar, my lord, why did I ever lay eyes on you?
I'd rather die quickly
670 than suffer this lingering torture.

My love, if I could escape,
I'd go to where you put out to sea
and drown myself." Then she got up;
in astonishment she went to the door
675 and found it unlocked;
by good fortune, she got outside—
no one bothered her.
She came to the harbor, and found the boat.
It was tied to the rock
680 where she had intended to drown herself.
When she saw it there, she went aboard;
she could think of only one thing—
that this was where her lover had perished.
Suddenly, she couldn't stand up.
685 If she could have gotten back up on deck,
she would have thrown herself overboard,
so great was her suffering.
The boat set out, taking her with it.
It came to port in Brittany,
690 beneath a strong, well-built castle.
The lord of the castle
was named Meriaduc.
He was fighting a war with a neighbor,
and had risen early that morning
695 because he wanted to dispatch his troops
to attack his enemy.
Standing at a window,
he saw the ship arrive.
He went downstairs
700 and called his chamberlain;
quickly they went to the ship,
climbed up its ladder;
inside they found the woman
who had a fairylike beauty.
705 He took her by the cloak
and brought her with him to his castle.

He was delighted with his discovery,
for she was incredibly beautiful;
whoever had put her on the boat,
710 he could tell she came from high lineage.
He felt for her a love
as great as he'd ever had for a woman.
He had a young sister,
a beautiful maiden, in his care;
715 he commended the lady to her attention.
So she was waited on and made much of;
the damsel dressed her richly.
But she remained constantly sad and preoccupied.
The lord often came to speak with her,
720 since he wanted to love her with all his heart.
He pleaded for her love; she didn't want it,
instead she showed him her belt:
she would never love any man
except the one who could open the belt
725 without breaking it. When he heard that,
Meriaduc replied angrily,
"There's another one like you in this land,
a very worthy knight,
who avoids, in a similar manner, taking a wife
730 by means of a shirt
the right tail of which is knotted;
it can't be untied
except by using scissors or a knife.
I think you must have made that knot!"
735 When the lady heard this, she sighed,
and almost fainted.
He took her in his arms,
cut the laces of her tunic,
and tried to open the belt.
740 But he didn't succeed.
There wasn't a knight in the region
whom he didn't summon to try his luck.

Things went on like this for quite a while,
up to the time of a tournament
745 that Meriaduc had proclaimed
against the lord he was fighting.
He sent for knights and enlisted them in his service,
knowing very well that Guigemar would come.
He asked him as a special favor,
750 as his friend and companion,
not to let him down in this hour of need,
but to come help him.
So Guigemar set out, richly supplied,
leading more than one hundred knights.
755 Meriaduc entertained him
as an honored guest in his stronghold.
He then sent two knights to his sister,
and commanded her
to prepare herself and come to him,
760 bringing with her the woman he so much loved.
The girl obeyed his order.
Lavishly outfitted,
they came hand in hand into the great hall.
The lady was pale and upset;
765 she heard Guigemar's name
and couldn't stand up.
If the damsel hadn't supported her,
she'd have fallen to the ground.
Guigemar arose when the women entered;
770 he looked at the lady and noticed
her appearance and behavior;
involuntarily, he shrank back a bit.
"Is this," he said, "my dear love,
my hope, my heart, and my life—
775 my beautiful lady who loved me?
Where did she come from? Who brought her here?
Now, that was a foolish thought!
I know it can't be she;
women often look alike—

780 I got all excited for no reason.
But because she looks like the one
for whom my heart aches and sighs,
I'll gladly speak to her."
Then the knight came forward,
785 he kissed her and sat her down beside him;
he didn't say another word,
except that he asked her to sit down.
Meriaduc looked at them closely,
upset by the sight of them together.
790 He called Guigemar cheerfully:
"My lord," he said, "please
let this girl try
to untie your shirt,
to see if she can manage to do it."
795 Guigemar answered, "Certainly."
He summoned a chamberlain
who was in charge of the shirt
and commanded him to bring it.
It was given to the girl,
800 but she couldn't untie it at all.
The lady knew the knot very well;
her heart is greatly agitated,
for she would love to try to untie it,
if she dared and could.
805 Meriaduc saw this clearly;
he was as sorry as he could be.
"My lady," he said, "now try
to untie it, if you can."
When she heard his order,
810 she took the shirttail
and easily untied the knot.
Guigemar was thunderstruck;
he knew her very well, and yet
he couldn't bring himself to believe firmly it was she.
815 So he spoke to her in this way:

"Beloved, sweet creature,
is that you? Tell me truly!
Let me see your body,
and the belt I put on you."
820 He put his hands on her hips,
and found the belt.
"My beautiful one," he said, "what a lucky adventure
that I've found you like this!
Who brought you here?"
825 She told him about the grief,
the great pains, the monotony
of the prison where she was held captive,
and everything that had happened to her—
how she escaped,
830 how she wished to drown, but found the ship instead,
and how she entered it and was brought to this port;
and how the lord of the castle kept her in custody,
guarding her in luxury
but constantly asking for her love.
835 Now her joy has returned:
"My love, take back your beloved!"
Guigemar got up.
"My lords," he said, "listen to me!
Here I have the mistress
840 I thought I had lost forever.
Now I ask and implore Meriaduc
to give her back to me out of kindness.
I will become his vassal,
serve him two or three years,
845 with one hundred knights, or more!"
Meriaduc answered,
"Guigemar," he said, "my handsome friend,
I'm not so harried
or so afflicted by any war
850 that you can bargain with me about this.
I found this woman and I propose to take care of her

and defend her against you."
When Guigemar heard that, he quickly
commanded his men to mount.
855 He galloped away, defying Meriaduc.[8]
It upset him to leave his beloved behind.
Guigemar took with him
every knight who had come
to the town for the tournament.
860 Each declared his loyalty to Guigemar;
they'll accompany him wherever he goes.
Whoever fails him now will truly be dishonored!
That night they came to the castle
of Meriaduc's opponent.
865 The lord of the castle put them up;
he was joyful and delighted
that Guigemar came over to his side, bringing help with him.
Now he's sure the war's as good as over.
The next morning they arose,
870 and equipped themselves at their lodgings.
They departed from the village, noisily;
Guigemar came first, leading them.
Arriving at Meriaduc's castle, they assaulted it;
but it was very strong and they failed to take it.
875 Guigemar besieged the town;
he won't leave until it has fallen.
His friends and other troops increased so greatly
that he was able to starve everyone inside.
He captured and destroyed the castle,
880 killed its lord.
Guigemar led away his mistress with great rejoicing;
all his pain was now at an end.
From this story that you have heard
the *lai* of Guigemar was composed,

8. The *defi* was a formal gesture, renouncing feudal bonds of alliance or dependency and making it possible for one knight to attack another (or a vassal his former lord) without incurring charges of treason.

885 which is now recited to the harp and rote;
the music is a pleasure to hear.

GUIGEMAR

IF WE JUDGE from its twenty-six-line prologue—in which Marie defends her art, and the continued practice of it, against the attacks of envious detractors—it seems that Marie intended *Guigemar* to stand at the head of her collection of *lais.* (Such an opening apologia was in fact an often-used convention of twelfth-century courtly narrative.) In *Guigemar,* Marie employs and synthesizes fairy-tale-like material (presumably of Celtic origin), contemporaneous love conventions, and situations basic to chivalric romances and *fabliaux* (short, cynical, frequently obscene tales), in order to represent metaphorically the process of growing up, and the central role desire plays in that process. The length of *Guigemar* (it is the second longest of the *lais*) allows Marie to trace the stages that bring her hero from a reflexive scorn for love, through the painful discovery of his sexuality and its powers to wound and heal, to the crisis of forming a love relationship. When the protagonist's love is tested by adversity, loyalty emerges as its crucial element, and a final twist of fortune gives the lovers a chance to seize happiness.

The story is placed in a vague Breton past, when Hoel ruled the land.[1] Guigemar, the well-beloved son of one of Hoel's vassals, finishes his apprenticeship to a king and sets out to seek honor (*pris*) as a mercenary knight.[2] His success in war contrasts sharply with his complete indifference to women and love. This rejection of the possibility of a relationship that would offer purely private fulfillment (as opposed to the public rewards of prowess: i.e., honor and fame) and the resultant deepening of self-awareness mark Guigemar as sexually and psychologically immature. In modern terms, he is engaged in the dangerous enterprise of avoiding or repressing the passionate, instinctual side of himself, which is a form of psychic self-mutilation. His refusal to be involved with women also allows Guigemar to avoid locating the source of his happiness outside himself, as would be the case if he loved, and therefore to forestall vulnerability to circumstances beyond his control, or Fortune. He chooses instead to create his own "fortune" by forcing others to submit to his strength in battle.

To dramatize the consequences and the abrupt conclusion of Guigemar's mode of living, Marie seizes upon the emblem of his penchant for hunting—a symbol, at least as old as the classical myth of Hippolytus, of aggressive self-sufficiency and repressive chastity, because in the hunt the bestial part of nature is confronted and destroyed. Guigemar encounters a white female deer with the antlers of a male, accompanied by a fawn.[3] Guigemar unleashes an arrow that wounds the hind and rebounds, severely injuring him in the thigh. This is a symbolic representation of his life to date: the hind is an image of the full sexual existence—the recognition of one's impulses toward passion as well as toward mastery (hence the creature's bisexuality)—that Guigemar has attempted to stifle and "kill" in himself, and the twin wounds suggest the deleterious effects of this policy. (Here, as in *Chaitivel,* the thigh wound is a euphemism.) Furthermore, the hind's prophecy that Guigemar will not be healed until he finds a woman, who, in curing him, will share with him a new suffering in love, would appear to represent Guigemar's concurrent awareness of the tremendous potential his newly perceived sexuality has for harm and health; it is a force that simultaneously gives and assuages misery.[4] Finally, the presumed death of the hind implies that Guigemar has ended his phase of asexual self-sufficiency. In short, the hunt of the white hind allows Marie to portray metaphorically a crisis of sexual growth and awareness in Guigemar that we associate today with adolescence.

Guigemar's realization that his wound requires treatment by an unknown woman signals his alienation from the all-male world of the hunt, with its assumption that man can seek out and control his fate, and his entry into the world of fortune with its surprises and uncertainties. Accordingly, he steals away from his companions and boards a mysterious ship, emblem of the chance (*aventure*) to which he must now consign himself in hopes of surviving. The land to which the ship brings him is the spatial embodiment of social conventions that deny and repress the love impulse from outside. A jealous old husband holds a beautiful young wife virtually captive in her chambers. Guigemar, seeking his own relief, enters this world and revives the wife by fulfilling the need for love she cannot satisfy in her loveless marriage.

If the situation of the imprisoned wife recalls the plot of many a *fabliau,* the clearly marked stages by which she and Guigemar recognize and consummate their mutual love show Marie following literary conventions developed in chivalric romances and Ovidian love tales of her day. With a characteristic blend of sentimental involvement and witty detachment, she records Guigemar's sleepless night and gradual realization of its cause; his agonized wavering between resolve to tell the lady of his desire and resignation to suffer all in silence; the exquisite moment in which the two terrified lovers make their confessions; and the brief debate (recalling the analogous but longer love dialogues of Andreas Capellanus' pseudo-textbook *De arte honeste amandi*) during which he convinces her, using delightfully spurious reasoning, that if she intends to be a loyal lover, she should grant him her favors at once—only inconstant women hesitate, to hide their lasciviousness!

The discovery of the lovers after eighteen months of secret pleasure is preceded by Marie's reference to Fortune's ever-turning wheel and by the lady's own premonition that they are about to be separated. Her fear prompts their exchange of vows of eternal loyalty, sealed and symbolized by the knot that can only be untied by the lover who made it. The change of Fortune's symbol from the ship to the wheel suggests that the lovers can no longer count on fortune for progress and continuity in their relationship, but must now transcend its hostility by drawing on the resources of the love itself. Similarly, the lady's realization that the love can no longer be kept secret reflects Marie's contention that love cannot forever remain static, secure, and untested within a womblike private world. Instead, it must grow by testing itself in the world of chance and hostile values. If love is to survive in such a world, a new virtue, loyalty, must complement and preserve passion. When the furious husband breaks in on the lovers, Guigemar reacts courageously and thus saves his life; the husband puts him back in the marvelous boat and adventure takes the grieving knight back to his own land, where his friends make much of him, but where he lives in sorrow, as unwilling as before to marry, though for a completely different reason. (The device of using repeated external situations to set off the evolving inner state of the protagonist occurs frequently in romance.)

Guigemar's insistence on marrying only the woman who will untie the knot in his shirt makes him famous and sets up the climax of the *lai,* in which he is reunited with his beloved at the castle of Meriaduc, when each unties the other's knot. Meriaduc, having taken the lady into custody after she escaped from the tower her husband had imprisoned her in and sailed away in the mysterious boat, has summoned Guigemar specifically to see if he can undo the knotted belt around the lady's body, and she his. Despite this overwhelming proof that the lovers belong only to each other, Meriaduc refuses to surrender the lady. Guigemar wins her once and for all by an act of prowess (he besieges Meriaduc's castle) that recalls his warrior life at the beginning of the *lai,* but Marie recalls his warrior consciousness only to emphasize the difference between his earlier and his later self: the knight who scorned love has become the knight who fights under its banner; his impulse to dominate is now wholly subservient to his desire to possess a woman without whom he remains incomplete.

Marie's mastery of romance conventions and her convincing, metaphoric anatomy of the stages by which love comes to dominate a life make *Guigemar* one of the most satisfying of all medieval short narratives.

1. Marie borrowed Hoel from Wace's *Roman de Brut,* a contemporary French adaptation of Geoffrey of Monmouth's fanciful *Historia regum Britanniae* (*History of the Kings of Britain*).

2. On the existence of a large floating population of young soldiers of fortune in Marie's day, see G. Duby, "Au XIIe siècle: les 'jeunes' dans la société aristocratique," *Annales* 19 (1964), 835–846.

3. Cf. Chrétien de Troyes' *Erec* and the anonymous *Partonopeu de Blois* for other twelfth-century uses of marvelous animals to activate a chivalric narrative.

4. The image of Love's medicine-tipped arrow that wounds and heals simultaneously is a commonplace of medieval love literature. Cf. Marie's comment on love's wound, 1. 483 f.

Equitan

Most noble barons
were those Bretons of Brittany.
In the old days they were accustomed, out of bravery,
courtliness, and nobility,
5 to create *lais* from the adventures they heard,
adventures that had befallen all sorts of people;
they did this as a memorial,
so that men should not forget them.
They made one that I heard—
10 it should never be forgotten—
about Equitan, a most courtly man,
the lord of Nauns, a magistrate and king.[1]

Equitan was a man of great worth,
dearly loved in his own land.
15 He loved sport and lovemaking;
and so he kept a body of knights in his service.
Whoever indulges in love without sense or moderation
recklessly endangers his life;
such is the nature of love
20 that no one involved with it can keep his head.[2]
Equitan had a seneschal,
a good knight, brave and loyal,
who took care of his land for him,
governed and administered it.
25 Unless the king was making war,
he would never, no matter what the emergency,
neglect his hunting,

1. The meaning and location of Nauns are subjects of scholarly dispute. Conjectures range from Nantes, in Brittany, to the kingdom of the dwarfs (*nains*). Equitan's name may, as Mickel suggests, contain a play on the Latin word for horse (*equus*), appropriate for a huntsman. Cf. further the endnote to *Milun* (note 3).

2. There is a play in the text on two meanings of *mesure,* rendered "moderation" in l. 17 and "nature" in l. 19.

his hawking, or his other amusements.
This seneschal took a wife
30 through whom great harm later came to the land.
She was a beautiful woman
of fine breeding,
with an attractive form and figure.
Nature took pains in putting her together:
35 bright eyes in a lovely face,
a pretty mouth and a well-shaped nose.
She hadn't an equal in the entire kingdom.
The king often heard her praised.
He frequently sent his greetings to her,
40 presents as well;
without having seen her, he wanted her,
so he spoke to her as soon as he could.
For his private amusement
he went hunting in the countryside
45 where the seneschal dwelt;
in the castle, where the lady also lived,
the king took lodging for the night
after he had finished the day's sport.
He now had a good chance to speak to the wife,
50 to reveal to her his worth, his desires.
He found her refined and clever,
with a beautiful body and face,
and a pleasing, cheerful demeanor.
Love drafted him into his service:
55 he shot an arrow at the king
that opened a great wound in the heart,
where Love had aimed and fixed it.
Neither good sense nor understanding were of use to the king
now;
love for the woman so overcame him
60 that he became sad and depressed.
Now he has to give in to love completely;
he can't defend himself at all.

That night he can't sleep or even rest,
instead he blames and scolds himself:
65 "Alas," he says, "what destiny
led me to these parts?
Because I have seen this woman
pain has struck at my heart,
my whole body shivers.
70 I think I have no choice but to love her—
yet if I love her, I'm doing wrong;
she's the wife of my seneschal.
I owe him the same faith and love
that I want him to give me.
75 If, by some means, he found out about this
I know how much it would upset him.
Still, it would be a lot worse
if I went mad out of concern for him.
It would be a shame for such a beautiful woman
80 not to have a lover!
What would become of her finer qualities
if she didn't nourish them by a secret love?[3]
There isn't a man in the world
who wouldn't be vastly improved if she loved him.
85 And if the seneschal should hear of the affair,
he oughtn't be too crushed by it;
he certainly can't hold her all by himself,
and I'm happy to share the burden with him!"
When he had said all that, he sighed,
90 and lay in bed thinking.
After a while, he spoke again: "Why
am I so distressed and frightened?
I still don't even know
if she will take me as her lover;
95 but I'll know soon!
If she should feel the way I do,

3. The French text refers to *druerie,* extramarital passion that would, of course, be kept secret from the husband.

I'd soon be free of this agony.
God! It's still so long till morning!
I can't get any rest,
100 it's been forever since I went to bed."
The king stayed awake until daybreak;
he could hardly wait for it.
He rose and went hunting,
but he soon turned back
105 saying that he was worn out.
He returns to his room and lies down.
The seneschal is saddened by this;
he doesn't know what's bothering the king,
what's making him shiver;
110 in fact, his wife is the reason for it.
The king, to get some relief and some pleasure,
sends for the wife to come speak with him.
He revealed his desire to her,
letting her know that he was dying because of her;
115 that it lay in her power to comfort him
or to let him die.
"My lord," the woman said to him,
"I must have some time to think;
this is so new to me,
120 I have no idea what to say.
You're a king of high nobility,
and I'm not at all of such fortune
that you should single me out
to have a love affair with.
125 If you get what you want from me,
I have no doubt about it:
you'll soon get tired of me,
and I'll be far worse off than before.
If I should love you
130 and satisfy your desire,
love wouldn't be shared equally
between the two of us.
Because you're a powerful king

and my husband is your vassal,
135 I'm sure you believe
your rank entitles you to my love.
Love is worthless if it's not mutual.
A poor but loyal man is worth more—
if he also possesses good sense and virtue—
140 and his love brings greater joy
than the love of a prince or a king
who has no loyalty in him.
Anyone who aims higher in love
than his own wealth entitles him to
145 will be frightened by every little thing that occurs.
The rich man, however, is confident
that no one will steal a mistress away
whose favor he obtains by his authority over her."
Equitan answered her,
150 "Please, my lady! Don't say such things!
No one could consider himself noble
(rather, he'd be haggling like a tradesman)
who, for the sake of wealth or a big fief,
would take pains to win someone of low repute.
155 There's no woman in the world—if she's smart,
refined, and of noble character,
and if she places a high enough value on her love
that she isn't inconstant—
whom a rich prince in his palace
160 wouldn't yearn for
and love well and truly,
even if she'd nothing but the shirt on her back.
Whoever is inconstant in love
and gives himself up to treachery
165 is mocked and deceived in the end;
I've seen it happen many times like that.
It's no surprise when someone loses out
who deserves to because of his behavior.
My dear lady, I'm offering myself to you!
170 Don't think of me as your king,

but as your vassal and your lover.
I tell you, I promise you
I'll do whatever you want.
Don't let me die on your account!
175 You be the lord and I'll be the servant[4]—
you be the proud one and I'll be the beggar!"
The king pleaded with her,
begged her so often for mercy,
that she promised him her love
180 and granted him possession of her body.
Then they exchanged rings,
and promised themselves to each other.
They kept their promises and loved each other well;
they died for this in the end.
185 Their affair lasted a long time,
without anyone hearing of it.
At the times set for their meetings,
when they were to speak together at the king's palace,
the king informed his followers
190 that he wanted to be bled privately.
The doors of his chamber were closed,
and no one was so daring,
if the king didn't summon him,
that he would ever enter there.
195 Meanwhile, the seneschal held court
and heard pleas and complaints.
The king loved the seneschal's wife for a long time,
had no desire for any other woman;
he didn't want to marry,
200 and never allowed the subject to be raised.
His people held this against him,
and the seneschal's wife
heard about it often; this worried her,
and she was afraid she would lose him.
205 So when she next had the chance to speak to him—

4. The French text has *dame* and *servant*.

when she should have been full of joy,
kissing and embracing him
and having a good time with him—
she burst into tears, making a big scene.
210 The king asked
what the matter was,
and the lady answered,
"My lord, I'm crying because of our love,
which has brought me to great sorrow:
215 you're going to take a wife, some king's daughter,
and you will get rid of me;
I've heard all about it, I know it's true.
And—alas!—what will become of me?
On your account I must now face death,
220 for I have no other comfort than you."
The king spoke lovingly to her:
"Dear love, don't be afraid!
I promise I'll never take a wife,
never leave you for another.
225 Believe me, this is the truth:
If your husband were dead,
I'd make you my lady and my queen;
no one could stop me."
The lady thanked him,
230 said she was very grateful to him;
if he would assure her
that he wouldn't leave her for someone else,
she would quickly undertake
to do away with her lord.
235 It would be easy to arrange
if he were willing to help her.
He agreed to do so;
there was nothing she could demand of him
that he wouldn't do, if he possibly could,
240 whether it turned out well or badly.
"My lord," she says, "please
come hunting in the forest,

out in the country where I live.
Stay awhile at my husband's castle;
245 you can be bled there,
and on the third day after that, take a bath.[5]
My lord will be bled with you
and will bathe with you as well;
make it clear to him—and don't relent—
250 that he must keep you company!
I'll have the baths heated
and the two tubs brought in;
his will be so boiling hot
that no man on earth
255 could escape being horribly scalded
as soon as he sat down in it.
When he's scalded to death,
send for his men and yours;
then you can show them exactly how
260 he suddenly died in his bath."
The king promised her
that he'd do just as she wished.
❧ Less than three months later,
the king went out into the countryside to hunt.
265 He had himself bled to ward off illness,
and his seneschal bled with him.
On the third day, he said he wanted to bathe;
the seneschal was happy to comply.
"Bathe with me," said the king,
270 and the seneschal replied, "Willingly."
The wife had the baths heated,
the two tubs brought;
next to the bed, according to plan,
she had them both set down.
275 Then she had boiling water brought
for the seneschal's tub.

5. Baths were taken much less frequently in the Middle Ages than now and would normally be planned in advance.

The good man got up
and went outside to relax for a moment.
His wife came to speak to the king
280 and he pulled her down beside him;
they lay down on her husband's bed
and began to enjoy themselves.
They lay there together.
Because the tub was right before them,
285 they set a guard at the bedroom door;
a maidservant was to keep watch there.
Suddenly the seneschal returned,
and knocked on the door; the girl held it closed.
He struck it so violently
290 that he forced it open.
There he discovered the king and his own wife
lying in each other's arms.
The king looked up and saw him coming;
to hide his villainy
295 he jumped into the tub feet first,
stark naked.
He didn't stop to think what he was doing.
And there he was scalded to death,
caught in his own evil trap,
300 while the seneschal remained safe and sound.
The seneschal could see very well
what had happened to the king.
He grabbed his wife at once
and thrust her head first into the tub.
305 Thus both died,
the king first, the wife after him.
Whoever wants to hear some sound advice
can profit from this example:
he who plans evil for another
310 may have that evil rebound back on him.
It all happened just as I've told you.
The Bretons made a *lai* about it,

about Equitan, his fate,
and the woman who loved him so much.

EQUITAN

EQUITAN has been criticized by some scholars for its unsympathetic protagonists and for the doggedly didactic tone in which it tells the story of their illicit love and its punishment. That the *lai* is admonitory cannot be denied. The *fabliau*-like story of a king who betrays his own seneschal by loving the latter's wife, and then plots with her the seneschal's death only to have the plan backfire fatally, allows Marie to draw an unequivocal concluding moral: he who plans evil for another may find the evil falling upon himself. At the beginning of the tale, she had already signaled its exemplary nature by another sententious statement about love: those who love irrationally, and excessively, court danger, for love prevents the lover from acting reasonably in the best of circumstances. Connecting the two framing *sententiae,* the intervening narrative illustrates with pitiless clarity the inevitable progress from the king's passion—which he cannot or will not control, though he knows it violates the loyalty he owes a devoted vassal—to his involvement in the murder plot. When, just before the murder is to take place, the king once again gives in to his passion, and makes love with the seneschal's wife on her husband's bed, he seals his own fate: the seneschal bursts into the chamber, and the king, in total confusion, leaps into the bathtub of scalding water intended for the victim. Equitan, that is, becomes the victim of his own plot, as he has been the victim of his own irresistible desire. The tub of boiling water thus becomes a double emblem: of the trickster tricked, and of the immoderate lover fatally burned by his ungoverned passion.

Marie's artistic intent functions at two levels besides the didactic-exemplary in *Equitan*. First, the *lai* functions as a negative version of some of the twelfth-century love conventions sympathetically represented in *Guigemar*. The situations of the two protagonists are similar: both are hunters; both experience the first sufferings of love during a sleepless night and soliloquize about their pains and fears; the commonplace of love as a wound is applied to both; both woo married women and overcome their objections in dialogues of a casuistical type that were popular in the twelfth century. Finally, after a long, happy period of secret liaisons, each pair of lovers is discovered by the husband.

Within this network of parallels, Marie subverts or inverts in *Equitan* the attitudes of *Guigemar*. In the king's love monologue, he blames destiny for leading him to the wife's land (cf. Guigemar's ship), whereas he had deliberately come to the seneschal's castle, ostensibly on a hunting trip, but actually to meet the woman of whose beauty he had heard so much. (The hunt, in *Equitan,* leads not to a symbolic encounter, as it does in *Guigemar,* but to a real one; the king's "hunt" for sexual gratification reminds us that there was a substantial medieval literature in which love was represented allegorically as a hunt.)[1] The theme of loyalty in love, emblematically represented by the knots tied by the protagonists in *Guigemar,* receives dubious scrutiny in *Equitan:* the king recognizes at once that he will do wrong in loving the wife of a man to whom he owes the same faith he expects from him, but he beats back this knowledge with cynical arguments that his own sanity and the lady's *courtoisie* both require the love affair for their continuity. He even tells himself, with mock earnestness, that he is only going to help the seneschal bear the burden of his beautiful wife—an obvious double entendre.

Later, when the wife parries Equitan's declaration of love by saying that she would rather love a poor but loyal man than a powerful one who feels his rank entitles him to abandon her whenever he wishes, the king insists that only *her* loyalty matters to him, not any difference in their fortunes. In fact, in receiving him as her lover, she is joining Equitan in a monumental act of disloyalty to her husband. Later, in the face of his barons' plea that he marry, the wife forces Equitan to prove his fidelity to her by agreeing to help her kill the seneschal so he can marry her. Thus love-loyalty and vicious disloyalty to the marriage bond are inextricably linked. As a final, negative counterpoint to *Guigemar,* Marie depicts Equitan, when he is discovered by the seneschal, not as one emboldened by desperate love, but as a panic-stricken criminal who rushes in confusion to his own doom.

A further level of meaning in *Equitan* comprises an examination of the king's surrender of various facets of his public and private identities in his dealings with the other characters. Equitan is introduced as king and *jostise,* or administrator of justice to his people. Yet at once we are told that the king refused to leave his life of hunting and pleasure for any reason but war, and that, in his absence, the loyal seneschal protected the land and *justisoit,* administered justice. In other words, the seneschal had assumed a good part of the burdens of kingship, a fact that makes Equitan's offer to assume part of the burden of his wife an ironic completion of an exchange of roles. (The seneschal's assumption of the king's identity as judge reveals an excess, as it were, of loyalty, while the king's assumption of the seneschal's role of husband reveals a deficiency of loyalty.)

Later, in response to the lady's doubts about becoming the mistress of a king who could tyrannize over her, Equitan urges her to think of herself as a proud lady, and him a vassal, servant, and petitioner. To assuage his passion, Equitan surrenders his status to the wife, as he has previously surrendered his judicial role to the husband. Once the love affair has begun in earnest, the king enjoys his mistress behind closed doors, while outside the seneschal holds court and hears claims—again fulfilling the *judicial* function the king has abdicated to him, while Equitan assumes the role of husband the seneschal has (unknowingly) abdicated to him!

This exchange of identities—the king's public for the seneschal's private—continues until the king and the wife make love on the seneschal's own bed; Equitan has at this point gone further than ever before toward assuming the seneschal's identity. But in doing so, he exposes himself to maximum danger. The seneschal barges back into the chamber—not, presumably, because he suspects anything, but because he has been commanded by the king to be with him in private. The king, discovered in his adultery, completes his assimilation of the seneschal's identity with a final leap into the other's tub, thus appropriating the seneschal's death as well. Meanwhile, the seneschal kills the wife—an act of retribution that finalizes his assumption of the king's public identity as meter-out of justice. (Of course, at his death, the king also for the first time earns his title of *jostise* by condemning himself to death; but, as opposed to the seneschal's deliberate act of judgment, his is accidental.) The deepest irony of *Equitan* is therefore that the king's escape from the responsibilities of his public identity, already clear when the *lai* begins, is paralleled, as the *lai* unfolds, by a similar escape into the private identity of the seneschal, and that, when the process is complete, the king has destroyed himself physically as well as metaphysically.

The tight and multileveled construction of *Equitan* would seem to belie, at least in part, the contention by some critics that it is an early and inferior work of Marie. In its own fashion, it is a highly accomplished poem.

1. Mickel, in his essay on irony (see bibliography), explores the implications of the hunting metaphor for this *lai*.

Le Fresne (*The Ash Tree*)

I shall tell you the *lai* of Le Fresne
according to the story as I know it.
In olden days there lived in Brittany
two knights who were neighbors;
5 both were rich men,
brave and worthy knights.
They lived close by, within the same region;
each was married.
Now one of the wives became pregnant;
10 when her time came
she gave birth to twins.
Her husband was absolutely delighted;
in his joy at the event
he sent word to his good neighbor
15 that his wife had had two sons—
he had that many more children now.
He would send one to him to raise,
and name the child after him.
The rich neighbor was sitting down to eat
20 when the messenger arrived;
he knelt before the high table
to announce his news.
The lord thanked God for it
and rewarded him with a fine horse.
25 The knight's wife laughed
(she was seated next to him at dinner)
because she was deceitful and proud,
evil-tongued and envious.
She spoke very foolishly,
30 saying, for all her household to hear,
"So help me God, I can't imagine
where this worthy man got such advice
to announce to my lord,
to his own shame and dishonor,

35 that his wife has had twin sons.
Both he and she are disgraced by this;
we know the truth of the matter all too well:
it never was and never will be
possible for such a thing to happen[1]—
40 that a woman could have
two sons in one birth—
unless two men had lain with her."
Her lord stared fiercely at her,
reproached her bitterly for what she said.
45 "Wife," he said, "stop that!
You mustn't talk that way!
The fact is that she's a woman
who's always had a good reputation."
But the people in the household
50 repeated the wife's words;
the matter was widely spoken of
and became known throughout Brittany.
The slanderous wife was hated for it,
and later made to suffer for it.
55 Every woman who heard about it,
rich or poor, hated her.
The messenger who had brought the news
went home and told his lord everything.
When he heard the messenger's report,
60 he became so sad he didn't know what to do.
He hated his worthy wife because of it,
strongly suspected her,
and kept her under strict guard,
even though she didn't deserve it.
65 The wife who had spoken so evilly
became pregnant herself that same year,
and was carrying twins—

1. Marie uses the word *aventure* here and throughout the *lai* to refer to unexpected circumstances of the kind that test the endurance and moral worth of human beings, and bring them to happiness if they deserve it.

now her neighbor has her vengeance.
She carried them until her time came;
70 then she gave birth to two daughters; she was extremely upset,
and terribly sad about the situation.
She lamented bitterly to herself:
"Alas!" she said, "what shall I do?
I'll never get any honor out of this!
75 I'm in disgrace, that's certain.
My lord and all his kin
will never believe me
when they hear about this bad luck;[2]
indeed, I condemned myself
80 when I slandered all womankind.
Didn't I say it never happened—
at least, we've never seen it happen—
that a woman could have twins
unless she had lain with two men?
85 Now that I have twins, it seems to me
my words have come back to haunt me.
Whoever slanders another
never knows when it will rebound on him;
he may speak badly about someone
90 who's more deserving of praise than he.
Now, to keep from being disgraced,
I'll have to kill one of my children!
I'd rather make that up to God
than live in shame and dishonor."
95 Those of her household who were in the bedchamber with her
comforted her and said
they wouldn't allow her to do it;
killing somebody was no joke.
The lady had an attendant
100 who was of noble birth;
the lady had raised and taken care of her
and was very attached to her.

2. The French text has *aventure*.

This girl heard her mistress crying,
bemoaning her situation;
105 it bothered her terribly.
She came and comforted her:
"My lady," she said, "it's not worth carrying on so.
Stop grieving—that's the thing to do.
Give me one of the babies;
110 I'll take care of her for you,
so that you won't be disgraced;
you'll never see the child again.
I'll abandon her at a convent,
to which I'll carry her safe and sound.
115 Some good person will find her,
and, God willing, he'll raise her."
The lady heard what she said;
she was delighted with the idea, and promised her
that if she did her this service
120 she'd be well rewarded for it.
They wrapped the noble child
in a linen garment,
and then in an embroidered silk robe,
which the lady's husband had brought back to her
125 from Constantinople, where he had been.
They had never seen anything so fine.
With a piece of ribbon
she tied a large ring onto the child's arm;
it contained a full ounce of pure gold,
130 and had a ruby set in it,
with lettering around the rim of the setting.
Wherever the little girl might be found,
everyone would know beyond doubt
that she came from a noble family.
135 The damsel took the baby
and left the chamber with her.
That night, after dark,
she left the town
and took the highroad

140 that led into the forest.
She went right through the woods
with the baby, and out the other side,
without ever leaving the road.
Then, far off to the right, she heard
145 dogs barking and cocks crowing;
she knew she would be able to find a town over there.
Quickly, she went in the direction
of the barking.
Soon she came
150 to a fine, prosperous town.
There was an abbey there,
a thriving, well-endowed one;
I believe it held a community of nuns
supervised by an abbess.
155 The damsel saw
the towers, walls, and steeple of the abbey,
and she hastened toward it,
stopping at the front gate.
She put down the child she was carrying
160 and knelt humbly
to say a prayer.
"O God," she prayed, "by your holy name,
if it is your will,
protect this infant from death."
165 When she'd finished praying,
she looked behind her,
saw a broad-limbed ash tree,
its branches thick with leaves;
its trunk divided into four boughs.
170 It had been planted as a shade tree.
The girl took the baby in her arms
and ran over to the ash tree,
placed the child up in its branches and left her there,
commending her to the true God.
175 Then the girl returned to her mistress
and told her what she'd done.

There was a porter in the abbey,
whose job it was to open the abbey gate,
to let in the people who had come
180 to hear the early service.
That morning he rose as early as usual,
lit the candles and the lamps,
rang the bells and opened the gate.
He noticed the clothes up in the ash tree,
185 and thought that someone must have stolen them,
and then left them there.
He didn't notice anything else.
As quickly as he could, he went over to the tree,
touched the clothes, and found the child there.
190 He gave thanks to God;
he did not leave the child, but took her with him
to his own dwelling.
He had a daughter who was a widow;
her husband was dead and she had a child,
195 still in the cradle, whom she was nursing.
The good man called her:
"Daughter," he said, "get up!
Light the candle, start the fire!
I've brought home a baby
200 that I found out there in the ash tree.
Nurse her for me,
then get her warm and bathe her."
The daughter obeyed him;
she lit the fire and took the baby,
205 made her warm and gave her a good bath,
then nursed her.
On the child's arm they discovered the ring,
and they saw her costly, beautiful clothes.
From these they were certain
210 that she was born of noble lineage.
The next day, after the service,
when the abbess came out of the chapel,

the porter went to speak to her;
he wanted to tell her how, by chance,
215 he had found the child.
The abbess ordered him
to bring the child to her
just as she was found.
The porter went home,
220 willingly brought the child back,
and showed her to the abbess.
She examined the baby closely
and said she would raise her,
would treat her as her niece.
225 She strictly forbade the porter
to tell the truth about the child's discovery.
She raised the child herself,
and because she had been found in the ash tree
the abbess decided to name her "Fresne" [Ash].
230 And so people called her.
The abbess did indeed treat her as a niece,
and for a long time she grew up in privacy;
she was raised
entirely within the walls of the abbey.
235 When she reached the age
where nature creates beauty,
in all of Brittany there wasn't such a beautiful
or so refined a girl;
she was noble and cultivated
240 in appearance and speech.
Everyone who saw her loved her,
praised her to the skies.
Now at Dole there lived a good lord—
there's never been a better, before or since—
245 whose name I'll tell you here:
they called him Gurun in that region.
He heard about the young girl
and he fell in love with her.
He went to a tournament,

250 and on his way back passed the abbey,
where he stopped to ask after the damsel.
The abbess introduced her to him.
He saw that she was beautiful and cultivated,
wise, refined, and well educated.
255 If he couldn't win her love
he'd consider himself very badly off indeed.
But he was at a loss about how to proceed;
if he came there often,
the abbess would notice what was going on,
260 and he'd never lay eyes on the damsel again.
He hit upon a scheme:
he would become a benefactor of the abbey,
give it so much of his land
that it would be enriched forever;
265 he'd thus establish a patron's right to live there,
so that he could come and stay whenever he chose.
To be a member of that community
he gave generously of his goods—
but he had a motive
270 other than receiving pardon for his sins.
He came there often
and spoke to the girl;
he pleaded so well, promised so much
that she granted him what he desired.
275 When he was sure of her love,
he spoke seriously with her one day.
"Beautiful one," he said, "now that
you've made me your lover,
come away from here and live with me.
280 I'm sure you know
that if your aunt found out about us
she'd be upset,
especially if you became pregnant right under her roof.
In fact, she'd be furious.
285 If you'll take my advice,
you'll come away with me.

I'll never let you down—
and I'll take good care of you."
Since she loved him deeply,
290 she willingly granted what he desired.
She went away with him;
he took her to his castle.
She brought her silk swaddling cloth and her ring with her;
that could turn out to be very fortunate for her.
295 The abbess had given them to her
and told her the circumstances
in which she had been sent to her:
she was nestled up in the ash tree,
and whoever had abandoned her there
300 had bestowed on her the garments and the ring.
The abbess had received no other possessions with her;
she had raised her as her niece.
The girl kept the tokens,[3]
locked them in a chest.
305 She took the chest away with her;
she'd no intention of leaving it behind.
The knight who took her away
loved and cherished her greatly,
and so did all his men and servants.
310 There wasn't one, big or little,
who didn't love her for her noble character,
and honor her as well.
She lived with him for a long time,
until the knight's vassals
315 reproached him for it.
They often urged him
to marry a noble woman,
and to get rid of this mistress of his.
They'd be pleased if he had an heir
320 who could succeed to
his land and inheritance;

3. The translation follows Rychner's emendation of *l'esgardat* to *les gardat*.

it would be much to their disadvantage
if he was deterred by his concubine
from having a child born in wedlock.
325 They would no longer consider him their lord
or willingly serve him
if he didn't do what they wanted.
The knight agreed
to take a wife according to their wishes,
330 so they began to look about for one.
"My lord," they said, "quite near by
lives a worthy man of your rank;
he has a daughter who is his heiress.
You'll get much land if you take her.
335 The girl's name is Codre [Hazel];
there isn't one so pretty in this region.
In exchange for the ash, when you get rid of her,
you'll have the hazel.
The hazel tree bears nuts and thus gives pleasure;
340 the ash bears no fruit.
Let us make the arrangements for the daughter;
God willing, we will get her for you."
They arranged the marriage,
obtained everyone's promise.
345 Alas! what a misfortune
that these good men didn't know
the real story about these girls[4]—
they were twin sisters!
Fresne was hidden away,
350 and her lover was to marry the other.
When she found out that he had done this,
she didn't sulk about it;
she continued to serve her lord well
and honored all his vassals.
355 The knights of the household,
the squires and serving boys

4. Again, the text has *aventure*.

were all very sad on her account;
sad because they were going to lose her.
❧ On the day of the betrothal,
360 her lord sent for his friends.
The archbishop of Dole,
another of his vassals, was there as well.
They all brought his fiancée to him.
Her mother came with her;
365 she worried about this other girl
whom the lord loved so much,
because she might try to cause trouble, if she could,
between Codre and her husband.
The mother wants her expelled from the house;
370 she'll tell her son-in-law
that he should marry her off to some good man;
that way he'll be rid of her, she thinks.
❧ They held the betrothals in grand style;
there was much celebrating.
375 Fresne was in the private chambers.
No matter what she saw,
it didn't seem to bother her;
she didn't even seem a bit angry.
She waited on the bride-to-be
380 courteously and efficiently.
Everybody who saw this
thought it a great marvel.
Her mother inspected her carefully,
and began to love and admire her.
385 She said to herself that if she'd known
what kind of a person Fresne was,
she wouldn't have let her suffer on account of her daughter Codre,
wouldn't have taken Fresne's lord away from her.
❧ That night, Fresne went
390 to make up the bed
in which the new bride was to sleep;
she took off her cloak,

and called the chamberlains to her.
She instructed them concerning the manner
395 in which the lord liked things done,
for she had seen it many times.
When they had prepared the bed,
they threw a coverlet over it.
The cloth was some old dress material;
400 the girl looked at it,
it seemed to her poor stuff;
that bothered her.
She opened a chest, took out her birth garment,
and put it on her lord's bed.
405 She did it to honor him;
the archbishop would be coming there
to bless the newlyweds in bed.
That was part of his duty.
When the chamber was empty,
410 the mother led her daughter in.
She wished to prepare her for bed,
and told her to get undressed.
She looked at the cloth on the bed;
she'd never seen such a fine one
415 except the one she'd given
to her infant daughter when she abandoned her.
Then she suddenly remembered the castaway;
her heart skipped a beat.
She called the chamberlain:
420 "Tell me," she said, "on your honor,
where was this fine silk cloth found?"
"My lady," he replied, "I'll tell you:
the girl brought it,
and threw it over the coverlet
425 because the coverlet didn't seem good enough to her.
I think the silk cloth is hers."
The mother now called Fresne,
and Fresne came to her;
she removed her cloak,

430 and the lady began questioning her:
"My dear, don't hide anything from me!
Where did you find this beautiful cloth?
How did you come by it? Who gave it to you?
Tell me at once where it came from!"
435 The girl answered her,
"My lady, my aunt, who raised me—
she is an abbess—gave it to me
and ordered me to take good care of it;
whoever sent me to be raised by her
440 had given me this, and also a ring."
"Fair one, may I see the ring?"
"Yes, my lady, I'll be happy to show you."
Then Fresne brought her the ring;
she examined it carefully.
445 She recognized it very well,
and the silk cloth too.
No doubt about it, now she knew—
this was her own daughter.
She didn't hide it, but cried out for all to hear,
450 "My dear, you are my daughter!"
Out of pity for Fresne
she fell over in a faint.
When she regained consciousness,
she quickly sent for her husband,
455 and he came, all in a fright.
When he entered the bedroom,
his wife threw herself at his feet,
hugged and kissed him,
asked his forgiveness for her crime.
460 He didn't know what this was all about;[5]
"Wife," he said, "what are you talking about?
There's been nothing but good between us.
I'll pardon you as much as you please!
Tell me what's bothering you."

5. The reading follows MS (S).

465 "My lord, since you've forgiven me,
I'll tell you—listen!
Once, in my great wickedness,
I spoke foolishly about my neighbor,
slandering her because she had twins.
470 I was really wronging myself.
The truth is, I then became pregnant
and had twin daughters; so I hid one,
had her abandoned in front of an abbey,
wrapped in our brocaded silk cloth,
475 wearing the ring that you gave me
when you first courted me.
I can't hide this from you:
I've found the ring and the cloth,
and also discovered our daughter,
480 whom I lost through my folly;
and this is she, right here,
the brave, wise, and beautiful girl
loved by the knight
who has married her sister."
485 Her husband said, "I'm delighted by this news;
I was never so pleased.
Since we've found our daughter,
God has given us great joy,
instead of doubling the sin.
490 My daughter," he said, "come here!"
The girl was overjoyed
by the story she'd heard.[6]
Her father won't wait any longer;
he goes to get his son-in-law,
495 and brings in the archbishop too—
he tells him the adventure.
When the knight heard the story
he was happier than he'd ever been.
The archbishop advised

6. "Story" renders *aventure*.

500 that things should be left as they were that night;
in the morning he would separate
the knight from the woman he had married.
They agreed to this plan.
Next morning, the marriage was annulled
505 and the knight married his beloved;
she was given to him by her father,
who was well disposed toward her;
he divided his inheritance with her.
The father and his wife remained at the festivities,
510 for as long as they lasted, with their daughter.
When they returned to their land,
they took their daughter Codre with them;
later, in their country,
she made a rich marriage too.
515 When this adventure became known
just as it happened,
the *lai* of Fresne was made from it.
It was named after its heroine.

LE FRESNE (*The Ash Tree*)

VIRTUALLY ALL readers of Marie's *lais* agree on the charm and effectiveness of *Le Fresne*. Its adroit combination of three durable motifs in European folktale and fiction pays tribute to Marie's craftsmanship as a storyteller, for the interaction among the three elements of the plot is as unforced as it is dramatic. The first motif is the romance of a heroine (or hero) who is abandoned, in infancy, by her noble parents, is found and raised by benevolent foster parents, and who then falls in love, only to be threatened with the loss of her beloved to a rival of higher rank. The protagonist's true station in life is discovered at the last minute, thanks to the identification of tokens left in her possession when she was abandoned, and the story ends with a double "recovery"—marriage to the beloved and reconciliation with the repentant parents. (A popular version of this plot is embodied in the Greek romance *Daphnis and Chloe.*) In the second of Marie's plot motifs, a wicked woman who falsely accuses another of a crime is placed by fortune in the position of appearing to have committed the same crime. To protect herself (or as a punishment) she loses her child, and years later, when she accidentally finds the child again, is impelled to repentance and confession, thereby winning the right to keep her offspring. The final motif of *Fresne* is the female Job or patient Griselda, as she is called in the later medieval versions of Boccaccio, Petrarch, and Chaucer. A young woman of low rank is chosen by a nobleman as his consort; her devotion is severely tested by the husband or by fortune, but she remains faithful in adversity and her virtue is suitably recognized at the story's happy ending.

In *Le Fresne,* the heroine's growth from helpless infant-foundling to a young woman of great beauty and moral stature provides her circular journey away from and back to her parents with a strong element of progress;[1] it imparts to the fortuitous events of the conclusion a moral force and, above all, permits a seamless joining of the three plot elements. At the beginning of the story, Fresne's mother slanderously accuses a neighbor of adultery for bearing twin children (according to the popular belief that two children in one birth point to two fathers); when she herself bears twins, she realizes she has brought about her own disgrace. Since she prefers offending God to shaming herself, she prepares to murder one of the children. She is dissuaded by one of her damsels, who volunteers instead to leave the child at the gate of a monastery (a not uncommon fate for unwanted children in the Middle Ages), where it will receive a good upbringing without bringing grief to its mother.

The selfless offer of the *meschine,* the girl, which saves Fresne's life and her mother's reputation, embodies a mature, deeply moral response to life's chances and human relationships: having been nurtured by her mistress, who has loved and cherished her, the girl is now in a position to repay that earlier protection with a reciprocal manifestation of love at the moment when it will do her lady the most good. Her gesture prefigures Fresne's crucial response of selfless devotion to her lord, Gurun, out of gratitude for his love. Even though Gurun is about to marry Codre and abandon Fresne, Fresne, to dignify it, places her prized possession, the luxurious coverlet in which she was wrapped by her mother, on the nuptial bed of Gurun and Codre. By this gesture, Fresne makes possible her mother's discovery of her identity and thus brings about the *lai*'s double denouement: the mother confesses her sin to her husband and receives her lost daughter back into the family, and Fresne, her noble lineage thus revealed, recovers Gurun in marriage.

The symbolic act of covering the bed of her apparently faithless lover is an emblem of Fresne's self-sacrifice, which, paradoxically, wins her back her full identity as daughter and as wife. It also stands as testimony to her capacity for love and action based on gratitude—an element of moral growth in her character that imposes linearity on the cycles of fortune in this romance. Finally, the placing of the swaddling robe on the marriage bed is an image of the continuity from generation to generation of the impulse to shelter those closest to us—and, ideally, all our fellow humans—in the protective envelope of love. This impulse to protect and nurture runs through the *lai,* exemplified not only by Fresne and the *meschine,* but by the abbess, and even by the old porter of the abbey who discovers the infant Fresne and brings her at once to his own widowed daughter so the infant can be nursed. (The juxtaposition of lost husband and found child suggests the rhythm of this romance world in which love and nurture must operate in order to give moral meaning to the cycle of death and birth.) Even Fresne's mother, in an earlier time, had nurtured the *meschine,* and the vassals who force Gurun to abandon Fresne for Codre (unknown to them, Fresne's sister) are moved by the desire that their lord have children who will assume his heritage and protect them from harm: i.e., be their feudal foster parents.

All these instances of nurture find their central symbol in the great shade tree that gives Fresne her name. Gurun's followers interpret Fresne's name in a negative sense, as a tree that, unlike the hazel (*la Codre*), bears no fruit; Marie, however, intends us to see the name proleptically: as the ash tree once protected its namesake, and as she has been nurtured by the abbess, so will she, in "protecting" Gurun with her mantle, establish her right to become his wife and the nurturer of his children.[2] Set in the midst of such a pervasive pattern, Fresne's mother's refusal to nurture her daughter at birth appears as a violation of the *lai*'s fundamental moral principle. Fortunately, in the optimistic world of *Le Fresne,* it is a breach that can be mended and repented at the right moment.

Marie encloses the main movement and theme of her miniature romance in a world of charming, sentimental details: the tableau of village sounds that tells the *meschine* she has come to the end of her search for a place to leave her infant charge; her prayer as she deposits the foundling in the tree; and the routine of the porter, interrupted by his discovery of the foundling. Marie's portrait of Gurun, the young lord who falls in love with Fresne without ever having seen her (cf. Equitan's similar passion from afar, and the troubadour tradition of distant love, *amor de lonh*) and later arranges to give large donations to the abbey as an excuse to see her regularly, is also affectionate and sentimental. His love for Fresne is pure and complete, and when he takes her away from the abbey to live with him as his mistress, Marie uses the same words to describe his treatment of her—*mut la cheri e mut l'ama*—that she has used to describe Fresne's mother's conduct toward the *meschine: et mut [l'ot] amee e mut cherie* ("and he [she] loved and cherished her much").

The harmony of plot motifs and (themes) endows *Le Fresne* with gemlike perfection, as Marie celebrates the triumph of protective love over the obstacles of human weakness, social circumstance, and fortune.

1. The interaction of circular and linear elements is a mark of the sophisticated romance plot. The element of movement away from and back to stasis (represented by a stable situation involving family ties, a well-defined social rank, or the like) reflects a perception of the cyclicality of human experience, often represented iconographically in the Middle Ages by the revolving wheel of fortune. The protagonist's endurance of this circular movement can coexist with an irreversible process of physical or moral growth, so that while he may seem merely to return to his starting point by the end of the romance, he has in fact become a very different person in the process, and therefore sees his old situation through new eyes, as it were.

2. On the significance of Fresne's name, see R. W. Hanning, "Uses of Names in Medieval Literature," *Names* 16 (1968), 337–338, and the article by Mickel on Marie's irony, cited in the bibliography.

Bisclavret *(The Werewolf)*

Since I am undertaking to compose *lais,*
I don't want to forget Bisclavret;
In Breton, the *lai*'s name is *Bisclavret*—
the Normans call it *Garwaf* [*The Werewolf*].
5 In the old days, people used to say—
and it often actually happened—
that some men turned into werewolves
and lived in the woods.
A werewolf is a savage beast;
10 while his fury is on him
he eats men, does much harm,
goes deep in the forest to live.
But that's enough of this for now:
I want to tell you about the Bisclavret.

15 In Brittany there lived a nobleman
whom I've heard marvelously praised;
a fine, handsome knight
who behaved nobly.
He was close to his lord,
20 and loved by all his neighbors.
He had an estimable wife,
one of lovely appearance;
he loved her and she him,
but one thing was very vexing to her:
25 during the week he would be missing
for three whole days, and she didn't know
what happened to him or where he went.
Nor did any of his men know anything about it.
One day he returned home
30 happy and delighted;
she asked him about it.
"My lord," she said, "and dear love,
I'd very much like to ask you one thing—
if I dared;

35 but I'm so afraid of your anger
that nothing frightens me more."
When he heard that, he embraced her,
drew her to him and kissed her.
"My lady," he said, "go ahead and ask!
40 There's nothing you could want to know,
that, if I knew the answer, I wouldn't tell you."
"By God," she replied, "now I'm cured!
My lord, on the days when you go away from me
I'm in such a state—
45 so sad at heart,
so afraid I'll lose you—
that if I don't get quick relief
I could die of this very soon.
Please, tell me where you go,
50 where you have been staying.
I think you must have a lover,
and if that's so, you're doing wrong."
"My dear," he said, "have mercy on me, for God's sake!
Harm will come to me if I tell you about this,
55 because I'd lose your love
and even my very self."
When the lady heard this
she didn't take it lightly;
she kept asking him,
60 coaxed and flattered him so much,
that he finally told her what happened to him—
he hid nothing from her.
"My dear, I become a werewolf:
I go off into the great forest,
65 in the thickest part of the woods,
and I live on the prey I hunt down."
When he had told her everything,
she asked further
whether he undressed or kept his clothes on [when he became a werewolf].
70 "Wife," he replied, "I go stark naked."

"Tell me, then, for God's sake, where your clothes are."
"That I won't tell you;
for if I were to lose them,
and then be discovered,
75 I'd stay a werewolf forever.
I'd be helpless
until I got them back.
That's why I don't want their hiding place to be known."
"My lord," the lady answered,
80 "I love you more than all the world;
you mustn't hide anything from me
or fear me in any way:
that doesn't seem like love to me.
What wrong have I done? For what sin of mine
85 do you mistrust me about anything?
Do the right thing and tell me!"
She harassed and bedeviled him so,
that he had no choice but to tell her.
"Lady," he said, "near the woods,
90 beside the road that I use to get there,
there's an old chapel
that has often done me good service;
under a bush there is a big stone,
hollowed out inside;
95 I hide my clothes right there
until I'm ready to come home."
The lady heard this wonder
and turned scarlet from fear;
she was terrified of the whole adventure.
100 Over and over she considered
how she might get rid of him;
she never wanted to sleep with him again.
There was a knight of that region
who had loved her for a long time,
105 who begged for her love,
and dedicated himself to serving her.
She'd never loved him at all,

nor pledged her love to him,
but now she sent a messenger for him,
110 and told him her intention.
"My dear," she said, "cheer up!
I shall now grant you without delay
what you have suffered for;
you'll meet with no more refusals—
115 I offer you my love and my body;
make me your mistress!"
He thanked her graciously
and accepted her promise,
and she bound him to her by an oath.
120 Then she told him
how her husband went away and what happened to him;
she also taught him the precise path
her husband took into the forest,
and then she sent the knight to get her husband's clothes.
125 So Bisclavret was betrayed,[1]
ruined by his own wife.
Since people knew he was often away from home
they all thought
this time he'd gone away forever.
130 They searched for him and made inquiries
but could never find him,
so they had to let matters stand.
The wife later married the other knight,
who had loved her for so long.
135 A whole year passed
until one day the king went hunting;
he headed right for the forest
where Bisclavret was.
When the hounds were unleashed,
140 they ran across Bisclavret;
the hunters and the dogs
chased him all day,

1. Hereafter Bisclavret will be treated as a proper name, and the definite article omitted.

until they were just about to take him
and tear him apart,
145 at which point he saw the king
and ran to him, pleading for mercy.
He took hold of the king's stirrup,
kissed his leg and his foot.
The king saw this and was terrified;
150 he called his companions.
"My lords," he said, "come quickly!
Look at this marvel—
this beast is humbling itself to me.
It has the mind of a man, and it's begging me for mercy!
155 Chase the dogs away,
and make sure no one strikes it.
This beast is rational—he has a mind.
Hurry up: let's get out of here.
I'll extend my peace to the creature;
160 indeed, I'll hunt no more today!"
Thereupon the king turned away.
Bisclavret followed him;
he stayed close to the king, and wouldn't go away;
he'd no intention of leaving him.
165 The king led him to his castle;
he was delighted with this turn of events,
for he'd never seen anything like it.
He considered the beast a great wonder
and held him very dear.
170 He commanded all his followers,
for the sake of their love for him, to guard Bisclavret well,
and under no circumstances to do him harm;
none of them should strike him;
rather, he should be well fed and watered.
175 They willingly guarded the creature;
every day he went to sleep
among the knights, near the king.
Everyone was fond of him;
he was so noble and well behaved

180 that he never wished to do anything wrong.
Regardless of where the king might go,
Bisclavret never wanted to be separated from him;
he always accompanied the king.
The king became very much aware that the creature loved him.
185 Now listen to what happened next.
The king held a court;
to help him celebrate his feast
and to serve him as handsomely as possible,
he summoned all the barons
190 who held fiefs from him.
Among the knights who went,
and all dressed up in his best attire,
was the one who had married Bisclavret's wife.
He neither knew nor suspected
195 that he would find Bisclavret so close by.
As soon as he came to the palace
Bisclavret saw him,
ran toward him at full speed,
sank his teeth into him, and started to drag him down.
200 He would have done him great damage
if the king hadn't called him off,
and threatened him with a stick.
Twice that day he tried to bite the knight.
Everyone was extremely surprised,
205 since the beast had never acted that way
toward any other man he had seen.
All over the palace people said
that he wouldn't act that way without a reason:
that somehow or other, the knight had mistreated Bisclavret,
210 and now he wanted his revenge.
And so the matter rested
until the feast was over
and until the barons took their leave of the king
and started home.
215 The very first to leave,
to the best of my knowledge,

was the knight whom Bisclavret had attacked.
It's no wonder the creature hated him.
Not long afterward,
220 as the story leads me to believe,
the king, who was so wise and noble,
went back to the forest
where he had found Bisclavret,
and the creature went with him.
225 That night, when he finished hunting,
he sought lodging out in the countryside.
The wife of Bisclavret heard about it,
dressed herself elegantly,
and went the next day to speak with the king,
230 bringing rich presents for him.
When Bisclavret saw her coming,
no one could hold him back;
he ran toward her in a rage.
Now listen to how well he avenged himself!
235 He tore the nose off her face.
What worse thing could he have done to her?
Now men closed in on him from all sides;
they were about to tear him apart,
when a wise man said to the king,
240 "My lord, listen to me!
This beast has stayed with you,
and there's not one of us
who hasn't watched him closely,
hasn't traveled with him often.
245 He's never touched anyone,
or shown any wickedness,
except to this woman.
By the faith that I owe you,
he has some grudge against her,
250 and against her husband as well.
This is the wife of the knight
whom you used to like so much,

and who's been missing for so long—
we don't know what became of him.
255 Why not put this woman to torture
and see if she'll tell you
why the beast hates her?
Make her tell what she knows!
We've seen many strange things
260 happen in Brittany!"
The king took his advice;
he detained the knight.
At the same time he took the wife
and subjected her to torture;
265 out of fear and pain
she told all about her husband:
how she had betrayed him
and taken away his clothes;
the story he had told her
270 about what happened to him and where he went;
and how after she had taken his clothes
he'd never been seen in his land again.
She was quite certain
that this beast was Bisclavret.
275 The king demanded the clothes;
whether she wanted to or not
she sent home for them,
and had them brought to Bisclavret.
When they were put down in front of him
280 he didn't even seem to notice them;
the king's wise man—
the one who had advised him earlier—
said to him, "My lord, you're not doing it right.
This beast wouldn't, under any circumstances,
285 in order to get rid of his animal form,
put on his clothes in front of you;
you don't understand what this means:
he's just too ashamed to do it here.
Have him led to your chambers

290 and bring the clothes with him;
then we'll leave him alone for a while.
If he turns into a man, we'll know about it."
The king himself led the way
and closed all the doors on him.
295 After a while he went back,
taking two barons with him;
all three entered the king's chamber.
On the king's royal bed
they found the knight asleep.
300 The king ran to embrace him.
He hugged and kissed him again and again.
As soon as he had the chance,
the king gave him back all his lands;
he gave him more than I can tell.
305 He banished the wife,
chased her out of the country.
She went into exile with the knight
with whom she had betrayed her lord.
She had several children
310 who were widely known
for their appearance:
several women of the family
were actually born without noses,
and lived out their lives noseless.

315 The adventure that you have heard
really happened, no doubt about it.
The *lai* of Bisclavret was made
so it would be remembered forever.

BISCLAVRET (*The Werewolf*)

In *Bisclavret,* Marie turns to the folklore of lycanthropy—a subject of deep fascination for European culture. Antecedents of Marie's story include versions in Pliny's *Historia naturalis* and Petronius' *Satyricon;* her version seems in turn to have influenced episodes in the later medieval *Lai de Melion* and *Roman de Renart le Contrefait.* In Marie's hands, the story of the man compelled by fortune (*aventure*) to spend part of his existence as a beast of prey in the forest becomes a parable about the forces of bestiality that exist within human nature and how they should (and should not) be confronted, used, or transcended. None of the *lais* is more deeply concerned with the fragility of social existence, given the battle within men and women between their higher and baser impulses, but *Bisclavret* is also concerned with the human capacity to manifest nobility even under the most trying conditions, and thus to transcend the animal part of our nature and garner the hard-won benefits of civilization.

Marie plays upon and reverses our expectations in the exposition of *Bisclavret,* so that, unlike the case in *Equitan* (for example), the moral point of the story only gradually emerges from its twistings and turnings and is never pressed overtly upon us. The effect of this technique is to establish a parallel between Bisclavret's *aventure*—his fall into and then rescue from bestial shape—and the audience's struggle to free itself from its initial misapprehensions and attain a clear understanding of the significance of the werewolf's emblematic career.

The *lai* opens with a word picture of the werewolf, stressing his man-eating brutality. (Ironically, the closest the protagonist will come to such behavior is biting off his disloyal wife's nose, a gesture of justifiable revenge rather than of uncontrolled savagery.) This evocation of the werewolf as the beast that lurks within a man and breaks out periodically prompts our initial sympathy with the wife's reaction of fear and loathing when she learns that her husband is such a creature—a reaction that leads her to betray him in her desire to escape.

Yet Marie also makes it clear that the protagonist, in his human phase, is noble, a trusted companion of his lord, and a man beloved of his neighbors. His one failing, aside from the lycanthropy that is beyond his control, is his inability to keep his secret from his wife, although he knows that his confession, in response to her entreaties, may well cause him to lose her, and his human shape, forever. He loves not wisely but too well; she, on the other hand, does not love, or trust, enough. Faced with the dark side of her husband's nature, she forgets all his virtues, as enumerated by Marie in the passage cited above, and desperately arranges to free herself by a double betrayal. She accepts the favors of a suitor she has hitherto scorned, and exploits his desire to serve her by instructing him to steal the werewolf's hidden clothes, thereby preventing his return to his human shape. Her husband thus disposed of, she marries the suitor.

By this point, our original responses to the werewolf and his wife have undergone a transformation to sympathy for the betrayed man-beast and disapproval, if not disgust, for the wife. Marie's intention has also emerged: the werewolf is an image of human nature, capable of nobility, but also of irrationality and bestiality. His wife sees him only through a self-centered haze of idealizing love; her main worry about his absences is that he is betraying her with another woman, which is another irony, considering her subsequent behavior. His revelation of the full ambiguities of his nature, far from prompting sympathy and aid, sends her reeling, unable to face the truth. Her absolute love turns at once to absolute loathing; she can now see only his bestial side (though it has never harmed her), and, seeking to destroy this knowledge that has contaminated her vision of life, she turns to another man who has wooed her in the ideal manner of stereotypical, troubadour-like courtly love. She takes refuge in this partial vision and, in fact, uses it to put the now blighted husband out of her life and sight forever. The wife's failure of trust results from her obsession with her husband's potential for evil; her abandonment of him, with the theft of his clothes, is thus a self-fulfilling prophecy, imprisoning him forever (as it seems) within the bestial self she so fears. The wife's treason and the loss of the werewolf's clothing are reciprocal metaphors; both embody a loss of that civilizing force in life—symbolized at the surface level by apparel, at a deeper level by the love relationship—which saves humanity from perpetual servitude to its lower, amoral impulses, and allows it to engage in the satisfying social relationships enumerated in Marie's opening statement about the protagonist.

The victimization of the man-beast is not, however, the end of the story; more reversals are in store. The werewolf is discovered by the king he served in human form, while the latter is out hunting. When the beast makes motions of obeisance and begs for mercy, the king, despite initial fear, recognizes human awareness (*sen de hume*) in the creature, and saves him from the hunting dogs. In this scene, the narrative, which till now has presented the human condition as the beast that lurks within man (and woman, for the wife's fear and disloyalty are equally "bestial"), asks us to look anew at that condition and discover the man that lurks within the beast, to wit, the potential for graceful ingenuity in adversity manifested by the werewolf, and for mercy in the face of fear manifested by the king (though not the wife). The werewolf answers the king's compassion with further civilized behavior: he becomes the king's inseparable companion and acts nobly to all the courtiers, who recognize his love for the king who has saved him (another implied comment on the wife).

Only when the werewolf encounters his wife's new husband, and then the wife herself, does he behave "bestially," by attacking them. But a perceptive courtier (yet another foil to the imperceptive wife) realizes there must be a reason for this departure from the creature's normal behavior; by putting the savagery into perspective, the court recognizes that the werewolf can make moral distinctions between good and bad, friend and foe. This moral awareness allows him to channel his capacity for violence into the appropriate, civilized punishment of evil. By this demonstration of his powers of discrimination, the werewolf wins the chance to recover his human form: the king, following his councillor's advice, forces a confession from the wife, and forces her to produce her husband's clothes as well. As the wife's betrayal was metaphorically linked to the husband's loss of his clothing and thus his human shape, so now does his recovery of them follow on, and express metaphorically, his reintegration back into a human community founded on the perception, compassion, and love shown to him by the king and his court.

Before his final metamorphosis, the werewolf demonstrates a final civilized virtue, shame: he refuses to don his clothes in public. This reticence, which the councillor sympathetically understands but which probably strikes us as amusing, if not absurd, has a double significance. First, the cultivation of shame—the unwillingness to fall below a certain level of behavior in the presence of one's peers—is a mark of human social awareness, of sensitivity to others. Second, the werewolf's reluctance to let others see him changing his form reverses his foolish willingness to reveal this shape-shifting to his wife at the beginning of the *lai*. He has, in effect, learned his lesson about the need for privacy, and thus fully deserves to return to full humanity and social integration.

Thus the king, by his trust in the man-in-beast, wins back a noble vassal; his human treatment of the werewolf is another self-fulfilling prophecy, while the wife sees her prophetic fear of the beast-in-man come true in becoming the victim of the werewolf's only bestial deed (the loss of her nose). In *Bisclavret,* Marie argues that human beings are defined not only by their inherent potential for good or evil but also by their fellow humans' responses of trust or fear to that potential. Thus love is lauded as a socializing force in the *lai,* and its betrayal condemned as the ultimate antisocial act.

Lanval

I shall tell you the adventure of another *lai,*
just as it happened:
it was composed about a very noble vassal;
in Breton, they call him Lanval.

5 Arthur, the brave and the courtly king,
was staying at Cardoel,
because the Scots and the Picts
were destroying the land.
They invaded Logres[1]
10 and laid it waste.
At Pentecost, in summer,[2]
the king stayed there.
He gave out many rich gifts:
to counts and barons,
15 members of the Round Table—
such a company had no equal[3] in all the world—
he distributed wives and lands,
to all but one who had served him.
That was Lanval; Arthur forgot him,
20 and none of his men favored him either.
For his valor, for his generosity,
his beauty and his bravery,
most men envied him;
some feigned the appearance of love
25 who, if something unpleasant happened to him,
would not have been at all disturbed.
He was the son of a king of high degree

1. Logres is England.

2. In medieval poetry, only two seasons are usually recognized, summer and winter. The feast of Pentecost is frequently the starting point of an Arthurian adventure.

3. Equal in number as well as in worth: cf. Ewert, "There was no equal number of such knights in all the world" (p. 173).

but he was far from his heritage.
He was of the king's household
30 but he had spent all his wealth,
for the king gave him nothing
nor did Lanval ask.
Now Lanval was in difficulty,
depressed and very worried.
35 My lords, don't be surprised:
a strange man, without friends,
is very sad in another land,
when he doesn't know where to look for help.
The knight of whom I speak,
40 who had served the king so long,
one day mounted his horse
and went off to amuse himself.
He left the city
and came, all alone, to a field;
45 he dismounted by a running stream
but his horse trembled badly.
He removed the saddle and went off,
leaving the horse to roll around in the meadow.
He folded his cloak beneath his head
50 and lay down.
He worried about his difficulty,
he could see nothing that pleased him.
As he lay there
he looked down along the bank
55 and saw two girls approaching;
he had never seen any lovelier.
They were richly dressed,
tightly laced,
in tunics of dark purple;
60 their faces were very lovely.
The older one carried basins,
golden, well made, and fine;
I shall tell you the truth about it, without fail.
The other carried a towel.

65 They went straight
to where the knight was lying.
Lanval, who was very well bred,
got up to meet them.
They greeted him first
70 and gave him their message:
"Sir Lanval, my lady,
who is worthy and wise and beautiful,
sent us for you.
Come with us now.
75 We shall guide you there safely.
See, her pavilion is nearby!"
The knight went with them;
giving no thought to his horse
who was feeding before him in the meadow.
80 They led him up to the tent,
which was quite beautiful and well placed.
Queen Semiramis,
however much more wealth,
power, or knowledge she had,
85 or the emperor Octavian
could not have paid for one of the flaps.
There was a golden eagle on top of it,
whose value I could not tell,
nor could I judge the value of the cords or the poles
90 that held up the sides of the tent;
there is no king on earth who could buy it,
no matter what wealth he offered.
The girl was inside the tent:
the lily and the young rose
95 when they appear in the summer
are surpassed by her beauty.
She lay on a beautiful bed—
the bedclothes were worth a castle—
dressed only in her shift.
100 Her body was well shaped and elegant;
for the heat, she had thrown over herself,

a precious cloak of white ermine,
covered with purple alexandrine,
but her whole side was uncovered,
105 her face, her neck and her bosom;
she was whiter than the hawthorn flower.
The knight went forward
and the girl addressed him.
He sat before the bed.
110 "Lanval," she said, "sweet love,
because of you I have come from my land;
I came to seek you from far away.
If you are brave and courtly,
no emperor or count or king
115 will ever have known such joy or good;
for I love you more than anything."
He looked at her and saw that she was beautiful;
Love stung him with a spark
that burned and set fire to his heart.
120 He answered her in a suitable way.
"Lovely one," he said, "if it pleased you,
if such joy might be mine
that you would love me,
there is nothing you might command,
125 within my power, that I would not do,
whether foolish or wise.
I shall obey your command;
for you, I shall abandon everyone.
I want never to leave you.
130 That is what I most desire."
When the girl heard the words
of the man who could love her so,
she granted him her love and her body.
Now Lanval was on the right road!
135 Afterward, she gave him a gift:
he would never again want anything,
he would receive as he desired;

however generously he might give and spend,
she would provide what he needed.
140 Now Lanval is well cared for.
The more lavishly he spends,
the more gold and silver he will have.
"Love," she said, "I admonish you now,
I command and beg you,
145 do not let any man know about this.
I shall tell you why:
you would lose me for good
if this love were known;
you would never see me again
150 or possess my body."
He answered that he would do
exactly as she commanded.
He lay beside her on the bed;
now Lanval is well cared for.
155 He remained with her
that afternoon, until evening
and would have stayed longer, if he could,
and if his love had consented.
"Love," she said, "get up.
160 You cannot stay any longer.
Go away now; I shall remain
but I will tell you one thing:
when you want to talk to me
there is no place you can think of
165 where a man might have his mistress
without reproach or shame,
that I shall not be there with you
to satisfy all your desires.
No man but you will see me
170 or hear my words."
When he heard her, he was very happy,
he kissed her, and then got up.
The girls who had brought him to the tent
dressed him in rich clothes;

175 when he was dressed anew,
there wasn't a more handsome youth in all the world;
he was no fool, no boor.
They gave him water for his hands
and a towel to dry them,
180 and they brought him food.
He took supper with his love;
it was not to be refused.
He was served with great courtesy,
he received it with great joy.
185 There was an entremet
that vastly pleased the knight
for he kissed his lady often
and held her close.
When they finished dinner,
190 his horse was brought to him.
The horse had been well saddled;
Lanval was very richly served.
The knight took his leave, mounted,
and rode toward the city,
195 often looking behind him.
Lanval was very disturbed;
he wondered about his adventure
and was doubtful in his heart;
he was amazed, not knowing what to believe;
200 he didn't expect ever to see her again.
He came to his lodging
and found his men well dressed.
That night, his accommodations were rich
but no one knew where it came from.
205 There was no knight in the city
who really needed a place to stay
whom he didn't invite to join him
to be well and richly served.
Lanval gave rich gifts,
210 Lanval released prisoners,

Lanval dressed jongleurs [performers],
Lanval offered great honors.
There was no stranger or friend
to whom Lanval didn't give.
215 Lanval's joy and pleasure were intense;
in the daytime or at night,
he could see his love often;
she was completely at his command.

In that same year, it seems to me,
220 after the feast of St. John,
about thirty knights
were amusing themselves
in an orchard beneath the tower
where the queen was staying.
225 Gawain was with them
and his cousin, the handsome Yvain;
Gawain, the noble, the brave,
who was so loved by all, said:
"By God, my lords, we wronged
230 our companion Lanval,
who is so generous and courtly,
and whose father is a rich king,
when we didn't bring him with us."
They immediately turned back,
235 went to his lodging
and prevailed on Lanval to come along with them.
At a sculpted window
the queen was looking out;
she had three ladies with her.
240 She saw the king's retinue,
recognized Lanval and looked at him.
Then she told one of her ladies
to send for her maidens,
the loveliest and the most refined;
245 together they went to amuse themselves

in the orchard where the others were.
She brought thirty or more with her;
they descended the steps.
The knights came to meet them,
250 because they were delighted to see them.
The knights took them by the hand;
their conversation was in no way vulgar.
Lanval went off to one side,
far from the others; he was impatient
255 to hold his love,
to kiss and embrace and touch her;
he thought little of others' joys
if he could not have his pleasure.
When the queen saw him alone,
260 she went straight to the knight.
She sat beside him and spoke,
revealing her whole heart:
"Lanval, I have shown you much honor,
I have cherished you, and loved you.
265 You may have all my love;
just tell me your desire.
I promise you my affection.
You should be very happy with me."
"My lady," he said, "let me be!
270 I have no desire to love you.
I've served the king a long time;
I don't want to betray my faith to him.
Never, for you or for your love,
will I do anything to harm my lord."
275 The queen got angry;
in her wrath, she insulted him:
"Lanval," she said, "I am sure
you don't care for such pleasure;
people have often told me
280 that you have no interest in women.
You have fine-looking boys
with whom you enjoy yourself.

Base coward, lousy cripple,
my lord made a bad mistake
285 when he let you stay with him.
For all I know, he'll lose God because of it."
When Lanval heard her, he was quite disturbed;
he was not slow to answer.
He said something out of spite
290 that he would later regret.
"Lady," he said, "of that activity
I know nothing,
but I love and I am loved
by one who should have the prize
295 over all the women I know.
And I shall tell you one thing;
you might as well know all:
any one of those who serve her,
the poorest girl of all,
300 is better than you, my lady queen,
in body, face, and beauty,
in breeding and in goodness."
The queen left him
and went, weeping, to her chamber.
305 She was upset and angry
because he had insulted her.
She went to bed sick;
never, she said, would she get up
unless the king gave her satisfaction
310 for the offense against her.
The king returned from the woods,
he'd had a very good day.
He entered the queen's chambers.
When she saw him, she began to complain.
315 She fell at his feet, asked his mercy,
saying that Lanval had dishonored her;
he had asked for her love,
and because she refused him
he insulted and offended her:

320 he boasted of a love
who was so refined and noble and proud
that her chambermaid,
the poorest one who served her,
was better than the queen.
325 The king got very angry;
he swore an oath:
if Lanval could not defend himself in court
he would have him burned or hanged.
The king left her chamber
330 and called for three of his barons;
he sent them for Lanval
who was feeling great sorrow and distress.
He had come back to his dwelling,
knowing very well
335 that he'd lost his love,
he had betrayed their affair.
He was all alone in a room,
disturbed and troubled;
he called on his love, again and again,
340 but it did him no good.
He complained and sighed,
from time to time he fainted;
then he cried a hundred times for her to have mercy
and speak to her love.
345 He cursed his heart and his mouth;
it's a wonder he didn't kill himself.
No matter how much he cried and shouted,
ranted and raged,
she would not have mercy on him,
350 not even let him see her.
How will he ever contain himself?
The men the king sent
arrived and told him
to appear in court without delay:
355 the king had summoned him

because the queen had accused him.
Lanval went with his great sorrow;
they could have killed him, for all he cared.
He came before the king;
360 he was very sad, thoughtful, silent;
his face revealed great suffering.
In anger the king told him:
"Vassal, you have done me a great wrong!
This was a base undertaking,
365 to shame and disgrace me
and to insult the queen.
You have made a foolish boast:
your love is much too noble
if her maid is more beautiful,
370 more worthy, than the queen."
Lanval denied that he'd dishonored
or shamed his lord,
word for word, as the king spoke:
he had not made advances to the queen;
375 but of what he had said,
he acknowledged the truth,
about the love he had boasted of,
that now made him sad because he'd lost her.
About that he said he would do
380 whatever the court decided.
The king was very angry with him;
he sent for all his men
to determine exactly what he ought to do
so that no one could find fault with his decision.
385 They did as he commanded,
whether they liked it or not.
They assembled,
judged, and decided,
than Lanval should have his day;
390 but he must find pledges for his lord
to guarantee that he would await the judgment,

return, and be present at it.
Then the court would be increased,
for now there were none but the king's household.
395 The barons came back to the king
and announced their decision.
The king demanded pledges.
Lanval was alone and forlorn,
he had no relative, no friend.
400 Gawain went and pledged himself for him,
and all his companions followed.
The king addressed them: "I release him to you
on forfeit of whatever you hold from me,
lands and fiefs, each one for himself."
405 When Lanval was pledged, there was nothing else to do.
He returned to his lodging.
The knights accompanied him,
they reproached and admonished him
that he give up his great sorrow;
410 they cursed his foolish love.
Each day they went to see him,
because they wanted to know
whether he was drinking and eating;
they were afraid that he'd kill himself.
415 On the day that they had named,
the barons assembled.
The king and the queen were there
and the pledges brought Lanval back.
They were all very sad for him:
420 I think there were a hundred
who would have done all they could
to set him free without a trial
where he would be wrongly accused.
The king demanded a verdict
425 according to the charge and rebuttal.
Now it all fell to the barons.
They went to the judgment,
worried and distressed

for the noble man from another land
430 who'd gotten into such trouble in their midst.
Many wanted to condemn him
in order to satisfy their lord.
The Duke of Cornwall said:
"No one can blame us;
435 whether it makes you weep or sing
justice must be carried out.
The king spoke against his vassal
whom I have heard named Lanval;
he accused him of felony,
440 charged him with a misdeed—
a love that he had boasted of,
which made the queen angry.
No one but the king accused him:
by the faith I owe you,
445 if one were to speak the truth,
there should have been no need for defense,
except that a man owes his lord honor
in every circumstance.
He will be bound by his oath,
450 and the king will forgive us our pledges
if he can produce proof;
if his love would come forward,
if what he said,
what upset the queen, is true,
455 then he will be acquitted,
because he did not say it out of malice.
But if he cannot get his proof,
we must make it clear to him
that he will forfeit his service to the king;
460 he must take his leave."
They sent to the knight,
told and announced to him
that he should have his love come
to defend and stand surety for him.
465 He told them that he could not do it:

he would never receive help from her.
They went back to the judges,
not expecting any help from Lanval.
The king pressed them hard
470 because of the queen who was waiting.
When they were ready to give their verdict
they saw two girls approaching,
riding handsome palfreys.
They were very attractive,
475 dressed in purple taffeta,
over their bare skin.
The men looked at them with pleasure.
Gawain, taking three knights with him,
went to Lanval and told him;
480 he pointed out the two girls.
Gawain was extremely happy, and begged him
to tell if his love were one of them.
Lanval said he didn't know who they were,
where they came from or where they were going.
485 The girls proceeded
still on horseback;
they dismounted before the high table
at which Arthur, the king, sat.
They were of great beauty,
490 and spoke in a courtly manner:
"King, clear your chambers,
have them hung with silk
where my lady may dismount;
she wishes to take shelter with you."
495 He promised it willingly
and called two knights
to guide them up to the chambers.
On that subject no more was said.
The king asked his barons
500 for their judgment and decision;
he said they had angered him very much
with their long delay.

"Sire," they said, "we have decided.
Because of the ladies we have just seen
505 we have made no judgment.
Let us reconvene the trial."
Then they assembled, everyone was worried;
there was much noise and strife.
While they were in that confusion,
510 two girls in noble array,
dressed in Phrygian silks
and riding Spanish mules,
were seen coming down the street.
This gave the vassals great joy;
515 to each other they said that now
Lanval, the brave and bold, was saved.
Gawain went up to him,[4]
bringing his companions along.
"Sire," he said, "take heart.
520 For the love of God, speak to us.
Here come two maidens,
well adorned and very beautiful;
one must certainly be your love."
Lanval answered quickly
525 that he did not recognize them,
he didn't know them or love them.
Meanwhile they'd arrived,
and dismounted before the king.
Most of those who saw them praised them
530 for their bodies, their faces, their coloring;
each was more impressive
than the queen had ever been.
The older one was courtly and wise,
she spoke her message fittingly:
535 "King, have chambers prepared for us
to lodge my lady according to her need;

4. Ewert gives Yweins; Warnke, Walwains. Gawain seems more likely, since he is the one most concerned with Lanval throughout and since he always moves with his companions, as in this case.

she is coming here to speak with you."
He ordered them to be taken
to the others who had preceded them.
540 There was no problem with the mules.[5]
When he had seen to the girls,
he summoned all his barons
to render their judgment;
it had already dragged out too much.
545 The queen was getting angry
because she had fasted so long.[6]
They were about to give their judgment
when through the city came riding
a girl on horseback:
550 there was none more beautiful in the world.
She rode a white palfrey,
who carried her handsomely and smoothly:
he was well apportioned in the neck and head,
no finer beast in the world.
555 The palfrey's trappings were rich;
under heaven there was no count or king
who could have afforded them all
without selling or mortgaging lands.
She was dressed in this fashion:
560 in a white linen shift
that revealed both her sides
since the lacing was along the side.
Her body was elegant, her hips slim,
her neck whiter than snow on a branch,
565 her eyes bright, her face white,
a beautiful mouth, a well-set nose,
dark eyebrows and an elegant forehead,
her hair curly and rather blond;
golden wire does not shine

5. The following two lines are added in (S) to explain this remark: "There were enough men to care for them / and put them into the stables."

6. Warnke and Rychner give *jeünot;* Ewert, *atendeit,* "waited," which is not quite as callously selfish.

570 like her hair in the light.
Her cloak, which she had wrapped around her,
was dark purple.
On her wrist she held a sparrow hawk,
a greyhound followed her.[7]
575 In the town, no one, small or big,
old man or child,
failed to come look.
As they watched her pass,
there was no joking about her beauty.
580 She proceeded at a slow pace.
The judges who saw her
marveled at the sight;
no one who looked at her
was not warmed with joy.
585 Those who loved the knight
came to him and told him
of the girl who was approaching,
if God pleased, to rescue him.
"Sir companion, here comes one
590 neither tawny nor dark;
this is, of all who exist,
the most beautiful woman in the world."
Lanval heard them and lifted his head;
he recognized her and sighed.
595 The blood rose to his face;
he was quick to speak.
"By my faith," he said, "that is my love.
Now I don't care if I am killed,
if only she forgives me.
600 For I am restored, now that I see her."
The lady entered the palace;
no one so beautiful had ever been there.

7. (S) adds the following attractive if doubtful lines: "A noble youth led her / carrying an ivory horn. / They came through the street, very beautiful. / Such great beauty was not seen / in Venus, who was a queen, / or in Dido, or in Lavinia."

She dismounted before the king
so that she was well seen by all.
605 And she let her cloak fall
so they could see her better.
The king, who was well bred,
rose and went to meet her;
all the others honored her
610 and offered to serve her.
When they had looked at her well,
when they had greatly praised her beauty,
she spoke in this way,
she didn't want to wait:
615 "I have loved one of your vassals:
you see him before you—Lanval.
He has been accused in your court—
I don't want him to suffer
for what he said; you should know
620 that the queen was in the wrong.
He never made advances to her.
And for the boast that he made,
if he can be acquitted through me,
let him be set free by your barons."
625 Whatever the barons judged by law
the king promised would prevail.
To the last man they agreed
that Lanval had successfully answered the charge.
He was set free by their decision
630 and the girl departed.
The king could not detain her,
though there were enough people to serve her.
Outside the hall stood
a great stone of dark marble
635 where heavy men mounted
when they left the king's court;
Lanval climbed on it.
When the girl came through the gate
Lanval leapt, in one bound,

640 onto the palfrey, behind her.
With her he went to Avalun,
so the Bretons tell us,
to a very beautiful island;
there the youth was carried off.
645 No man heard of him again,
and I have no more to tell.

LANVAL

IN THIS *lai,* Marie presents a contrast between the world which love enables lovers to create for themselves and the world of ordinary human society, where they must otherwise live. The world of love is complete in itself; secular society, even in its noblest form, the Arthurian court, is shown to be severely limited. The hero is mistreated at Arthur's court, despite his valuable service to the king and his generous spending of his fortune. The king forgets him when he distributes wives and lands, and other knights envy him. A stranger in Arthur's land, Lanval is further isolated by the neglect of the court, which forces him to turn inward. He goes off alone and finds or imagines a love that gives him all that he lacked in the world and more.

Like the bird-knight who comes to the imprisoned lady in *Yonec,* Lanval's love comes to him because he needs her and whenever he needs her, but she remains invisible to everyone else, as though she were the creation of his fantasy. Indeed, even when she does appear to the court at the end of the *lai,* she is the climax of a wonderful and otherworldly procession of beauty and wealth. Her rich clothes and trappings, the hawk and the hunting dog, suggest an allegorical figure, a personification of Love, and all who see her perceive her as their ideal beauty. She offers Lanval enormous wealth, enabling him to help others, but he is concerned only with her love. Her beauty is never described without reference to her fabulous wealth; Arthur's world is impressed with both, Lanval only with her.

Ironically, love gives him the means to win attention at court, but it also destroys his interest in such attention. Henceforth he chooses to keep himself apart from others so that he can think about his love, and the others must seek him out. Lanval's desire to be alone provides another contrast with the Arthurian world, where fellowship was valued, a point Marie underlines rather humorously by having Gawain take two or three companions wherever he goes. But now, when Lanval would be happier by himself, he is not left alone. Love seems also to make him more attractive to others and even the queen begins to make advances to him. This puts the hero in a difficult predicament: he must reject the queen out of loyalty to his love, but his rejection offends her and she insults him. Her insults provoke him to boast about his love and in so doing he betrays his vow of secrecy and thus forfeits the love.

As in so many of Marie's *lais* (cf. *Yonec, Laustic*), once the love is known to others it is lost, as though it can only exist as the private possession of the lovers and is somehow demeaned when brought into contact with the outside world. But in contrast to *Yonec* and *Laustic,* Marie permits the love to triumph in this *lai*. The lady returns to rescue Lanval despite his betrayal of their secret, because his love for her has not wavered. His only concern when he is accused is that he has lost her—his disgrace at court does not trouble him at all. Her mercy, despite his fault, is in sharp contrast to the king's attempt to condemn Lanval for an act he did not commit.

The superficiality, perhaps even falseness, of the court's values, which was apparent in the mistreatment of Lanval at the beginning, is revealed particularly in the accusation and trial of the hero. The queen, offended by his rejection, first accuses him of homosexuality, a conclusion the court has leapt to because he takes no interest in women there. When that is answered by Lanval's boast about the superior beauty of his love and of the least of her servants over the queen's, the queen takes revenge, like Potiphar's wife, and accuses Lanval of trying to make love to her. The contrast between the pettiness, the vulgarity, and the immorality of the queen and the perfection of the woman Lanval loves is obvious. The queen's charge causes the king to accuse Lanval, publicly, of wronging him, although Lanval had protested his loyalty to Arthur as the first reason for not acceding to the queen's wishes. This leads to the formality of a trial, which further reveals the inadequacy of the court. The king and the barons are all careful to observe the proper procedure, but the king is also anxious to have a verdict against Lanval in order to satisfy the queen, and some of the barons, although they all seem to be aware of Lanval's innocence, are ready to condemn him just to please the king. Ultimately, the legal system works only because the lady appears, making herself visible to all, and forcing them to see the truth physically. If she had not come, injustice would have prevailed again as it did at the beginning of the story.

The lady's appearance at the court comes after a suspenseful buildup: the arrival of a series of girls, each lovelier than the last, a motif that is probably borrowed from the Tristan stories. It serves both to increase our sense of the lady's beauty and to suggest the way the mind works, beginning with the perception of conventional visible beauty and rising to the concept of ideal beauty. The lady's approach is a slow and stately public progress, in contrast once again to Arthur's anxious attempts to hasten the deliberations of justice. The girls who preceded the lady had all insisted on special preparations, as if Arthur's court were not fit to entertain their mistress, and indeed when she does come she refuses to stay, despite the preparations and the evident desire of all there to serve her. The love she represents cannot be contained in such a world. The hero, who has known the advantages of one and the limitations of the other, makes a total commitment to love: he leaps on her horse as she leaves (from a mounting stone that is used by the heavier men of the court, a sly reminder perhaps of the lightweight nature of most of Arthur's world) and follows her to Avalun, a land that is not of this world.

Les Deus Amanz (*The Two Lovers*)

There happened once in Normandy
a famous adventure
of two young people who loved each other;
both died because of love.
5 The Bretons composed a *lai* about it;
and they gave it the title, *The Two Lovers.*

The truth is, that in Neustria,
which we call Normandy,
there's a wondrously great, high mountain:
10 the two youngsters lie buried up there.
Near one side of that mountain,
with much deliberation and judgment,
a king who was lord of the Pistrians
had a city built;
15 he named the city after the Pistrians—
he called it Pistre.
The name has lasted ever since;
the town and its dwellings still remain.
We know the region well:
20 it's called the valley of Pistre.
The king had a beautiful daughter,
an extremely gracious girl.
He found consolation in the maiden
after he had lost his queen.
25 Many reproached him for this—
even his own household blamed him.[1]

1. The reason for this attitude on the part of the household is made clearer by the following lines added after 24 in MSS (S) and (N):

> Except for her he had neither son nor daughter;
> he cherished her and loved her deeply.
> She was wooed by rich men
> who would willingly have wed her,
> but the king didn't want to give her away

When he heard that people were talking about his conduct
he was saddened and troubled;
he began to consider
30 how he could avoid
anyone's seeking to marry his daughter.
So he sent word far and near, to this effect:
whoever wanted to win his daughter
should know one thing for certain:
35 it was decreed and destined that he
would have to carry her in his arms
to the summit of the mountain outside the city
without stopping to rest.
When the news was known
40 and spread throughout the region,
many attempted the feat,
but couldn't succeed at all.
There were some who pushed themselves so hard
that they carried her halfway up the mountain;
45 yet they couldn't get any farther—
they gave up there.
So, for a long time, he put off giving her away,
because no one wanted to ask for her.
There was a young man in that country,
50 the son of a count, refined and handsome;
he undertook great deeds
to win renown beyond all other men.
He frequented the court of the king—
He stayed there quite often
55 and he came to love the king's daughter,
and many times he pleaded with her
to grant him her love
and become his mistress.
Because he was brave and refined,

---

for he could not do without her.
The king had no other solace;
she was near him night and day.

60 and because the king thought highly of him,
she granted him her love
and he humbly thanked her for it.
They often conversed together
and they loved each other truly,
65 and as much as they could they hid their love
so that no one would discover it.
This restraint disturbed them greatly;
but the young man made up his mind
that he would rather suffer such hardships
70 than be too hasty in his love and thus lose everything.
He was hard pressed by love for her.
So it chanced one day
that the young man—who was so wise, so brave, and so handsome—
came to his beloved
75 and made his complaint to her:
he earnestly begged her
to run away with him—
he couldn't stand the pain any longer;
if he asked her father for her,
80 he knew that the king loved her so much
that he'd refuse to give her up,
unless the suitor could carry her
in his arms to the summit of the mountain.
The maiden answered him:
85 "Dearest," she said, "I know very well
that you couldn't carry me up there for anything:
you aren't strong enough.
If I ran away with you,
my father would be grief-stricken and angry;
90 he would suffer the rest of his life.
Certainly, I love and cherish him enough
that I would never want to upset him.
You'll have to think of another scheme,
because I don't want to hear any more of this one.
95 I have a relative in Salerno,

a rich woman with lots of property;
she's lived there more than thirty years.
She's practiced the medical arts for so long
that she's an expert on medicines.[2]
100 She knows herbs and roots so well
that if you want to go to her
bringing a letter from me with you,
and tell her your problem,
she'll take an interest in it;
105 then she'll make up such prescriptions
and give you such potions
that they'll fortify you,
give you lots of strength.
When you return to this region,
110 you'll ask my father for me;
he'll think you're just a child,
and he'll tell you the agreement—
that he won't give me away to any man,
whatever pains he may take,
115 if he can't carry me up the mountain
in his arms, without stopping to rest."
❦ The youth listened to the idea
and the advice of the maiden;
it delighted him, and he thanked her.
120 He took leave of his mistress,
and went off to his own country.
Quickly he supplied himself
with rich clothes, money,
palfreys and pack mules;
125 only the most trustworthy of his men
did the youth take with him.

2. According to many medieval writers, women studied and practiced medicine at Salerno from the eleventh century onward. A gynecological treatise from this period, the *Trotula,* has frequently (but not without objection) been attributed to a Salernitan woman doctor. See A. B. Cobban, *The Medieval Universities* (London, 1975), 40, and works cited in Cobban's notes.

He went to stay in Salerno,
to consult his beloved's aunt.
On her behalf he gave her a letter.
130 When she had read it from one end to the other,
she kept him with her
until she knew all about his situation.
She strengthened him with medicines
and gave him such a potion that,
135 no matter how fatigued he might be,
no matter how constrained, or how burdened,
the potion would still revive his entire body—
even the veins and the bones—
so that he would have all the strength he needed,
140 the moment he drank it.
She poured the potion into a bottle;
he took it back to his own land.[3]
The young man, joyful and happy,
wasted no time at home
145 on his return.
He went to the king to ask for his daughter:
if the king would give her to him, he would take her
and carry her to the summit of the mountain.
The king made no attempt to refuse him,
150 though he took him for a great fool,
because the lover was so young.
Many great men, hardy and wise,
had undertaken this task
and none could accomplish it at all!
155 The king named and set a date;
then sent for his vassals, his friends,
everybody he could get;
he wouldn't let anyone stay behind.
Because of his daughter, and the young man
160 who was taking the chance

3. We follow Rychner, who reverses 141 and 142 in MS (H).

of carrying her to the mountain's top,
they came from everywhere.
The damsel prepared herself:
she fasted and dieted,
165 cut down on her eating,
because she desired to help her lover.
On the day when everyone arrived,
the youth was there first;
he didn't forget to bring his potion.
170 Toward the Seine, out in the meadow,
and into the great crowd assembled there
the king led his daughter.
She wore nothing except her chemise;
her suitor lifted her into his arms.
175 The small phial containing his potion
he gave her to carry in her hand:
he knew well she'd no desire to cheat him.
But I'm afraid the potion did him little good,
because he was entirely lacking in control.
180 Off he went with her at top speed,
and he climbed until he was halfway up the mountain.
In his joy for his beloved
he forgot his potion.
She noticed he was growing weak:
185 "Love," she said, "drink!
I can tell you're getting tired—
now's the time to regain your strength!"
The youth answered:
"Sweetheart, my heart is very strong;
190 I wouldn't stop for any price,
not even long enough to take a drink,
so long as I can still move an inch.
The crowd below would raise a racket,
deafen me with their noise;
195 soon they'd have me all confused.
I don't want to stop here."

When they had gone two thirds of the way up,
he was on the verge of collapsing.
Again and again the maiden begged,
200 "Dearest, take your medicine!"
But he wouldn't listen or take her advice;
in great anguish he staggered on.
He reached the top of the mountain in such pain
that he fell there, and didn't get up;
205 the life went out of his body.
The maiden looked down at her lover,
she thought he had fainted.
She knelt beside him,
attempting to give him his potion;
210 but he couldn't respond to her.
That's how he died, as I've told you.
She grieved for him with loud cries;
she emptied and threw away
the bottle that contained the potion.
215 The mountain got well doused with it,
and the entire region and countryside
were much improved thereby:
many a fine herb now found there
owes its start to the potion.
220 Now I'll tell you about the damsel:
when she knew she had lost her lover,
you never saw anyone so sad;
she lay down and stretched out beside him,
took him in her arms, pressed him to her,
225 kissed his eyes and lips, again and again;
sorrow for him struck deep in her heart.
She died there too,
that maid who was so brave, so wise, so beautiful.
The king and the others who were waiting for them,
230 when they saw that they weren't returning,
went after them and found them.
The king fell down in a faint.

When he could speak again, he grieved greatly,
and so did all the strangers.
235 They stayed there mourning for three days.
Then they ordered a marble tomb
and placed the two youngsters inside it.
On the advice of everyone present
they buried them on the mountain's summit,
240 and at last they went away.

Because of the sad adventure of the young folk,
the place is now called the Mount of the Two Lovers.
It happened just the way I've told you;
the Bretons made a *lai* about it.

LES DEUS AMANZ (*The Two Lovers*)

LES DEUS AMANZ (*The Two Lovers*) takes its name from a mountain near Pitres, in Normandy, known as the Mont des Deux Amants, at the top of which remain, to this day, the ruins of a twelfth-century priory dedicated to "the two lovers." The lovers thus memorialized were a holy couple, Injuriosus and Scholastica, who, legend had it, had retired to monastic life together. Marie borrowed the mountain and its name and attached to them a fanciful tale of young love thwarted by parental obstacles and by its own immoderate exuberance. *Les Deus Amanz* is also a tissue of literary borrowings from stories well known to Marie and her audience; by juxtaposing these often disparate materials—or rather, by crowding them upon each other within the *lai*'s less than 250 lines—Marie creates narrative imbalances and uncomfortably sudden shifts of perspective that undermine the story's potentially serious impact. Since the *lai* is also full of anticlimax and other comic manipulations of its characters and situations, there is every reason to believe that Marie undertook to parody her own art, and that of other tellers of noble love stories, in *Les Deus Amanz.*

The story of the king who cannot bear to part with his only daughter, and so invents a test that any prospective suitor must pass before marrying her, is a domesticated version of the widely diffused romance of Apollonius of Tyre; in the original, the king's relationship with his daughter is incestuous, and the test, in the form of a riddle, carries with it the death penalty for those who do not solve it. Marie excises both disgust and peril from the story, and thereby trivializes it: the king is a bereaved widower with an understandable, though selfish, desire to retain the consoling presence of his only daughter, and the trial he devises carries with it no penalty for failure save loss of the princess. The ordeal itself is faintly ludicrous: the suitor must carry the princess in his arms to the top of a nearby mountain. Marie proceeds to exploit this situation for comic effect. The young hero of the *lai,* although he is anxious to win surpassing renown by great deeds, is too weak to carry the princess the required distance, as she candidly admits. The impact of this failure of prowess is considerably dulled by the boy's being able to persuade the princess to enter into a secret love relationship with him, thanks to his valor(!), his courtesy, and—most ironic of all—his good standing with the king. After having prudently suffered for a while the inconveniences of such a love, the young man proposes the (unheroic) expedient of elopement, which the princess vetoes on the grounds of her unwillingness to hurt her father. Yet she is quite willing to propose that her lover cheat to pass the ordeal (by means of a strength potion obtained from her aunt in Salerno, a famous medieval center of medical studies), although this ruse proves to hurt her father far more than elopement would have—she dies.

The strength potion is a down-to-earth (and therefore parodistic) version of the love philter or strength-giving magic ring that figures in many medieval romances; a further bathetic touch is the letter of introduction the hero brings with him, on his quest for triumph in love, to Salerno. Meanwhile, as the hour of trial approaches, Marie subverts the heroic enterprise with yet another anticlimactic novelty: the princess undertakes to aid her lover by going on literature's first crash diet. (In fact, if the potion works as planned, the diet will be as unnecessary as it is incongruous.)

Once the young man sets out up the mountain carrying his beloved, Marie's literary model changes from romance to epic—from Apollonius to *The Song of Roland*. Marie signals the change by warning us portentously that the potion won't work because the hero lacks *mesure*—the virtue of moderation inevitably absent from the character of great heroes like Achilles or Roland. The climax of the *lai* comes when the youth, staggering ever more weakly up the mountain, still refuses (for the curious reason that the roar of the crowd of spectators would confuse him if he paused) to drink the potion urged ever more insistently upon him by the princess, who is carrying it for him in a little bottle. The princess's plea, *bevez vostre mescine* ("take your medicine"), echoes Oliver's plea that Roland sound his horn to summon Charles and the Frankish army back to Roncesvalles to save the rearguard; the difference in circumstance defines the distance between heroic intensity and heroic parody. The weight of a fasting princess is neither an expected nor an acceptable instrument of heroic self-confrontation through self-destruction, nor can we suppress the awareness that the princess's exhortations sound uncomfortably like those of a worried mother dosing a sick and cantankerous child.

Having brought her lovers to the summit of their passion, literally and figuratively, Marie has the hero succumb to exhaustion, and, immediately thereafter, the heroine to grief. This bathetic denouement, in which the young lovers are discovered dead by the grieving father (the ultimate cause of their death) and interred in a single tomb, deliberately recalls Ovid's story of Pyramus and Thisbe (*Metamorphoses,* Bk. 4), which was retold as a courtly fable in Marie's day. Marie parodies her "source" by a final, comic metamorphosis when the princess discards the potion; though unused in the cause of love, it proves to be excellent plant food, and causes new, efficacious herbs to grow in the region where it is spilled. (In Ovid's version, Thisbe, before committing suicide over Pyramus's body, prays that the mulberry tree's fruit may become dark red to memorialize the double death; her prayer is granted.) The *lai* ends as it began, in a transparently allusive and euphemistic relationship to literary tradition.

The ostensible message of *Les Deus Amanz* is that love, by inspiring in lovers transcendent joy and daring—the hero forgets the potion in his joy at his beloved—forces them beyond the limits imposed on them by the exigencies of social and familial relationships, and thus destroys them. More persistently, the *lai* urges the fragility of the literary tradition of ennobling, tragic love by hedging the love affair about with details and stratagems that curb its flight toward heroism or even pathos. The potion, intended within the story to bridge the gap between the hero's love aspirations and human limitations, is also a symbol of love's inability to thrive without recourse to trickery and art. The refusal of the potion is at once the triumph and the death of childhood's exalted vision—but the acceptance of the potion would spell the end of the illusion from another point of view. In illustrating the limits of the courtly love vision, Marie demonstrates artistic *démesure*—the use of too many conflicting story models, too tamely retold in too little space—analogous to that of her hero. As a result, the story staggers, as it were, under the weight of its borrowings, and falls repeatedly from the heights of intensity into the valley of anticlimax. Nowhere does Marie show her artistic mastery more clearly than in this joke she plays on herself.

Yonec

Now that I've begun these *lais*
the effort will not stop me;
every adventure that I know
I shall relate in rhyme.
5 My intention and my desire
is to tell you next of Yonec,
how he was born and how his father
first came to his mother.
The man who fathered Yonec
10 was called Muldumarec.

There once lived in Brittany
a rich man, old and ancient.
At Caerwent, he was acknowledged
and accepted as lord of the land.
15 The city sits on the Duelas,
which at one time was open to boats.
The man was very far along in years
but because he possessed a large fortune
he took a wife in order to have children,
20 who would come after him and be his heirs.
The girl who was given to the rich man
came from a good family;
she was wise and gracious[1] and very beautiful—
for her beauty he loved her very much.
25 Because she was beautiful and noble
he made every effort to guard her.
He locked her inside his tower
in a great paved chamber.
A sister of his,
30 who was also old and a widow, without her own lord,
he stationed with his lady
to guard her even more closely.

1. *curteise:* courtly.

There were other women, I believe,
in another chamber by themselves,
35 but the lady never spoke to them
unless the old woman gave her permission.
So he kept her more than seven years—
they never had any children;
she never left that tower,
40 neither for family nor for friends.
When the lord came to sleep there
no chamberlain or porter
dared enter that room,
not even to carry a candle before the lord.
45 The lady lived in great sorrow,
with tears and sighs and weeping;
she lost her beauty,
as one does who cares nothing for it.
She would have preferred
50 death to take her quickly.

It was the beginning of April
when the birds begin their songs.
The lord arose in the morning
and made ready to go to the woods.
55 He had the old woman get up
and close the door behind him—
she followed his command.
The lord went off with his men.
The old woman carried a psalter
60 from which she intended to read the psalms.
The lady, awake and in tears,
saw the light of the sun.
She noticed that the old woman
had left the chamber.
65 She grieved and sighed
and wept and raged:
"I should never have been born!

My fate is very harsh.
I'm imprisoned in this tower
70 and I'll never leave it unless I die.
What is this jealous old man afraid of
that he keeps me so imprisoned?
He's mad, out of his senses;
always afraid of being deceived.
75 I can't even go to church
or hear God's service.
If I could speak to people
and enjoy myself with them
I'd be very gracious to my lord
80 even if I didn't want to be.
A curse on my family,
and on all the others
who gave me to this jealous man,
who married me to his body.
85 It's a rough rope that I pull and draw.
He'll never die—
when he should have been baptized
he was plunged instead in the river of hell;
his sinews are hard, his veins are hard,
90 filled with living blood.
I've often heard
that one could once find
adventures in this land
that brought relief to the unhappy.
95 Knights might find young girls
to their desire, noble and lovely;
and ladies find lovers
so handsome, courtly, brave, and valiant
that they could not be blamed,
100 and no one else would see them.
If that might be or ever was,
if that has ever happened to anyone,
God, who has power over everything,
grant me my wish in this."

105 When she'd finished her lament,
she saw, through a narrow window,
the shadow of a great bird.
She didn't know what it was.
It flew into the chamber;
110 its feet were banded; it looked like a hawk
of five or six moultings.
It alighted before the lady.
When it had been there awhile
and she'd stared hard at it,
115 it became a handsome and noble knight.
The lady was astonished;
her blood went cold, she trembled,
she was frightened—she covered her head.
The knight was very courteous,
120 he spoke first:
"Lady," he said, "don't be afraid.
The hawk is a noble bird,
although its secrets are unknown to you.
Be reassured
125 and accept me as your love.
That," he said, "is why I came here.
I have loved you for a long time,
I've desired you in my heart.
Never have I loved any woman but you
130 nor shall I ever love another,
yet I couldn't have come to you
or left my own land
had you not asked for me.
But now I can be your love."
135 The lady was reassured;
she uncovered her head and spoke.
She answered the knight,
saying she would take him as her lover
if he believed in God,
140 and if their love was really possible.

For he was of great beauty.
Never in her life
had she seen so handsome a knight—
nor would she ever.
145 "My lady," he said, "you are right.
I wouldn't want you to feel
guilt because of me,
or doubt or suspicion.
I do believe in the creator
150 who freed us from the grief
that Adam, our father, led us into
when he bit into the bitter apple.
He is, will be, and always was
the life and light of sinners.
155 If you don't believe me
send for your chaplain.
Say that you've suddenly been taken ill
and that you desire the service
that God established in this world
160 for the healing of sinners.
I shall take on your appearance
to receive the body of our lord God,
and I'll recite my whole credo for you.
You will never doubt my faith again."
165 She answered that she was satisfied.
He lay beside her on the bed
but he didn't try to touch her,
to embrace her or to kiss her.
Meanwhile, the old woman had returned.
170 She found the lady awake
and told her it was time to get up,
she would bring her clothes.
The lady said she was ill,
that the old woman should send for the chaplain
175 and bring him to her quickly—
she very much feared she was dying.

The old woman said, "Be patient,
my lord has gone to the woods.
No one may come in here but me."
180 The lady was very upset;
she pretended to faint.
When the other saw her, she was frightened;
she unlocked the door of the chamber
and sent for the priest.
185 He came as quickly as he could,
bringing the *corpus domini*.[2]
The knight received it,
drank the wine from the chalice.
Then the chaplain left
190 and the old woman closed the doors.
The lady lay beside her love—
there was never a more beautiful couple.
When they had laughed and played
and spoken intimately,
195 the knight took his leave
to return to his land.
She gently begged him
to come back often.
"Lady," he said, "whenever you please,
200 I will be here within the hour.
But you must make certain
that we're not discovered.
This old woman will betray us,
night and day she will spy on us.
205 She will perceive our love,
and tell her lord about it.
If that happens,
if we are betrayed,
I won't be able to escape.
210 I shall die."

2. The body of the Lord, the eucharistic host.

With that the knight departed,
leaving his love in great joy.
In the morning she rose restored;
she was happy all week.
215 Her body had now become precious to her,
she completely recovered her beauty.
Now she would rather remain here
than look for pleasure elsewhere.
She wanted to see her love all the time
220 and enjoy herself with him.
As soon as her lord departed,
night or day, early or late,
she had him all to her pleasure.
God, let their joy endure!
225 Because of the great joy she felt,
because she could see her love so often,
her whole appearance changed.
But her lord was clever.
In his heart he sensed
230 that she was not what she had been.
He suspected his sister.
He questioned her one day,
saying he was astonished
that the lady now dressed with care.
235 He asked her what it meant.
The old woman said she didn't know—
no one could have spoken to her,
she had no lover or friend—
it was only that she was now more willing
240 to be alone than before.
His sister, too, had noticed the change.
Her lord answered:
"By my faith," he said, "I think that's so.
But you must do something for me.
245 In the morning, when I've gotten up
and you have shut the doors,

pretend you are going out
and leave her lying there alone.
Then hide yourself in a safe place,
250 watch her and find out
what it is, and where it comes from,
that gives her such great joy."
With that plan they separated.
Alas, how hard it is to protect yourself
255 from someone who wants to trap you,
to betray and deceive you!

Three days later, as I heard the story,
the lord pretended to go away.
He told his wife the story
260 that the king had sent for him by letter
but that he would return quickly.
He left the chamber and shut the door.
The old woman got up,
went behind a curtain;
265 from there she could hear and see
whatever she wanted to know.
The lady lay in bed but did not sleep,
she longed for her love.
He came without delay,
270 before any time had passed.
They gave each other great joy
with word and look
until it was time to rise—
he had to go.
275 But the old woman watched him,
saw how he came and went.
She was quite frightened
when she saw him first a man and then a bird.
When the lord returned—
280 he hadn't gone very far—
she told him and revealed
the truth about the knight

and the lord was troubled by it.
But he was quick to invent
285 a way to kill the knight.
He had great spikes of iron forged,
their tips sharpened—
no razor on earth could cut better.
When he had them all prepared
290 and pronged on all sides,
he set them in the window—
close together and firmly placed—
through which the knight passed
when he visited the lady.
295 God, he doesn't know what treachery
the villains are preparing.
The next day in the morning
the lord rose before dawn
and said he was going hunting.
300 The old woman saw him to the door
and then went back to bed
for day was not yet visible.
The lady awoke and waited
for the one she loved faithfully;
305 she said he might well come now
and be with her at leisure.
As soon as she asked,
he came without delay.
He flew into the window,
310 but the spikes were there.
One wounded him in his breast—
out rushed the red blood.
He knew he was fatally wounded;
he pulled himself free and entered the room.
315 He alighted on the bed, in front of the lady,
staining the bedclothes with blood.
She saw the blood and the wound
in anguish and horror.
He said, "My sweet love,

320 I lose my life for love of you.
I told you it would happen,
that your appearance would kill us."
When she heard that, she fainted;
for a short while she lay as if dead.
325 He comforted her gently,
said that grief would do no good,
but that she was pregnant with his child.
She would have a son, brave and strong,
who would comfort her;
330 she would call him Yonec.
He would avenge both of them
and kill their enemy.
But he could remain no longer
for his wound was bleeding badly.
335 He left in great sorrow.
She followed him with loud cries.
She leapt out a window—
it's a wonder that she wasn't killed,
for it was at least twenty feet high
340 where she made her leap,
naked beneath her gown.
She followed the traces of blood
that flowed from the knight
onto the road.
345 She followed that road and kept to it
until she came to a hill.
In the hill there was an opening,
red with his blood.
She couldn't see anything beyond it
350 but she was sure
that her love had gone in there.
She entered quickly.
She found no light
but she kept to the right road
355 until it emerged from the hill

into a beautiful meadow.
When she found the grass there wet with blood,
she was frightened.
She followed the traces through the meadow
360 and saw a city not far away.
The city was completely surrounded by walls.
There was no house, no hall or tower,
that didn't seem entirely of silver.
The buildings were very rich.
365 Going toward the town there were marshes,
forests, and enclosed fields.
On the other side, toward the castle,
a stream flowed all around,
where ships arrived—
370 there were more than three hundred sails.
The lower gate was open;
the lady entered the city,
still following the fresh blood
through the town to the castle.
375 No one spoke to her,
she met neither man nor woman.
When she came to the palace courtyard,
she found it covered with blood.
She entered a lovely chamber
380 where she found a knight sleeping.
She did not know him, so she went on
into another larger chamber.
There she found nothing but a bed
with a knight sleeping on it;
385 she kept going.
She entered the third chamber
and on that bed she found her love.
The feet of the bed were all of polished gold,
I couldn't guess the value of the bedclothes;
390 the candles and the chandeliers,
which were lit night and day,

Like Corpus Christi Carol!

were worth the gold of an entire city.
As soon as she saw him
she recognized the knight.
395 She approached, frightened,
and fell fainting over him.
He, who greatly loved her, embraced her,
lamenting his misfortune again and again.
When she recovered from her faint
400 he comforted her gently.
"Sweet friend, for God's sake, I beg you,
go away! Leave this place!
I shall die within[3] the day,
there will be great sorrow here,
405 and if you are found
you will be hurt.
Among my people it will be well known
that they have lost me because of my love for you.
I am disturbed and troubled for you."
410 The lady answered: "Love,
I would rather die with you
than suffer with my lord.
If I go back to him he'll kill me."
The knight reassured her,
415 gave her a ring,
and explained to her
that, as long as she kept it,
her lord would not remember
anything that had happened—
420 he would imprison her no longer.
He gave her his sword
and then made her swear
no man would ever possess it,
that she'd keep it for their son.
425 When the son had grown and become

3. Rychner, following (P) and (Q), gives *en mi*, "in the middle of the day"; Ewert, with (H) and (S), gives *devant*, "before."

a brave and valiant knight,
she would go to a festival,
taking him and her lord with her.
They would come to an abbey.
430 There, beside a tomb,
they would hear the story of his death,
how he was wrongfully killed.
There she would give her son the sword.
The adventure would be recited to him,
435 how he was born and who his father was;
then they'd see what he would do.
When he'd told her and shown her everything,
he gave her a precious robe
and told her to put it on.
440 Then he sent her away.
She left carrying the ring
and the sword—they comforted her.
She had not gone half a mile
from the gate of the city
445 when she heard the bells ring
and the mourning begin in the castle,
and in her sorrow
she fainted four times.
When she recovered from the faints
450 she made her way to the hill.
She entered it, passed through it,
and returned to her country.
There with her lord
she lived many days and years.
455 He never accused her of that deed,
never insulted or abused her.
Her son was born and nourished,
protected and cherished.
They named him Yonec.
460 In all the kingdom you couldn't find
one so handsome, brave, or strong,
so generous, so munificent.

When he reached the proper age,
he was made a knight.
465 Hear now what happened
in that very year.
To the feast of St. Aaron,
celebrated in Caerleon
and in many other cities,
470 the lord had been summoned
to come with his friends,
according to the custom of the land,
and to bring his wife and his son,
all richly attired.
475 So it was; they went.
But they didn't know the way;
they had a boy with them
who guided them along the right road
until they came to a castle—
480 none more beautiful in all the world.
Inside, there was an abbey
of very religious people.
The boy who was guiding them to the festival
housed them there.
485 In the abbot's chamber
they were well served and honored.
Next day they went to hear Mass
before they departed,
but the abbot went to speak to them
490 to beg them to stay
so he could show them the dormitory,
the chapter house, and the refectory.
And since they were comfortable there,
the lord agreed to stay.
495 That day, after they had dined,
they went to the workshops.
On their way, they passed the chapter house,
where they found a huge tomb
covered with a cloth of embroidered silk,

500 a band of precious gold running from one side to the other.
At the head, the feet, and at the sides
burned twenty candles.
The chandeliers were pure gold,
the censers amethyst,
505 which through the day perfumed
that tomb, to its great honor.
They asked and inquired
of people from that land
whose tomb it was,
510 what man lay there.
The people began to weep
and, weeping, to recount
that it was the best knight
the strongest, the most fierce,
515 the most handsome and the best loved,
that had ever lived.
"He was king of this land;
no one was ever so courtly.
At Caerwent he was discovered
520 and killed for the love of a lady.
Since then we have had no lord,
but have waited many days,
just as he told and commanded us,
for the son the lady bore him."
525 When the lady heard that news,
she called aloud to her son.
"Fair son," she said, "you hear
how God has led us to this spot.
Your father, whom this old man murdered,
530 lies here in this tomb.
Now I give and commend his sword to you.
I have kept it a long time for you."
Then she revealed, for all to hear,
that the man in the tomb was the father and this was his son,
535 and how he used to come to her,
how her lord had betrayed him—

she told the truth.
Then she fainted over the tomb
and, in her faint, she died.
540 She never spoke again.
When her son saw that she had died,
he cut off his stepfather's head.
Thus with his father's sword
he avenged his mother's sorrow.
545 When all this had happened,
when it became known through the city,
they took the lady with great honor
and placed her in the coffin.
Before they departed
550 they made Yonec their lord.

Long after, those who heard this adventure
composed a lay about it,
about the pain and the grief
that they suffered for love.

YONEC

YONEC begins with what appears to be a conventional literary situation, an old and jealous husband keeping his young wife under close guard. The audience expects a plot to deceive the husband and smuggle in a young lover. A young lover does indeed make his way to the wife, but otherwise, in all the details and in the overall tone of the story, the treatment is quite unusual. The lovers do not use their wits to deceive the husband—it is the husband who plots to trap and kill the lover, while the wife uses her imagination to create the kind of love she needs.

The wife is young and lovely, with all the social graces, but these are wasted in the tower in which she is imprisoned; the husband, wanting to keep her charms all to himself, only destroys them. He is too old, a point underlined in the French by the repetition of the word *trespas* (l. 16) in *trespassez* (l. 17): the river of his city once offered a *trespas,* "passage," to boats, that is, it has since dried up; and the husband is *mult trespassez,* "very far along in years," presumably also dried up. Furthermore, his love is possessive, life-denying—he married supposedly to have heirs, but the marriage is childless—and ultimately evil. He will not allow his wife even to go to church and she accuses her family of committing a grave sin in marrying her to this man; she suspects that he was baptized in the waters of hell. As if to emphasize the husband's evil, the lover's first act when he comes to the lady is to ask for a priest and take the host.

The love, in other words, is not a sin. In fact, it restores the lady's beauty and joy (joy is the dominant theme in the love scenes, the word *joie* is constantly repeated), so that even the husband notices the change. That is what drives him to search out and destroy the lover who is the source of it. The husband is a hunter—he is always leaving to go off to the forest—and he sets a particularly vicious trap for his prey, the lover who comes to the lady in the shape of a bird. The bird, a hawk, is at once the only creature who could gain entrance to the tower and a symbol of the lover in lyric poetry. He is also, by nature, a predator, a hunter, but the bird-knight of this story, in another reversal of expectation, is a gentle, tame creature who comes at the lady's call to bring her love and joy.

The lady, forced inward on herself by the lack of love in her marriage and the absence of family or friends to console her, escapes into her imagination. She thinks of adventures, which she associates with blameless love between knights and ladies; she prays for one to come to her, and the bird appears. As she stares at it, it becomes a handsome man. That is, her will brings him, and her look gives him form. But when the reality of her world intrudes on her fantasy, when the husband discovers the existence of the bird, the dream is shattered, destroyed by his envy. The bird, wounded by the husband's trap, withdraws forever. But love has given the lady the power to overcome the problems of her life. She is able to leave her prison (she leaps from a window of the tower without injury), follow her dying lover to his land, and then return to her husband, but she is never again to be imprisoned by him.

The lover's land is a kind of dream world, a city of silver that she reaches by making her way through a long, dark tunnel. When she enters his palace, she goes through room after room of sleeping knights. Her own life is in danger here, as her lover's was in her husband's tower; when her dream is taken from her, she loses the desire to live. But her lover tells her that she will have a son and gives her a sword to keep for him, so that he can one day avenge them and their love. It is the child who gives reality to the love; it is through him that the love can endure.

What Marie seems to be saying in this *lai,* as in several others, is that the world can imprison the body but not the mind, once the mind wills itself free. Love gives the lady the power, by giving her the will, to free herself.

Laustic (*The Nightingale*)

I shall tell you an adventure
about which the Bretons made a *lai*.
Laüstic was the name, I think,
they gave it in their land.
5 In French it is *rossignol,*
and *nightingale* in proper English.
At Saint-Malo, in that country,
there was a famous city.
Two knights lived there,
10 they both had strong houses.
From the goodness of the two barons
the city acquired a good name.
One had married a woman
wise, courtly, and handsome;
15 she set a wonderfully high value on herself,
within the bounds of custom and usage.
The other was a bachelor,
well known among his peers
for bravery and great valor;
20 he delighted in living well.
He jousted often, spent widely
and gave out what he had.
He also loved his neighbor's wife;
he asked her, begged her so persistently,
25 and there was such good in him,
that she loved him more than anything,
as much for the good that she heard of him
as because he was close by.
They loved each other discreetly and well,
30 concealed themselves and took care
that they weren't seen
or disturbed or suspected.
And they could do this well enough
since their dwellings were close,

35 their houses were next door,
and so were their rooms and their towers;
there was no barrier or boundary
except a high wall of dark stone.
From the rooms where the lady slept,
40 if she went to the window
she could talk to her love
on the other side, and he to her,
and they could exchange their possessions,
by tossing and throwing them.
45 There was scarcely anything to disturb them,
they were both quite at ease;
except that they couldn't come together
completely for their pleasure,
for the lady was closely guarded
50 when her husband was in the country.
Yet they always managed,
whether at night or in the day,
to be able to talk together;
no one could prevent
55 their coming to the window
and seeing each other there.
For a long time they loved each other,
until one summer
when the woods and meadows were green
60 and the orchards blooming.
The little birds, with great sweetness,
were voicing their joy above the flowers.
It is no wonder if he understands them,
he who has love to his desire.
65 I'll tell you the truth about the knight:
he listened to them intently
and to the lady on the other side,
both with words and looks.
At night, when the moon shone
70 when her lord was in bed,

she often rose from his side
and wrapped herself in a cloak.
She went to the window
because of her lover, who, she knew,
75 was leading the same life,
awake most of the night.
Each took pleasure in the other's sight
since they could have nothing more;
but she got up and stood there so often
80 that her lord grew angry
and began to question her, to ask
why she got up and where she went.
"My lord," the lady answered him,
"there is no joy in this world
85 like hearing the nightingale sing.
That's why I stand there.
It sounds so sweet at night
that it gives me great pleasure;
it delights me so and I so desire it
90 that I cannot close my eyes."
When her lord heard what she said
he laughed in anger and ill will.
He set his mind on one thing:
to trap the nightingale.
95 There was no valet in his house
that he didn't set to making traps, nets, or snares,
which he then had placed in the orchard;
there was no hazel tree or chestnut
where they did not place a snare or lime
100 until they trapped and captured him.
When they had caught the nightingale,
they brought it, still alive, to the lord.
He was very happy when he had it;
he came to the lady's chambers.
105 "Lady," he said, "where are you?
Come here! Speak to us!

I have trapped the nightingale
that kept you awake so much.
From now on you can lie in peace:
110 he will never again awaken you."
When the lady heard him,
she was sad and angry.
She asked her lord for the bird
but he killed it out of spite,
115 he broke its neck in his hands—
too vicious an act—
and threw the body on the lady;
her shift was stained with blood,
a little, on her breast.
120 Then he left the room.
The lady took the little body;
she wept hard and cursed
those who betrayed the nightingale,
who made the traps and snares,
125 for they took great joy from her.
"Alas," she said, "now I must suffer.
I won't be able to get up at night
or go and stand in the window
where I used to see my love.
130 I know one thing for certain:
he'd think I was pretending.
I must decide what to do about this.
I shall send him the nightingale
and relate the adventure."
135 In a piece of samite,
embroidered in gold and writing,
she wrapped the little bird.
She called one of her servants,
charged him with her message,
140 and sent him to her love.
He came to the knight,
greeted him in the name of the lady,

related the whole message to him,
and presented the nightingale.

145 When everything had been told and revealed to the knight,
after he had listened well,
he was very sad about the adventure,
but he wasn't mean or hesitant.
He had a small vessel fashioned,
150 with no iron or steel in it;
it was all pure gold and good stones,
very precious and very dear;
the cover was very carefully attached.
He placed the nightingale inside
155 and then he had the casket sealed—
he carried it with him always.

This adventure was told,
it could not be concealed for long.
The Bretons made a *lai* about it
160 which men call *The Nightingale*.

LAÜSTIC (*The Nightingale*)

Laüstic offers us an unusual variation on the idea of art as the preserver or embodier of love. In this *lai,* the dead bird in the jeweled casket is the symbol of a love that had little substance to begin with. The love has no apparent reason for beginning or continuing, except for the amusement of the two lovers. The lady accepts the man's love as much because he is her next-door neighbor as because he has a good reputation. Their physical proximity makes it easy for them to talk and even to toss gifts back and forth, despite the husband's close guarding of his wife. At the same time, the lovers are confined by the very walls that bring them together.[1] The lady can look out from her room into another life, but she is not able to enter it. Since, in other *lais,* the will to go is enough (*Guigemar, Yonec, Lanval*), we must assume that her love lacks force. It ends symbolically confined in an even smaller space, the casket.

The love that is carried on over or through a wall separating two houses is, of course, reminiscent of the Pyramis and Thisbe story, but Marie has changed the innocent affection of two children to a self-indulgent flirtation between two adults, the man a friend of the woman's husband. The lovers indulge themselves like children: the lady gets up so often in the middle of the night to speak with her lover that her husband becomes suspicious. Marie seems to feel little sympathy for this love—for the man it means the betrayal of a friend; for the woman, the deceiving of a husband. The phrase "he also loved his neighbor's wife" (l. 23) suggests a moral criticism as well.

Disapproval of the lovers does not mean that we are to take the husband's part. His reaction to his wife's story about the nightingale is so cruel, so gratuitously vicious, that even though his victim is a bird and not the lover (in contrast to *Yonec*),[2] we are shocked. Marie tells us that one who loves understands the songs of the bird, so when the husband kills the bird, we infer how impossible it is for him to understand love. His actions are so exaggerated in view of the aim—traps are made and set in every tree in order to capture one small bird, the bird is murdered in front of the wife and the bloody body tossed on her breast—that we can only be horrified and disgusted. And yet the effect on his wife is much slighter than we might have expected: only a little blood stains her shift; she weeps and curses but she accepts the situation very quickly. No plots are devised, no new ways to communicate are sought. Both lovers give up quite easily.

This is a very different ending from the analogous story about the poet Guilhem de Cabestaing as it is told in his *vida;* there the lover is killed in an ambush by the lady's husband, who feeds the lover's heart to his wife. When he tells her what it was, she vows never to eat any other food and throws herself from the balcony.[3] Although this version is later than Marie's, there are similar folktales which Marie might well have known. In any case, the difference in her version shows that she is not concerned here with a tragic tale of passion but with a short-lived, self-indulgent affair. At the end of her *lai,* all that remains of the love is the bird that lies with his neck broken in a splendid coffin of gold and jewels, an artifact which, like the love, displays all its wealth on the surface. Because it is a self-indulgent love, it cannot bear fruit. The bird symbol cannot be replaced by or live on in a son, as in *Yonec* and *Milun;* it can only die.

Since the nightingale is also a symbol of the poet, the singer of love songs, Marie may be saying that art, too, preserves dead events in an elaborate setting. This rather negative view of her art, not unusual in medieval literature, is unusual for Marie, but we will find it again in *Chaitivel.* Presumably, if the subject of the art, in this case the love, has no substance, the art that re-creates it can be only an empty shell.

1. R. D. Cottrell suggests that Marie concentrates on the area of drama by progressively delimiting the geographical confines. "As the spatial dimension of the story contracts, the lovers' frustration increases" ("'Le Lai du Laüstic': From Physicality to Spirituality," *Philological Quarterly* 47 (1968), 502.

2. J. Ribard points out that the lover is a shadowy figure until the end of the *lai,* that he is almost a figment of the imagination like the bird-knight in *Yonec,* but he does not materialize ("Le lai du Laostic: Structure et signification," *Le Moyen Age* 76 [1970], 269).

3. Boccaccio tells the same story in the *Decameron,* IV, 9. It is also told in the twelfth-century poem *The Owl and the Nightingale;* the owl tells how the husband catches his nightingale and draws and quarters it (ll. 1049–62) and later the nightingale tells how the husband was punished (ll. 1075–1110). There are other versions in which the death of the nightingale leads the lover to kill the husband and marry the lady.

Milun

Whoever wants to tell a variety of stories
ought to have a variety of beginnings,
and speak so intelligently
that people will enjoy listening.
5 Now I'll begin *Milun*
and show, in a brief discourse,
why and how the *lai*
called by that name was written.[1]
Milun was born in South Wales.
10 From the day he was dubbed knight
he couldn't find a single opponent
who could knock him off his horse.
He certainly was a good knight:
generous and strong, courteous and proud.
15 He won fame in Ireland,
in Norway and Gothland;
in Logres and in Albany
many envied him.
He was well beloved
20 and honored by many princes.
There was a baron in his country—
I don't know his name—
who had a daughter,
a beautiful and most refined girl.
25 She had heard of Milun,
and began to love him.
She sent a messenger to him,
to say that, if it pleased him, she would love him.
Milun was happy with the news,
30 and thanked the girl;
he willingly granted her his love,
and said he would never leave her;

1. The French term, *trovez,* could also be rendered "composed," if Marie is referring to a musical setting.

his response to her was very courtly,
and he gave rich gifts to the messenger,
35 promising him his friendship.
"My friend," he said, "please undertake
to help me speak to my beloved
and to keep our communications secret.
Carry my gold ring to her
40 and tell her on my behalf:
whenever she wants, she can send you for me
and I'll go with you."
The messenger took his leave and soon went away;
he returned to his lady.
45 He gave her the ring and told her
that he had done what she had asked.
The girl was delighted
at the love she was being offered.
Outside her room, in a grove
50 where she went to amuse herself,
she and Milun, very often,
had a rendezvous.
Milun came there so often and loved her so much
that the girl became pregnant.
55 When she realized this,
she sent for Milun and made her lament.
She told him what had happened;
she had lost her honor and her good name
when she got herself into this situation.
60 She would be grievously punished:
tortured by the sword
or sold into slavery in another land.
Such were the ancient customs
observed in those days.
65 Milun answered that he would do
whatever she counseled.
"When the child is born," she said,
"you must bring him to my sister,
who is married and living in Northumbria;

70 she is a rich woman, worthy and prudent.
And send word to her, in writing
and also orally
that this child belongs to her sister,
who has endured great grief because of him.
75 She should make sure that he's well nourished,
whatever it may be, son or daughter.
I shall hang your ring around his neck
and send a letter with it,
in which will be written his father's name
80 and the unfortunate story of his mother.[2]
When he is full grown,
and has arrived at the age
when he can listen to reason,
she should give him the ring and the letter
85 and command him to keep them
so that he can find his father."
They abided by this plan,
and the time eventually came
for the girl to have her baby.
90 An old woman who watched over her,
to whom she had disclosed her entire situation,
covered things up so well
that she was never discovered,
by her words or appearance.
95 The girl had a beautiful son.
They hung the ring around his neck,
and also a silken wallet
with the letter in it, so that no one could see it.
Then they laid the child in a little cradle,
100 wrapped in a white linen cloth;
beneath his head
they placed a fine pillow
and over him a coverlet,
hemmed all around with marten fur.

2. Once again, Marie uses the key term *aventure*.

105 The old nurse gave him to Milun,
who was waiting for her in the grove.
He turned the child over to some trustworthy retainers
who would take him to his destination.
As they traveled from town to town,
110 they stopped to rest seven times a day;
they had the child nursed,
changed, and bathed.
They took their job so seriously
that they had brought a wet nurse with them.[3]
115 They stayed on the right road
until they reached the sister and gave the child to her.
She took him from them, and was very pleased with him.
She also took the letter with its seal.
When she knew who he was,
120 she cherished him even more.
Then the men who had brought the child
returned to their own land.
Milun left his homeland
to seek honor through martial exploits.[4]
125 His mistress remained at home
and her father gave her in marriage
to a rich lord of the region,
a powerful man of great repute.
When she found out about this turn of events,[5]
130 she was grief-stricken,
and she cried for Milun.
She was especially worried about being blamed
for having had a child already;
her husband would discover that soon enough.
135 "Alas," she said, "what can I do?
Must I be married? How can I?
I'm no longer a virgin,

3. Lines 113–114 are omitted by Rychner and Warnke from their editions.

4. The text uses the term *sudees,* meaning paid military service. Cf. the endnote to *Guigemar,* note 2.

5. French: *aventure.*

I'll have to be a servant all my life.
I didn't know it would be like this;
140 rather, I thought I could have my love,
that we could keep it a secret between us,
that I'd never hear it bruited about.
Now I'd rather die than live,
but I'm not even free to do that,
145 since I have guardians all around me,
old and young; my chamberlains,
who hate a noble love,
and take their delight in sadness.
Now I have to suffer like this—
150 if only I could die!"
The time came for her to be married,
and her father led her to the altar.
Milun came back to his land;
he was sad and upset—
155 he gave himself up to grief.
He took some comfort from the fact
that the one he loved so much
was still in her country, nearby.
Milun undertook to plan
160 how he could send word to her—
without being discovered—
that he had come home.
He wrote a letter and sealed it.
He had a swan of which he was very fond;
165 he tied the letter to its neck,
hid it among the feathers.
He summoned one of his squires
and made him his messenger.
"Go immediately and change your clothes," he said.
170 "I want you to go to my mistress' castle,
and take my swan with you.
Make arrangements
for the swan to be given to her
by a servant or a maid."

175 The squire did his duty.
He went off quickly, taking the swan with him;
by the most direct route he knew
he came to the castle.
He went through the village
180 directly to the main gate,
called out to the porter:
"Friend," he said, "listen!
This is how I make a living:
I go around catching birds.
185 In a meadow outside Caerleon
I captured a swan in my net.
To earn her goodwill and support,
I want to make a present of it to the lady of the castle,
so that I won't be bothered
190 while I'm working in this area."
The porter replied,
"Friend, no one can speak to her;
but nonetheless, I'll go find out:
if I can find a place
195 that I can bring you to,
I'll arrange for you to speak with her."
The porter went to the main hall
and found only two knights there,
seated at a big table
200 amusing themselves at chess.
Quickly he returned to the messenger,
and brought him in in such a way
that he wasn't seen
or disturbed by anyone.
205 He came to the lady's chamber, and called;
a girl opened the door for them.
They came into the lady's presence,
presented her with the swan.
She called one of her valets
210 and said to him, "Make it your business
to take good care of my swan;

be sure he has enough food."
"My lady," said the messenger who brought the swan,
"No one but you should have him;
215 this is indeed a royal present—
see how fine and handsome a bird he is!"
He placed the bird in her hands.
She accepted it quite willingly,
petted its neck and head,
220 and felt the letter among the feathers.
Her blood ran cold; she shivered,
realizing the letter was from her lover.
She had some money given to the messenger,
and told him to go.
225 When the chamber was empty
she called one of her maids.
She detached the letter,
broke the seal.
She read at the top of the sheet, "Milun,"
230 and when she saw her lover's name
she kissed it a hundred times, crying,
before she could read further.
At the beginning of the letter she read
what he had written
235 of the great sadness
from which he was suffering night and day.
Now it was entirely in her power
to kill or cure him.
If she could think of a scheme
240 whereby he could speak with her,
she should let him know in a letter
and send the swan back to him.
First she should have the swan well guarded,
then keep him fasting
245 three days without any food.
Then the letter should be hung on his neck,
and he should be released; he would fly

to where he had formerly lived.
When she had looked at the whole letter,
250 and heard the contents,
she had the swan well taken care of
with abundant food and drink;
she kept him in her chamber for a month.
Now listen to what happened!
255 She used her ingenuity so well
that she obtained some ink and parchment;
she wrote the letter she wanted to,
and sealed it with a ring.
Then she made the swan go hungry,
260 hung the letter on his neck, released him.
The bird was famished—
he really wanted food;
so he quickly returned
to where he had come from—
265 the same town, the same household—
there he landed at Milun's feet.
When Milun saw him, he was very joyful;
he quickly grabbed him by the wings,
he called his steward,
270 had him give the swan some food,
and meanwhile took the letter from his neck.
He read it from one end to the other,
noting all the words that he found in it,
and rejoicing at her message:
275 "She couldn't have any pleasure without him,
and now he should send back his feelings to her,
by the swan, the same way she had done."
He'll do that right away!
For twenty years they lived like this,
280 Milun and his mistress.
The swan was their messenger,
they had no other means of communication,
and they always made him fast
before they let him go on his errand;

285 whoever the bird came to,
you can be sure, fed it well.
They met together several times.
(No one can be so constrained
or so closely guarded
290 that he can't find a way out.)
Meanwhile, the lady who had raised their son
had him dubbed a knight;
he had been with her long enough
to come of age.
295 He had become a fine young man.
She gave him the letter and the ring,
told him who his mother was,
and his father's story as well:
how his father was a good knight,
300 so bold, hardy, and proud
that there was none who exceeded him
in worth or valor anywhere.
When the lady had told him all this
and he'd listened carefully to her,
305 he rejoiced in his father's virtues;
he was delighted with what he had learned.
He said to himself,
"A man oughtn't to think he's worth much,
being born in such a manner
310 and having such a famous father,
if he doesn't seek out even greater renown
away from home, in foreign lands."
He had everything he needed;
he didn't stay beyond that night,
315 but took his leave next morning.
His foster mother admonished him,
urging him to do good deeds;
she also gave him plenty of money.
He went to Southampton to get under way;
320 as quickly as he could he set out to sea.

He arrived at Barfleur
and went right to Brittany.
There he spent lavishly and tourneyed,
and became acquainted with rich men.
325 In every joust he entered,
he was judged the best combatant.
He loved poor knights;
what he gained from rich ones
he gave to them and thus retained them in his service;
330 he was generous in all his spending.
He would never willingly stay long in one place;
in all those foreign lands
he won renown for his heroic virtues.
He also excelled in refined and honorable behavior.
335 Because of his excellence and fame
the news spread to his own country
that a young knight of that land,
who had gone abroad to seek honor,
had so excelled in prowess,
340 goodness, and generosity
that those who didn't know his name
called him, everywhere, "the knight without equal."
Milun heard this stranger praised
and his virtues recounted.
345 He was saddened, and complained to himself
about this knight who was worth so much
that, so long as he traveled,
fought in tournaments, and bore arms,
no one else born in that land
350 would be praised or honored.
Milun came to a decision:
he would quickly cross the sea
and joust with this knight,
in order to do some harm to him and his reputation.
355 Anger spurred him on
to try to unhorse the knight—

that would put him to shame!
Then he would go look for his son
who had left the country;
360 Milun did not know what had become of him.
He let his mistress know his scheme,
and asked her leave to go;
he revealed his intentions
by sending her a sealed letter,
365 by the swan, I believe;
now she had to let him know how she felt.
When she heard his wish,
she thanked him, expressing her gratitude
that he wanted to leave the country
370 to find their son,
and to find out about his fortunes;
she wouldn't interfere with his plans.
Milun got her message,
then dressed himself richly
375 and went over to Normandy,
whence he traveled to Brittany.
He made many acquaintances,
sought out many tournaments;
his lodgings were usually luxurious,
380 and he gave suitably generous gifts.
Through an entire winter, I believe,
Milun stayed in that land.
He obtained the services of many good knights,
until Easter came,
385 when tournaments began again,
as well as wars and other battles.[6]
A tournament was held at Mont Saint Michel;
Normans and Bretons,
Flemings and Frenchmen all came,

6. During much of the Middle Ages, the times of year when the Church permitted warfare and tournaments were strictly limited, by the concept of the "truce of God." Lent, the period of penance before Easter, was one such time of truce. (The Church's ban was not always observed.)

390 though there were few English knights.
Milun came early,
good knight that he was.
He inquired after the knight without equal;
there were plenty of knights who could tell him
395 where he had come from.
By his arms and shield
he was pointed out to Milun,
who observed him carefully.
The tournament began.
400 Whoever wanted to joust quickly found the opportunity;
he need only search the ranks a bit
to find a companion
in the quest for victory or defeat.
This much I'll tell you about Milun:
405 it went very well with him in combat
and he was highly praised that day.
But the young man of whom I've told you—
he was acclaimed beyond all others;
none could equal him
410 in tourneying and jousting.
Milun watched him perform,
riding and attacking so well;
although he was Milun's rival,
he pleased Milun greatly.
415 Milun rushed into the ranks against him,
and the two jousted together.
Milun struck him so hard
that his lance splintered,
but he didn't unhorse him.
420 The other knight struck Milun so hard
that he knocked him right off his steed.
Beneath Milun's visor,
he saw his beard and white hair;
he was sorry to have made him fall.
425 He took Milun's horse by the reins,
and presented it to him,

saying, "My lord, remount;
I'm saddened
that I should have so humiliated
430 a man of your age."
Milun leaped up, highly pleased,
for he had recognized the ring on the other's finger
when he gave Milun his horse.
He spoke to the young man.
435 "My friend," he said, "listen to me!
For the love of almighty God
tell me your father's name!
What is yours? Who is your mother?
I want to know the truth about this.
440 I've seen a lot, wandered a lot,
searched in many lands
in tournaments and wars;
I never once fell from my war-horse
because of a blow from another knight.
445 You knocked me down in a joust—
I could love you a great deal."
The other answered, "I'll tell you
about my father, as much as I know of him.
I think he was born in Wales
450 and is named Milun.
He loved the daughter of a rich man
and secretly conceived me with her.
I was sent to Northumbria,
and there I was raised and educated
455 by my aunt.
She kept me with her,
then gave me a horse and my arms,
and sent me to this land,
where I have long resided.
460 It is my desire and intent
to go back across the sea quickly
and return to my own land;

I wish to find out who my father is,
and how he is behaving toward my mother.
465 I'll show him my gold ring
and tell him my story;
he will certainly not reject me,
rather, as a loving father he'll make much of me."
When Milun heard him say all this
470 he didn't wait to hear any more;
he quickly leapt forward
and took the other by the skirt of his hauberk.
"God!" he cried, "I'm a new man!
By my faith, friend, you are my son!
475 It was to look for you
that I left my homeland this year."
When the young knight heard him, he got down from his horse
and kissed his father warmly.
They both looked so happy
480 and said such things to each other
that all the others watching them
began to cry from joy and pity.
When the tournament broke up,
Milun went away, very anxious
485 to speak at leisure with his son,
to find out what his pleasure was.
They spent the night in a hostel
where there was much celebrating
being done by a large number of knights.
490 Milun told his son
how he loved the boy's mother,
and how her father had given her
to a baron of that region,
and how he had continued loving her,
495 and she him, with all her heart,
and how he used the swan as a messenger,
having the bird carry his letters,
since he couldn't trust anyone else.
The son responded, "Indeed, my good father,

500 I'll bring you and my mother together;
I shall kill her husband
and see you married."
They spoke no more about it;
the next day they made ready to leave.
505 They said good-bye to their friends,
and returned to their own land.
Their crossing was speedy,
thanks to a good strong wind.
As they went on their way
510 they met a boy
coming from Milun's mistress;
he was on his way to Brittany,
for she had dispatched him to go there.
Now his trip was shortened.
515 She was sending Milun a sealed letter
with a message telling him
that he should come to her without delay:
her husband was dead—now was the time to make haste!
Milun heard the news,
520 and it seemed wonderful to him.
Then he told his son.
Nothing held them back now;
they pushed on until they came
to the lady's castle.
525 She was delighted with her son,
who was so worthy and well behaved.
Without consulting any relatives,
with no advice from anyone else,
their son brought them together,
530 gave his mother to his father.
In great happiness and well-being
they lived happily ever after.

The ancients made a *lai*
about their love and good fortune;

535 and I who have put it down in writing
have thoroughly enjoyed retelling it.

MILUN

Milun is one of Marie's more precisely localized *lais*. The hero and heroine come from South Wales;[1] the child of their love match is sent to be raised by an aunt in Northumbria; Milun—and later his son—goes to Brittany by way of Southampton, seeking *pris,* the honor that comes from the successful exercise of prowess in chivalric combat. Within this circumstantial setting, Marie develops a story of chivalry, love, and a family divided and reconciled. *Milun* resembles *Yonec* in many particulars, but its characters and situations are treated in a strikingly different fashion.

One of the peculiarities of *Milun* is its central concern with communication. The relationship between Milun and his mistress is sustained for twenty years by means of a swan that flies back and forth with a message hidden beneath its feathers. The other important means of communication is the gold ring that Milun sends to his mistress (when she first seeks his love) as a sign that he will come to her whenever she wishes. The ring functions as a symbol of the fulfilled relationship; it is used to set up meetings that lead to the girl's pregnancy, and when her son is born and sent north, it goes with him, to be given him (along with a letter revealing his parents' identity) when he comes of age. Eventually, the ring will reveal the son to his father during the tournament where they meet and fight each other.

The climactic encounter between son and father has clear implications for the view of chivalry and love advanced by the *lai*. Milun and his son are the best knights of their respective generations; neither is ever unhorsed in combat until the younger so humbles the father in the joust just mentioned. The "law" of chivalry, with its relentless quest to gain and maintain *pris,* forces each new generation into combat with the one before. In its pure form, such chivalry takes no heed of other forms of relationship that might modify or cancel its sole criterion of categorization: winners and losers. Though Milun admires the young "knight without equal" when he observes him at a tournament, his pleasure is mingled with resentment that the other is threatening his preeminence among knights; accordingly, he must challenge him, and so the son comes to defeat his father—a moment of potential pathos and outrage recalling the ousting, in Greek mythology, of the ruler of the gods by the hero of the next generation of Olympians (Uranus by Cronos, Cronos by Zeus). The armored knight sees in other knights only foes; the battle between Milun and his son shows how total commitment to prowess and *pris* blinds one to crucial differences of individual identity in others, while obscuring one's own identity as well.[2]

When he sees his rival's white hair, Milun's son—who is, we have been told, of noble character—regrets his deed of violence and holds out to the fallen knight the reins of his horse. By this anticompetitive gesture of compassion, the son reveals the ring and his identity to his father. Discovery of kinship halts a rivalry that would never have taken place had not the two men put the quest of honor above all else in their lives. Marie indicates this dubious set of priorities by telling us that the son, upon learning who his father is, sets out, not to find his parents, but to win fame greater than his father's, i.e., to compete with the preceding generation (as will literally happen when he meets Milun) instead of being united to it by ties of love. When Milun, on the other hand, hears of this (unrecognized) knight's prowess in Brittany, he grieves that there is now a better knight than he, and sets out to challenge him, *after* which he will seek his missing son. (The son mentions his intent to seek his parents only in telling Milun his life history after their joust.) Only the ring prevents patricidal tragedy and brings about the reunion the two knights have delayed in seeking. Love, with its legacy from one generation to the next (symbolized by the ring), neutralizes the dangerous legacy of chivalric *pris*.

Until this climactic moment, love is not a strong enough force in the *lai* to counter either Milun's prowess impulse or his mistress' social bondage. The lovers meet in secret, and make no attempt to marry or run away when their son is conceived; they never defy the social forces threatening or hindering their love. Instead, they send their son away, further sundering the love unit. Then, in a gesture that both symbolizes their separation and contrasts Milun's boldness in chivalry with his furtiveness in love, he leaves his mistress and seeks *pris* once again.[3] While Milun is away, his mistress is forced into a loveless and dangerous marriage—dangerous because her husband may discover she is not a virgin. Milun returns to find even greater obstacles than before to seeing and communicating with his beloved, and solves them ingeniously by using the swan as a messenger. During their twenty-year (!) dependence on the swan, they also meet several times, despite the close surveillance over the wife.[4] This seems small reward for their love; in fact, the starved swan, bringing messages to and from the love-starved pair, becomes a symbol of their undernourished relationship that survives on words alone because of Milun's passivity.

Only at the end of the *lai* does the son, after his reunion with Milun, suggest an active response to the forces that have splintered the love unit: he will do what his father has not done—kill the husband and arrange his parents' marriage. His resolution and vigor imply Marie's criticism of Milun's dilatoriness in his own cause. The message that the two knights receive on their way to South Wales—the husband is dead; Milun should return at once—serves Marie not simply as a device to avoid unpleasant bloodshed and a reliance on the same denouement as *Yonec*'s, but as a way of suggesting that as soon as love begins to control prowess, directing its energies to bind together rather than to separate the love unit, the apparently insuperable social obstacles to love's fulfillment simply disappear.

Milun, then, is an anti-*Yonec* (as *Equitan* is an anti-*Guigemar*), in which the father-lover remains alive and the husband dies conveniently instead of being killed by a vengeful stepson. Neither *lai,* of course, expresses Marie's last word on the subject; each responds to an imaginative view about the power and fruitfulness of love in a world dominated by other value systems—in *Milun,* especially chivalry—that exert centrifugal force on the love relationship.

1. It has been argued that the lovers' use of a swan is a realistic touch since swans breed in certain parts of South Wales.

2. The limitations of a life dedicated to prowess are similarly explored in twelfth-century chivalric romances by Chrétien de Troyes and Hue de Roteland, among others.

3. The emphasis on Milun's inseparability from his horse in battle at the beginning of the *lai* is perhaps intended as a contrast to the easy separability of Milun from his mistress; the parallel would derive force from the literary convention of referring to sexual relations under the metaphor of horse riding, as in a troubadour lyric of Guillaume IX, and possibly the protagonist's name in *Equitan*.

4. Marie may be thinking in these lines of the separated lovers Pyramus and Thisbe, whose story, borrowed from Ovid, Marie parodies in the conclusion of *Les Deus Amanz*.

Chaitivel (*The Unfortunate One*)

It is my desire to bring to mind
a *lai* that I have heard about.
I shall tell you the adventure,
its name, and the city
5 where it was born.
Men call it *The Unfortunate One,*
but there are many
who call it *The Four Sorrows.*

In Brittany, at Nantes, there lived
10 a lady, respected
for her beauty, her education,
and the very best manners.
There wasn't a knight in that land
who had ever done anything praiseworthy,
15 who, if he saw her but once,
did not love and court her.
She could not love them all,
but she didn't want to refuse them either.[1]
It would be better to seek the love
20 of all the ladies in one land
than to separate a single fool from his rag,
for he wants to strike out at once.[2]
The lady grants her favor
according to her goodwill;
25 however, if she doesn't want to hear someone,
she shouldn't abuse him with words
but honor him, hold him dear,

1. *reuser,* "refuse," in Warnke's text; *tuer,* "kill," according to both Ewert and Rychner.

2. The courting may be as futile as the attempt to take a worthless object from a fool, but the fool will fight while the lady may accept; meanwhile, presumably, the courting itself can give some pleasure. The passage has never been satisfactorily explained.

serve his pleasure and be grateful.
The lady I wish to tell you of
30 was so sought after in love,
for her beauty and her merit,
that men thought about her day and night.

In Brittany there were four barons
whose names I do not know;
35 they were not very old
but they had great beauty,
and they were brave, valiant knights,
generous, courtly, open-handed;
they were widely esteemed,
40 noble men of that land.
These four loved the lady,
and took pains to do good deeds;
to win her and her love[3]
each did his utmost.
45 Each one sought her for himself,
put all his efforts into his suit.
There was not one who didn't think
that he was doing better than the others.
The lady had good sense:
50 she took her time to consider,
to find out and to ask
which of them it would be best to love.
They were all of such great merit
one could not choose the best.
55 She didn't want to lose three in order to have one,
so she was nice to each of them;
she gave them all tokens of love,
she sent them all messages.
None of them knew about the others;

3. *Pur li e pur s'amur aveir:* the first five words suggest simple love inspiration, "for her and her love," but the last word *aveir* makes it clear that it is for tangible reward, possession of the lady.

60 but no one was able to leave her;
with his service and his prayers
each thought he was succeeding.
At the assembly of knights,
each one wanted to be first,
65 to do well, if he could,
in order to please the lady.
They all considered her their love,
all carried her token,
a ring, or sleeve, or banner,
70 and each one cried her name.
She loved all four and held them all
until one year, after Easter,
a tournament was called,
before the city of Nantes.
75 To meet the four lovers,
men came from other lands:
French and Normans,
Flemish, Brabants,
Boulognese, Angevins,
80 and near neighbors too.
All were anxious to go.
They had stayed there a long time;
then, on the evening of the tournament,
they exchanged blows furiously.
85 The four lovers armed,
left the city;
their knights followed them,
but the burden fell on those four.
Those outside knew them[4]
90 by their tokens and shields;
they sent knights against them,
two from Flanders and two from Hainault,
ready to strike.
There was no one there who did not want to fight.

4. For purposes of the tournament, the knights were apparently divided into inner and outer armies. Cf. Wolfram's *Parzival*.

95 The four saw them approaching,
they had no desire to flee.
Lance lowered, at full speed,
each one chose his partner.
They struck with such vehemence
100 that the four outsiders fell.
The others did not worry about their horses,
but left them riderless;
they took their stand against the fallen
and their knights came to their aid.
105 With their advent, there was a great melee,
many blows struck with swords.
The lady was in a tower,
she knew which were her knights and which their men;
she saw her lovers helping each other
110 and did not know which one to praise most.

The tournament began,
ranks grew and swelled.
Several times that day
combat was joined before the gate.
115 Her four lovers fought so well,
that they won honor beyond all the others,
until night began to fall
when they should have separated.
But they kept on, recklessly,
120 far from their people, and they paid for it.
For three of them were killed
and the fourth wounded and hurt:
the tip of the lance shot through his thigh
into his body: it came out the other side.
125 They were pierced straight through
and all four fell.
Those who struck them dead
threw their shields onto the ground;
and grieved for them—
130 they had not meant to kill them.

The noise began and the cries,
such mourning was never heard.
The people from the city came
without a thought for the others.[5]

135 In sorrow for these knights,
two thousand
undid their visors,
drew out their hair and beards;
all felt a common grief.

140 Each one was placed upon his shield
and carried to the city
to the lady he had loved.
As soon as she knew the adventure
she fell, fainting, on the hard ground.

145 When she recovered from her faint,
she mourned for each by name.
"Alas," she said, "what shall I do?
I'll never be happy again.
I loved these four knights

150 and desired each one for himself;
there was great good in all of them;
they loved me more than anything.
For their beauty, their bravery,
their merit, their generosity,

155 I made them fix their love on me;
I didn't want to lose them all by taking one.
I don't know which I should grieve for most;
but I cannot conceal or disguise my grief.
I see one wounded, three are dead;

160 nothing in the world can comfort me.
I shall see that the dead are buried
and if the wounded one can be healed,
I shall willingly undertake it,
and find a good doctor for him."

5. The "others" are the outside, or enemy, knights.

165 She had him brought to her chambers;
then she had the others prepared
with great love, nobly
and richly fitted out.
She made great offerings and gifts
170 in a very rich abbey
where they were buried.
God have mercy on them!
She sent for wise doctors
and assigned them to the knight
175 who lay wounded in her chamber
until he could be healed.
She went to see him often
and comforted him gently;
but she mourned for the other three
180 and suffered great grief for them.
One summer day, after dinner,
the lady was talking to the knight;
then she remembered her great sorrow,
hid her head and her face,
185 she lost herself in her thoughts.
He looked at her
and saw that she was thinking.
He addressed her in a proper way:
"Lady, you are upset.
190 What are you thinking? Tell me.
Give up your sorrow.
You must find comfort somewhere."
"Friend," she said, "I was thinking,
remembering your companions.
195 Never did a lady of my position,
however beautiful, noble, or wise,
love four such men at once,
only to lose them all in a day
except for you, who were wounded;
200 you were in great danger of dying.

Because I have loved you so,
I want my grief to be remembered:
I shall compose a *lai* about the four of you
and call it *The Four Sorrows*!"
205 When he heard her,
the knight quickly answered:
"Lady, compose the new *lai*
but call it *The Unfortunate One*!
and I'll show you why
210 it should have such a name.
The others have been dead some time;
they spent their lives
in great pain that they suffered
because of their love for you;
215 but I, who escaped alive,
am confused and miserable—
the one I could love most in the world
I see coming and going frequently,
speaking with me morning and evening,
220 but I can have no joy from her,
from kisses or embraces,
nor any other good but talk.
You make me suffer a hundred such ills,
that it would be better for me to die.
225 If the *lai* is to be named for me,
let it be called *The Unfortunate One*.
Whoever calls it *The Four Sorrows*
will be changing its real name."
"By my faith," she said, "I like that.
230 Let's call it *The Unfortunate One*."
So the *lai* was begun
and then perfected and performed.
Of those who traveled about with it,
some called it *The Four Sorrows;*
235 either name is apt,
both suit the subject.

The Unfortunate One is the common name.
Here it ends, there is no more;
I've heard no more and I know no more about it;
240 I shall tell you no more of it.

CHAITIVEL (*The Unfortunate One*)

In Chaitivel, Marie writes a *lai* about a lady who writes a *lai* about her four lovers, who would have done better to write poetry themselves, instead of fighting, to impress their lady. The *lai* is really about the kind of love found in courtly lyrics: devotion to the ideal and apparently inaccessible lady who is loved by all the worthy men who know her, but particularly by the poet who writes poetry to praise her and at the same time to relieve and describe his own suffering. Marie takes the clichés of lyric poetry to their extremes, and makes fun of the tradition. The *lai* has two names, *Le Chaitivel* (*The Unfortunate One*) and *Les Quatre Dols* (*The Four Sorrows*), not in two languages, as in *Chevrefoil* and *Laustic,* but from two different perspectives, as in *Eliduc,* his and hers. *Chaitivel* is the name given to it by the one surviving lover, to describe his distress. *Quatre Dols* is the lady's name for it, to commemorate her achievement in having won the love of four such men.

The story shows up the futility and perhaps the hypocrisy of the men's love service: three of the four lovers die in a tourney, showing off before the lady and taking excessive risks in order to impress her, and the fourth is badly wounded, probably castrated, and therefore unable to possess her even if she were willing. Tourneys are meant for display: men should not be killed in them; and it is clear in the poem that the knights responsible for the deaths did not intend them, that it was the recklessness of the lovers that brought them about. Thus, for all the talk of their great deeds, their deaths serve no purpose. And, ironically, the one who is left alive might as well be dead for all the satisfaction he gets from the lady. Of course, he does have her daily attention and conversation, which is what courtly lovers pretend to want, but which, in fact, is not enough.

The focus of attention in the *lai,* however, is on the lady, and this in itself is a comment on the lyric tradition, in which the lady is the excuse for the poetry and the apparent subject of it, but in reality has little existence within it. Here Marie's emphasis on the object of all their devotion helps to show up the foolishness of such devotion. The lady is most concerned with her prestige as the inspiration for their love. When they are alive she is concerned with which one would be best for her love (l. 52), which is doing best in the fighting (l. 110), and, when they are dead, which she should grieve for most (l. 157). She was unwilling to choose one of them because that would have meant giving up the other three, so she kept them all, but without letting them know about one another, deceiving them all into thinking they were her favorite. She keeps mourning the loss of the three, remembering that the fourth is still alive only as an afterthought (see lines 197–9), and thinking of him still as one of them (l. 203: "I shall make a *lai* about the four of you" "vus quatre")—hardly flattering or comforting to him. Indeed one wonders if she would have been happier had he also died. She is certainly concerned with the dead, giving them sumptuous funerals and burials, but that is because they enable her to make the most of her own emotions: she composes the *lai* in order to record her love and her grief, not their suffering or death: "Because I loved you so, I want my grief to be remembered" (ll. 201–2). This is another clever twist of the conventional lyric situation, in which the man pretends to write about the lady he loves, but in fact writes about his own emotions, his joy and suffering, his hopes and frustrations.

The *lai* ends with the love situation unresolved, as it usually is in the lyric. Marie repeats four times in the last three lines that there is "no more" to it. We are left to assume that the surviving lover continues to worship the lady without fulfillment, and she to glory in her conquest.

Chevrefoil (*The Honeysuckle*)

I should like very much
to tell you the truth
about the *lai* men call *Chevrefoil*—
why it was composed and where it came from.
5 Many have told and recited it to me
and I have found it in writing,
about Tristan and the queen
and their love that was so true,
that brought them much suffering
10 and caused them to die the same day.
King Mark was annoyed,
angry at his nephew Tristan;
he exiled Tristan from his land
because of the queen whom he loved.
15 Tristan returned to his own country,
South Wales, where he was born,
he stayed a whole year;
he couldn't come back.
Afterward he began to expose himself
20 to death and destruction.
Don't be surprised at this:
for one who loves very faithfully
is sad and troubled
when he cannot satisfy his desires.
25 Tristan was sad and worried,
so he set out from his land.
He traveled straight to Cornwall,
where the queen lived,
and entered the forest all alone—
30 he didn't want anyone to see him;
he came out only in the evening
when it was time to find shelter.
He took lodging that night,
with peasants, poor people.

35 He asked them for news
of the king—what he was doing.
They told him they had heard
that the barons had been summoned by ban.
They were to come to Tintagel
40 where the king wanted to hold his court;
at Pentecost they would all be there,
there'd be much joy and pleasure,
and the queen would be there too.
Tristan heard and was very happy;
45 she would not be able to go there
without his seeing her pass.
The day the king set out,
Tristan also came to the woods
by the road he knew
50 their assembly must take.
He cut a hazel tree in half,
then he squared it.
When he had prepared the wood,
he wrote his name on it with his knife.
55 If the queen noticed it—
and she should be on the watch for it,
for it had happened before
and she had noticed it then—
she'd know when she saw it,
60 that the piece of wood had come from her love.
This was the message of the writing[1]
that he had sent to her:
he had been there a long time,
had waited and remained

1. There are several possible explanations of this line: that Tristan had sent a message to her before she arrived in the forest, which seems least likely since it is not otherwise mentioned; that his name on the wood told her everything because of the understanding that existed between them; that the message was written on the wood in runic inscriptions which only the specially trained could read (see M. Cagnon, "*Chievrefoil* and the Ogamic Tradition," *Romania* 91 [1970], 238–55).

65 to find out and to discover
how he could see her,
for he could not live without her.
With the two of them it was just
as it is with the honeysuckle
70 that attaches itself to the hazel tree:
when it has wound and attached
and worked itself around the trunk,
the two can survive together;
but if someone tries to separate them,
75 the hazel dies quickly
and the honeysuckle with it.
"Sweet love, so it is with us:
You cannot live without me, nor I without you."
The queen rode along;
80 she looked at the hillside
and saw the piece of wood; she knew what it was,
she recognized all the letters.
The knights who were accompanying her,
who were riding with her,
85 she ordered to stop:
she wanted to dismount and rest.
They obeyed her command.
She went far away from her people
and called her girl
90 Brenguein, who was loyal to her.
She went a short distance from the road;
and in the woods she found him
whom she loved more than any living thing.
They took great joy in each other.
95 He spoke to her as much as he desired,
she told him whatever she liked.
Then she assured him
that he would be reconciled with the king—
for it weighed on him
100 that he had sent Tristan away;

he'd done it because of the accusation.
Then she departed, she left her love,
but when it came to the separation,
they began to weep.
105 Tristan went to Wales,
to wait until his uncle sent for him.
For the joy that he'd felt
from his love when he saw her,
by means of the stick he inscribed
110 as the queen had instructed,
and in order to remember the words,
Tristan, who played the harp well,
composed a new *lai* about it.
I shall name it briefly:
115 in English they call it *Goat's Leaf*
the French call it *Chevrefoil.*
I have given you the truth
about the *lai* that I have told here.

❦ CHEVREFOIL *(The Honeysuckle)*

CHEVREFOIL presents one moment of the famous love story of Tristan and Isolt—a meeting in the woods, a moment that has little importance in longer versions of the story. Marie repeats a motif from an earlier episode of the Tristan legend, the name written on a piece of wood as a secret signal between the lovers, but transposes it from the intrigue of a rendezvous in the early period of their affair to a reunion after a long and painful separation. Marie alludes to a number of details in the story that her audience would recognize: the king's anger over the affair, the envious barons, and the loyal servant Brenguein, all of which evoke the world that was hostile to the love. She makes no reference to the potion, either because it is too obvious to mention or, more likely, because she is emphasizing a different aspect of their love: not the fatal passion that binds their lives together, like the honeysuckle and the hazel tree that cannot live when separated, but the perfect understanding and joy they share when they are together, and which sustain them when they are apart.

In a sense, Marie has substituted the natural image of the honeysuckle for that of the magic love potion to explain the binding nature of the love, the mutual dependence which draws them together despite all the obstacles the world sets in their way; but what she emphasizes in the *lai* is the joy of the moment of reunion, the one happy moment in lives that are not only filled with sorrow but destined to end tragically. Although Marie allows the lovers to look forward to a formal reconciliation with the king—to live on that hope—we know it will never occur because she has told us that they will die on the same day. But she chooses to show us what she considers the essence of a love that is the subject of one of the most popular romances of the Middle Ages: the understanding and sensitivity that sets the two lovers apart from others and enables Tristan to leave a sign that only Isolt will see and comprehend; and the deep affection that makes a snatched moment of conversation a joyful scene of love. That essence is the "truth" Marie assures us she is telling at the beginning and the end of the *lai,* which is the same whether the story is told in English, and called *Goteslef,* or in French, and called *Chevrefoil.* It is what Tristan captures in the *lai* he composes for himself to remember that meeting, and it is what Marie preserves in the *lai* she composes for us.

Finally, perhaps, it is only art that can capture such perfect love and joy in life, which, in earlier *lais,* seemed to issue from the imagination of the lover when it existed, and in the last *lai, Eliduc,* will be real and permanent only in the love of God. If Marie means that such love as she describes in *Chevrefoil* is only possible in the mind of the lover, that may explain why, in a *lai* that makes much of mutual feeling and that draws on a tradition in which Isolt is a major force in the story, Marie does not even name the heroine; she simply calls her "the queen," the title which, because it reminds us of her position and responsibility, also tells us how impossible their love must be in the world.

Eliduc

I shall tell you, as I understand
the truth of it, and as I know it,
a very old Breton *lai,*
its story and all its substance.
5 In Brittany there was a knight,
brave and courtly, bold and proud;
Eliduc was his name, it seems to me,
no man in the country was more valiant.
He had a wife, noble and wise,
10 of high birth, of good family.
They lived together a long time
and loved each other loyally;
but then, because of a war,
he went to seek service elsewhere.[1]
15 There, he fell in love with a girl,
the daughter of a king and a queen.
Guilliadun was her name,
no girl in the kingdom was more beautiful.
Eliduc's wife was called
20 Guildeluec in her country.
From these two the *lai* is named
Guildeluec and Gualadun.[2]
At first the *lai* was called *Eliduc,*
but now the name has been changed,
25 for it happened to the women.
The adventure behind the *lai,*
I shall relate to you, as it occurred,
and I shall tell you the truth.

Eliduc had a lord,
30 a king of Brittany,

1. *soudees querre* literally means to hire himself out to fight for a lord in return for pay and maintenance. I am translating *soudees* as "service" throughout the *lai,* and *soudeur* as "soldier."

2. The spelling of the name in the alternate title differs from the name of the character as it is otherwise given in the *lai* (*Guilliadun*).

who loved and cherished him—
Eliduc served him loyally.
Whenever the king had to travel,
Eliduc guarded the land for him;
35 he was retained because of his valor.
Much good came to him from that:
he could hunt in the forests,
there was no forester bold enough
to dare try and stop him,
40 nor did one ever grumble about it.
But envy of his success,
which often happens among people,
caused trouble between him and his lord.
He was slandered and accused
45 until the lord sent him away from his court
without a formal accusation.
Eliduc did not know why.
He asked the king many times
to listen to his defense,
50 not to believe the slander,
for he'd always served the king willingly;
but the king would not respond.
Since he would hear none of it,
Eliduc had to leave.
55 He went to his home
and sent for all his friends;
Eliduc told them all about the king, his lord,
about the anger he now showed toward him;
he had served him as well as he was able
60 and did not deserve the king's ill will.
The peasant proverb says,
when it admonishes the ploughman,
that the love of a lord is not a fief:
he is wise and clever
65 who gives loyalty to his lord,
and love to his good neighbors.

Eliduc doesn't want to remain in the country
but will, he says, cross the sea;
he will go to the kingdom of Logres,
70 where he will enjoy himself for a while.
He will leave his wife at home [in his own land]
commending her to his men,
to guard her loyally,
and to all his friends as well.
75 With that counsel he stopped,
and attired himself richly.
His friends were very sad
because he was leaving them.
Eliduc took ten knights along,
80 his wife escorted him,
revealing enormous sorrow
at her husband's departure.
But he assured Guildeluec
that he would be faithful to her.
85 Then he departed,
and began his journey straightaway;
he came to the sea, crossed it,
and arrived at Totnes.
Several kings in that land
90 were fighting among themselves.
Near Exeter, in that country,
there was a very powerful man,
old and ancient.
He had no male heir of his own flesh,
95 but a daughter of marriageable age.
Because he did not want to give her
to his peer, the latter made war on him,
laying waste his whole land.
He had cut him off inside a castle;
100 no man in the castle was so bold
that he dared go out against him,
dared meet him in battle or in combat.

Eliduc heard about it;
he didn't want to go any farther,
105 since he had found a war.
He wanted to remain in that country.
To the king who was most pressed
and injured and hurt,
he'd give all the help within his power
110 and remain in that king's service.
He sent his messengers
and informed him, by letter,
that he had left his country,
that he had come to help him.
115 The king should make his pleasure known by return messenger
and, if he did not want to have him,
he should grant him an escort through his land;
Eliduc would travel farther to seek service.
When the king saw the messengers,
120 he loved and cherished them.
He called his constable,
commanded him quickly
to prepare an escort
and bring the baron to him,
125 and to have lodgings made ready
for him and his men to stay in,
and to give them
as much as they might want to spend in a month.
The escort was prepared
130 and sent for Eliduc,
who was received with great honor—
exceedingly welcome to the king.
His lodging was with a bourgeois,
who was very wise and courtly;
135 his lovely, curtained room
he turned over to his guest.
Eliduc had himself well served
and invited to his dinner
the poor knights

140 who were lodged in the town.
He forbade all his men
to be so bold,
in the first forty days,
as to take any gifts or money.
145 On the third day that he was there,
the cry was raised in the city
that their enemies had arrived
and had spread throughout the countryside;
they wanted to assail the city,
150 to reach its gates.
Eliduc heard the noise,
the populace in confusion.
He armed himself without delay
and his companions did the same.
155 Fourteen mounted knights
were staying in the city—
several were wounded,
many were prisoners—
they saw Eliduc mount;
160 they went to arm at their lodgings
and rode out the gate with him,
without awaiting a summons.
"Sire," they said, "we'll go with you
and whatever you do we shall do."
165 He answered: "I thank you.
Does any one of you
know a narrow spot or ambush
where we can stop them?
If we wait for them here,
170 it may be that we shall joust,
but that serves no purpose;
there must be another way."
They tell him: "Sire, in faith,
near this wood, in that thicket,
175 there is a narrow cart road

by which they return
when they've taken their booty;
they'll return that way,
unarmed on their mounts;
180 they ride back often
and risk the chance
of dying outright."
We could swiftly damage them,
injure and hurt them there.
185 Eliduc said to them: "Friends,
I pledge you my faith:
who does not often go
where he may expect to suffer a loss
will never gain anything,
190 never win great renown.
You are all the king's men,
and owe him great faith.
Come with me where I go,
do what I do.
195 I assure you, faithfully,
you will come to no harm
as long as I can help.
If we can gain anything there,
it will win us great fame
200 to have hurt our enemies."
They accepted his assurance
and led him to the wood;
they hid themselves near the road
until the others returned.
205 Eliduc showed them everything,
instructed and planned
in what way they would ride against them,
how they would shout.
When they had entered the pass,
210 Eliduc shouted at them.
He called all his companions

and exhorted them to do well.
They struck hard,
spared nothing.
215 The others were completely surprised,
quickly routed and dispersed,
conquered, in a short time.
Their constable was captured
and many other knights;
220 they were all entrusted to the squires.
There were twenty-five of them
and they captured thirty of the others.
They also took armor to their profit.
They made exceptional gains there
225 and came back very happy:
they had done very well.
The king was in a tower,
in great fear for his men;
he complained about Eliduc,
230 he thought and feared
that he had endangered
his knights in order to betray them.
The knights were approaching in a crowd
all burdened and loaded down.
235 There were many more returning
than had gone out;
that's why the king didn't know them,
why he doubted and suspected.
He commanded the gates to be shut,
240 told the people to mount the walls
to shoot and throw things at the knights;
but there will be no need for that.
They had sent
a squire ahead, riding hard,
245 to tell them the adventure
all about the new soldier,
how he conquered the others,

and how he behaved;
there was never such a knight.
250 He captured their constable,
took twenty-nine others,
and wounded and killed many more.
The king, when he heard the news,
rejoiced wonderfully.
255 He descended from the tower
and went to meet Eliduc.
He thanked him for his deeds.
Eliduc turned the prisoners over to the king,
then he divided the booty among the others;
260 for his own use he kept only three horses,
which were allotted to him;
he divided and gave everything,
his own share as well,
to the prisoners and the men.
265 After the feat that I have described to you,
the king loved and cherished Eliduc.
He kept him a whole year—
and those who had come with him—
and accepted his oath of loyalty;
270 he made him protector of his land.
Eliduc was courtly and wise,
a handsome knight, brave and generous.
The king's daughter heard him spoken of,
his virtues described.
275 Through one of her trusted chamberlains
she asked Eliduc, begged and summoned him
to come visit her,
to speak with her and become acquainted;
she was quite astonished
280 that he had not come.
Eliduc answered that he would go,
that he would willingly make her acquaintance.
He mounted his horse,
taking one knight with him,

285 and went to speak to the girl.
When he was about to enter the chamber,
he sent the chamberlain ahead.
Eliduc delayed somewhat,
until the other returned.
290 With a sweet look, with a simple expression,
and with very noble behavior,
he spoke politely;
he thanked the girl,
Guilliadun, who was very lovely,
295 that she had been pleased to summon him
to come and speak with her.
She took him by the hand
and they sat on a bed,
they spoke of many things.
300 She looked at him intently,
at his face, his body, his appearance;
she said to herself there was nothing unpleasant about him.
She greatly admired him in her heart.
Love sent her a message,
305 commanding her to love him,
that made her go pale and sigh
but she didn't want to speak of it
in case he might hold it against her.
He stayed there a long time;
310 then took his leave and went away;
she gave the leave most unwillingly,
nonetheless he left
and returned to his lodging.
He was gloomy and worried,
315 concerned about the lovely girl,
the daughter of his lord, the king,
because she had summoned him so sweetly,
because she had sighed.
He thought it unfair
320 that he'd been so long in the country
and had not seen her often.

But when he said that, he was sorry;
for he remembered his wife
and how he had assured her
325 that he'd be faithful to her,
that he'd conduct himself loyally.
The girl who had seen him
wanted to make him her lover.
She'd never thought so well of anyone;
330 if she could, she would have him.
All night she was awake,
she couldn't rest or sleep.
The next day, in the morning, she got up
and went to a window;
335 she summoned her chamberlain,
and revealed her condition to him.
"By my faith," she said, "this is terrible.
I have gotten myself into a sorry mess.
I love the new soldier,
340 Eliduc, the good knight.
Last night I had no rest,
I couldn't close my eyes to sleep.
If he wants to give me his love[3]
and promise his person to me,
345 I shall do whatever he likes;
great good will come to him:
he will be the king of this land.
He is so wise and courtly
that, if he does not love me with real love,
350 I must die in great sorrow.
When she had said what she wished,
the chamberlain she'd called
gave loyal advice;
no one should criticize him for it.

3. The expression Guilliadun uses throughout this passage is *par amur amer,* "to love with love," presumably with passion, desire, not just as a vassal would his lord's daughter.

355 "Lady," he said, "since you love him,
send something to him,
a belt, a ribbon, or a ring;
send it, he will like that.
If he receives it well,
360 if he is happy that you sent it,
you may be sure of his love.
There is no emperor on earth,
who, if you wanted to love him,
should not be happy [to have your love]."
365 When she heard his advice
the girl answered:
"How can I know from my present
if he has any desire to love me?
I've never seen a knight
370 who had to be begged—
whether he loved or hated—
who would not willingly take
a present that was offered to him.
I would hate to have him make fun of me.
375 But still, by a reaction
one can know something.
Get ready, then, and go to him."
"I am," he said, "all ready."
"You will bring him a gold ring
380 and give him my belt.
You will greet him a thousand times in my name."
The chamberlain left.
She remained in such a state
that she almost called him back;
385 but she let him go
and then began to carry on:
"Oh, how my heart was assaulted
by a man from a strange land.
I don't even know if he is nobly born,
390 he left so quickly.
I shall remain in grief.

I've fixed my desires foolishly.
I never spoke to him before yesterday
and now I'm asking for his love.
395 I think he will blame me;
but if he is courtly, he will be grateful.
Now everything is up to chance [*aventure*].
And if he has no interest in my love,
I shall be miserable,
400 never in my life shall I have any joy."
While she was carrying on,
the chamberlain was moving quickly.
He came to Eliduc
and greeted him in secret
405 with what the girl had sent;
he presented the ring
and gave him the belt.
The knight thanked him.
He put the gold ring on his finger
410 pulled the belt around him;
the youth said no more,
nor did Eliduc ask anything,
except that he offered him something of his.
But the chamberlain took nothing and departed;
415 he returned to his mistress,
whom he found in her chamber;
he brought her Eliduc's greeting
and his thanks for the present.
"Come, now," she said, "don't hide anything from me.
420 Does he really want to love me?"
He answered: "So it seems to me.
The knight is not frivolous;
I find him courtly and wise,
one who knows how to hide his feelings.
425 I brought him your greetings
and presented your things.
He put on your belt,
pulled it tight around him;

he placed your ring on his finger.
430 I said nothing more to him nor he to me."
"He didn't receive it as a love token?
If that is so, I am betrayed."
He told her, "By my faith, I don't know,
but listen to what I have to say:
435 if he didn't really wish you well,
he wouldn't want anything of yours."
"You are," she said, "making fun of me.
I know perfectly well that he doesn't hate me.
I've never done him any harm
440 except that I love him so intensely;
if he hates me nonetheless,
then he ought to die.
Never, through you or anyone else,
until I speak to him myself,
445 do I want to ask him for anything;
I want to show him myself
how love for him tortures me.
But I don't know if he'll remain."
The chamberlain answered:
450 "Lady, the king holds him
by an oath until a year from now—
that he will serve the king loyally.
You'll have sufficient time
to show him what you please."
455 When she heard that Eliduc would remain,
she was filled with joy,
very happy about Eliduc's remaining.
She knew nothing of the distress
he felt since he'd seen her.
460 He had no joy or pleasure
except when he thought of her.
But he considered himself unfortunate
because, before he left his own country,
he had promised his wife
465 that he'd love no one but her.

His heart was now in great turmoil.
He wanted to keep his faith,
but he couldn't keep himself
from loving the girl,
470 Guilliadun, who was so lovely;
or from seeing and addressing,
kissing and embracing her;
but he would not pursue the love
that would dishonor her
475 because of the faith he awed his wife
and because he served the king.
Eliduc was in great distress.
He mounted with no more delay,
calling his companions to him.
480 At the castle he went to speak to the king:
he would see the girl if he could—
that's the reason he bestirred himself.
The king had gotten up from dinner
and entered his daughter's chambers.
485 He began to play chess
with a knight from overseas
who, on the other side of the chess board,
was teaching his daughter.[4]
Eliduc went forward;
490 The king received him well
and sat him down beside him.
He called his daughter and said:
"Young lady, you should certainly
know this knight,
495 and show him great honor;
in five hundred there is none better."
When the girl heard
what her father commanded,
she was very happy.

4. Chess is often an allegory of the love game. Note that Guilliadun is learning to play from a stranger.

500 She rose and called Eliduc,
they sat down far from the others;
both were fired with love.
She didn't dare broach the subject
and he was afraid to speak,
505 except to thank her
for the present she had sent:
he'd never had anything more precious.
She answered the knight
saying that she was very pleased,
510 that was why she'd sent the ring
and the belt as well,
for he had taken possession of her being.
She loved him with such love
that she wanted to make him her lord;
515 and if she could not have him,
he could be sure of one thing:
she would never have a living man.
Now let him tell her his desire.
"Lady," he said, "I am very grateful to you
520 for your love, it gives me great joy.
Since you hold me in such high esteem,
I must be happy.
I shall not forget it.
I've been retained by the king for one year;
525 he has accepted my pledge,
I shall not leave him under any condition
until the war is over.
Then I shall return to my country
if I can get your leave,
530 because I don't want to remain."
The girl answered:
"Love, I thank you.
You are so wise and courtly,
by then you will have decided
535 what you want to do with me.
I love and trust you more than anything."

They made their pledges to each other;
they spoke no more that time.
Eliduc went to his lodging;
540 he was filled with joy, he had done well.
He was often able to speak to his love,
there was great affection between them.
Meanwhile he took such pains with the war
that he captured and held
545 the one who was waging war on the king
and set the whole land free.
He was highly respected for his bravery,
his wisdom, and his generosity;
everything went well for him.
550 Within the term [of his service]
the king of Brittany sent to find him[5]
three messengers from his land:
he was being hard pressed and hurt,
damaged and harmed;
555 he was losing all his castles
and his land was being laid waste.
He had often been sorry
that Eliduc had left him;
he'd been badly advised,
560 he'd been wrong about him.
The traitors who accused Eliduc,
slandered and made trouble for him,
the king had thrown out of the country
and sent into exile for ever.
565 Because of his great need, he was sending for Eliduc,
summoning and begging him—
in the name of the alliance that bound them
when the king received homage from Eliduc—
to come and help him,
570 for the king needed him badly.
Eliduc heard the news.

5. This is the lord who had exiled him at the beginning of the story.

He was upset because of the girl;
for he loved her painfully
and she him, as much as one could.
575 But there was no folly between them,
no frivolity, no shame:
When they were together,
their lovemaking consisted
of courting and speaking
580 and giving fine gifts.
This was her intention and her hope:
she thought to have him completely
and to hold him, if she could;
she didn't know he had a wife.
585 "Alas," he said, "I have acted very badly.
I have been in this country too long.
If only I had never seen this land.
I have loved a girl here—
Guilliadun, the king's daughter—
590 very much, and she me.
If I have to leave her,
one of us must die,
or perhaps both.
Nonetheless, I have to go;
595 my lord has sent for me by letter
appealed to me by my oath
and my wife, too, for her part.
Now I must be careful.
Certainly, I can not remain,
600 I am forced of necessity to go.
If I were to marry my love,
Christianity would not allow it.
This is bad in every way.
God, how hard it is to part.
605 But whoever may blame me for it,
I shall always do right by her;
I shall do whatever she wills,
act as she advises.

The king, her lord, has a secure peace,
610 I don't think anyone will make war with him again.
For my own lord's need
I shall ask for leave before the day
fixed by my term
for me to remain here.
615 I shall go and speak to the girl,
reveal my situation to her;
she will tell me her wish
and I shall do it, as far as I can."
The knight waited no longer,
620 he went to get his leave from the king.
He told and related the adventure to him,
showed and read him the letter
his lord had sent,
by which, in his distress, he had summoned Eliduc.
625 The king heard the summons
and that he would not remain;
he was very sad and disturbed.
He offered much of what he had,
a third of his inheritance
630 and the whole of his treasure;
to keep him, the king would do so much for him
that Eliduc would praise him forever.
"By God," he said, "this time,
since my lord is harassed
635 and has summoned me from so far,
I must go to help him in his need;
I cannot remain, no matter what.
But if you need my service,
I shall willingly return to you
640 with a great force of knights."
For that the king thanked him
and graciously gave him leave.
All the possessions of his household
the king put at his disposal,
645 gold and silver, dogs and horses,

and cloth of silk, good and fine.
Eliduc took in moderation;
then he said, in a fitting way,
that if it pleased the king
650 he would go and speak most willingly with his daughter.
The king answered: "That pleases me very much."
He sent a boy ahead
to open the chamber door for him.
Eliduc went to speak to her.
655 When she saw him, she called him,
greeted him six thousand times.
He consulted her about his affairs,
and briefly revealed the news of his journey.
Before he'd told her everything,
660 taken or asked for her leave,
she fainted in sorrow
and lost all her color.
When Eliduc saw her faint
he began to lose his mind;
665 he kissed her mouth again and again
and wept quite tenderly;
he took her and held her in his arms,
until she recovered from her faint.
"By God," he said, "my sweet love,
670 listen to me for a little:
You are my life and my death,
in you is all my comfort.
That's why I am consulting you,
because there is an understanding between us.
675 I am returning to my country out of necessity.
I have taken my leave of your father,
but I shall do what you wish
whatever may come of it."
"Take me," she said, "with you,
680 since you don't want to remain.
If you don't, I shall kill myself;
I will never have joy or good."

Eliduc answered gently
that he loved her with good love:
685 "Sweet, in truth I am pledged
by my word to your father—
if I took you with me
I would betray my faith to him—
until my term is over.
690 I swear and pledge loyally to you:
if you want to give me leave
and set a time and name a day,
if you want me to come back,
there is nothing in the world that will stop me
695 as long as I am alive and healthy;
my life is completely in your hands."
She had great love for him;
she gave him a term and named the day
for him to come and take her.
700 There was great sorrow when they parted;
they exchanged gold rings
and kissed each other sweetly.
He went as far as the sea;
the wind was good, he crossed it quickly.
705 When Eliduc returned,
his lord was joyful and happy
his friends and his relatives
and all the others too,
above all his good wife,
710 who was very lovely, wise, and worthy.
But he was always preoccupied
because of the love that had seized him.
Nothing that he saw
gave him joy or a happy look,
715 he would never have joy
until he saw his love.
He behaved furtively.
His wife had a heavy heart,
she didn't know why this was;

720 and worried about it to herself.
She asked him often
if he'd heard from anyone
that she had done something wrong
while he was out of the country;
725 she would willingly defend herself
before his people, whenever he desired.
"Lady," he said, "I don't accuse you
of any fault or misdeed.
But in the country where I stayed,
730 I pledged and swore to the king
that I would return to him;
for he has great need of me.
If the king, my lord, were at peace,
I would leave within a week.
735 I should have to endure great hardship
before I could come back.
Indeed, until I return
I can find no joy in anything I see
because I don't want to betray my faith."
740 Then the lady left him alone.
Eliduc was with his lord;
he had helped him and had been of great use to him.
The king followed his advice
as he kept watch over the whole country.
745 But when the time
that the girl had set approached,
he undertook to make peace;
he reconciled all the king's enemies.
Then he prepared to travel [on his own]
750 and chose the people he would take.
He took two of his nephews, whom he very much loved,
and one of his chamberlains—
the one who knew the situation,
who had carried his messages—
755 and his squires only;

he didn't want anyone else.
He had them pledge and swear
to keep his whole affair secret.
He put to sea without delay,
760 crossed it quickly,
and arrived in the country
where he was so eagerly awaited.
Eliduc was very clever:
he took lodging far from the harbor;
765 he didn't want to be seen,
or found or recognized.
He prepared his chamberlain
and sent him to his love,
to tell her that he had come,
770 that he had kept his promise.
At night, when it was dark,
she should leave the city;
the chamberlain would go with her
and he would meet her.
775 The chamberlain had changed all his clothes;
he went slowly on foot
straight to the city
where the king's daughter was.
He asked and sought
780 until he got inside her room.
He greeted the girl
and told her that her love had come.
Before she heard the news
she was gloomy and troubled,
785 then she wept tenderly for joy
and kissed him often.
The chamberlain told her that in the evening
she was to go with him.
All day they stayed there
790 and planned their journey carefully.
At night, when it was dark,

they left the city,
the youth and the girl,
only those two.
795 She was very much afraid that someone would see her.
She was dressed in a silk gown,
finely embroidered with gold,
and wrapped in a short cloak.
Far from the gate, the distance of an arrow shot,
800 there was an enclosed wood.
Waiting for them beneath the hedge
was her love, who had just arrived.
The chamberlain brought her,
Eliduc dismounted and kissed her.
805 Their joy at meeting was great.
He helped her mount a horse,
mounted himself, took her rein,
and went off quickly with her.
They came to the harbor at Totnes
810 and entered a boat immediately;
there was no one there except his men
and his love Guilliadun.
They had good wind
and good weather.
815 But when they were about to arrive,
a storm broke out at sea—
a wind rose before them,
driving them far from the harbor;
it broke and split their mast
820 and tore their sail.
They called on God devoutly,
on Saint Nicholas and Saint Clement,
and on my lady Saint Mary,
to seek help from her son
825 to save them from dying
and let them reach the harbor.
One hour backwards, another forwards,

they moved along the coast;
they were on the verge of shipwreck.
830 Then one of the sailors, loudly,
cried: "What are we doing?
Sire, you have inside with you
the one who is causing our deaths.
We'll never reach land.
835 You already have a faithful wife
but you're bringing another back
in defiance of God and the law
of right and of faith.
Let us throw her into the sea,
840 so we can get home safely."
Eliduc heard what he said
and almost went mad with anger.
"Son of a bitch," he said, "rotten,
filthy traitor, be silent!
845 If you had let my love go
I'd have made you pay for it."
But he held her in his arms
and comforted her as well as he could
from the distress she felt from the sea[6]
850 and from what she'd heard
of her lover having a wife
other than herself in his country.
She fell faint on her face,
all pale and without color.
855 And she remained in a faint
without recovering or sighing.
He who was bringing her back with him
really thought that she was dead.
His grief was terrible; he got up,
860 moved swiftly toward the sailor,

6. Her distress from the sea, *mal . . . en mer,* probably involves a pun on *amer* to love, as in Chrétien's *Cligès* and Gottfried's *Tristan,* the latter presumably from Thomas.

and struck him so hard with an oar
that he knocked him down.
He grabbed his feet and threw him overboard;
the waves carried the body away.
865 After Eliduc had tossed him into the sea,
he took over the helm.
He continued to pilot the boat
until he reached the harbor and brought it to land.
When they arrived,
870 they lowered the gangplank and dropped anchor.
She was still unconscious
and appeared to be dead.
Eliduc was very unhappy;
if he could have had his way, he would have died with her.
875 He asked his companions
what advice each could give him
about where to take the girl;
for he would not leave her
until she was buried,
880 and laid with great honor, with a fine service,
in a consecrated cemetery.
She was the daughter of a king and had a right to that.
They were all confused,
had no advice to give.
885 Eliduc began to consider
where he might take her.
His home was close to the sea,
he could be there for dinner.
There was a forest around it,
890 thirty leagues long,[7]
where a holy hermit lived,
and there was a chapel.
He'd been there forty years;
Eliduc had often spoken with him.
895 He would, he said, bring Guilliadun to him,

7. About ninety miles.

and bury her in the chapel;
he would give enough of his land
to found an abbey
and would establish a convent of monks,
900 or of nuns or canons,
who would always pray for her.
God have mercy on her!
He had his horse brought to him,
commanded all his men to mount.
905 But he had them all swear
not to betray him.
Before him on his palfrey
he carried his love.
He traveled straight along the road
910 until they entered the wood.
They came to the chapel,
called out and beat on the door;
they found no one to answer them
or to open the door.
915 Eliduc had one of his men make his way in,
to open and unlock the door.
Eight days before, the perfect,
the holy, hermit had died.
He found the new tomb;
920 he was very sad, quite dismayed.
The men wanted to dig a grave
in which he might bury his friend,
but he made them hold back.[8]
He told them: "That won't do.
925 First I must seek the advice
of the wise people of the land,
to learn how I can glorify a place
with an abbey or a church.
We shall lay her before the altar
930 and commend her to God."

8. I have reversed the order of these two lines.

He had cloths brought
and a bed made up immediately.
The girl was placed on it
and left there for dead.
935 But when it came to leaving,
he thought he would die of grief.
He kissed her eyes and her face.
"Lovely one," he said, "may God never
let me bear arms again
940 or live or endure in the world.
Lovely friend, to your harm you saw me,
sweet love, to your harm you followed me.
Lovely one, if you had been queen,
the love, with which you loved me faithfully,
945 could have been no more loyal and true.
My heart is filled with sorrow because of you.
The day I bury you
I shall become a monk;
each day on your tomb
950 I shall make my grief resound."
Then he left the girl,
shut the door of the chapel.
He sent a messenger
to his home, to announce
955 to his wife that he was coming
but that he was exhausted and upset.
When she heard [that he was coming] she was very happy,
she prepared herself for him
and received her lord well.
960 But little joy awaited her,
for he never showed a pleasant countenance,
never said a good word.
No one dared to speak to him about it.
He was in the house two days;
965 then he heard Mass early in the morning
and set out on the road.

In the wood he went to the chapel
where the girl lay.
He found her unconscious:
970 she did not recover or sigh.
It seemed a great wonder to him
that she was still white and red;
she never lost her color
except that she was a bit paler.
975 He wept in anguish
and prayed for her soul.
When he had said his prayer,
he returned home.
One day when he left the church
980 his wife had him watched
by one of her valets; to him she promised a great deal
if he went and saw from afar
which way his lord turned;
she would give him horses and arms.
985 He did as she commanded.
He went to the woods and followed Eliduc
so that he was not noticed.
He watched well, saw
how he entered the chapel;
990 he heard the sorrow Eliduc gave vent to.
Before Eliduc came out again,
the valet had returned to his lady.
He related everything he heard,
the grief and the noise and the cries
995 of her lord in the hermitage.
Her heart was quite moved.
The lady said: "Let us go right away.
We will search the whole hermitage.
My lord must, I think, travel;
1000 he is going to court to speak to the king.
The hermit died a while ago—
I know that Eliduc loved him

but he wouldn't do that for him,
he wouldn't show such grief."
1005 That's how she left it that time.

That very day, after noon,
Eliduc went to speak to the king.
His wife took the valet with her
and brought him to the hermitage.
1010 When she entered the chapel
and saw the bed of the girl,
who resembled a new rose,
she uncovered her,
saw the body so slender,
1015 the long arms and white hands,
slim fingers, long and smooth;
now she knew the truth,
the reason her lord had felt such grief.
She called the valet
1020 and showed him the wonderful sight.
"Do you see," she said, "this woman
whose beauty resembles a jewel?
This is my lord's love
for whom he feels such grief.
1025 By my faith, I'm not surprised,
if such a lovely woman has perished.
As much for pity as for love
I shall never have joy again."
She began to weep
1030 and to mourn for the girl.
As she sat, weeping, before the bed,
a weasel came running;
it had come out from beneath the altar
and the valet had hit it
1035 because it ran over the body;
he killed it with a stick.
Then he threw it on the floor.

In very little time
her mate ran up[9]
1040 and saw where she lay;
he went around her head
prodded her several times with his foot.
When he couldn't get her up,
he gave signs of grieving.
1045 He left the chapel
and went to the wood for herbs;
he took a flower in his teeth,
a red one,
and came back quickly;
1050 he put it in such a way
inside his companion's mouth,
whom the valet had killed,
that she revived at once.
The lady watched it all,
1055 she cried to the valet: "Hold her.
Throw something, good man, she mustn't get away."
And he threw, striking her
so that the flower fell.
The lady got up and retrieved it
1060 and went back quickly.
Inside the girl's mouth
she placed the very lovely flower.
After a short while
Guilliadun revived and sighed;
1065 then she spoke and opened her eyes.
"God," she said, "I've slept so long."
When the lady heard her speak

9. I use the masculine and feminine pronouns here where it is important to show the relationship of the weasels, not before where it might have led to confusion with the humans in the scene. It is difficult not to make a connection between the episode of the weasels and the main plot, though one hesitates to carry it too far. The lover who grieves for his dead mate seems to represent Eliduc, but the "flower" *he* finds to bring her back to life is his wife's charity.

she began to thank God.
She asked who she was
1070 and the girl replied:
"Lady, I was born in Logres,
the daughter of that country's king.
I have loved a knight very much,
Eliduc, the good soldier;
1075 he brought me here with him.
But he sinned when he deceived me:
he had a wife, but he didn't tell me
or ever give me any idea about that.
When I heard about his wife
1080 I fainted from the grief.
Villainously, he has abandoned me,
friendless, in a strange land.
He has betrayed me, I don't know why.
Whoever believes in a man is very foolish."
1085 "Lovely one," the lady answered,
"there is no living thing in all the world
that can give him joy;
I can assure you of that.
He thinks that you are dead
1090 and is quite disconsolate.
Each day he has come to look at you;
I think he found you unconscious.
I am his wife, in truth,
I have a very heavy heart for his sake,
1095 because of his grief.
I wanted to know where he was going:
I came after him, that's how I found you.
That you are alive gives me great joy;
I shall take you with me
1100 and give you back to your love.
I want to leave him completely free,
and I shall take the veil."
The lady so comforted the girl
that she finally took her away with her.

1105 She had her valet make ready
and sent him for her lord.
He traveled until he found him;
he greeted him fittingly
and told him the adventure.
1110 Eliduc mounted a horse
without waiting for any companion.
By night he had reached home.
When he found his love alive
He thanked his wife sweetly.
1115 Eliduc was very pleased,
he had never been so happy;
he kissed the girl again and again
and she him, very sweetly;
together they felt great joy.
1120 When the lady saw how they looked,
she addressed her lord;
she sought and asked his leave
to depart from him,
she wanted to be a nun, to serve God.
1125 Let him give her a piece of his land
to establish an abbey;
then let him take Guilliadun, whom he so loved,
for it is neither good nor fitting
to keep two wives,
1130 nor should the law consent to it.
Eliduc made her a promise
and graciously gave her leave:
he would do what she desired,
he would give her land.
1135 Near the castle, in the woods,
at the chapel of the hermitage,
he had her place her church,
and build her houses;
he put much land and wealth into it:
1140 she would have whatever she needed.
When everything was well prepared,

the lady took the veil
and thirty nuns with her;
she established a rule of life for herself and her order.

1145 Eliduc took his love;
with great honor and a lovely service
the feast was celebrated
on the day he married her.
They lived together many days;
1150 there was perfect love between them.
They gave great alms and did great good,
so much so that they turned to God.
Near the castle, on the other side,
after great care and deliberation
1155 Eliduc founded a church
to which he gave most of his land
and all his gold and silver.
To maintain the order and the house,
he placed his men in it, and other people
1160 devout in their religion.
When he had prepared everything,
he delayed no longer;
with the others he gave and rendered himself up
to serve almighty God.
1165 With his first wife
he placed the wife whom he so cherished.
She received her as her sister
and gave her great honor;
she encouraged her to serve God
1170 and instructed her in her order.
They prayed to God for their friend—
that He would have mercy on him—
and he prayed for them.
He sent messages to them
1175 to find out how they were,
how each was doing.
Each one took great pains

to love God in good faith
and they made a very good end,
1180 thanks to God, the divine truth.

From the adventure of these three,
the ancient courtly Bretons
composed the *lai*, to remember it,
so that no one would forget it.

ELIDUC

ELIDUC, by far the longest of Marie's *lais,* is a more complex story than it may appear. It brings together the various human emotions of selfless affection, loyalty, romantic love, desire, self-indulgence; the bonds between a man and his wife, a man and his love, and a man and his lord. The only love that can resolve the conflicts between the others is the love of God, and that is the solution offered in this, the last *lai*. The story tells of a man caught between two women, his wife and his new love, and two lords, the old one who exiles him but to whom he always feels bound, and the new one, who takes him in. Such a conflict of loyalties often occurs in medieval romance (see *Tristan, Horn, Ille et Galeron, Li Biaus Desconneus*), where it usually indicates a problem in the man—uncertainty about himself or about his love, an inability to commit himself entirely or to deny himself anything, an internal conflict externalized. *Eliduc* is related to at least two of these romances: it probably influenced the author of *Ille* and was itself influenced by *Tristan* (most likely the version by Thomas). The differences between Marie's treatment and the other two tell us a number of things about Marie's intentions.

In *Ille et Galeron* the hero leaves his first wife because he thinks he is not worthy of her and he cannot believe in her love. He becomes involved with the second woman when he defends her land, but then he encounters his wife again in circumstances that permit no doubts of her love for him. He would rather return to her, but he is now committed to the other woman, and he spends most of the remaining story torn between the two until his wife becomes a nun, leaving him free to marry the other woman and discharge his obligation to her. One is left with the distinct feeling that the first woman is his real love, but that he cannot hold her because of his own failure to trust her love. The author of *Ille,* Gautier d'Arras, retains the basic story line of the *Eliduc* plot, but changes the hero's preference and keeps us more sympathetic to the hero. In *Eliduc,* the hero prefers the new love but the audience sees how superior his wife is, and must feel not only that he has made the wrong decision but that he does not, in fact, deserve his wife.

We see this even more clearly in Marie's treatment of the Tristan material. She reverses the Tristan situation in order to show that Eliduc has made the wrong choice. We know, from the previous *lai, Chevrefoil,* that Marie thinks of the Tristan-Isolt love as a nearly perfect communion, so we can assume that she applauds Tristan's loyalty to his first love, the queen. Marie borrows much of the plot line from Tristan: the hero's exile from his lord, his journey to find adventure and serve other lords (Eliduc's journey, like his loves, is the reverse of Tristan's, moving from Brittany to England), winning the love of the daughter of the lord he serves, their exchange of gifts, his tacit encouragement of her affection by not actively discouraging it, and his secret return to his love (the first Isolt). Eliduc's daily visits to the body of his love in a chapel in the woods recall Tristan's visits to the statue of Isolt in the Hall of Statues, located in a cave in the woods; the chapel which had housed a religious man, a hermit, may also recall the visits to the hermit during the forest exile in Béroul's *Tristan,* but with a significant difference: the hermit recalled Tristan and Isolt to their duty and tried to persuade them to renounce their sin. The main difference between Tristan and Eliduc is that

Tristan, despite his marriage to the second Isolt, which is never consummated, remains loyal to the queen. His affections never swerve from the woman who deserves his loyalty. Even his dalliance with the other woman is occasioned by his love for the queen—he tries unsuccessfully to make himself forget his love by concentrating on another woman, and he pays for that attempt with his death. Here, too, the contrast is significant: Tristan's wife betrays him out of jealousy, while Eliduc's wife spies in order to help her husband; she restores her rival to life and removes herself in order to make way for her. Marie's emphasis is on the selflessness and generosity of real love. It may be to call attention to the significant differences between the two stories that Marie tells us that the name of the *lai* was changed from *Eliduc,* the hero's name, to *Guildeluec and Gualadun,* the names of two women.

Comparison with related stories indicates that Marie does not approve of her hero's actions, but there are similar indications within the story. The first thing we learn about Eliduc is calculated to win our sympathy; he is exiled by his lord through the envy and slander of other barons, punished like Lanval for something he did not do. And yet his behavior through the rest of the *lai* suggests that he is capable of the kind of action for which he is punished, without perhaps even recognizing himself that what he does is wrong. Marie slowly reveals the defects of her hero. His first military exploit is an ambush in which he takes the unarmed enemy unawares, an effective maneuver, but scarcely heroic. When the princess, who is impressed with his exploits, summons him, he hesitates at first to go in to her, but then stays a long time with her. After he has met her, he regrets the long time he has been in that land without knowing her—that is, he resents what he has missed—and only then does he remember that he had promised to be faithful to his wife. Later, when he has received gifts from the princess, he begins to feel himself ill used because he had made that promise. He continues to encourage the girl's affection for him, doing everything short of sleeping with her:

"he couldn't keep himself / from loving the girl . . . from seeing and addressing, / kissing and embracing her" (l. 468 ff.) and the gifts he receives from the girl, the ring and belt, are highly suggestive and certainly signify to her a promise of that kind of love. He refrains only from the final act and thinks that by doing so he remains faithful to his wife and to his new lord, the girl's father. He observes the letter but not the spirit of his vow. The same is true of his loyalty to her father: he will not abduct the girl during his specified term of service, but once that term is over, he feels free to carry her off, even though he cannot hope to marry her. But he does not hesitate to bind himself to her by a set of pledges which must conflict at least in spirit with his marriage vows. Forced by the demands of his first lord to return home, he actually lies to his wife in order to leave her again, telling her the lord he served in the land of his exile still needs him. And finally, when he brings the girl back home with him, endangering the lives of all who accompany him—his sinful act occasions the storm at sea—he murders the sailor who speaks the truth.[1] Thus he betrays the trust of both the women who love him, and there is even some question about his relations with his two lords. He remains loyal to the first lord, despite the unfair treatment, but betrays the second lord by stealing his daughter, although this lord had always treated him well. Perhaps, in some way, his behavior to the second justifies the way the first behaved toward him. Eliduc's loyalty, like his love, is misplaced.

In contrast to the hero's actions, the women never fail in their devotion. The young girl loves purely; she is unable to accept a life of sin and remains unconscious until she is revived by the wife and given the means to regularize her position. The wife behaves with perfect loyalty, generosity, and charity. She is never jealous or vindictive. Hers is an ideal love, which turns finally to God, as it must, since no human object can properly deserve it. And her example leads even the others eventually to turn to God. They end their lives sharing a religious vocation, communicating by letter and praying for each other, rather like Abélard and Héloïse, perhaps the only possible solution in life (death resolves Tristan's conflict) to the problems of secular love.

1. H. S. Robertson suggests that Eliduc tries to operate in a sphere of total unreality, trying to preserve his love in isolation. The sailor's accusation is a brutal intrusion of reality, revealing the extent of Eliduc's trespass into the other world. ("Love and the Other World in Marie de France's 'Eliduc,'" in *Essays in Honor of Louis Francis Solano,* eds. R. J. Cormier and U. T. Holmes, 174.)

SELECTIVE BIBLIOGRAPHY

THE FOLLOWING list of editions and secondary materials is far from complete. (Fuller bibliographies can be found in Ewert's edition and in Mickel's book-length study, the latter with annotations.) We include here those works we have found particularly useful, as well as some that are generally considered important for the study of the *Lais*.

EDITIONS

Marie de France, *Lais*. Ed. A. Ewert. Oxford, 1947, repr. 1965.

Les lais de Marie de France. Ed. J. Rychner. Paris, 1969.

Die Lais der Marie de France. Ed. K. Warnke. Halle, 1925.

Die Fablen der Marie de France. Ed. K. Warnke. Halle, 1898.

Marie de France, *Fables* (selected). Eds. A. Ewert and R. C. Johnston. Oxford, 1942.

Das Buch vom Espurgatoire S. Patrice der Marie de France und seine Quelle. Ed. K. Warnke. Halle, 1938.

Marie de France, *L'Espurgatoire Saint Patriz*. Ed. T. A. Jenkins. Chicago, 1903.

SCHOLARLY AND CRITICAL STUDIES

A. Ahlström. *Marie de France et les lais narratifs*. Göteborg, 1925.

H. Baader. *Die Lais. Zur Geschichte einer Gattung der altfranzösischen Kurzerzählungen*. Frankfurt, 1966.

R. Baum. *Recherches sur les oeuvres attribuées à Marie de France*. Heidelberg, 1968.

J. Bédier. "Les lais de Marie de France." *Revue des deux mondes* 107 (1891), 835–63.

G. Brereton. "A 13th Century List of French Lays and Other Narrative Poems." *Modern Language Review* 45 (1950), 40–45.

K. Brightenback. "Remarks on the 'Prologue' to Marie de France's *Lais*." *Romance Philology* 30 (1976), 168–77.

R. Bromwich. "A Note on the Breton Lays." *Medium Aevum* 26 (1957), 36–38.

E. Brugger. "Eigennamen in den *Lais* der Marie de France."

Zeitschrift für französische Sprache und Literatur 49 (1927), 201–52, 381–484.

C. Bullock-Davies. "The Love Messenger in 'Milun.'" *Nottingham Medieval Studies* 16 (1972), 20–27.

R. Cargo. "Marie de France's 'Le Laüstic' and Ovid's *Metamorphoses.*" *Comparative Literature* 18 (1966), 162–66.

R. D. Cottrell. "'Le lai du Laüstic': From Physicality to Spirituality." *Philological Quarterly* 47 (1968), 499–505.

S. F. Damon. "Marie de France, Psychologist of Courtly Love." *PMLA* 44 (1929), 968–96.

M. Delbouille. "Le nom et le personage d'Equitan." *Le Moyen Age* 69 (1963), 315–23.

M. H. Ferguson. "Folklore in the *Lais* of Marie de France." *Romanic Review* 57 (1966), 3–24.

B. E. Fitz. "The Prologue to the *Lais* of Marie de France and the *Parable of the Talents* and Monetary Metaphor." *Modern Language Notes* 90 (1975), 558–64.

P. N. Flum. "Additional Thoughts on Marie de France." *Romance Notes* 3 (1961), 53–56.

L. Foulet. "Marie de France et les lais bretons." *Zeitschrift für romanische Philologie* 29 (1905), 19–56, 293–322.

J. C. Fox. "Marie de France." *English Historical Review* 25 (1910), 303–6.

———. "Mary Abbess of Shaftesbury." *English Historical Review* 26 (1911), 317–26.

E. A. Francis. "Marie de France et son temps." *Romania* 72 (1951), 78–99.

———. "The Trial in 'Lanval,'" in *Studies . . . Presented to M. K. Pope.* Manchester, 1939, 115–24.

———. "A Commentary on Chevrefoil," in *Medieval Miscellany Presented to Eugene Vinaver.* Manchester, 1965, 136–45.

J. Frappier. "Remarques sur la structure du lai, essai de definition et de classement," in *La litterature narrative d' imagination.* Paris, 1961, 23–39.

J. A. Frey. "Linguistic and Psychological Couplings in the Lays of Marie de France." *Studies in Philology* 61 (1964), 3–18.

R. B. Green. "The Fusion of Magic and Realism in Two Lays of Marie de France." *Neophilologus* 59 (1975), 324–36.

F. Hodgson. "Alienation and the Otherworld in *Lanval, Yonec,* and *Guigemar.*" *Comitatus* 5 (1974), 19–31.

E. Hoepffner. "Pour la chronologie des *Lais* de Marie de France." *Romania* 59 (1933), 351–70; 60 (1934), 36–66.

———. "La tradition manuscrite des lais de Marie de France." *Neophilologus* 12 (1927), 1–10, 85–96.

———. "Marie de France et les lais anonymes." *Studi Medievali* 4 (1931), 1–31.

———. *Les Lais de Marie de France*. Paris, 1935.

———. "Le geographie et l'histoire dans les lais de Marie de France." *Romania* 56 (1930), 1–32.

U. T. Holmes. "New Thoughts on Marie de France." *Studies in Philology* 29 (1932), 1–10.

R. N. Illingworth. "La chronologie les *Lais* de Marie de France." *Romania* 87 (1966), 433–75.

A. Knapton. "A la recherche de Marie de France." Paper read to the Courtly Literature Society seminar, Modern Language Association meeting, San Francisco, December 1975.

A. Knapton. "La Poésie enluminée de Marie de France." *Romance Philology* 30 (1976), 177–87.

M. Lazar. *Amour courtois et "fin'amours" dans la littérature du XIIe siècle*. Paris, 1964.

E. Levi. "Il Re Giovane e Maria di Francia." *Archivum Romanicum* 5 (1921), 448–71.

———. "Maria di Francia e le abbazie d'Inghilterra." *Archivum Romanicum* 5 (1921), 472–93.

———. "Sulla cronologia delle opere di Maria di Francia." *Nuovi Studi Medievali* 1 (1923), 40–72.

C. Martineau-Génieys. "Du 'Chievrefoil,' encore et toujours." *Le Moyen Age* 78 (1972), 91–114.

E. J. Mickel. "A Reconsideration of the *Lais* of Marie de France." *Speculum* 46 (1971), 39–65.

———. "Marie de France's Use of Irony as a Stylistic and Narrative Device." *Studies in Philology* 71 (1974), 265–90.

———. "The Unity and Significance of Marie's Prologue." *Romania* 95 (1974), 83–91.

———. *Marie de France*. New York, 1974.

S. Painter. "To Whom were Dedicated the Fables of Marie de France?" *Modern Language Notes* 48 (1933), 367–69.

D. W. Robertson. "Marie de France, *Lais,* Prologue 13–15." *Modern Language Notes* 64 (1949), 336–38.

———. "Love Conventions in Marie's *Equitan.*" *Romanic Review* 44 (1953), 241–45.

H. S. Robertson. "Love and the Other World in Marie de France's 'Eliduc,'" in *Essays in Honor of Louis Francis Solano.* Chapel Hill, 1969, 167–76.

F. Schürr. "Komposition und Symbolik in den Lais der Marie de France." *Zeitschrift für romanische Philologie* 50 (1930), 556–82.

C. Segre, "Per l'edizione critica dei *lai* di Maria di Francia." *Culture Neolatina* 19 (1959), 215–37.

L. Spitzer. "Marie de France, Dichterin von Problem-Märchen." *Zeitschrift für romanische Philologie* 50 (1930), 29–67.

———. "The Prologue to the *Lais* of Marie de France and Medieval Poetics." *Modern Philology* 41 (1943), 96–102.

J. Stevens. "The *granz biens* of Marie de France," in *Patterns of Love and Courtesy,* ed. J. Lawlor. Evanston, 1966, 1–25.

K. Warnke. "Über die Zeit der Marie de France." *Zeitschrift für romanische Philologie* 4 (1880), 223–48.

J. Wathelet-Willem. "Equitan dans l'oeuvre de Marie de France." *Le Moyen Âge* 69 (1963), 325–45.

R. D. Whichard. "A Note on the Identity of Marie de France," in *Romance Studies in Honor of W. M. Dey.* Chapel Hill, 1950, 177–81.

B. Wind. "L'idéologie courtoise dans les lais de Marie de France," in *Mélanges . . . Delbouille,* Vol. 2. Gembloux, 1964, 741–48.

E. Winkler. *Marie de France.* Vienna, 1918.

W. Woods. "Marie de France's 'Laüstic.'" *Romance Notes* 12 (1970), 203–7.